I0762751

Advance Praise for *Salomé*

"Baird's prose is a bit like descending into a Parisian catacomb—at once darkly terrifying, and somehow simultaneously, bewitching. *Salomé* is equal parts viscerally sharp and cloyingly subtle; scenes of swiftly fading girlhood, with its nostalgia and romances, are met by unexpected interludes on the science of immortality and the peril of extremist ideologies, all blurring elegantly into a scintillating balm which belies the desperate, cathartic honesty at the novel's center. The highest praise I can give any work of art is that it has made me think. And Leslie's novel has given me thoughts for many years to come."

—Eilish Quin, author of *Medea*

"Leslie Baird's *Salomé* is a gripping, sensual thriller about the perils of charm and unexpected connection. It explores the complicated space where hospitality threatens to tilt into control, where generosity cannot untangle itself from ulterior motives. *Salomé* is an engrossing debut novel about the impact of technological progress on family, mourning, and love."

—Isle McElroy, author of *People Collide*

"Leslie Baird's debut is an alluring exploration of ambition, friendship, and secrets. If you had the chance to go on an unexpected adventure in a gorgeous place, wouldn't you consider taking it? Baird gives us this delicious opportunity from the first pages. This atmospheric, evocative novel will be a hit with readers everywhere. I can't wait to read what Baird writes next!"

—Saumya Dave, author of *The Guilt Pill*

"A thrilling story of desire and deception set against the intoxicating backdrop of Paris. . . . A wild ride in every way—a seductive thriller where astral realms collide with bodily desires, where beauty masks malevolence, where science borders on sorcery, where nefarious billionaires reach new depths of depravity, and the line between victim and willing participant vanishes completely. Breathless, electric, and utterly consuming. I was addicted."

—Lisa Gabriele, author of *The Winters*

"Wonderful and compelling, well-drawn and riveting. The book has everything—France, a mysterious town, a seductive friend/lover, a menacing mother, a cult—all moving toward a beautiful description of loss, being present, and how to live a life. A beautiful and original book!"

—Karen E. Bender, author of *Refund* and *The Words of Dr. L*

"*Salomé* reinvents the gothic . . . blending the moodiness and suspense of the genre's origins with a modern social consciousness. Baird's novel explores lust and friendship alongside the perils of today's world: corporate and technological greed; the erosion of privacy; the widening wealth gap. The result is a smart, thoughtful, and sensual retelling of a classic tale."

—Chloe Benjamin, *New York Times* bestselling author of *The Immortalists*

"Reading this book feels like sitting on a velvet couch and drinking absinthe. Part gothic seduction, part cult psychology, *Salomé* reckons with how easily smart, searching women can be pulled toward the promise of transcendence . . . and what it costs when the fantasy talks back. I loved it."

—Amanda Montell, *New York Times* bestselling author of *Wordslut*, *Cultish*, and *The Age of Magical Overthinking*

"Set in a secluded French town, *Salomé* is a hauntingly seductive exploration of desire, grief, and avarice. Baird's lush, hypnotic prose had me in a trance from the very first page. A riveting debut!"

—Monika Kim, internationally bestselling author of *The Eyes Are the Best Part*

"Sexy, bold, and impossible to put down. *Salomé* is an exhilarating and original reimagining of the young American in France, told through a seductive friendship between two women. Leslie Baird builds suspense with remarkable control as she explores the delicious thrills and dangers of obsession."

—Sanaë Lemoine, author of *The Margot Affair*

SALOMÉ

SALOMÉ

A NOVEL

LESLIE BAIRD

G. P. Putnam's Sons
New York

PUTNAM
— EST. 1838 —

G. P. Putnam's Sons
Publishers Since 1838
An imprint of Penguin Random House LLC
1745 Broadway, New York, NY 10019
penguinrandomhouse.com

Book design by Laura K. Corless

LIBRARY OF CONGRESS CATALOGING-IN-PUBLICATION DATA

Names: Baird, Leslie author
Title: Salomé : a novel / Leslie Baird.
Description: New York : G. P. Putnam's Sons, 2026.
Identifiers: LCCN 2025033675 (print) | LCCN 2025033676 (ebook) |
ISBN 9798217045938 hardcover | ISBN 9798217045952 ebook
Subjects: LCGFT: Novels
Classification: LCC PS3602.A5735 S25 2026 (print) |
LCC PS3602.A5735 (ebook) | DDC 813/.6—dc23/eng/20250808
LC record available at https://lccn.loc.gov/2025033675
LC ebook record available at https://lccn.loc.gov/2025033676

Printed in the United States of America
1st Printing

The authorized representative in the EU for product safety and compliance is Penguin Random House Ireland, Morrison Chambers, 32 Nassau Street, Dublin D02 YH68, Ireland, https://eu-contact.penguin.ie.

For Marie

You must not shrink.

The mystery of love is greater than the mystery of death.

—Oscar Wilde, *Salomé*

SALOMÉ

CHAPTER 1

June 19, 2018

In college, I lived in the 18th arrondissement of Paris above a locksmith shop—a *serrurerie*, which is considered to be the most difficult word for Americans to pronounce in the French language. The verb *serrer* means to tighten or to squeeze, among other things. *Serrure* is the lock itself, from the Latin *sera*: a bolt or crossbar.

The word, for me, took on its own meaning, as words are apt to do. To think of *serrurerie* placed me so fully in a time and space not exactly in the past or the future, and certainly not the present as I experienced it. *Serrurerie* became a portal of sorts into an alternative world in which I'd never left Paris. Now I spent most of my time saving up for my next trip back.

Once I'd bought a plane ticket, I ticked the days off on the calendar and wrote *serrurerie* lovingly in the margins of my notebook, the way people tended to their gardens in anticipation of the harvest. Perhaps that's how everyone felt about vacations—but I would never consider my trips to France as vacations. They were somewhere between a homecoming and a compulsion satisfied.

As I shuffled down the plane's center aisle, stopping to wait for other passengers to lift their bags into the overhead bins, my fingers tapped gently against my thigh. *S-E-R-R-E-R.* My going-to-Paris word. The two *R*s, a double tap on the middle finger, naturally.

I found my row, deep in basic economy. There was a woman around my age in the window seat. I lifted my backpack into the overhead compartment before taking my seat next to her. She was looking down at her hands, which were folded neatly in her lap, her thumbs side-by-side. One thumb slid over to the other and smoothed the nail.

Two tears dripped from her chin and onto her thigh. She must've felt me looking. Her watery eyes turned to me, but she didn't seem ashamed, and maybe only partially aware of how obvious it was that she was crying.

"I'm sad," she said with a small shrug.

"I'm sorry," I said. "I won't bother you." I plugged in my headphones and started a podcast before I realized she was still looking at me. I paused the podcast and removed my earbuds.

"I don't love to fly," she said. She had an accent. She couldn't be French, could she? French people weren't typically as quick as Americans to strike up conversations with strangers.

"Neither do I," I said. "But I love to travel, so I have to."

She angled her body toward me. "Same, same."

"I'm Courtney."

She slipped her hand, soft and cool, into mine. "Salomé." *Se serrer la main.*

I'd always wanted to meet someone named Salomé.

She was prettier than me, but not by a lot. Her hair was dark blonde, parted down the middle and cut into a long bob with curtain bangs. Each time she tucked her bangs behind her ear, they fell right back out, dusting her cheek. It was more the way she moved that gave me the sense that she was beautiful, some sort of sensual lag behind the beat.

There were a number of normal responses for a situation like this: "Oh, what a lovely name," or even, "I've always wanted to meet a Salomé."

But I said, "You aren't going to behead me, are you?"

Her mouth fell open.

"I'm sorry, you probably hear that all the time."

She tilted her head slightly to the side. "No, I don't. And never before from a young person."

"I'm a recovering Catholic," I said. "And I'm not that young."

She squinted and leaned a little closer. "I think we are the same age."

"I'm thirty-one."

"I'm twenty-nine," she said.

"Well. I'm actually thirty. My birthday is on Sunday. It's Saint John the Baptist Day, which is why I knew that whole thing about your name."

"*Joyeux anniversaire*," she said.

"Thank you." I didn't want the conversation to switch to French, though it was unlikely she expected it to. It wasn't that my French was rusty. I was afraid to make mistakes.

Salomé lifted the window shade to look down where the airline workers were bustling around the exterior of the plane and immediately closed it again. Somehow, I knew how the next exchange would unfold, though I tried to talk myself out of it at first. I always chose the aisle seat. The window was too claustrophobic, and I could never bring myself to wake a sleeping passenger to slide past to go to the bathroom. But mostly I avoided that seat because in my worst moments of plane anxiety I would imagine the glass bursting open and sucking my body out, where I would still be conscious as I started to fall.

I knew she didn't want the window seat either. I couldn't stop myself; I asked, "Would you like to switch seats?"

She raised her eyebrows in pleasant surprise. "Oh, how did you know? Yes, thank you, I don't like the window. It was the only seat available. I just bought my ticket yesterday."

I almost had the row to myself. And now I was voluntarily giving up my seat because a pretty young woman seemed to want it. How chivalrous. We awkwardly switched seats. My new seat was still warm where her narrower hips had been. One by one, she handed me my cell phone, hand sanitizer, and bottle of water from the seat back pocket so delicately you'd think she was handling butterflies. I did the same with hers.

The last item was the notebook I'd hoped to use as a journal but which was mostly filled with to-do lists. She ran her fingertips over its embossed cover, swirling gold and green. It was a Christmas gift from my dad, who had gotten the idea years before that I liked Celtic stuff, which was neither true nor untrue.

"Pretty," she said, before handing it to me.

The flight attendant came by and pressed the overhead bin closed. The engines rumbled to a new frequency. I spelled *serrer* across my fingers a few times and tried not to hold my breath. If I used the right distractions, it wouldn't be so bad. I spelled through the flight attendant's safety spiel, first in English and then in halting French, and through the Delta commercial that played involuntarily on our screens. I got my stopwatch ready as the plane rolled forward and picked up speed, and pressed "start" as soon as the wings caught air. The plane tilted dramatically to the left at twenty-two seconds. I just had to keep my eyes trained on the stopwatch for two more minutes. The Concorde flight 4590 crashed on July 25, 2000, two minutes after taking off from Charles de Gaulle Airport. So after two and a half minutes, I would consider myself safe until landing.

You need to meditate. That's what they all said. Friends, boyfriends, all of them, and every last drop of advice unsolicited. Meditating involved *going in there* and that's the last place I ever wanted to be. Imagine it's snowing. You decide to give in to the whimsical moment and open your mouth to let a snowflake land on your tongue. But instead of a snowflake, an entire battlefield's worth of bullets rains down on your open mouth and pummels you into the ground. That's what it felt like to go in there. But it was okay. I'd learned to circumvent the battlefield.

I tried spelling "Salomé" across my fingers, but it didn't fit well. It had a silvery quality, like water moving beneath the surface of a frozen river. What a beautiful name. Was she named after the biblical Salomé, who'd ordered the head of John the Baptist brought to her on a plate? She obviously understood my reference. The name was too distinct to not be deliberate.

Maybe Salomé was thinking of how my name didn't suit me. In French, *court* means "short." Maybe she could feel my thoughts snaking out like tendrils and filling up the plane. The ones that got close all felt it eventually.

Right at two minutes and thirty seconds, there was a ding. The flight attendant's voice came across the intercom. "On behalf of Delta, we want to thank you for flying with us. Our priority is your safety and comfort . . ."

I stopped my timer and slipped my phone into the seat back pocket. Salomé was watching *Bridesmaids* with French subtitles.

I often made ridiculous goals for flights, like reading an entire book or writing the first draft of an article, which I was never able to accomplish. It was a demoralizing cycle: I'd make a goal, get too nervous to perform, then feel guilty for resorting to the in-flight entertainment. But Salomé had just gone for it. She probably hadn't worried I'd judge her for her film selection, either.

There was something inviting about her that suggested she wouldn't mind being politely observed—or perhaps that she already assumed she was being observed. I scrolled through the films and chose *Bridesmaids* with French subtitles.

Not a minute later, I felt her cool fingers on my arm. She pointed to my screen.

"I love this movie," I said.

She paused her screen. "I will wait for you. You are like two minutes behind."

"We can discuss it afterward."

"Yes, like a film club."

"I'm sure this film will require a lot of heavy discussion of themes, you know. It looks pretty dense," I said, right as the electric gate Kristen Wiig had climbed trying to leave her fuckboy's house jolted into motion with her on it.

She nodded, watching my screen for it to catch up with hers.

We laughed at the same parts. When the crew of bridesmaids got food poisoning at a dress fitting, Salomé covered her whole face with her hands and shook her head. A couple of times during a particularly funny moment we looked at each other, and I was struck by how natural it felt to be hanging out with her. My friend in Raleigh had recently adopted the word "vibing" into her vocabulary. I'd thought it was stupid at first, but it seemed to fit here.

The flight attendants rolled dinner carts through the aisles. Salomé got the vegetarian option, and I got the same. I usually thought airplane meals were pretty good, considering. But I was no foodie. Would Salomé be a picky eater and be put off by me eating airplane food?

She didn't peel the film back on her dinner until her drink arrived. She got red wine, and I did too. She turned to me and mimed a little cheers with her plastic cup. She made a face to indicate that it wasn't the world's best wine, but it was a good-natured expression. With synchronized fingers, we unpaused the movie.

I could get used to this dinner and movie club, held somewhere above the North Atlantic, en route to France. I'd gladly endure the stress of takeoff for this.

When the credits scrolled, we both removed our headphones.

"What did you think?" I asked.

"I liked it. Very funny. But you know, this jealousy is weird. Like, can you not have more than one friend?"

Before I could respond, the plane hit a patch of turbulence so rough that the woman behind us screamed. Wine leapt over the lip of my plastic cup and pooled onto my tray table. The seat belt light dinged on and a flight attendant hurried down the aisle to get back to her seat. A baby wailed. Salomé wiped up my spilled wine with her napkin.

I watched the napkin turn purple as her hand moved back and forth. My vision tunneled backward, blackening at the edges. My hands were going numb. I spelled *serrer*, not even trying to hide the movement in my fingers.

"Do you play the piano?" Salomé asked.

It took me a second to realize why she was asking. I shook my hands at the wrists. "Oh, no."

The plane lurched again, dropping my stomach. Our hands instinctively found each other. Mine were so sweaty, I was sure she regretted touching me.

"Let's just talk a little while," she said. I pulled my attention to her. There was a small spatter of freckles on the bridge of her nose, with three dark ones that formed a perfect isosceles triangle.

"Where are you from?" She kept her eyes fixed on mine, a spotlight guiding a tightrope walker to the other end of the wire.

"Raleigh." I hoped she couldn't hear how my voice wavered over the sound of the engines. "Where are you from?" We hadn't actually established that she was French; I just assumed. She could be Belgian or Swiss or something.

"I'm from Paris. But I am going to stay with my mother in a little town called Châteaubriant. Do you know it?"

I shook my head.

"I would think it very weird if you knew it," she said.

"Where is it?"

"It is between Rennes and Nantes. Southwest of Paris."

I wasn't very familiar with that region. "What were you doing in the States?"

She made a very French expression, blowing a puff of air upward. "Bah, well. Nothing. I was in Raleigh since three months, and there, I did nothing. Some babysitting." She put the emphasis on the second syllable of Ra*leigh.*

"What brought you to Raleigh?"

"I went to stay with my boyfriend."

"Is he going to come see you in France?"

She looked at her thumbnail, and that's when I remembered the crying. "No, I will not see him again. He decided it was too difficult, with the distance. But before I am even on the plane, he has another woman. It's terrible. It sucks."

Granted, I'd only known her for three hours, but I couldn't imagine someone rejecting her. This did, however, give us something in common, if you considered someone remaining devotedly neutral about you for months as rejection. "His loss," I said.

"His what?"

"Loss. He's an idiot," I said.

She cut me a glance from under her bangs. "He's an eediot."

"That's why you're sad?"

"Mostly."

"If it makes you feel better, I recently got my feelings hurt by a guy, too. And you know what always helps? Talking about why he sucks. What's the most annoying thing about him?"

"Justin . . . 'e was allergic to everything. Flowers, bees, grass. I am surprised not air."

"So he's an indoor kid. Are *you* an indoor kid?"

She laughed. "Me, I am not like that. I like to be outside. I love to be with nature and animals. Justin could not have a pet."

"Yeah, so see, maybe it wasn't a good match."

Her eyes roamed down to my chin and back to my eyes. She hesitated, but didn't say whatever she was thinking. I realized the turbulence was over. We let go of each other's hands.

"What?" I said.

She smiled. "I was trying to help *you*."

"It's okay. You did help. Thank you. I was kind of freaking out."

"I know. And when you first see me, I am crying," she said. "We are a mess!"

I smiled at her. It was nice not to be the only mess. For a moment it seemed that we'd stop talking. I didn't want to risk coming off as an annoying American by making small talk. What if she was too nice to brush me off and ended up having to tolerate me for the rest of the flight?

She spoke next. "I was thinking I would meet so many friends in America because Americans are friendly, but you are the first person in three months to be so nice to me, and we are on the plane to France."

"Yeah, Americans are friendly, but I'm not sure we're very good at being friends."

"What do you mean?"

"I don't know. We feel competitive a lot. And I feel like our society doesn't actually value closeness as much as it values proximity. Like, social proximity, not physical. We aren't good at that, either. But that's just my take on it."

"The French like to say that we are hard on the outside and soft on the inside, but with Americans it is the opposite," she said.

"Yeah, I've heard that too. Do you think it's true?"

"Before I was here, I didn't believe it. But now, I think maybe," she said.

"Yeah. It does seem true at face value. But I don't know. I'm a journalist and I spend so much time agonizing over what's a stereotype and what's a general cultural comment or idea worth exploring."

A flight attendant passed, collecting garbage. Salomé handed over her tray and dropped her cup into the trash bag. I did the same. She looked like she was carefully considering what she would say next. I hoped I hadn't offended her by suggesting that she was stereotyping. I was about to clarify when she turned toward me and leaned her temple against the seat.

"Will you be in Paris only?" she asked.

"Yes, until next Wednesday." I laughed and added, "I guess that's pretty stereotypical—only going to Paris."

She didn't laugh with me. "Will you be alone?"

"Well, not really. I studied there in college. My roommate never left, so I come every other year, sometimes every year if I can afford it, and stay with her to go to museums and eat and stuff. It's not luxurious or anything, I mean I'm sleeping on a futon . . ." And, in all likelihood, I wouldn't be coming back next year. By then, I'd probably be taking care of my mom full-time. I should've been with her now instead of on a plane to Paris.

My face must've betrayed my thoughts. She narrowed her eyes. "What?"

I didn't want to say anything about my mom's Alzheimer's diagnosis. But that wasn't the only reason this trip felt a little different, so

I could still answer honestly without bringing it up. "Oh, well, it's kind of funny. My old roommate, Kylie, she's trying to be an influencer now, so she actually does try to make everything look luxurious, or maybe 'effortless' is a better word."

"Like on Instagram?"

"Yeah, and YouTube. She was just starting this up last year, and I felt like she was using me for content. She was constantly on her phone. And she filmed me a lot, but I'm not good at that stuff so she had to direct me. Then she got a little frustrated that I wasn't going to yield any good content."

She nodded slowly. If I didn't stop talking, I'd launch into a well-rehearsed rant. Salomé seemed interested, though. I couldn't stop myself.

"She's trying to do these comedic France versus America posts, but they're just not funny. To watch her stuff, you'd think that no French people actually go to work and that everyone's just smoking and having casual sex all the time. I don't know. It just feels cheap."

Salomé clicked her tongue. "Ah, just what you don't like."

"Yeah, but honestly, she's a great person. I don't like her social media presence, but I like her. We're friends," I said. What I didn't say was that I had it in the back of my mind to write a story about the rise of influencer culture, particularly as it related to consumerist travel. I hadn't decided yet. But I would certainly observe Kylie through a different lens than I had last time.

Salomé pressed her lips together. I was about to try to keep convincing her that I liked Kylie when she said, "I thought Americans weren't so good at being friends."

I gave her a bemused shrug. "Yeah, I mean, this is a pretty good example of that."

"Do you want to come to Châteaubriant?" She said it casually, as if she were asking if I wanted to grab a coffee.

Had I heard her correctly? "Now?"

"Yes, now. You can come for a day or two if you like. It is not a far ride on the TGV, just like two hours."

If she'd asked me to hang out in Paris, I wouldn't hesitate. "Well, Kylie . . . she would be mad if I changed my plans."

"You will be in just Paris for more than a week? And she will be mad that you don't stay on her futon the entire time?" Her accent was cute on "futon."

"Well," I said. "There's a part of me that was hoping to get inspired to write something new, and I think Paris is the best place for that."

"What do you write?"

"I freelance for a newsmagazine in Raleigh. The *Raleigh Scene*, do you know it?"

"The one inside every store and restaurant?" she said, referring to the magazine stands where the *Scene* was dropped off weekly.

"Yeah. But I also write other stuff on my own. I'm trying to get into cultural commentary . . . whatever that means."

Salomé looked away for a second, then met my gaze with a little smirk. "So, you are going to write about the influencer?"

How did she know? I felt slightly disgusting for the way I'd planned to study Kylie, but I didn't feel like Salomé was trying to call me out. "I don't know. It does seem like an interesting topic. But, you know, I don't blame people for using these platforms to make money. It's empowering in a way. But then again, it's just another form of consumerism."

"I hate it." She brushed her bangs away from her face. "My town, it has a very interesting history. Do you know Guy Môquet, who is a symbol of the Résistance?"

"I guess that's who the Métro stop in Paris is named after?"

"Yes. He was executed at an internment camp in Châteaubriant. I think there is something you can write about to compare with American politics. Americans don't really know about him. Could be interesting."

Kylie and I used to live near that Métro stop. I remembered Guy's image inside the station, a black-and-white photograph of a teenage boy. The last thing I was interested in writing was a World War II piece. But I felt a bit embarrassed over the Kylie thing, so I pretended to consider it.

"And I promise, I won't put you on Instagram. I don't have it."

I didn't have any concrete plans in Paris, but it felt wrong to spontaneously agree to change everything. I laughed uncomfortably. "You really want me to come?"

"I am about to be there with only my mother and her stupid boyfriend for I don't know 'ow long, so would be nice to have a friend. And to keep speaking English."

"Your mother wouldn't mind?"

She thought for a second. "I think she will understand."

Maybe her small-town mother didn't speak English and I would be forced to practice my French. That would be good for me, even though I wasn't very comfortable with the idea. "Okay, I'll get your contact information and maybe I'll come over there after I talk to my friend. Or maybe she'll be up for a little trip and we'll come together."

She shrugged. "Okay, but will be better just you, I think. I don't want to be on YouTube, either."

I wrote my name, email address, and phone number in my notebook and ripped off the page.

She folded it crisply down the center and stuck it in the seat back pocket. "Okay, I will try to sleep a little." She inflated her neck pillow and settled in with her head facing the aisle, so I couldn't see if her eyes were closed.

I turned away too, lifting the window shade. Sunlight dappled the tops of the clouds. I focused on the prism of frozen condensation between the panes. Last year when I visited Paris, I walked by the apartment I used to share with Kylie above the *serrurerie.* It looked the same, but when I tried to imagine the inside, all I saw were the pictures I'd put on Facebook. I could no longer remember the sensation of the herringbone floorboards under my feet or the exact layout of the tiny kitchen. From the sidewalk, I saw the locksmith in his shop, bent over the desk. He was older now, with glasses far down his nose and a shiny bald spot on the back of his head. We'd spoken many times as I'd come and gone from my door right next to his. I considered going in to say hello, but couldn't bring myself to do it. I couldn't remember his name.

There were other things that marred the trip with an unexpected heaviness. Cigarettes bothered me now. So did the dog shit on literally every walking surface, in all levels of decomposition: fresh *crottes*, tracked-through, rained-on, sunbaked. Everywhere. Then there were the tourists, choking some streets until they were impassable. I'd become so claustrophobic while following Kylie across one of the bridges over the Seine that I'd almost fainted. The experience had made me worry that my attraction to Paris was more an attraction to my own youth. But I had to try again. All love affairs faltered from time to time, right?

The intercom announced the breakfast service. Salomé stirred awake. She tapped the screen on the seat in front of her, scrolling over so that it showed our time until landing. Two hours, twelve minutes to go. I was watching random episodes of *It's Always Sunny in Philadelphia.*

She pulled her phone out from under her thigh and scrolled

through a few photos. She paused on a picture of herself and a late-twenties guy and turned the phone so I could see it.

"Zis is 'im."

"Who?" I hadn't meant to be so obviously watching her. The guy in the photo was skinny with a big Adam's apple. "Oh wait, I know that guy. He works at Uncommon Ground, right?"

"Yeah."

"I go there all the time to work. Wow, small world."

"Well when you will be back next time, you will see the girl he prefers than me. She works there too."

"Wait, is she the one who always wears pigtails?"

"What is this?"

"Oh, umm, *queues de—?*" I knew the word for pigtails was not a direct translation from English, but I couldn't remember which animal it was. I defaulted to hand gestures.

"Yes, this is her."

I made a face like the one she'd made after tasting the airplane wine. "She probably just caters to his ego and makes him feel like a man despite the fact that he's deeply insecure. It doesn't have anything to do with you."

She was listening, but didn't say anything back.

"What kind of music does he play, anyway?" I asked. "He's a musician, right?"

"How did you know?"

"His left shoulder is like this." I jacked my shoulder up.

She laughed. "You notice this?"

"Well, I mean, I've dated a guitar player before." "Dated" was a generous word.

"He does like punk rock, like the Pixies kind of, but more angry."

I groaned. "I know exactly what you mean. Let me guess, he's the lead singer too?"

"He used to be, but now this girl is added to the group and she screams into the microphone and like . . . makes out with it. She holds like . . ." She held her fist close to her mouth. "And is like, 'baaaah baaa baaaa babaaahhh' and I am like, it's not a dick, you know? But she wants everybody to think of her as 'olding a penis. I saw the microphone after a show one time and it had lipstick all over."

I laughed louder than I meant to and covered my mouth in case I had morning breath. "Did you ever try to be her friend?"

"Well, every time I talk to her she was like, 'What? What are you saying, I am not understanding you,' and so I stopped. At the same time she is saying to my boyfriend, 'Sa-loam does not like me.' Like she cannot say 'Sa-lo-may.'"

"Girl, bye."

She laughed. "I like this, 'girl, bye.'" She waved her hand like she was swatting a gnat from her face. She bit her bottom lip, then deleted the picture. "And, boy, bye," she said.

How could this American guy have considered replacing her? "I mean, I hardly know you, but I can tell he doesn't deserve you."

She smiled with her lips closed. "You're right, you do not know me. But thank you."

It could've sounded dismissive, but I felt another small tug of invitation. I didn't care about her mother's small town or its macabre history. But I did want to know her, if she was offering. "Hey, so, I've been thinking, and . . ."

"Breakfast?" The flight attendant appeared behind her shoulder. She handed us each a plastic-wrapped croissant with a pad of butter and a plastic knife.

Once that cart had passed, another attendant gave us Styrofoam cups of weak coffee. Our eyes settled back on each other, the steam from our cups rising between us.

She blew a gentle ripple across her coffee. “You will come with me.”

“I think I’d like to. If the offer still stands.”

“Then it’s good.” She took a sip of coffee. “We will have fun for a day or couple of days, and then you can go to Paris.”

“Perfect,” I said.

For the first time in a long time, it felt like France wanted me, too.

CHAPTER 2

"*Bienvenue à Paris*," the flight attendant said to Salomé as she stepped through the airplane door. "Welcome to Paris," she said to me without hesitation. What made me so obviously American?

Salomé and I walked along the ramp together in silence and emerged into a quiet section of Charles de Gaulle Airport. We followed the flow of passengers into the large room with immigration lines.

"Meet me by the trains?" Salomé said, lightly touching my upper arm before splintering off toward the EU citizens line.

I did dread breaking the news to Kylie that I wasn't coming today. It wasn't spending less time with me that would bother her; it was the change of plans. Whenever I visited, I reminded Kylie that I wasn't a typical tourist and she didn't need to escort me around, but she usually did anyway, performing her deeply ingrained rendition of A Good Hostess. It exhausted me and it had to exhaust her, too, though she never admitted it. Now A Good Hostess was amplified through the lens of Influencer Effortlessly Living Her Best Life, which would be even more YouTube-able when juxtaposed with a disappointing sidekick: The One Who Didn't Leave America. It was true, but I didn't need the reminder.

In the passport line I opened Instagram. Kylie had posted a new story, a Boomerang video of her spinning in a circle in front of the Eiffel Tower. "THIS is your reminder to book a ticket to PARIS!"

I guess people needed a reminder to book a trip to the literal tourism capital of the world.

I texted her.

Just landed! So something strange happened and I hope you won't be mad, but I got invited to go to a little farm in the Loire for a couple of nights, and I really want to do it. It will be kind of a writing retreat for me. If I got to Paris on Friday would that be okay? I'm sure Mari wouldn't mind not having someone on the futon for two extra nights ☺

Love you and can't wait to see you on Friday ♡

I couldn't tell her I'd simply made a new friend. I worried she would find that unlikely. Bleak as it was, I assumed I wasn't the only person who didn't feel an authentic connection to many of their friends. In my experience, people revolved around each other like electrons attracted to the same nucleus, that nucleus being arbitrary: a shared last name, Francophilia, a dorm room, Harry Potter fandom. Humans were designed to cling to the others that kept being around.

The line inched forward. I definitely wouldn't tell Mom about my change of plans. It would prove stressful for her, as she had my itinerary printed out and taped to her refrigerator so she wouldn't forget where I was. At her doctor's suggestion she had programmed her routine into her Alexa, which reminded her to eat, brush her teeth, and do her other daily activities. Most of the time it annoyed her, she said. But it didn't annoy her as much as when she forgot something and her sister gave her a "knowing glance," so she kept Alexa. The plan was for me to move in with her whenever she started to struggle to take care of herself. At the moment she still lived on her own, though my aunt Trudy and I both lived minutes away.

Mom encouraged me to go on this trip, knowing that I might not be as untethered next year. I had felt confident in my decision to travel until last week when Mom and I were grocery shopping. She went to get something from another aisle but never returned. I found her one aisle over, touching the face of a child sitting cross-legged in a grocery cart. The child's mother had just noticed when I came rushing into the aisle. I apologized and explained my mother's condition, but the woman gave me a horrible look and threatened to call security. My mom was confused about why she couldn't touch the child. When I tried to explain it to her, for the first time, I felt like I was looking at a stranger.

I ruminated over the scene for hours afterward. I considered canceling my trip. But Mom's next few days were good, and Aunt Trudy assured me they'd be fine. And here I was, inching closer to the immigration officer who would add the last République Française stamp to my passport for many years.

Once I got the stamp, I followed the signs for the trains, walking as quickly as I could. I'd been in the immigration line for over an hour.

When I got to the train station waiting area, I scanned the people sitting on benches, buying espresso from vending machines, lining up behind the RER kiosks. Debussy's "Arabesque" floated through the room. It sounded like a real piano. Maybe it was Salomé playing?

She'd asked me if I played the piano. I followed the sound of the music until I found an upright piano near the escalators with a sign that said "*à vous de jouer*." The dark-haired player also had a violin case at her feet.

Salomé leaned against a pillar, the pianist's only stationary audience member. The expression on her face was one of enjoyment, but perhaps some recognition, too. Though I might have imagined the recognition because the music fit her so perfectly. I almost didn't want to interrupt, but I called her name.

Americans supposedly smile too much, but she smiled now, too. Her two front teeth overlapped a bit.

"I am so glad you're here!" she said. "I bought tickets and the train will leave in ten minutes. We have to go!"

We turned together and walked as fast as we could, following signs for "*trains grandes lignes*," weaving in and out of people, dodging luggage carts.

We passed platforms one and two. "I don't have any euros yet," I said. "I'll pay you back."

She shrugged. "You are my guest." She looked at her phone. "Sheet, we are at *voie* twenty-two. And we have six minutes."

She started running, her rolling bag rocking wildly from wheel to wheel. I followed, weighed down by my backpack. "*Attendez, attendez!*" she called to the uniformed man scanning tickets. He waved at us to hurry. He scanned the tickets on her phone, and we jumped on the first car seconds before the train lurched into motion. We had to inch our way down the center aisle of sixteen cars, knocking a few passengers' knees and shoulders with our bags.

"Oh fuck, they are backwards," she said when we reached our seats. "This always 'appens. It makes me so sick."

I slid my backpack onto the overhead rack, legs braced against the movement of the train. "It's okay. We won't look out."

I took the window seat and she took the aisle, both of us smiling as we hurtled backward toward Nantes.

I woke to total darkness. It took me a couple of seconds to remember where I was. I jutted my arm out to the right, knocking an empty water glass. My fingers found the familiarity of my phone and punched the center button: 2:53 a.m. Seemed about right. After we'd gotten to Salomé's mother's house the day before, we'd slept all afternoon. The "short ride" on the TGV Salomé had mentioned turned out to include a transfer in Nantes to a regional TER to Châteaubriant, which added another couple of hours to our trip. Salomé explained that you take the TGV to either Nantes, Rennes, or Angers, whichever the app says is fastest or cheapest, and then the TER from there. By the time we arrived at her house, we were exhausted.

I wasn't going to fall back asleep. If I held my breath, I could hear Salomé breathing in her bed, a tiny, faint whistling. I Googled the name Salomé. I read on Wikipedia that Salome's (with no accent aigu) stepfather, King Herod Antipas, offered her anything she wished for if she would dance for him at his birthday celebration. She obliged with a seductive dance, and asked for John the Baptist's head on a platter in return. That's about what I had already associated with the name. But I still didn't understand why John the Baptist was there in the first place.

The name and story had inspired centuries of art depicting a teenage girl holding a platter with a severed head on it. A play by Oscar Wilde presented her as an archetypal temptress whose lust for John the Baptist resulted in her death. An opera by Richard Strauss followed the same plot. There were many film adaptations over the past century, but I'd never seen one.

I resigned myself back to my pillow and closed my eyes against the bright rectangular scar the phone left across my vision. It was weird to be awake alone in someone else's house. I didn't want to lie here with my thoughts until morning with nothing to do but look at my phone. Even if this had happened in Kylie's living room, I could turn on a light or walk around without worrying about disturbing someone. *Serrer* flitted across my fingers. I wanted to get some water from the kitchen but couldn't convince myself to move. I turned onto my stomach, but my heartbeat was so loud against the mattress I could hear it through the pillow. Why had I come here? It had seemed so spontaneous at the time, something a younger version of myself would've done. But now I had to lie here in the dark and wait out the night.

I thought about Luke. The last time I'd seen him was about three months ago. He invited me over "for cocktails," which meant we drank whiskey on the rocks out of plastic cups in the dingy room he rented at the back of a house owned by a man who was almost twice our age but didn't act like it. Luke had just rolled off of me when the dryer buzzed. He left me lying on my side near the edge of the bed. He returned, still naked, holding a bear hug of clean, warm laundry, which he dropped on top of me. He pulled a plaid shirt off my face and smiled, the edges of his bright blue eyes crinkling.

"Don't you love that?" he said.

I burrowed into the warmth, breathed in the fragrance of his detergent. The tight knot in my center loosened a bit. "I do," I said.

He slid his arms through the fabric and around me. "That's why they call it Snuggles," he said, and kissed me.

The memory ended there, followed by the guilt of a woman who wanted to be more independent than she was.

Luke and I were just friends who got together a few times a month. I never spent the night at his place, mostly to save him the trouble of acting like he wanted me to. But we had a connection. His dad was sick; my mom was sick. We were both struggling to find our footing in dying creative industries. A few days after the Snuggles, he announced that he was moving to Nashville to be a full-time musician. I held up my plastic cup—another "cocktail"—and said, "Cheers," forcing myself to smile. Even as recently as a couple of years ago, I'd have held on to the hope that he'd come back to me or ask me to go with him, though he'd never promised me more. I knew better now. If Luke was going to live so unattached, then so should I. Except I wasn't going to be untethered for a long time. I consoled myself by booking a plane ticket to Paris, the real love of my life. That's how I'd unironically referred to Paris for the past decade. It only now occurred to me that it might be cringey.

I pressed my palms into my eyelids until the colors started. I imagined them snaking across the dark room, searching the corners until they found Salomé, then enveloping her in the warmth of clean laundry right out of the dryer.

When I opened my eyes to the light of morning, I didn't feel like I had slept. Salomé was gone. I heard clinking and murmuring coming from the kitchen. I got up and followed the sounds.

Salomé and her mother, Nathalie, leaned against the counter by the stove, bare feet on the tile. Blue flames leapt at the metal bottom of a stovetop percolator. They hadn't seen me yet.

Salomé wore a loose T-shirt and large, high-waisted panties—what I would consider granny panties—but she somehow looked glamorous in them. She was crying again. Probably, I hoped, about her ex-boyfriend. Nathalie reached out and cupped Salomé's face in her palms. My mother hadn't seen me in my underwear since I was a child;

nor had she touched my face since then. I would never allow either. A billow of grief threatened to overtake me. What if she'd thought that child in the grocery cart was me? You'd think that watching the recognizable pieces of her slip away would provide the framework we needed to get close, but it hadn't.

Nathalie removed her hands from Salomé's face. Salomé's jaw was clenched, more defiant than sad. She wasn't crying about a guy. Nathalie spoke in a hushed tone, barely audible over the hiss of the gas stove. Maybe I was wrong, but I thought I heard: ". . . *pourquoi . . . journaliste . . .*"

A sickly feeling spread through my stomach. Were they talking about me? I shifted my weight, and my foot made a small squeak against the tile.

Nathalie whipped around to face me. "*Coucou, Cour-ten-ey!*" I startled when she looked at me, but I didn't think she noticed. Her singsongy tone felt somewhat inauthentic, though I was glad to hear it after what I'd just seen.

"*Bonjour,*" I said. I couldn't pull off "*coucou.*"

"Did you sleep well?" Nathalie asked. When we'd briefly met before Salomé and I fell asleep yesterday, I was surprised by Nathalie's nearly fluent English. She said she traveled to England often to visit Salomé's older sister, Élise. But her vocabulary extended far beyond what she would need to travel. When I asked her where she'd learned, she said, "I learned it at university," with an air of wistfulness.

"I slept really well, thank you. The room is so quiet," I said, still feeling the need to redeem myself for intruding on them. Nathalie seemed pleased with my answer, as if she prided herself on the house's silence.

The first thing anyone would notice about Nathalie Leduc was that she was alarmingly thin—far past what typical dieting for aesthetic purposes would lead to. I found it hard to look directly at her, all tendons and metacarpals and puffy blue veins. She had a striking resemblance to Audrey Hepburn, but with Jackie Kennedy's wide-set, almost inanimate eyes, which appeared wet and lifeless at the same time, like a stuffed animal's. She seldom blinked, and when she did, her gaze often shifted, so I never knew where she would be looking when her eyes opened. Her dark brown hair was cut short. A family portrait in the living room from the early nineties revealed that she'd worn her hair short even as a younger woman. She was thin in the portrait, too, but not in the way she was now. I wondered if Nathalie wanted to be so thin or if she was sick. A few times, I'd detected an eerie desperation behind her eyes that was immediately negated by the inflection of her voice or what she said. This tension reminded me more of the Southern ladies I grew up around than it did the directness I associated with French women.

"Do you want coffee?" Salomé asked, her tone friendly. She wiped her eyes on the back of her wrist, making no effort to conceal her tears.

"Yes, please."

Salomé brought me a tiny espresso cup, steam rising off the top. There were goose bumps on her thighs; it was chilly in the stone house. France was expecting a heat wave later that week, and like most French homes, the Leducs' did not have an air conditioner. The stone was a fantastic natural insulator, Nathalie had explained last night. In the past, people knew how to design things to work with nature, not against it. The houses on this street were all built at a precise angle to limit how much direct sunlight came through the windows during the summer.

The kitchen and *salon* were one big room spanned by the thick, dark wooden beams crossing the ceiling, typical of a French country home. What was not typical were the security cameras situated in the upper corner of every room. This had seemed strange to Salomé as well. She'd noticed the cameras immediately upon arrival, but Nathalie brushed off her questions: "I'm here alone a lot, you know."

I hated security cameras. I went through paranoid phases from time to time, thinking I was being watched to the point that I would search a room for hidden cameras. As a kid, *The Truman Show* sent me into a full spiral, going so far as to surgically open the back of my teddy bear's head in search of a nanny cam. I stole a lace doily from Gran's linen closet and covered my face with it like a beekeeper as I walked the hallway of my own home. (The adults thought I was practicing for my future wedding—*aww.* I didn't correct them.)

I'd always had these paranoid tendencies, and they were rarely, if ever, correct. Maybe Salomé and Nathalie hadn't been talking about me. I must've misheard them. Despite her odd mannerisms, Nathalie seemed to like me.

Salomé took her coffee over to the couch, where she sat next to Louis, their black-and-white cat. I couldn't go sit next to Salomé without disturbing Louis, which I thought better of, so I stayed in the kitchen with Nathalie.

To avoid making eye contact with Nathalie, I looked at the beams crossing the ceiling. "I love these ceilings," I said.

"The beams are original," Nathalie said in French. "Almost three hundred years ago, someone chopped down these trees under a full moon and submerged them in a muddy offshoot of the Loire River for seventy-five years, where they were slowly preserved in a low-oxygen environment. Then they were retrieved, dried, and used to build the house. That's how they built things to last."

"That's older than my country."

"America is a teenager," Nathalie said in English, still looking upward. Her dry tone hinted at politics. She blinked, and when she opened her eyes, her gaze was fixed on me. "When my daughters were teenagers, I let them run wild and be 'umbled by life."

Heat rose to my cheeks. I looked back up at the beams. I hadn't wanted to discuss American politics in France, because what could I say? I didn't vote for him, but my dad did? That I was often consumed with trying to piece together how seemingly intelligent people could fall for an obvious narcissist? "Unfortunately it will take something really big to humble America."

"Oh, and France is not the same?" Salomé said from the couch. "We don't do the same sheet, we don't make laws for the rich only? We don't steal land? We don't put our soldiers everywhere?"

"I forgot that Salomé loves America," Nathalie said, almost teasing.

"I don't love America. I just don't think there is a very big difference between them as institutions of power," Salomé said in French.

I wasn't going to disagree with her this early in the morning, but I thought she'd probably have a different view if she had to pay for a shitty health insurance plan that valued shareholder profits over her actual health, or if she had been paying hundreds of dollars per month purely in interest on a student loan for the past ten years like many of my friends.

I said, "Let me know if you want to trade health care plans. Mine only costs three hundred dollars per month and you can only use it at like two places in North Carolina, and if you try to use it anywhere else, they'll send you a fifty-thousand-dollar bill." I hoped to diffuse the situation, not heighten the debate.

Nathalie laughed. Salomé scratched under Louis's chin. I wasn't sure how much she was listening to us.

Nathalie said, "You are both right. The United States and France both commit atrocities to gain and retain their power. And there are problems with every system, though some appear to value their citizens more than others. When you live somewhere long enough, you learn the problems, and think it must be better anywhere else. I tell my daughters, who are always running away, going all over the world—" She hesitated, translating in her head. "Somezing like, 'Where you go, you will be there also.'"

"Wherever you go, there you are," I offered.

"*Voilà*," said Nathalie.

We were silent for a few seconds. I hoped the conversation was over. Salomé's eyes flicked to the camera in the corner and lingered there an extra beat. Then she looked at me. "Okay, let's go see amazing France. I will show you the most boring town in the world." There was a small, almost caustic lilt to her voice that I wasn't sure was meant for me or Nathalie. Either way, it caught me off guard.

I laughed, hoping she was joking. "Wait, when you told me about it on the plane, you didn't say it was the most boring town in the world."

Nathalie, too, seemed to notice her small tonal shift. "What do you mean? Today is la Fête de la Musique."

Every year on June 21, France celebrates World Music Day as a holiday with free concerts on basically every street corner. I'd been in France several times for the Fête, as I often traveled over my birthday week, but only in Paris. "Will the Fête be big here?"

"Everybody will be in the streets," Nathalie said. Then to Salomé, she said in French, "If Châteaubriant is good enough for me, it should be good enough for you, Salomé. I stay busy enough, I assure you."

"I'm sure you do," Salomé muttered in English as she and I left the room. I felt certain the hint of irritation was meant for Nathalie, not me. Either way, I was ready to get out of the house.

I dug around in my backpack and pulled out a sleeveless top and a black pleated skirt I'd planned to wear for my birthday dinner. I'd packed for a much cooler France, but the forecast showed 34 degrees Celsius, which was over 90 degrees Fahrenheit, tomorrow. Why had

I brought two pairs of jeans? Before I took off my pajama shorts, I glanced at the security camera. Last night, Salomé had stood on a chair and slipped a sock over it, saying, "This is Marco, my mother's stupid boyfriend. He thinks he is so smart with this technology but all I need is a sock to ruin it." The blue light glowed through the fabric.

Nathalie said she put the camera in the bedroom because normally no one slept there, but someone could break a window and enter through this room. My dad and stepmom also had a state-of-the-art security system that they armed even when they took a shower, despite living in an incredibly safe suburb. I'd never seen something like this in France. Maybe Salomé was right. There wasn't a big difference.

I turned my back to Salomé and changed my clothes.

"I can't believe you have only a backpack," she said.

I did better with fewer choices. I'd end up wearing the same outfit for days no matter how much I packed. Plus, Kylie usually wanted to dress me from her own closet for anything special.

"Do I look like a tourist?" I asked.

Salomé wore a tank top and cuffed denim shorts. "You do, a little. Do I?"

"Somehow, no," I laughed. I'd learned that shorts were a faux pas in Paris, but maybe that didn't extend to all of France.

"It's okay, Châteaubriant has no tourists so they will feel lucky. Ready?"

She called "*À plus, Maman!*" as we walked toward the front door. The keyhole was leaking a slow drip of condensation onto the off-white tile. It was more humid here than in Paris. Salomé opened the door and we stepped out onto the sidewalk. As with many of the houses on the street, the sidewalk ran directly along the exterior walls.

Purple wisteria petals littered the sidewalk. The vine grew up the side of the house and into the eaves, where the blooms dangled luxuriously like clusters of grapes. A few petals dislodged, fluttering down.

The word "eavesdrop" came to mind, one of my favorites. *Écouter aux portes*, in French. Listening at the doors, exactly what I'd done this morning. *Journaliste.* I couldn't have heard that.

We walked single file down the slanted sidewalk, Salomé leading, me following. Two cars whizzed by, clattering across the cobblestones. "Was everything okay this morning? It seemed really tense when I came into the kitchen. I hope it's okay that I'm here."

"Oh, yeah. We were fighting. But not about you. She likes you," she said over her shoulder.

Maybe Salomé brought me here to act as a culturally obtuse buffer between the two of them, or to siphon some of her mother's attention away from her. I could play that role.

"Are we going anywhere in particular?" I asked.

"Yes," she said. "But first, we will walk past the château, which is not very pretty. It is over a thousand years old."

The downtown area was almost as quiet as the residential streets. Salomé offered commentary about spending her high school years here. Her narration got a tad louder when we passed a couple of people, perhaps showing off her skills in English. If she had been a man, this hint of showiness would've annoyed me. But I could see myself doing the same if giving a tour of Raleigh in French, if I were brave enough to do something like that. Why shouldn't she be proud?

We approached the château. Several men were setting up a soundstage on the lawn. Salomé was right; the château wasn't beautiful, especially compared to some of the others in the region. She didn't ask if I wanted to go in, which was good because I didn't. Castles can be Googled. What couldn't be Googled was the lightness in her step and the gentle, fluid way she used her hands when she talked, like she was subtly underscored by the Debussy song from the airport. The grace of her movements didn't feel uniquely feminine. I could easily imagine her father, whom I'd seen in the living room portrait, moving like this.

Thierry Leduc had passed away four years before from pancreatic cancer at seventy-four years old. He was at least twenty years older than Nathalie. A professor and a scientist. His several diplomas hung on the living room wall in dusty frames. When Salomé spoke of him, she held a certain reverence in her tone, lightly touching her sternum as if fingering a necklace that wasn't there. She did this now, when she asked if I wanted to see the old school where M. Leduc had taught once the family relocated from Paris. It was also relevant to my article about Guy Môquet, she assured me.

She led me to the far side of the château. Ahead of us lay a long, pebbled driveway that disappeared into a thick row of trees and brush. The sign read "Lycée Môquet."

My foot snagged in the tangle of wild grasses covering the pebbles. Salomé steadied me, placing a hand against my arm, and left it there for a few seconds. It was getting warm outside, but her hand was cool. There was something unique about her touch. But then again, I hadn't been touched by women very often outside of perfunctory hugs. Maybe all women had a coolness to them.

"*Hop*, here we are. This is my high school."

"You went to school here?"

"... *Oui* ..." she said on an inhale, a mannerism I'd mostly observed in older French women.

"How long ago?"

The building was in complete disrepair. The thin roof sagged, the top windows were boarded up, and ivy had taken over the left side so much that the pinkish brick, which was uncommon in this region, was barely visible.

"It closed five years ago."

"It looks like it's been empty for fifty years."

"I know, it's so strange."

"It looks haunted."

"It is. This is the field where the Résistance fighters were executed. The one I told you about, Guy Môquet, was only seventeen years old."

I didn't want to tell her now, but I was quite sure I wasn't going to write about the French Résistance, not because I didn't find it relevant, but because I was afraid. I was trying to fit into a lane that wasn't overtly political, nor particularly journalistic. I didn't want to get pigeonholed as a politics writer, where my every opinion or prediction would be on record in perpetuity. My recent interest in politics was by necessity, not by nature. I would've loved to get out of writing "articles" altogether in favor of longer, nuanced essays, like the human profiles in *The New Yorker.* Anything that didn't have to adhere to the inverted pyramid. I was one of the few *Raleigh Scene* writers who hadn't studied journalism in college and often had to revise my articles to be "less editorial." My editor complained that he couldn't easily lob off my final two paragraphs to save space. I was eventually moved to the online-only version of the magazine and, after a series of funding cuts, was removed from the permanent staff and made a freelancer. I still wrote my local features column, but now for a flat fee and without benefits.

I took on other gigs to bolster my income, which also allowed me to shift into more of the type of work I hoped would populate my portfolio of bylines. I'd had one such publication, in *Slate*, which caused a rift in my dad's side of the family, who did not share my politics.

Salomé stepped off the driveway and stomped through the knee-high grass toward the nearest ground-floor window. I followed her. She leaned close enough to the window that her breath fogged in two distinct streaks below her nostrils. "This was the . . . looby?"

"Lobby."

"Lobby, yes." She pressed her forehead against the glass.

I did the same. There was a grand staircase that opened in a flourish, the center of each step worn down from a century of footsteps. It was hard to imagine students climbing these elegant stairs to their classrooms, when all I had known were grimy, homogeneously speckled linoleum floors and buzzing fluorescent lights that always had dead bugs in them. The floors were stone as well, with cracks that crisscrossed like ley lines.

"Schools are usually not this pretty in the States."

Salomé looked through the window, shielding the sun from her eyes with a flat hand. "They are usually not this pretty here, either. But this is very old." Tiny beads of sweat had formed on her nose. "Oh, something moves!" she whispered.

In the center of the ceiling, the chandelier rocked gently, casting glints of sunlight across the back wall. "The chandelier!"

Salomé grasped my forearm. It was lovely how easily she did things like that.

"Is it a ghost?" I asked. Her hand was still on my arm.

"I am serious with you, when I was at school here, there was scary sheet happening all the time. It was like . . . *avoir la poisse, c'est quoi*?"

"I don't know."

"Comme un sort . . ."

"A curse?"

"Yes, it is a curse."

"Was it cursed by the resistance?"

"No, this spot has always been cursed since the *Moyen Âge* . . . what is this?"

"The Middle Ages."

"You know a lot of French, Cour-ten-ey," she said.

"In theory," I said, and laughed lightly. "I know a lot of things in theory." After a moment, I said, "I used to want to be a translator.

But . . . I don't know what happened. I didn't find work." I was tempted to blame the recession I graduated into, but it was more likely caused by my own inadequacy.

She looked at me, her head tilted slightly to the side. "You still could, I think."

I hadn't thought about it for a while, but now, spending time with a French peer, I realized how right that felt. I would love getting into the mindset of an author to the point of obsession, poring over nuance and lyricism, to create a collaborative piece of literature.

"You're right," I said. Why hadn't I realized that before? I had done the work to make that dream a possibility. It was just up to me to make a change.

She went back to looking through the window. I did the same.

I didn't feel this drawn to any of my friends at home. They had started to seem pretty lackluster, always trying to scaffold a get-together with something like a *Bachelor* watch party, which was fun, but we usually just exchanged the bullet point highlights of our lives, and rarely anything of substance. Did I know who my friends truly were? I knew I loved them, but what did I love *about* them?

I couldn't recall Salomé mentioning any friends. "Do any of your friends who went to school here with you still live in town? Or have they all moved away?"

She kept looking through the window. "I don't have any friends in Châteaubriant."

"Are they mostly in Paris?" I asked.

"No."

Just then a black bird swooped in from the lobby and landed on the chandelier, jolting it into motion. We screamed and scrambled back onto the driveway, laughing, our hands over our hearts.

As we started back down the path, Salomé's mind seemed to be elsewhere. A couple of times she looked back as if she'd heard her name called from the direction of the school. But when I followed her gaze, I saw nothing but an old building in shambles, receding behind the trees.

Viande?" Salomé picked a thin strip of pork fat out of her quiche.

She and Nathalie had a quick exchange in French: Basically, "Salomé can cook her own food if she is going to be picky. Plus, lardons are only fat, not actual meat. So, there."

Salomé shook her head and kept picking the bacon out of her quiche. It tasted like meat to me.

Nathalie blinked, opening her eyes to look at me. "I like Courten-ey very much, you know, she *eats*." She emphasized the last word in a way that made me self-conscious. I'd only eaten twice in front of her.

"And when do you eat, Maman?" Salomé said in French.

Nathalie waved away the accusation with a bony hand. "Nothing tastes good," she said in English. She must've said it hundreds of times before, because the comment came across as rote. "What did you see in the most boring French town?"

Salomé told Nathalie about going to the school because I was considering writing an essay on the French *résistance.* Nathalie stepped over to the sink, her arm raised with the back of her hand against her mouth, as if bracing against a wave of nausea. Perhaps it was painful for her to remember when her late husband taught there. Or was it the suggestion of me writing something that gave her pause? *Journaliste.*

Nathalie turned back toward us, her face composed and newly authoritative. "Okay, *les filles.* Today, I 'ave to do many things, and I will take the car." She dusted her hands off on her pants as if she were wearing an apron.

"Maman, are you not going to eat anything?" Salomé asked in French, her voice now verging on annoyance.

Nathalie dramatically popped a little tomato into her mouth and left the kitchen. As she strode through the living room, her hand traveled to her mouth and back to her side, and in a split second I saw the red flesh of an uncrushed tomato tucked into the crease of her palm.

CHAPTER 3

While Salomé showered, I glanced over the dust-covered objects on the bookshelves in the living room. An old wooden pipe, a set of fabric-bound books, three large rodent skulls, a bronze candle snuffer. I was tempted to categorize the decor as Dark Academia, but as soon as I had the thought, it would be offset by something truly familial, such as a professional photo of Salomé and Élise as shirtless young children with chocolate all over their mouths. The sisters were almost identical, though Élise's face was a little more square. They grinned at the camera, clinging to each other. Élise was missing a front tooth.

This was Thierry's childhood home. When Salomé was twelve, the family left Paris and came here to live with Thierry's father. It wasn't clear where they all slept, as the house only had two bedrooms.

I had also grown up with a grandparent in the house. When my parents divorced, Mom and I went to her mother's big yellow Victorian in Raleigh's Historic Oakwood neighborhood. I loved Gran's house, which was a good thing, because that's where I'd be moving shortly to take care of Mom. Someday, it would be mine, though it wouldn't come with a monetary inheritance large enough to afford its upkeep.

I slid a random book from the bookshelf. It was a print-on-demand book with a horrible cover design titled *Manger moins pour vivre plus.* Eat less to live longer. Maybe that was why Nathalie was so thin?

Three copies of another book were side-by-side on the shelf. I tilted my head to read the spines. *La science de l'immortalité* by Thierry Leduc. I slid one of the copies out. It was a slim book, only about one hundred pages, with a shiny black cover and white text. Salomé had told me Thierry was a scientist. What kind of scientist studies immortality? The back cover bio said he was a *gérontologue.* I assumed that meant he studied aging. That seemed like an interesting, if perhaps depressing, field of study. If Thierry were alive, I would've loved to ask if he had any insights into why the brain and the body seemed to age at different rates. Why do some people with sharp minds become entombed in their failing bodies, while others, like my mother, have good physical health with minds that turn on them? I flipped through the pages without trying to read anything. The French would surely go over my head.

My eyes rested on a jelly jar filled with thick, clear liquid. There was something floating in it—a pale, soft form that curled in on itself. I couldn't tell what it was. I set Thierry's book down to reach for it. I nearly dropped the jar when, out of the confusion, I perceived a face. Huge, blue-lidded eyes and a stiff, pale beak. An embryonic bird. A few sad feathers floated serenely, barely attached to the skin.

I looked over my shoulder at the white security camera in the corner, its eye trained on the bookshelf.

I heard Salomé approaching, her feet still damp on the tile. I felt like I was about to be caught, but Salomé said, "Oh, yes, *l'oiseau.*"

She took the jar from me and held it up to the light, giving it a gentle flick of the wrist to spin the bird around in the liquid, its tiny feathers quivering.

"I found 'im, when I was young, outside, on the . . . *trottoir*?"

"Sidewalk."

"I tried to get Papa to save 'im, but you know, he was already dead."

I took another close look at the bird. It made me sad the way Pluto made me sad. Suspended, alone, very cold.

"He used to make me sad, too." She ran her finger over the glass, then touched the jar to the center of her forehead, her eyelids so lightly closed that her lashes fluttered. She handed the jar to me, and I touched it to my forehead, too.

She watched me place the bird back where I'd found it. Her eyes landed on the displaced copy of Thierry's book. Something in her face sharpened—a pulse of the jaw muscles or a quick purse of the lips—but it was gone so immediately I doubted if I'd seen it.

I picked the book up. "It says on the back that your dad was a gerontologist," I said. "Was he really studying immortality?"

She paused, chewing the inside of her lip. Why did I mention immortality about someone so recently deceased? I went to reshelve the book.

She shook her head and touched my wrist to stop me from putting it away. "No, it's okay. He . . . was more interested in helping people age better, not making them live forever. The title is not really accurate."

I set the book on the shelf next to the bird, which felt like neutral territory. "I really didn't mean to pry."

"You can look," she said, gesturing to the book with her head. "Just don't write about it."

For the first time, I noticed a resemblance between her and Nathalie. A stillness in the way she held my gaze that made the air between us feel charged, something I couldn't decipher.

"What do you mean?"

"Nothing. I'm sorry." She stepped back, granting me permission to pick up the book.

I didn't reach for it. I didn't know what to say, so I asked if I could shower.

The tiny tub had a handheld showerhead and only a small pane of glass to contain the spray. The whole time I showered, I couldn't stop thinking about the weird interaction around the book. Write about what? Salomé's father? Or his book? I suppose I had told her I was trying to get inspired to write something, but I hadn't considered writing about her or her family. There must be a story here, otherwise she wouldn't have said that.

I turned off the water. From far away, I could hear the beat of live music from la Fête. I dried off and wrapped myself in a threadbare towel that smelled like it had dried in the sun. My armpits were getting spiky and I didn't have a razor, since I was convinced I couldn't bring one in my carry-on. My legs needed shaving, too. But even after I'd shaved there'd be a shadow. Salome's legs and armpits seemed effortlessly hairless. She didn't have to try. Her shins were smooth and tan; her feet had perfect arches and unpainted toenails. I wished I could be one of those women who unapologetically didn't shave. But I couldn't pull it off. Not the hair, but the un-apology.

On the bathroom shelf I found a small tube of body lotion. I squeezed some out onto my fingertips and breathed in the familiar, almost herbal smell of Salomé. There was something slightly transgressive about rubbing her lotion into my skin. Next to that was a bottle of air-dry hair serum. It had to be Salomé's. Nathalie's hair was too short. I shouldn't use all her stuff. It was tempting, though, to see what they smelled like, felt like. She'd chosen them intentionally. I squirted a bit into my palms and worked it through my hair. The only other product on the shelf was a little jar of face cream that smelled like flowers. I patted this onto my face with my fingertips. What if Salomé smelled her products on me? She wouldn't mind, would she? I should go by a pharmacy and pick up some of my own products and stop being a leech. I changed into the clothes I'd brought with me into the bathroom.

When I passed through the living room, *La science de l'immortalité* was still out on the shelf. What could be in this book that she felt she needed to guard? Or, perhaps, I realized with a pang of discomfort, it might not be the contents of the book she was protecting. It could simply be that I hadn't yet earned her trust. But there wouldn't be anything in these pages that I couldn't handle. I could impress her, even, by understanding the text, if I worked hard enough at it. I debated for a moment by the shelf. When my hair started dripping onto the floor, I made the quick decision to grab the book and carry it with me into the bedroom, hoping whoever was on the other side of the camera didn't see me take it.

Salomé sat cross-legged on her bed, her hair wet but drying. She was looking at her phone. I set Thierry's book on top of my bag. I didn't want her to see that I had it, but it didn't feel right to hide it from her, either.

"Do you want to go drinking?" she asked without looking up.

"Sure . . ." I said.

Salomé looked pissed. It seemed to be directed at whatever she was reading rather than at me. Still, I wanted to make sure I hadn't upset her with the book.

"What did you see?" I asked.

"Instagram. He has brought that girl to the party of someone I know."

"God, that's the worst. You should probably unfollow him. Wait, I thought you didn't have an Instagram?" I combed my fingers through my hair, which I hoped wouldn't spread the scent of her air-dry serum across the room. I sat down next to her on the edge of the bed.

"I don't. But sometimes I look at the page for his band. It is public." She didn't seem at all ashamed to be going out of her way to keep track of him.

"Can I see?"

She turned the phone, where Instagram was open on her internet browser. It was a circle of guys playing some dorky game like Dungeons & Dragons with their pads of paper and pencils in hand, and one girl with chunky blonde braided pigtails sitting toward the middle. She was captured mid-sip of a Coors Light, her eyes red from the flash, bottom jaw and hand out of focus, pinkie garishly extended. She looked like a sorority girl who'd dropped out of college.

The guys in the circle were all tall and skinny, wearing graphic T-shirts from high school, and had the vibe of self-important musicians. Justin sounded like he was from New York, or maybe Boston, I recalled. Something nasal.

"She called him when she was upset and he would never say, 'Sorry, I can't talk, I am with Salomé.' He liked that she needed him to save her." She lifted her finger to her mouth and bit at a cuticle. "I tell him, you want to be my 'ero, why don't you just not lie to me?"

"Men are trash, you know."

It wasn't the most worldly advice, but her eyes lit up. "Trash?"

"Yes, trash. *Déchets. Poubelle.*"

She laughed. "Men are trash. Yes. What did your guy do?"

"He was . . . also a self-important musician. He didn't really do anything terrible. He spent a year acting interested in me and then just moved to Nashville without even considering me. I mean, I don't know what I expected. It's not like I could've gone with him anyway, so maybe he did me a favor by not asking." That's all I wanted to say about Luke. I didn't deserve to be angry at him. We were not in love.

She shifted around on the bed. "It feels so strange to be in my room again."

"How long were you gone?"

"I moved back to Paris in 2007. I have only been here once since Papa died."

"You left Paris for Raleigh?"

"Yes, I went to university there and then was working."

"So you left a job to go to the States?"

"Euh . . . well, I was a waitress before I met Justin." She flopped backward onto the bed, draping her forearm across her eyes. "I will tell you later."

We heard the sound of drums and the throb of a bass, disjointed over the distance.

"Okay, let's go drinking," I said.

It was almost 20h and the sun was still high. This far west and on the longest day of the year, the sun wouldn't fully set until almost midnight.

The music grew louder as we neared the château. It was a big band playing swing. People danced in front of the château, mostly in pairs, occasionally bumping into each other and laughing. We stood and watched them until the song ended. The music was nice, but I wasn't in the mood to be in a crowd. Salomé wasn't either, apparently, and gestured with her head for me to walk with her behind the château. We followed the stone wall around the back to a filmy pond and sat in the limp grass near the water, listening to the cacophony of the music echo off the château's walls.

"Happy solstice," I said.

"Ah, *ouais, le solstice d'été*!"

I wanted to love the summer solstice. Three days before my birthday, during the week called the "cusp of magic." But it was the summer solstice, twenty-one years ago, when my dad left. Or when my mom and I left my dad. I always tried to frame it like that, but in truth, we all left.

I wondered if my mother could remember that day now. I only remembered fragments: the church ladies' smug faces as they strode across the yard, how after they told her about the affair, I found her crumpled next to her bed and brought her a glass of water. I knew she didn't want me to see her like that, even now. If any of her memories had to go, I hoped that one was first.

Salomé rested her forehead on her bent knees. She looked like a paper crane, gentle and delicate and exact. It had been a long time since I liked a person as much as I liked her. I wondered if I would've been so drawn to her if we'd met in another scenario. She might not have spoken to me first if she hadn't been in such a vulnerable state. And I may not have taken the time to connect with her if I hadn't been sequestered on a flight. If we'd met in Raleigh, I might've been in a hurry or pushing toward a deadline. She must've felt my attention on her, because she looked up. We'd been sitting in silence for longer than I realized.

"What were you thinking?" she asked.

I'd been snapped at by two different boyfriends for asking this. "I hate that question," they'd both said, as if they'd read in a forum somewhere that you should never allow a woman to know what goes on in the fortress of your man mind. Fuck those guys.

"On the summer solstice when I was nine, my mom found out that my dad was having an affair, which totally unraveled our lives. It was a few days before my birthday, which is probably why I remember exactly when it was. The day felt really, really long."

She placed her hand on my back and her eyes roamed my face. For a moment it felt like she might drop a line of genius, something that summed it all up in the most perfectly human way. But she said, "Wine?" That worked, too.

We walked through a few crowded blocks to a little wine bar with a courtyard, warmly lit by string lighting and real candles on all the tables. There was a four-piece band with a female singer.

The courtyard was full of older women, laughing, lifting their glasses, spinning around with their dance partners. There was a confidence about them that I didn't see much of at home. France had the second-worst body image rating of any country, someone told me. I never asked for their sources, but it seemed right, considering how as a young student in Paris, I was bombarded by bus stop advertisements for diet pills with pictures of tape measures looped around thighs and stomachs. I also never found out which country was supposed to be number one on that list, but I assumed, given how many of my thoughts could be consumed with hating my body, that it was the US. Now, it all seemed wrong. If these French women poked and prodded their faces in the privacy of their bathroom mirrors, wishing if only this piece would defy gravity like it used to so they could earn the attention of men again, they hid it well.

Salomé found a little two-top near the back of the courtyard. Once we were seated, I said, "I so rarely see older women enjoying themselves like this in the States. I love it. They're stunning."

Salomé looked around. "Yes, they look good. Age is something we earn. It is what my father was working for. So that as we age, we are not . . . punished by our bodies."

"Back home, if a woman dares to age, even if her body doesn't punish her, society will. Our men are coddled to the point that they don't understand that time passes for women, too, and we don't seem to expect them to learn it. Instead of holding them accountable for wanting to date women half their age, as if that's some sort of symbol of worthiness, we are expected to look half their age. And if we don't want to spend thousands of dollars on a facelift, they'll date someone twenty years younger. It's a sick mind game."

Salomé teased her bangs with her fingers. "I know what you are saying. But you know, my mother was twenty years younger than my father, and they were really in love. Twenty-one, actually."

I'd forgotten that. "Oh, I'm sorry, I was talking about my dad, I didn't mean—"

"No, it's okay. I know what you mean. It happens in France, too, the beauty standards. But still, you see things like this"—she gestured to the other women in the courtyard—"and remember that we are young now, and when we are old, we will still be beautiful and fun."

"How did your parents meet?" I asked.

"They met when Maman was at university. Papa was her professor, but only for one class." She said this as if it weren't scandalous in the least. Maybe it wasn't at the time. It must've been the mid-eighties.

When the server came by, Salomé asked if the white wine was cold. He confirmed it was. We ordered a bottle. The server brought our wine and two glasses, along with a used ashtray. When the server left, Salomé slid the ashtray over to the far end of the table using the edge of her pinkie.

"You don't smoke at all?" I asked.

"Never," she said. "I think it's so gross."

"Me, too," I said. "I think smoking is the one criticism I have of the French."

"Well that means I am perfect, because I am French and I don't smoke," she said with a disarming smile.

She was right. I couldn't believe I'd met her and had been invited into her life.

We clinked our glasses together. *Santé.*

I asked about her time in Paris.

She told me that when she met Justin, she lived in an apartment in the 20th arrondissement with two other girls and had no money. The toilet wasn't even in their apartment, but down the hall. It didn't sound like her roommates had been very cool. They'd filled her room as soon as she left, even though she paid them to keep it empty for two months.

Her sister, Élise, lived in London and was married; Salomé was tepid toward her Scottish brother-in-law, whose name was so Scottish I didn't understand what she was saying. I couldn't imagine having married at twenty-four, especially to someone who didn't speak the same first language as me. I told Salomé about how in college, my French-major boyfriend and I decided to have our fights only in French to simplify the things we were capable of saying, so we wouldn't obsess over the minutiae, but that didn't help.

"Did Justin speak French?" I asked.

"*Bah, non*, well, a little. He knew *bonjour*, *au revoir*, *je t'aime*, and things like that."

"Did you love him?" I hoped it wasn't a rude question.

She picked up the wine bottle and refilled her glass. She sighed. "I wanted to."

"You moved to the US for him, though. That's a lot, right?"

She swatted the air playfully. "Cour-ten-ey, are you telling me that if a cute Frenchman offered for you to come live with 'im for free, that you would not give it a try? Or a woman, sorry, I should not assume."

I smiled at her. "No, you're right." I'd almost forgotten I hadn't come to France to visit her. We fit together, as if it had always been this way. I liked French Courtney, humbled by the language barrier, who didn't feel like she was on a TGV hurtling toward the end of her relevancy. What was relevancy, anyway? It was different here.

"So the one thing I've gotten published that I was proud of at all was this thing I wrote last year, this 'comfort-as-enemy' piece, basically about how the baseline comfort the average middle-class white American lives in, you know, streaming services, air-conditioning, home internet connection, fast food, all that, provides a false sense of security about the permanence of our way of life. Compared with much of the world, our day-to-day lives are pretty cushy. And because of that, we really have no idea how quickly things can change. We could elect a dictator after entertaining the wrong rhetoric for one generation."

Salomé was listening, nodding along. "This is absolutely true."

"And like, don't get me wrong, I'm proud of the article, but it also opened up this horrible insecurity in me. A lot of other 'think pieces'—I hate that term, but that's what they're called—came out around that time that touched on this same idea, and they were so much better than mine."

Salomé clicked her tongue. "Oh, *c'est normal.* I'm sure your article was good, or it would not be published."

I was tipsy, resting both of my elbows on the table to lean closer to her. "And the worst part, or maybe the next-to-worst part, was that it super pissed off my family."

"You are not serious! You are just doing your job!" she said.

She was right. I *was* just doing my job. Hadn't my dad always encouraged me to work hard? I worked my ass off. Besides my pilgrimages to France, I hadn't taken a weekend off in years. It wasn't my problem if he didn't like what I did for work, or the person I'd become in his absence.

"We were at Thanksgiving at my dad's house, and my half sister,

Hannah, who had just turned nineteen at the time, seized the opportunity to differentiate herself from me and became a 'no-nonsense' conservative. She's majoring in journalism, though I told her not to. I told her that reporters were doomed to be trapped in this special fucked-up limbo between the truth and whose incendiary headline can get the most clicks."

"What was the worst part?" she asked. She struggled to pronounce "worst" and we both giggled.

"The worst part was that the comments section below my article basically turned into a WWE match—do you know what that is?"

"No."

"Wrestling."

She laughed.

"A bunch of *Slate* subscribers got in all these stupid arguments with trolls and bots, which drove up engagement and pushed it up the SEO chain, which is actually what gets your article read, not the actual contents of it. So a lot of people read it. Which is, I guess, what I'm supposed to want?"

She shook her head. "I am honest with you, Cour-ten-ey, I had a 'real job' for a few years, and I realized that there is no end to . . . ah, fuck." She switched to French and said, "It doesn't matter what you do in a for-profit industry, you are and will forever be the little dog dancing next to the accordion man. And I couldn't do it anymore. I quit, and I became a waitress because at least then you know the parameters of your job."

"Is that your plan again, now?"

She blew a puff of air. "Bah. I guess so. I have no idea."

"What did you study in college?"

"*Pluridisciplinaire.* But my focus was philosophy," she said in a flat tone, as if that were nothing to be proud of. "And you?"

"French and English. Does that count as *pluridisciplinaire*?"

"I think yes."

I probably shouldn't have accepted that final glass she poured. I don't remember what we talked about at the end, but suddenly she stood up and said she wanted to show me the best thing about Châteaubriant. We pooled our money together. We only spent ten euros each.

As I rose from the table, I bumped my metal chair, sending it clattering across the ground. French Courtney wasn't as graceful as she could be. The musicians were between songs. "*Oh là là*," the singer said into the microphone. People looked at us. I hadn't been this drunk in a while. Salomé laughed, covering her mouth. I righted the chair and she grabbed my hand and we bolted out of the courtyard, giggling. We walked, arm in arm, through the throngs of people until Salomé took an abrupt turn into a narrow alleyway where we were alone. The clapping of our sandals echoed against the high walls flanking us, giving me the impression that we were walking into a cave. The muted sounds from another stage grew louder as we approached the end of the alley. We entered a square, bustling with people. Onstage a solo soprano performed an aria with a string quartet.

"*Hop*, 'ere we are," she said, stopping me with her arm. The white cathedral with its steeple sprawled upward, lit from below. Like everything I'd seen in this town, it wasn't spectacular. But in the moment, and scored by this music, I perceived it as glorious.

"Wow," I said, hoping I didn't sound drunk.

She was looking upward at the cathedral with the same expression she had while watching the airport pianist. "I've always seen it and it is so easy to lose your sense of . . . what is the word . . ."

"Awe?"

"Awe." Her gaze shifted to me, and she smiled.

"But you show it to someone new and you get to see it through their eyes," I said. She didn't seem to mind how cheesy that was.

She looked at me in a deeper way now that we were drunk. Her eyes moved from my eyes to my lips. "What?" she asked.

"I . . . I kind of want to be you." I was immediately embarrassed for saying this. I never would've said it sober.

"No, you don't!" Her tone was light, playful.

"I do. You're . . . so cool and smart, even though you don't have everything figured out, I feel like it's going to be okay for you, you know? And you get to live here."

"What is it in English . . . the grass is more greener . . . ?"

It was an apt usage. Even in my drunkenness I knew I was projecting. But still, in the glow of the cathedral's lighting, I swear there was a shimmer to her that I'd never have, not even if I got everything I wanted in life.

Instead, in French, I said, "If I were Justin, I would've learned your language."

"*Tu parles déjà ma langue*," she said.

We weren't looking at the cathedral anymore. We were standing so close the tips of our sandals were touching. People moved all around us, spinning like the inside of a snow globe. If she'd been a man, I would've been sure he'd kiss me then.

I took a step back, averting my gaze to the cathedral. I was supposed to leave tomorrow, but I couldn't imagine it. "Can you believe I'm leaving tomorrow?"

"Don't," she said. "We haven't gone to see the Guy Môquet stuff at the museum yet."

I almost forgot I was ostensibly here to do that. "I have to be honest, I don't think I'm going to write about that. But that's not why I want to stay."

She smiled. "You should know, I never did think you were going to write about it."

I didn't know what to say.

"Some people need a reason to do something, you know? Or a reason to tell themselves they are doing something."

"I mean, it worked."

She looked at the cathedral again. I didn't miss the pretense at all, now that it was gone. Once I left, whether that was tomorrow or just before I had to fly home, I knew I wouldn't stop thinking about seeing her again until I could make it happen.

We walked home, still linked at the elbow.

The room was spinning. I needed water, but I couldn't lift my head off the pillow. I ached all over, freezing, but the blanket hurt my skin. I closed my eyes to stop the ceiling from trembling. There was a song in my head. "Solitary Man" by Neil Diamond. Was Neil Diamond dead or alive? Please let him be alive. Dead people's songs always made me think about death in a way I wasn't prepared for in the middle of the night. My own, my mom's. I'd always been curious about the swell of endorphins the brain experienced upon death. Would it be psychedelic? How much would I feel like myself when it happened to me? Did people ever have songs stuck in their heads while they were dying? Stop it, stop it. I spelled *serrer.*

My mouth was parched. Getting water was a priority. I pressed myself upright and sat with my legs off the bed. Something hard touched my knee. Salomé, standing by my bed, her bony kneecap bumping mine. She handed me a cup. Water. I gulped it down and set the glass on the nightstand. I tried to thank her but the words wouldn't come out. She hadn't moved. What was she doing?

I reached my hands out and found her hips, pulled her toward me, pushed my face into the softness of her belly, maybe at first to ease the spinning. She pressed into me, not pushing me away, bringing me nearer and deeper into her skin, cool to the touch. Was she not wearing a shirt? My brain stopped whirring, the room stopped spinning. She slid her knee onto the bed between my thighs and gently pushed me backward. I was dizzy again for a second—I worried she was leaving but she slid on top of me, burying her head beside mine, down into my hair. I heard an inhalation, so sweet and lovely. She sat up, pressing her hands into my collarbones. She said, "Don't open your eyes," but it wasn't her voice. It was the most beautiful voice I'd ever heard, the color of snow, the thinness of pine needles. What was she saying? It was poetry, verses. I needed my notebook; how would I ever remember? "Don't open your eyes." I'd never had a woman on top of me before; she was so light, moving so gently, I wasn't going to get hurt, nothing was frightening. Did it feel good for her? The poem, the recitation, it was something ancient, not English, not French, but I knew it, I'd heard it before. I had to open my eyes. I had to see her, but they felt glued shut. I fought the pressure and opened my eyelids a sliver.

She was glowing. Her body was phosphorescent in the moonlight, and no, she didn't have a shirt on, she was completely naked. I worked my eyes open a little more. My hand was too heavy to lift to her face. I reached and reached and finally I felt her hair, cool—a mermaid. I pulled her toward me.

The words stopped. It was too dark without them. My chest was heavy and empty; my heartbeat sounded far away, from a different room. My lungs couldn't expand. She was pushing down on me. I couldn't see her face. It was so dark. Then, out of the darkness I saw it, but it wasn't Salomé. There was a hole where her face should've been. She plunged forward and tried to burrow through my mouth and wiggle into my throat. There was a shriek, a scream, maybe it was me, maybe it was her—

"Cour-ten-ey?"

It was still dark.

"Cour-ten-ey, are you okay?"

My arms couldn't move. I was encased in sand. The pressure.

"You're dreaming. I brought you water." She touched my shoulder.

Finally, my eyes unlocked. It was dawn; Salomé was perched on the edge of my bed, not naked, holding a cup of water. When I regained control of my arms, I sat up and took the glass.

"Did I wake you?" I asked.

"Yes, I am glad, though, because I could wake you." There was still a silvery tinge to her voice, something left over in my mind. This was the real Salomé, though. I smelled her lotion.

"Did I scream?"

She shook her head. "*Tu gémissais* . . . what is the word?"

I'd been whimpering. How embarrassing. "It must be jet lag. I'm sorry."

The water was perfect. My body was soaked with sweat, but still cold from her touch. I shivered. The dream was still too close.

Salomé watched me. "Do you think you'll go back to sleep?"

"I don't think so."

She left the room and bumped around in the kitchen. It still felt like I was clinging to the cold, slippery side of a well. But I also felt like I'd had a massive orgasm, and I worried that I hadn't so much whimpered as I had moaned. What if I'd touched myself in my sleep? Would she tell me if I had? But I was too exhausted to indulge in the worry. All I could manage was staring down the length of my body, kicking my legs free of the coarse blanket, and trying to get my wits about me.

A few minutes later Salomé came back with coffee.

I instinctively scooted over to make room for her, but then realized she wasn't trying to get into bed with me. She sat on the edge and sipped her coffee. I did the same. The warmth spread out over my throat, which felt a little scratchy.

"It's five-thirty. Do you want to watch something on my computer?" she asked. "Do you have rules against watching TV in the morning?"

I couldn't tell if she had a rule against this herself, or if she thought I was the type of person who would. "I'm traveling. There are no rules."

"Good," she said, retrieving her laptop. She climbed into bed with me and settled the computer against her bent knees. "Here is the show I like. I will start it over from the beginning for you."

It was *Broad City,* one of my favorites. "No, it's okay, just start it wherever you were. I've seen it."

"You like this show?"

"I love it."

She hit the space bar. I watched out the window as the first hints of sunrise blotted the sky, grateful that she shared this fleeting comfort.

CHAPTER 4

Nathalie was in her backyard flower garden, tending to a few young plants. Salomé sprawled across her bed, reading an article on her phone. The windows were fogged; the keyholes leaked. The cameras monitored the inside of the house, taciturn and unblinking.

I stood naked in front of the mirror in the *salle de bain*, looking at the reflection of my torso. Forty-eight hours of French food had done me some good, it appeared. My stomach was flatter, the skin on my collarbones soft and radiant. I'd never been particularly interested in beauty regimens outside of moisturizer. For the most part my eyebrows went unplucked and unfilled, and if I wore makeup, I was likely to sleep in it. Since turning twenty-eight I had become accustomed to small disappointments from the mirror. New lines, spots, slight droops; the tiniest emergence of what would someday be jowls. But today wasn't a disappointment. Today I got a glimpse of French Courtney.

What did it feel like for Salomé to look into the mirror? I assumed people like her would perceive a deep and ethereal beauty within themselves, something like I was seeing now. Someone with tangible purpose whose anxiety read as intelligence and exhaustion as depth. Was I seeing what people saw when they told me I was beautiful? Not that it mattered. No one would ever want me if they could see my mind as clearly as they could see my face.

I went into the bedroom and found Salomé lounging on her bed, scrolling a limp finger down her phone's screen. Sitting down on my bed—Élise's bed—I reached for my phone. I hadn't checked it last night or all morning, evidently. I had eight texts, five from my mom, the first of which came in at 2 a.m. my time.

Hope you're having fun!

How's Kylie? Tell her I said hi!

Hey, how is France?

☺☺☺

Hope you're having fun!

A few years ago, she might have sent me five texts if I didn't respond to the first one, but now instead of getting nervous at my lack of response, she just seemed to keep trying as if it were the first time.

When she first realized she was getting forgetful, she'd doubled down on checking in with me. My pulse was on her checklist. Probably literally, as she was now coping by leaving little notes all over the house. I wouldn't be surprised if "Courtney—alive?" was written down somewhere, or a reminder she programmed into Alexa.

Her texts juxtaposed with Salomé's silhouette in the background was such a dissonance I almost couldn't figure out what to say. I typed a quick response:

Sorry! I left my phone plugged in and haven't checked it this morning. We are having fun! Kylie says hi.

From Kylie, sent yesterday evening:

Hey, were you going to come tomorrow or Saturday?

Lemme know and I'll make a dinner reservation.

The tomorrow she mentioned was Friday, which was today. I scrambled to open my calendar. Perhaps I could extend my trip? Stay here a week or so? Mom seemed good, and Aunt Trudy was checking in with her every day. My hands got clammy as I considered it.

Let me talk to Salomé and get back to you. I think she might have something planned for today.

I looked at Salomé, catching her eye.

"Is something wrong?"

"No, just trying to figure out . . . to figure something out."

She stretched her arms overhead, becoming lavishly feline.

My notebook, mostly untouched since I'd arrived in Châteaubriant, sat on top of my backpack. I grabbed it and wrote the line: *Arms stretched overhead, a languid panther lounging in the crook of a branch.*

She watched me watch her. "What did you write?"

"Just something I need to remember."

She knew it was about her, but didn't press. "Well, what would you like to do today?"

"What would you be doing if I weren't here?"

"I would be very bored," she said.

"Could we go hiking?"

"Yes, but I think it will be very hot."

"I'm not exclusively an indoor kid," I said.

Nathalie interrogated Salomé about our lunch plans before we left. We'd decided on a picnic, but since there was very little food in the house, we'd have to stop at the *marché*.

Outside, Salomé said, "She wants me to eat all the time but to be also thin. Did you notice she never eats?"

I thought about mentioning the tomato, but I didn't. "My mom actually used to tell me that you could never be too rich or too thin."

Salomé opened the car door. I wasn't sure how to interpret her expression and wished I hadn't shared that. Inside the car, she said, "That is a very American thing to say." It was lighthearted, not accusatory.

"My mom is very American."

She pursed her lips and studied me for a moment. "You are not, I don't think."

My stomach turned a little and I struggled not to smile. She shifted the car into reverse and it shook until she pressed the gas pedal. I'd always wished I could drive a stick shift, but I didn't know anyone who drove one. That was pretty American of me.

We drove a few blocks and stopped at a tiny grocery store. Inside, we picked out a baguette, two cheeses, and a container of small bright red strawberries. Salomé consulted me by holding out each item for my inspection. I would nod yes to each, and she'd smile and nod back, placing it in the basket I held over my forearm. An effective team.

It only took a few minutes to drive to the outskirts of Châteaubriant. We parked in a gravel parking lot at a small nature reserve. Somewhere far in the distance, a cow was bellowing, or maybe it was the sound of a chain saw.

The trees weren't nearly as dense as the woods of North Carolina. The path was wide and starkly civilized compared to the root-studded trails I'd hiked at home. The entire length was paved in fine gray gravel that seemed permanently wet. Chalky pools collected in small craters, and the most perilous issue was dodging the mob of orange slugs, *les limaces*, that slimed across the path.

I'd already crafted "Not Very American" into some kind of banner to be flown pompously through all my future interactions. It occurred to me that Salomé could be my ticket back to France. We could get an apartment in Paris together. But I shouldn't think like that. I shouldn't make future plans. Making plans meant I was looking forward to Mom being gone.

Had Salomé and I been in the same room before, at that coffee shop? I struggled to conjure the memory of gangly, swoopy-haired, undeserving Justin. Even if she didn't really love him, he was someone she liked enough to try moving across the world to be with. I wondered what their sex had been like. He was probably the type to blame all his inadequacies and insecurities on her, while surreptitiously texting other women to bolster his ego. I bet he had a tattoo of the Giving Tree on his forearm.

Justin had invited her to come live with him, then replaced her before she was gone. Luke hadn't even discussed his plans to move with me, let alone asked me to come with him. Not that I would have, with my mom the way she was. But still, it would've been nice to be considered a more significant fixture in his life than the few pieces of furniture he'd sold before leaving. American Courtney had walked around with this thorn in her side for months, knowing she was never someone Luke had intended to keep. But the idea that I could be hurt by this man sounded almost satirical to French Courtney. When I returned home, I'd bring with me the idea that unless someone provided me with the level of ease I felt now, with Salomé, they didn't deserve my attention.

I broke the silence. "Do you think we were ever at Uncommon Ground at the same time?"

"This is what I am thinking too!" she said.

"It doesn't seem right that we wouldn't have known each other."

"*J'ai l'impression que je te connais depuis longtemps*," she said quietly, with a ferocity I knew she wanted me to detect. *I feel like I've known you for a long time.*

A small zing of energy traveled through my fingertips. "I know what you mean," I said, though I wished I could have phrased it more eloquently. We walked the trail for a few more minutes before we found a good place to picnic by the base of a large tree.

We spread the blanket and unpacked the basket. Salomé popped a strawberry into her mouth, tossing the little green top behind the tree. Normally I couldn't watch people eat without getting grossed out, but I didn't feel that way with her. There was something about her that could only be described as silver. It had little to do with her coloration and more a feeling, or maybe synesthetic association. A coolness, something shiny, reflective, like the undisturbed surface of a wishing well.

A throb in my thigh sent my hand there, where I found a tender bruise. The chair I'd knocked over. It was hard to believe we'd been so drunk the night before after sharing one bottle of wine. I didn't feel hungover at all. The cathedral, the walk home, nestled into each other, our sandals slapping the cobblestone. Then, later—the dream. How strange that our senses were alive in dreams. I could still feel the hardness of her pubic bone on me, the strength of her thighs around my hips. The memory made me dizzy. But it wasn't Salomé I was remembering; it was a conglomeration of my own experiences, fears perhaps, that my brain was shoving forward. I remembered the face, or rather the missing face, that woke me and my breath fell short. A demon. No, a succubus.

Thanks, Catholic school. It was a stress dream, not a succubus. *Don't open your eyes.* That sweet, airy, cool voice. The most pleasant voice I'd ever heard, I'd created in the unexplored depths of my imagination.

Salomé was looking at me. "What?"

"I was just thinking about that horrible dream I had last night." A shiver went up my arms.

A small, curious smile crossed her face. "You know, everybody has weird dreams in this house," she said.

"Really?"

"When we moved here from Paris, Élise had such bad dreams. When I heard you making noises, I remembered Élise sounding like that."

"Have you had bad dreams?"

"Sometimes. My grandfather Papi would tell us ghost stories sometimes. He said he was friends with the ghost."

"Really?"

"Well," she said. "I think he was joking with us, trying to scare us. And it was his way to complain about living with four people in the house where he lived alone for years." In French, she mimicked her grandfather's voice: "Who left these cabinets open? Was it you, *Philippe-le-fântome*?"

I laughed.

She laughed, too. "Do you want to hear something crazy?"

"Yes."

"When we were young, Élise and I thought we could play together in our dreams."

"Were you really playing together?"

"It felt like that," she said. "In the morning we would always remember the same things. But we were kids. We maybe made it up." Her bottom lip tensed as she searched for her next words. "Is that weird to tell you?"

"I have a huge threshold for weird."

"Oh, there is more weird."

I wanted to know what she meant by "more weird." I wanted to know everything. "If it's okay with you, could I stay here a few more days?"

"You know I want you to stay," she said. "But, I have some bad news."

"What's that?"

"My mother's stupid boyfriend will be back tomorrow."

"So I should leave?"

She thought for a moment. "No, but maybe we want to stay somewhere else. I don't have much money left, so I can't pay for a hotel or Airbnb for long. If I had money, believe me, I would be anywhere else in Europe rather than here." She ripped off another chunk of baguette. "But we can think about that, maybe, for tomorrow."

"What makes him so stupid?"

A little bird fluttered down and landed nearby. Salomé pinched a bit of bread off and tossed it to the bird, who snatched it and flew away. She leaned her head against the tree, closing her eyes. "I will tell you later."

I trusted she would. I reached into our tote bag and pulled out my notebook. I slipped the pen out of its elastic loop and hovered the tip over a fresh page. I wrote: *I'll see you in my dreams, hold you in my dreams.* I couldn't remember the next line to the song, but I could hear it. I didn't know who wrote the original. They were almost surely dead. But I wasn't going to let that bother me right now.

I lay sideways on the grass, my face only a few inches from Salomé's bare toes. There were two black hairs on her ankle. They were so lovely and natural, relieving in a way. Without thinking, I blew across the hairs, wanting to see them dance.

She jumped. "Ah! What are you doing?" She laughed.

Mortified, I sat upright. "Sorry, it was a bug."

She brushed her ankle twice. I couldn't believe I'd done that. I scooted over to the tree and leaned against it.

"Oh look, 'ere comes somebody!" Salomé said.

An unaccompanied dog trotted up the path. It was a big black-and-tan shepherd of some sort, kind of limping, with an ear turned inside out.

"*Hop*," she said, shoving away from the tree. "*Viens ici, ah, hop!*" She righted the ear. The dog stood by her, looking past me and panting.

The moment was an oil painting I wished I could create. I took a picture on my phone of Salomé standing in dappled sunlight, a finger resting on the dog. I felt a tinge of remorse for having taken the picture, as if it somehow cheapened the experience. I decided I would never share it on social media, so the memory would remain mine alone.

"La Loute!" a man's deep voice boomed in the distance. The dog turned and trotted away.

"*Loup?*" I asked.

"Loute, it's like a lady sweetheart, kind of, but a very old word."

"Do you know that dog?"

"No, but I like 'er!"

"She liked you too, I could tell," I said.

"It feels good to be liked," she said. "This is not something I feel often anymore." She looked down the trail in the direction Loute had trotted off.

She must've been talking about Justin. Or her lack of friends in Châteaubriant. It was obviously a sore subject for her. The only thing that seemed off-putting about her had to do with Nathalie, but it was unlikely that people would avoid being her friend because her mother was slightly creepy. The people she would've met in Paris wouldn't even know that. Maybe she didn't throw the word "friend" around as casually as I did.

"I like you a lot," I said, then instantly regretted my earnestness.

The statement landed with her, and she gave me a strange little look that I read as, *You don't have to say that.* She was right. I didn't have to say it. It had to be painfully obvious through everything I did. She bent down to adjust the strap of her sandal, and when she stood back up, she said, "It's hot! Do you want to go get ice cream?"

"Yes, let's do that," I said, thankful for the change of subject.

When we got back to the car, we had to leave the doors open for a minute to let the wavy-hot air escape. I got a text from Luke. It was 5 a.m. back home.

How are YOU?

He could feel me slipping further away. Interesting that he cared now that I was on another continent. I was surprised at how little I felt in hearing from him. I was almost annoyed.

Send me a picture?

I'm in rural France with a girl I met on the plane.

Salomé stared off into the woods, seemingly content to be far away in her thoughts. Why didn't she have any friends?

Send me a picture!

I'm drunk.

He probably meant a sexy picture. I was never into that even before he moved away, and he'd forfeited any right to ask for something like that when he left. I could send the picture I'd just taken of Salomé and Loute. Then he could see who I was spending time with in France—who I *was* in France. It would be interesting to see what he said. I sent it.

His response was about as perfect as could be:

I love the way you see things.

Maybe you could write a song about it.

What should I call it?

A string of words pushed their way into my mind. They were nonsensical but I sent them anyway:

Throw a hair to the magpies

I had no idea what it meant. This time, I could leave him hanging.

CHAPTER 5

A crack almost the length of the room bisected the plaster ceiling above Élise's bed. I studied it, my head against the pillow, arm draped overhead. I was a young art student; the crack, a nude model. I squeezed my eyes closed when I remembered my failure to write down any of the dream poem.

Don't open your eyes.

It's all I could remember. I could still hear the timbre of the voice, its needlelike thinness.

I checked my email for the first time since I'd been in France. My inbox was full of automated emails from the assignment platform that let hungry freelancers spar over the best filler gigs. I was skeptical that editors even read these assignments before hitting "publish." I could accept a web-only assignment for the "Top 10 Raleigh Neighborhoods" and write about Châteaubriant and see how long it took for anyone to notice. I doubted anyone read them after they were published, either.

An in-depth look at the name Salomé could make an interesting essay—its history, implications, pronunciations, and prevalence in different cultures. I could interview the parents of Salomés and ask them what considerations they'd taken when choosing the name. That was the lane I wanted to be in: cross-cultural, somewhat historical, looking at how art could influence people, not overtly political—but without shying away from the detrimental manner in which religion pigeonholed women. The only problem was: No publications would buy something like that.

My phone buzzed.

> Hey girl, you didn't get murded did you lol?

> Murdered*

No, Kylie. I didn't get "murded." I should've expected it. Kylie was the type of person who wanted to confirm dinner plans a week in advance, then forty-eight hours in advance, and then again, the day of. It was a quality that, on my better days, I appreciated. In past years, I had told myself I had a lot to learn from Kylie, *should've* done things like Kylie. I used to want her influence, back when it was optional.

Kylie had stayed in Paris and finished college at La Sorbonne, majoring in education, which I hadn't even realized was an option. After graduation she landed a great job teaching English in a fancy Parisian high school. Most of her friends were expats from England or the US. She was always single and thrived that way, though she got attention from most men she met. She had this type of effortless luck that revealed itself in small and large ways, such as having the Midas touch in a thrift store or only having to apply to one job straight out of college in the middle of a recession. She was unafraid to speak French with strangers, and was adorable if she got corrected. And now, of course, she had a burgeoning career as an influencer. Maybe it would work out for her, as everything always seemed to, but maybe this influencer thing would finally be the end of her winning streak. Not because she wasn't really cool, but because the qualities that made her cool weren't necessarily replicable. When it boiled down to it, she was trying to monetize the fact that people wished they had her life. When they ultimately realized they couldn't, they'd lose interest and unfollow her.

My perception of Kylie was reductive, but somehow, she made herself easy to reduce. Probably, I knew deep down, because she was very conventionally pretty—the real reason she was able to amass social media followers and brand sponsorships.

I composed a response that didn't let on what an actual bitch I was.

Sorry! Salomé did plan something for tonight. I think I need to stay here for a few more days. I'm loving it here. I'm writing a bunch and really getting to practice my French! Would Monday evening be okay for me to come to Paris? I fly out Wednesday morning.

Yeah, I guess that's fine. I was excited to see you for more than a day though!

☹

Gotta throw a hair to the magpies, you know?

Lol, What does that mean?

I locked my phone screen.

The room cracked and popped as if someone had entered. I sat up but saw no one. My eyes instinctively went to the camera, still rendered useless by the sock.

"Salomé?" I said, just loud enough for my voice to carry outside of the room. Then, still thinking it might be Salomé, I said, *"Philippe-le-fantôme?"* but even the joking suggestion that it could be a ghost made me more uncomfortable.

Thierry's book was on the floor next to my backpack. I picked it up and opened to the first page. To my surprise, the epigraph was in English:

> *Can death be sleep, when life is but a dream,*
> *And scenes of bliss pass as a phantom by?*
> *The transient pleasures as a vision seem,*
> *And yet we think the greatest pain's to die.*
>
> —JOHN KEATS

I didn't think much about what the verse was trying to convey. I was too surprised by seeing English in this book and the word "phantom" mere moments after saying it aloud. Maybe there was more English. I leafed through the pages (*feuiller* in French, literally "to leaf") but found nothing. It still didn't make sense to me why Salomé had insisted I didn't write about it. Even if I understood the book's contents, this was so far outside of my wheelhouse, I would never try to write about it. If she hadn't said anything, I probably wouldn't be interested at all.

I tried to read a paragraph somewhere in the middle. I saw the word *télomère*, which I recognized from a one-off blogging assignment I did for an anti-aging skin care line. In researching for the blog, I fell into a rabbit hole of science in which I'd learned that telomeres were little things on the ends of chromosomes that got shorter with every mitosis cycle until the cell died. The shorter the telomeres got, the more fragile the chromosomes, and therefore the DNA, became, which could lead to various age-related diseases. But I didn't write about telomeres for the skin care blog. No matter how much retinol or collagen or vitamin C or algae someone packed onto their face at night, it wouldn't slow down a telomere's fraying. We were all ticking time bombs no matter how diligently we applied night cream.

Toward the back of Thierry's book, there were black-and-white pictures of scanned Polaroids. A set of twins, photographed on July 11 each year from 1984 until 2010. For the first fifteen years they appeared identical, but around the year 2000, one of the twins started to look noticeably older, while the other had more or less stayed the same. I wanted to ask Salomé about it, but would she bristle again?

I set the book down and was met again by the eerie feeling of being alone in her house. I ventured into the kitchen, where the copper pots and pans hung serenely from their hooks. The kitchen was only two steps higher than the bedroom but noticeably hotter. Where were they? Nathalie's sun hat hung from the doorknob, so she probably wasn't in the garden. Her Peugeot was in the driveway, Louis was curled on the couch in the living room, and the bird floated in its formaldehyde tomb. Two oscillating fans in the living room blew at full capacity.

Over the whirring fans I heard something from down the hall, in Nathalie's room. Hushed voices, barely louder than a whisper. Salomé was probably in there, confronting Nathalie about whatever was going on between them that I was supposed to defuse. I listened harder. It wasn't her voice. It was deep, male. The second voice was a woman's, or was it? Was she being robbed? Held hostage? No, the cadence was familiar, but strained. They knew each other. I crept down the hall, holding my breath.

Stop. The mermaid's voice floated from somewhere between my ears. I obeyed. The hairs on my arms stood erect. I had the distinct feeling of just having rung a stranger's doorbell.

The speaking stopped. They had been speaking French, right?

Nathalie's boyfriend must have arrived, and I was about to be standing in the hall when they came out, which would be awkward. I wanted to back away, but I was fixed in place, my heart going wild. I tried to take a step backward. *Stop*, it said again, so I stopped . . . or did it stop me? It wasn't unlike the feeling of being buried in sand when I couldn't lift my arm off the bed.

The door swung open. Salomé gasped and dropped a spoon. The clatter of metal against the tile released me.

"*Putain!* Oh, Cour-ten-ey, you scared me!"

"I was looking for you . . ." I didn't want her to see the wetness in my eyes. I feigned a giggle and ducked into the *salle de bain*, where I spent a couple of seconds poking at my cheeks until the shock of the moment dissipated. Before when I'd looked in the mirror, I had seen a sexy, confident Courtney looking back. Now, the woman reflected was desperate and annoying.

I washed my hands and patted my cheeks. After a few deep breaths, I left the bathroom.

Salomé flopped down on the couch in the living room. I approached, but didn't sit next to her.

"Who's here?" I asked.

"My mother and me, and Louis, of course." She buried her face in his fur.

"I thought I heard a man talking."

"Umm, I think you are 'earing things, Court-en-ey." She smiled, but I felt betrayed.

"I guess," I mumbled.

"Or it was the radio," she said.

The radio. I'd gotten that freaked out over the radio? Sometimes I hated my brain.

"Tu veux faire quoi?" She asked what I wanted to do.

"What time is it?"

She looked at her phone. "Almost *quinze heures.* Three."

I crouched close to the floor and wrapped my arms around my knees. I wasn't sure why she translated to English and the twelve-hour clock for me. "I don't want to make a decision."

"Is everything okay?"

"Yeah. I uh, I just fell asleep and I feel a little weird now."

"I know what will make you feel better!"

"What?"

"Come here and get a kiss from Louis." She leaned over and kissed him again. His white whiskers quivered.

I didn't really want to kiss Louis, but I knelt by the couch and did as I was told. Salomé placed her hand on my head and smoothed my forehead with her thumb. A blush crept up from my neck into my cheeks.

Her hand lingered on my head for another moment, making my scalp grow hot, or was it cold? For a second, I thought that blood was pooling in my hair before the sensation became pleasant. I closed my eyes.

Don't open your eyes.

The mermaid's voice slipped around inside my head, but it was far away and unclear, like an echo without the original sound. Her hand would serve as a conduit, as long as it would stay.

Salomé removed her hand and rolled off the couch with a lazy groan. The voice stopped. I both missed it and was glad it was gone.

"I want a coffee. I need to wake up!"

Salomé's bare feet smacked the floor behind me as she retreated into our room. I knelt by the couch, wilted over, suddenly with very little energy to move. I looked up and found Louis staring at me with his snake-like yellow eyes.

I stood, and his gaze followed. He watched me back out of the room slowly, never blinking. I didn't break eye contact with him until

Salomé shuffled into the room in unbuckled sandals. Placing her hand on my arm for balance, she latched the strap at the back of her heel.

When I looked back at the couch, Louis was gone. Before I met him, I'd always thought I liked cats.

By the time we'd gotten to the brasserie, hot coffee sounded disgusting. We ordered kir royales, which came out warm in fancy cut-crystal flutes. Salomé asked if there were any ice cubes, and the waitress launched into an exasperated explanation of why that wasn't possible.

"Maybe something I like more about America. There is always ice," she said.

The kir was syrupy in my mouth, but I was glad to have it.

"So you're sure Nathalie's boyfriend wasn't at the house?"

"Tomorrow." She shifted uncomfortably, and I knew it wasn't only because the backs of her legs were sticking to the chair.

"Are you going to tell me why he's stupid?"

"He is stupid for many reasons. First, he fucking . . . *looks* at me. Like . . ." She gestured to her breasts in an obtuse way. They were fairly small, so it wasn't that she had cleavage.

"Oh, gross, I'm sorry. How long have they been together?"

"Just after my father died. But he is in our lives since a long time."

"I'm sorry, that's terrible," I said.

She rolled her eyes. "I learned this in English: 'It is what it is.'"

"Fuck that! You should not feel uncomfortable in your own house because some asshole can't refrain from objectifying you."

"I know, and this is only one reason why he is stupid."

"What's the other reason?"

"His stupid business."

"What's that?"

"The business is called ViPi. He sells vitamins. They are like . . . if you cut cardboard and make it into pills and sell it for a lot of money."

"I would've thought the regulations in France would make it hard to do something like that."

She blew an exhale upward. "*Bah ouais*, it is hard. But Marco is smart in that way. He gets away with sheet. And he is very good at selling. You should see these conferences he goes to, where he is talking to a big group saying things like, '*Vieillir est une maladie! Les maladies sont des choix!*'"

"Aging is a disease and diseases are choices?"

She nodded.

"Yeah, I'm sure if my mom took his shitty vitamins, she wouldn't have Alzheimer's. He can fuck all the way off with that."

"Your mom has *la maladie d'Alzheimer*?"

I forgot I hadn't told her. "Yes. She got diagnosed late last year."

"I'm sorry."

"Thanks. It happens in stages, and she's not really in the deep end yet." I didn't want to talk about it. "Let me guess, Marco also discourages modern medicine?"

"Well, kind of. He likes science very much. But he also says that many doctors are not fixing the real problem."

"Which, conveniently, ViPi does."

"Right," she said, swirling her kir.

"Does Nathalie realize he's a grifter? And a perv?"

"Bah. Good question. It is strange. She is one of the smartest people I know. I don't know what she sees in Marco. But he is very *charmant* too. I think being her partner is his biggest . . . what is the word you used? 'Grift'?"

I nodded. I decided to bring Thierry up gently, to see if she reacted defensively. "So is Marco a colleague of your dad's? Is he a gerontologist too?"

"He worked for my father as a lab assistant. But to say he is a scientist is not true. He like . . ." She finished the sentence in French, then asked, "How would you say this in English?"

I thought for a second. "He is exploiting his proximity to Thierry's work to give himself the facade of legitimacy?"

"This is very good," she said. "I like having a translator around."

I smiled. "I mean, I couldn't have come up with that sentence in French."

"If you are a translator, you don't have to," she said.

"I guess you're right. So Marco has created a whole snake-oil business on the foundation of your father's research, but he's not a scientist himself?"

"Basically." She shifted again, pulling the denim of her shorts away from her thighs. I sensed that she didn't want to talk about it anymore.

"How did you get your name?" I asked.

She smiled at the question. "There is a church near our house called l'Église Saint-Jean de Béré. My father grew up going to it."

"Even though Salomé was depicted as a murderer?"

In French, she said, "He said she was misunderstood. And that she was immortalized through art, but nobody really knew her."

I didn't have my notebook with me, or I would've written that down.

"Would you want to live forever?" I asked.

She sat back in her chair and thought about it. "I already feel like I can, in a way," she said.

"Because this consciousness is all you've ever known, so to imagine it being gone is impossible?"

"Yes, it is a feeling of *solipsisme* . . . but it is something else too. Like you know when you see somebody do something that you cannot do, like gymnastics or something? And your body knows it cannot do it?"

"Yeah, definitely."

"But then you see somebody do something like . . ." She hovered her finger over the rim of the crystal flute and drew a circle over it. "And you know how it will feel and sound like, just by a suggestion."

I nodded.

Without touching the glass, she brought her hand to her sternum. "Does it feel this way to you?"

I shook my head, just lightly. I hated to tell her no. I wanted to relate to everything she said. We both slid into our own thoughts and sat in silence.

I started to get the sense that Salomé was vastly more intelligent than me. Maybe she'd been holding back so as not to be off-putting. Perhaps she wanted a break from deep, heady conversations and just wanted to maintain the surface-level exchanges she was able to have with Americans.

But no, I didn't really believe that. I knew intuitively that wherever her mind went, I could learn to meet her there. A feeling spread through my lower abdomen like warm honey, sweet and somehow sickly. The feeling of anticipation, like when I'd wait and see if Luke would invite me to his place at the end of the night.

I finished my kir, licked my fingertip, and ran it across the crystal rim.

CHAPTER 6

A sniffing and gentle tousling of my hair made me think of a rodent sneaking into a garden at midnight, looking for something to steal. *Let down your hair*, the voice said.

Then I felt the weight of it on top of me—"slither" is the word I want. I'd heard of a python that had gotten lost in an apartment building and crashed through the ceiling of someone's room and suffocated them. But this wasn't a python. It was cool and serpentine, but not a snake. I couldn't raise my arms to touch it. I was pinned down, but I wasn't scared, as I'd worried I would be. She was back.

Who are you? I thought. An image of Salomé appeared, but she was older, wiser, with lovely lines around her eyes.

Let me in, she said, three perfect words like bubbles breaking at the water's surface.

Her finger dipped into my navel and caught the edge of my tank top. She ducked low and pressed her skin against mine, sliding herself into my shirt, bellies together, lips together, tongues together. We fit inside the shirt perfectly. She sniffed the rim of my ear. I wanted to smile, but the corners of my mouth were as weighted as my hands.

Sniff sniff sniff. It tickled. I couldn't move. I ached to throw my arms around her and pull her tighter and tighter. *Sniff sniff sniff.*

Kiss me again.

The rustling beside my ear continued.

Snip snip snip.

She wasn't sniffing, she was cutting.

I grew hot, every cell of my frozen body buzzing with potential energy that would culminate in an explosion.

What are you doing? I tried to scream. I pushed upward into my eyelids, trying to break free, but I was either underwater or under sand.

Don't open your eyes, she said. I could see the words like fireflies, blinking at inconsequential rhythms.

Your

Open

Don't

Eyes.

Eyes

Open

Your

Don't.

Eyes

Open

Then she was arching away from me, pulling the neck hole tight, lifting me up. The shirt slid over our heads, pulled from above. A firm hand on the back of my ribs settled me into the pillow.

Dis-moi ce que tu veux, Cour-ten-ey.

I want the words. You have them, aren't you offering them to me?

Her mouth found mine again and all I could do was kiss her back. It was a good kiss, deep and connected. The fireflies began to pulse in a discernible pattern. The poem was back, and it was coming from me; she was just showing me where to find it. The words projected from inside my mind, scrolling out like the title pages of a silent film. They spiraled into a snail shape, and she recited them in her angelic voice. What language was it? How could I understand?

I worked to free my arms and finally got one under my control. I touched the back of her head, but her teeth pulled savagely at my bottom lip, practically lifting me up again. My lip snapped closed and my head bounced against the wall. The words began to scatter.

Dis-moi.

I did . . . I'm trying . . .

I rushed after the dissipating words. The heaviness was wearing off. I tried to tell her to kiss me again. I forced my eyes open, and saw her outline in front of me. She had stopped moving, poised and perfectly still. She was unmistakably angry. She leaned closer, and I knew what I was about to see—the sunken spot, dark red and black, in the center of her skull, as if the face had imploded upon itself. My teeth instinctively tried to clamp but I felt them pried apart.

DON'T. The voice was right next to my ear, it was in my mouth—had I said it? There was something on my tongue, down my throat—scales like tiny barbs in my esophagus, choking me, urging my mouth open wider and wider. Wetness flooded into my ears. I heard a popping, a cracking, my jaw breaking.

Je ne le pardonnerai jamais. I don't know if I heard the words or saw them first. They were in my mind, but they hadn't come from me.

I was in the living room, but my vantage point was high, near the ceiling, looking down upon the room. Salomé, whose hair was much longer, and a young woman who I assumed was Élise were sitting on the couch. Nathalie, not quite as thin, lay across their laps. Salomé stroked Nathalie's hair near her temples. They were all crying.

"*Je ne le pardonnerai jamais*," Nathalie said several times. *I'll never forgive him.* I sensed that the "him" in this sentence was Thierry.

For what? I asked.

Salomé looked directly at me and said, "For dying."

Then it was over. All I heard was the tapping of the delirious moths outside swarming the light fixture over the living room window.

I wasn't in my bed. I was standing in the living room by the shelves, just like in the dream, but with my feet on the ground. My fingers had closed around something, but my eyes struggled to adjust to the darkness. I shifted to one leg and rubbed my prickly calves together. I had definitely woken up. The cool object in my hand came into focus. The bird. I set it down.

"Cour-ten-ey?"

The voice made me jump. I turned.

"What are you doing?" Nathalie whispered.

"Sorry, nothing, I was going to the bathroom."

She took a step back into the hallway and gestured at the door to the *toilette*.

"*Merci*," I breathed, and glided past her, avoiding her eyes in the dark. I locked the bathroom door and sat on the toilet. My thighs trembled as I tried to pee. When I came out, she was gone, and I slipped back to the bedroom.

I sat on the bed. I'd never sleepwalked before. I shook my hands at the wrists. I spelled *serrer*, *serrure*, *serrurerie*. I'd been drinking more on this trip than in my everyday life. That's why I sleepwalked. Or maybe it was because this room had no door. And everyone had bad dreams in this house, right? Even the mere suggestion could've triggered my own dreams. There was nothing actually wrong. But no matter how I tried to explain it away, nothing worked to unknot the feeling of dread that had settled in my stomach.

One moment at a time. I'd lie on my side until morning, not sleeping, doing everything I could to push the dream out of my mind like any other intrusive thought.

I had the urge to reach out to Luke, but it felt wrong. What would I even say? I'd left him hanging at the end of our last conversation. The image of him was less solid than it had been a couple of days ago. He had blue eyes, long eyelashes . . . but I couldn't remember if his teeth were crooked or if he was taller than me. He was slipping away, just as I'd wanted him to.

"Hey," I typed, then hesitated. I could do better than that. No, this wasn't the time to try to compose something brilliant. I sent it.

I wished I could text Salomé across the room to ask her if we could go to the beach tomorrow. I didn't even have her phone number. I pushed the blanket from my legs and put my feet on the floor. I listened for Salomé's breathing. There it was, light and peaceful. I stood, taking care not to make any noise, and tiptoed to the other side of the room. Her shape in the bed was curled, fetal, like the bird. I imagined wrapping myself around the crescent of her. I would form the outside, the first line of defense should we be attacked. Weird how that felt so gendered. Or in this case, ageist. But that's how it would be.

Salomé slept, and I stood over her, somewhat satisfied now that she was within my reach. Though, of course, I wasn't going to touch her. I just wanted to be nearby. The image of her from my dream returned to my mind, looking directly at me and saying, *For dying.* The hairs on my arms and legs stood up.

I heard the door to Nathalie's room open. I hurried back to my bed and pulled the blanket over my knees. Nathalie went into the bathroom and closed the door. The stream of pee hit the water. She cleared her throat. The toilet flushed. She went into the *salle de bain* and the faucet ran for a few seconds. Then the bathroom door opened, the light switch flipped off, but I heard no more movement.

Where was she? I strained my ears, trying to pinpoint her location in the hallway. Several seconds later, her bedroom door quietly clicked closed, as if she had deliberately made as little noise as possible. Had she stood there in the dark hall and heard me breathing, my heart pounding, knowing I was still awake? Had she expected me to be roaming again, touching her stuff? Maybe she'd felt dizzy for a moment and placed her hand on the wall for balance. Or she could've taken her phone with her and responded to a text at 4 a.m.

I used to do this kind of thinking when I was in college and thought my apartment was haunted. Was that a malevolent black shadow forming outside my door or simply the fallibility of the human eye in the dark?

My phone buzzed and made me jump.

Salut.

He had cooled down considerably since our last text.

Hello or goodbye?

Hello :)

He used an actual colon and parenthesis, not an emoji.

I just had a really bad dream and I . . .

Did he need to know this? What if he responded with aloofness or even got mad or something?

It's like 4 AM if you're still in France

His text came in before I could send mine.

I just had a really bad dream and I am afraid to try to sleep again.

Let's pretend that I'm there ;)

I already am.

Awww. You can tell me the dream if you want to.

I barely remember it now. It was one of those stress dreams I have sometimes.

It's weird to wake up first in someone else's house.

He was right. And so perceptive, and gentle, and understanding. I thought back to my conversations with Salomé and countless other women when I'd carelessly spouted off memetic phrases like "men are trash." Part of me wanted to admit to Luke that I'd done that, but he'd probably respond with the sound counterargument that I was only reacting to learned behavior. I *had* been abandoned, assaulted, cheated on, hadn't I? I thought about telling him about Nathalie going to the bathroom, but there was no way to convey that story appropriately over text.

Yeah, it really is.

I sleepwalked into the living room.

Well now you can add somnambulism to your list of awesome words.

I do like that word. Just not the act.

Auspicious.

That's the word you make me think of.

Because of my super promising career as a freelance journalist?

Haha I guess. Mostly the root.

What's the root?

I guess you'll just have to look it up, won't you ;P

"Cour-ten-ey?" This was Salomé, rubbing her eyes in the dark.

"Hey, sorry, did I wake you?"

"No, I don't think so. But I saw your face in the light of the phone."

"Are you still on American time too?"

"*Peut-être . . .*" she whispered, turned over, and went back to sleep.

Texting Luke felt wrong now that she'd seen. Did she know we were flirting? But it was okay for me to flirt with someone, I reminded myself.

So when do you get back?

I'm trying to figure out how to stay forever.

But my flight leaves Wednesday.

You should absolutely stay in France. I'll do a French tour and you can be my interpreter.

This would've felt like a real invitation a few weeks ago. But now, I didn't want to be with Luke in France. The thought of him being in the same room as Salomé felt like an impossible collision of worlds. What if he subtly rejected French Courtney and I came to find fault with her, too?

I spelled *serrer* a few times to stop the thoughts. I wasn't going to be able to go back to sleep. I crawled to the end of the bed and reached into my backpack for my headphones. Back under the covers, I Googled "Marco France longevity vitamin." I'd forgotten the name of the company.

A few things came up. I clicked over to "videos" and found several interview clips with Marco Angevine, founder of ViPi. I clicked on one that was obviously supposed to be an off-brand TED Talk. "Marco Angevine: les secrets de la longévité." Marco's face looked like a Guy Fawkes mask, with a pointy chin and a stringy dark mustache and goatee. His shoulder-length brown hair flipped up slightly at the ends, which somehow suited him, though I couldn't imagine many men could pull off that look. The video opened to scattered applause. Marco waited until the audience fell silent before he spoke. "The span of time between the first transatlantic flight and the first time man set foot on the moon was only forty-two years. The time between Dr. Alexis Carrel keeping an organ alive outside of a body to the present day is roughly twice that. Scientists have built upon each other's work for decades, such as adapting the model of an airplane to withstand the vacuum of space, and the same is true for medical science. Over the last hundred years, the human lifespan has roughly doubled, thanks to breakthroughs such as antibiotics, sterilization, nutrition, preventative testing, surgeries, organ transplants . . . the list goes on. So why would it shock you to learn that science is on the brink of tripling or quadrupling the human lifespan . . . or even delaying death indefinitely?"

He roamed the stage in careful, deliberate steps, speaking with authority. His French was easy to understand. The camera occasionally zoomed in on his face, and there was a look in his eye that I almost wanted to call a twinkle, but that felt too diminutive. It was the look people got when they spoke about their passion, their raison d'être.

"Scientists have mapped the genome and identified the physiological reasons for death—of which there are many. Now we are searching for a scientific way to delay death far beyond what has already been achieved. And just beyond that lies the answer to delaying death indefinitely. We're close." He went on to talk about certain molecular compounds and their efficacy in cellular regeneration, and I paused the clip. I couldn't understand him anymore.

I clicked on another video that was uploaded only four weeks ago and had 1,200 views. This was a low-budget podcast interview held over Skype. Marco's image took up half the screen and the host took up the other. Marco was in this house, in front of the bookshelf with the rodent skull. I saw Salomé's little bird embryo behind him.

Podcast host: *We're here today with Marco Angevine, founder of ViPi and a man who claims he will live forever. Is that correct, Marco?*

Marco: *It's true, it's true.*

Podcast host: *And besides a constant fear of your own mortality, how did you arrive at the idea that you should, or could, even, live forever?*

Marco: *Ever since I learned about death as a child, I'd look around myself and think, I'll never be done with this. There's no way I will let myself die. I very much felt addicted to life in an abnormal way that estranged me from other people. It wasn't an anxiety over the uncertainty of death that some religious story or tenacious belief could assuage. It was a true calling. As I got older, the feeling became stronger, and I realized that there were concrete physiological factors that determine our age, and they typically correspond with linear time, which is the process we call "aging." I realized it was only a matter of time before science was able to cure death, and if I wanted that to be in my lifetime, I'd have to make it my mission to contribute to this research. Of course, finding someone to take my ideas seriously was hard at first.*

Marco tilted his chin up to laugh at that last statement. The movement jarred me. I realized he'd been sitting incredibly still. My eyes hadn't left his face, not even when the podcast host spoke. Marco had a presence, that was sure. There was an authority about him, and when he laughed, he felt instantly more approachable—though it seemed more calculated than natural.

Maybe because I was just excited to be able to understand him, I thought his ideas about longevity weren't bad. The podcast host asked him what made his work different from that of his predecessor and teacher, Thierry Leduc.

At the mention of Thierry's name, Marco's face shone with reverence.

Marco: *Dr. Leduc was mainly interested in science that improved the quality of life during its final quarter. Which I believe is integral to my work as well. But the difference is that I do not stop at imagining that most nonagenarians could be as limber and mentally agile as they were in their thirties, almost up to the moment of death. I imagine that the person simply doesn't die. And I use the word "simple" purposefully, although the science is far from simple. But the concept of immortality is. Look at every Greek myth, or the promise of eternal life in Heaven, or even the presence of our survival instinct. It's ingrained in us. It's for that reason that I use the word "simple." You have to believe in this simplicity before you can allow your ideas to extend past the terrestrial plane, where the solution lies. The solution is bigger than one person's lifetime capabilities, as Dr. Leduc unfortunately discovered.*

Podcast host: *You've stated that philosophers and monks are just as integral to your research as biochemists. Why is this?*

Marco: *Because it is not just a question of science. Yes, we have to prime our bodies biologically, which is what the ViPi supplement is for, and exercise, and practices such as breathwork and caloric restriction, which ViPi also facilitates in our group experiences. But physiological priming is merely one step in a multidimensional space. It's the x-axis. The most obvious. I believe the answer to immortality lies on the w-axis, at the intersection of biology, physics, spirituality, and a psychological space that we don't have a sufficient word for at this point. What I've just described is far away from where scientists in their laboratories are operating. This is why I don't describe my real work as science. It is closer to art than it is to science. I have found more inspiration through studying the works of the early alchemists than I have in even my direct predecessor's findings.*

The video stopped here and the rest was available only to subscribers.

I remembered Salomé's hesitation surrounding *La science de l'immortalité.* Why was this so taboo? Maybe it had less to do with the research and more to do with Marco as a person.

Some writers would undoubtedly be scrambling for a story like this, but the amount of research I'd have to do to interview someone was enough to dissuade me, even if Salomé hadn't expressly asked me to stay out of it. I'd never heard of the w-axis before, but I figured it had to do with a fourth dimension.

I'd recently noticed a few headlines about Silicon Valley tech guys who were trying to live forever. I couldn't make it through those articles without feeling more disgust than intrigue. Some planned to cryogenically freeze their heads; some invested ungodly amounts of money into tech companies that promised eternal life . . . starting in twenty years or so, as long as their nascent technology developed as planned. There was a curious absence of a female voice in any of these articles. Women were too busy scrambling after aesthetic youth to consider trying to actually live forever—and would they even want to, given that so many existed in a Sisyphean nightmare of household chores and child-rearing alongside full-time jobs?

I could see myself writing an article about the difference between how men and women seek immortality. I could interview people. Sprinkle the essay with statistics. Find people who broke the mold—a woman who'd bought a plot in a cryogenic chamber and a man who'd had a facelift.

My mind tumbled for a while over this, but I must've fallen asleep on my side because when I awoke, it was light outside and my phone was still open to YouTube, which suggested two more episodes of the podcast. The battery was almost dead.

Salomé was still asleep. My head throbbed as if I'd had an entire bottle of wine myself. I plugged in my phone and went into the kitchen. It wouldn't be rude if I went ahead and made coffee, right? Surely not. I tapped the bottom of the percolator into the trash, filled it with fresh coffee grounds and water, and put it on the stove to brew.

I spent a few seconds looking in the *salle de bain* mirror before something in the sink caught my attention—a diluted pink streak about halfway down the porcelain basin. I cupped water in my hands and splashed it onto the streak. It disappeared down the drain.

I opened the door to find Nathalie outside, looking tired and even thinner than usual. Her eyelashes were plastered together with at least two days' worth of mascara.

"Ah, Cour-ten-ey, *pardon.*"

There was a bit of crusted blood under her right nostril.

"*Non, non, ça va,*" I managed.

"T'as déjà fait du café?"

"Oui."

"Merci, j'ai eu du mal à dormir." She'd had trouble sleeping. She went into the *salle de bain* and closed the door.

I hurried back through the kitchen and into the bedroom, where I purposefully made a little too much noise. Salomé stirred.

"*Coucou.*"

"Good morning," I said.

I went and stood by the edge of her bed, right where I'd been during the night. Was that creepy? It hadn't felt creepy then, but now I didn't feel great about it. I hadn't touched her, or had any intention of touching her. Now, out from under the sheet, I saw that she'd slept in a thin shirt with no bra, the dark outline of her nipples visible through the fabric. She raised her arms overhead, stretching the fabric further. I wished I could be so casually immodest. Or maybe "comfortable" was a better word. I didn't even like changing clothes in front of my friends.

"Let's go to the beach," she said. It sounded like "bitch" in her accent.

Of course she knew what I wanted. "Yes, but I don't have a swimsuit."

In the kitchen, the percolator rumbled. I heard Nathalie turn the burner off.

"That's okay. I don't want to do anything but walk on the water anyway," Salomé said.

"Like Jesus?" It slipped out.

She paused. "I didn't say the right word." She buried her face in the pillow.

I sat on the bed. "No no no, I made a bad joke, that's all. I'm sorry, it was stupid." I dared to lightly touch her leg through the sheet.

Her smile resurfaced from the pillow. "I'm not mad? Just still sleepy. You are funny, what you said." Then, examining my expression, she said, "Don't worry, Cour-ten-ey."

I tried to not be so obviously relieved. "I agree with you, I'd rather walk around on the beach than get into the ocean."

"Good, okay. We don't have to hurry, but it takes one and a half hours to get there, *environ*."

I went to my backpack to change clothes.

"You know, Cour-ten-ey, it is okay for you to correct my English. You shouldn't let me say things wrong. I will do the same for you in French, if you want."

"Actually—" I started, but at the same time, Salomé called for Nathalie. I was going to suggest switching to French. When Nathalie poked her head in the room, I busied myself with my bag, hoping she wouldn't direct a question at me. Salomé asked if we could use the car for the morning. There was a short exchange about where we were going and Salomé asked Nathalie if she'd like to come. I held my breath until Nathalie said no, she had a few things she needed to do before Marco got back. After pouring us each a small cup of coffee, she disappeared into her room with the percolator.

The Peugeot's door hit the wisteria blossoms as I squeezed myself inside, showering the windshield and my head with wet purple petals.

"Be careful to not let fall your coffee, Maman will not be happy with that," Salomé said, turning to toss a couple of beach towels into the back seat. She backed the car out of the driveway, handling the stick shift while balancing her cup and the steering wheel in her left hand.

Soon after pulling off of Rue de la Poterie, she steered the car into a roundabout, downshifting in the turn and then shifting again once she'd taken the exit. It seemed silly that I couldn't drive this car. How hard could it be?

"I wish I could drive a manual," I said. "I've always wanted to learn, but no one has them in America."

"Yes, I notice this," she said. "And so many times you 'ave to stop instead of *un rond-point.* What is this called?"

"A roundabout."

She laughed. "Hoh, that is funny sounding."

"It's so literal."

"You know what else I notice in America? This flag from the South . . . what is it called?"

"The Confederate flag."

"I saw it several times in North Carolina, it was so weird. I'm like . . . did you not know you lose?"

"Don't get me started on that. It's really fucked up. Sometimes I feel like breaking up with the US."

After the one roundabout, we were outside of Châteaubriant, driving west. The long stretch of highway was flanked by cornfields, so flat and straight the end of the road disappeared on the horizon. The sky was clear and there were very few other cars on the road. I'd momentarily forget where I was, and then a squatty little European car would remind me that I was in France.

I wanted to tell Salomé about the videos I'd watched, but I hesitated. I didn't want her to think I didn't believe that Marco was creepy to her. But I also suspected that at least part of her distaste for him and his work was rooted in her love for Thierry. I hoped to get her to say more about this, but now wasn't the moment.

"Is it something you want, to live in France?" Salomé asked.

"That's my dream. But I probably can't move away for a while. I think I'm going to have to move in with my mom later this year to take care of her. My landlord has let me go month-to-month with my lease in anticipation of it."

"And right now? How is she?"

"Right now it's not so bad. She *knows* she has it. It moves so quickly in some people that they don't have the cognitive ability to know what's happening to them. But she knows, which is kind of surreal and devastating in its own way, but I'm ultimately glad for it, I think. She tries to hide it from her sister and sometimes gets really emotional when she slips up in front of her. But with me, she's only been honest. I feel like it might be the most honest she's ever been with me my whole life. It kind of feels like her final act of service to me, being pragmatic about her decline, to the extent she can be." This wasn't what Salomé wanted to know when she asked. I cleared my throat. "But, yeah. Right now her sister is checking on her every day. She's been texting me, sounding pretty lucid and normal. She seems good." I paused for a moment, then added, "She encouraged me to come on this trip."

I almost expected her to say, *Are you kidding me? Your mother is sick with a terminal illness and you are squandering the last few weeks of her lucidity to travel to a country you've been to seven times?* But of course, she didn't say that.

"I'm sorry, Cour-ten-ey, that's really 'ard."

She must've intuited that I didn't want to talk about it more. "Where will you live in France?" she said. "In your dream?"

"Montmartre."

"Yes, I like this very much."

"I lived there in college," I said. I had struggled to remember it before, but now, talking to Salomé, the image of the little kitchen

I shared with Kylie materialized, with its tiny stove and stained countertops we often failed to wipe free of baguette crumbs. I had to look out of the window so she wouldn't see my eyes filling with tears. "It was the best time of my life."

"Why?"

I wasn't prepared to answer that. When I made that claim to other Americans, they seemed to take it as a given that living in Paris would be the best time of one's life. I found myself wanting to say, *I believe the answer lies somewhere on the w-axis, at the intersection between youth, autonomy, anonymity, and a psychological state that we don't have a sufficient word for at this time.* The thought made me laugh.

"What is funny?" she said.

"Nothing," I said, looking back at her. "I think I just felt like that was what the rest of my life would be like. I was excited for adulthood. But honestly, I haven't liked it very much since then." I paused. "Have you had a time like that?"

She thought about it. "I don't know. I only think of the times before Papa died. I was going to university, and I thought, Oh, it will just keep getting better from 'ere. Just to feel like I would never make a mistake too large, because he was there." After a moment of silence, she said, "Not a lot of people will say this to you, but I will say it. It is okay to have something you want in the future, even if the future also means your mom has died, you know? I did a bad job saying it, but you know?"

"Like, it's okay to have something to look forward to, even though that feels like I'm looking forward to her being gone?"

"Yes. Time is going to pass anyway. And if there is something in your own life that you want, that is a good thing. Maybe it will make this time more special."

"Thank you," I said. The fields blurred. I spelled my words until the tears stopped threatening.

"Maybe someday we can live in Paris together," she said. She took an exit toward Saint-Nazaire.

I knew she couldn't really mean it, but still I said, "That is something I could look forward to."

"Me too."

CHAPTER 7

Salomé led the way down a stone path, looking like a movie star in her cuffed shorts and linen shirt knotted at her belly button. I wore the same black skirt I'd been wearing for the past few days. A gust of hot wind hit us with such force that we teetered on our feet. The word *mistral* came to mind, but I wasn't sure that was correct for this region. We followed the curving pathway until it opened to the beach. Salomé stopped at the edge of the sand, hands on her hips. "Well, here it is. *Le Serpent d'Océan.*"

Out of the low tide rose an enormous, fanged skull, followed by curved vertebrae and a rib cage. A sculpture of a snake's skeleton, totally out of place on this obscure, rocky beach. Surely it was not meant to be a tourist attraction.

We tried to walk barefoot but the ground was hot and unforgiving, more rocks and shells than sand. Salomé rested a hand on my shoulder for balance as she strapped her sandals back on. We approached the statue, letting our shoes get soaked as the tide washed over our feet. The statue was bigger than it looked from the edge of the parking lot. Salomé stooped down and walked inside its open mouth.

"Maman loves *le Serpent*," she said, pinching a bit of dripping algae off a fang.

I placed my palm on a rib above the algae line. It was both warm and cool, almost electric, like the thing in my dream. I shuddered, and she noticed.

"I like it," I said quickly. "Is it aluminum?"

Salomé gave me a funny look. "Yes, I think." She got out of the skull and beckoned me to follow her onto the beach. We found a clean spot to lounge on our towels and watched a group of tourists approach the skeleton to take pictures of themselves crouching inside the mouth.

We started on our backs, eyes squinted against the sun. We hadn't thought to bring sunscreen, which would have really disappointed my mom if she knew.

I sat up and unburied a few blue-and-white shells whose ridges and coloration were so intricate that it was hard to believe they were created to protect such simple organisms, the lives they once contained long gone. The lifespan of the shell was exponentially longer than its purpose. I thought about what Marco said about an unnamed psychological space necessary for immortality. Maybe he meant that it was necessary to believe that your purpose never ended, which sounded a little narcissistic to me. Or maybe the psychological space was more a refusal to accept death by identifying a chemical aliveness in what appeared to be inert matter, like this shell. Had the shell ever been living at all, perhaps while it was forming?

Salomé followed my lead and made a line of shells along her shin like mismatched buttons up the front of a coat.

"Do you think this is alive?" I showed her one of the blue shells.

"Is there any part of it that remembers the little clam or whatever it was created to protect?"

She shielded her eyes and looked closely at the shell balanced on the end of my finger, sweat beading on her nose around the triangle of freckles. "Are you asking if it is alive, or if it is conscious?"

I placed it onto her kneecap in line with the others. "Both. Either."

She picked up the shell, looking somewhat amused. "See, this is very French."

"Hard on the outside?"

She laughed. "I think we are a lot the same, inside," she said.

"You and the shell?"

She laughed again. "You and me."

"Maybe. I don't think you're as neurotic as I am."

"You are not neurotic, Cour-ten-ey," she said.

"You only know traveling Courtney. You may not want to be friends with the *quotidienne* Courtney. She's always either thinking too much or trying to avoid thinking. Hard on the inside."

"I am so glad that you are American. A French person wouldn't be here with me after just meeting on the plane."

I tried not to let a foolish smile cross my face. "You wouldn't believe how much time I spend wishing I were French."

She blew a puff of air through her lips. "French people take themselves so seriously."

"I should probably take myself more seriously." I cleared my throat. "So earlier, I was trying to work up the nerve to ask you if we could speak French?"

"Of course," she said. "I know you are nervous, but don't be."

"I'll try," I said, but I was. "You start."

She rolled onto her back, draped her forearm across her eyes, and said in French: "I will tell you what I was thinking about a few minutes ago. One time, when I was little, in Paris, my family went to a restaurant with outdoor seating and live music. My mother and father drank wine and Élise and I danced to the band. Élise and I fought over getting a chance to dance with Papa. He got up and danced with us, one at a time, and we stood on his feet. I remember the string lights between the trees and the laughter and chatter of the patrons eating. Everyone was having a good time, all the strangers. We spun around and I caught a glimpse of Élise's face as she watched us, and she was seething with jealousy. She couldn't stand sharing him with me. I remember seeing her face and instead of it hurting me, I felt like I understood her better. I was only four years old or so."

"Et maintenant? Élise et toi . . . ?"

She continued in French. "We never talk. She does not like me."

"I'm sorry. Is there a reason for that?"

Salomé sighed. "It's complicated. And your sister, Haa-naah," she said, working hard for the *H*, "it is still strained between you?"

I could say a lot about this in French. "She doesn't like me, at all, it seems. I'm eleven years older than her. She's always resented me. And at our last Thanksgiving, when we were discussing my article, she accused me of being part of the liberal elite, as if our dad hadn't paid for her tuition too, at a much more expensive, out-of-state university. Which I did point out to her, and that didn't go well." I shook my head. In English, I said, "Sometimes I want to shake her by the shoulders and tell her she's enough, she doesn't have to be different from me for our dad to love her and think she's special. She doesn't need to throw other women under the bus and align herself with men to be protected. At work or in life."

"I know some of these women in France, too." Salomé sat up and brushed the sand off the bottoms of her feet.

"Really?"

"It is the country of Marine Le Pen, is it not?" she asked in French. "There are women who say they prefer tradition, even if tradition means having no rights. Like thirty percent of women voted for her last year."

"It's not even unique," I said, again in English. "There's a term for it. It's called making the patriarchal bargain."

She paused for a moment, seeming to deeply consider something. I worried that once she resumed the conversation, I'd be left behind. But she brushed her windswept hair from her eyes and asked, "What is 'throwing under a bus'?"

"Oh sorry, it's an idiom."

An empty soda can rolled by us, propelled by the wind. Salomé reached out to stop it, and put it under her bag. "I understand it," she said.

"The idiom or the patriarchal bargain?"

"Both."

A group of teenagers passed, speaking loudly. I didn't catch much of what they were saying. I couldn't recall if I was ever good enough at French to pick up on the out-of-context conversations of passersby, especially young ones. It was strange that I understood Marco's science talk but not a group of fifteen-year-olds.

"What is this word that means you are listening to someone else's conversation? I can never remember," Salomé asked.

"Eavesdrop." I'd been thinking of it yesterday or the day before. How did she know?

"Eavesdrop," she repeated. The word was candy shared between us, sweet and sacred.

"What were they saying?" I asked.

She squinted in their direction, though their voices were lost to the wind. "I think something about music. I already forgot." She kept her head turned away from me for a few seconds. The breeze blew her hair toward my face, carrying the scent of her air-dry serum.

"Was that a little café we passed? Want to go get something cold to drink?" I asked. For a moment I feared that when she turned back to me, she would be crying.

But she looked at me and smiled. "I was thinking the same!" Perhaps I seemed relieved, because she studied me for a brief moment before standing up and dusting off her legs. She offered a hand to help me up, and I took it.

The café was on the other side of the parking lot. Salomé threw the stray soda can in a recycling bin as we passed by. We sat at a table outside in the shade of a large umbrella sponsored by Aperol. There was an older couple sitting a table away, both drinking Orangina. I hadn't had a soft drink in years. It felt so childish.

"Would you think I was silly for getting an Orangina?"

She looked to the other table, then back to me. "Why would I think you are silly." It was a question phrased as a statement.

The server approached our table and Salomé ordered two Oranginas. Once the server had moved away, she sighed. She picked at the corner of a soggy coaster.

"What's worrying you?"

"My mother . . ."

"Because of how skinny she is?"

"Well, yes. That's one reason. But I'm thinking more about what you say . . . what did you call it? Patriarchal something?"

"The patriarchal bargain?"

"Yes. She does this. And I am so disappointed. Ever since university she is working with my father, and then, when he died, she went straight to Marco, thinking he can keep her safe, you know? And I understand it because I've done it, too."

I nodded. "Does your mom work with Marco? Like, professionally?"

"She works for ViPi," Salomé said. "And I know that every day, she is thinking of 'ow much this is a . . . what is the word? *Une trahison?*"

"A betrayal?"

"Yes. Of my father and his research." After a few seconds, she said, "She is always a . . . how do you say a *penseuse abstraite*?"

"An abstract thinker?"

"*Ouais.* But now, some of her ideas, they are getting too much."

"What do you mean by 'ideas'?"

She said in French, "She told me yesterday that she has figured out a way to visit my father." Her fingers fluttered to her face and pressed lightly into her cheeks.

"What? How?"

She shook her head. "She didn't say how she was doing it. Just that she knew how."

Could Nathalie be doing witchcraft or something? I thought about the blood in the sink, the absolute exhaustion behind her eyes when we crossed paths in the hallway that morning. She had this huge garden, but only grew herbs and flowers, no vegetables. Maybe she was creating potions or some sort of medicine. I stopped myself. That was crazy. But I remembered her voice from my dream. *I'll never forgive him.* I thought about telling Salomé about the dream, but I didn't want to upset her.

"If you need more private family time, I can go to Paris. I'd hate to keep you from having these conversations with her if you need to," I said, though I hoped that wasn't true.

"No, I would be very overwhelmed to be here alone," she said, looking down at her thumbs. "I hope you don't think I am here with you just to avoid being alone with her. But I want to admit to you that when I asked you to come, it was because I really liked you and wanted to spend more time with you, but also because I didn't want to be alone here."

"Honestly, I figured you wanted some sort of buffer. But it's okay, I understand. I'm so glad I came."

The server approached and set down our drinks. He asked if we wanted anything else but lingered for a couple of seconds after we'd said no, as if he had something to say. I realized I had turned to him, smiling, to welcome him into our conversation the way an American server would stand there and chitchat with us. I felt awkward when I squared my shoulders back toward Salomé. The server walked off. God, I was so devastatingly American.

Salomé looked amused. She understood every beat of that interaction. I didn't want to acknowledge it, so I asked, "In your absolute dream life, what would you do? Not even for work, but just what would you want to do with your time?"

"This will sound so stupid from someone in a family of scientists," she said. "But if I could do anything, it would be saving animals and 'elping them find families. This is really what makes me happy. I don't have to study the philosophies of all these dead men to know that treating animals with kindness is the best thing a society can do. Because, you know, if they are kind to animals, that usually means they are kind to people, too."

"You think that's less noble than spending your life in a lab coat? Or writing for a local publication that touts itself as being 'independent' but is wholly dependent on advertising revenue?"

Her mouth pulled into a tight smile. She said, in French, "So, when we are in Paris, can we have a cat? Or even two cats?"

"You can have as many cats as you want, as long as you're in charge of the litter box." And as long as one of those cats wasn't Louis.

She smiled and drank her Orangina, looking out toward the ocean.

We couldn't see the statue from here, only a stripe of faraway sea, dark and glistening. This little seed of a plan—Paris, an apartment with two cats—might be just what I needed to get through the next few months. But, if the past was any indication of the future, it would probably never be my life. Still, what could it hurt to dream?

CHAPTER 8

We drove back with the windows down. I reached my arm out and let the hot air flow between my fingers. Salomé did the same, and together we created a wingspan.

It didn't seem fair that this moment was subject to the constraints of time, that it wouldn't be available to revisit outside of my memory. I took another picture of her, elbow resting out of the window, her right thumb hooked to the steering wheel. Her chin was tilted slightly upward to keep the hair out of her eyes, but she looked defiant, like the famous Delacroix painting of La Marianne during the French Revolution, undeterred as she stepped over the bodies of soldiers with the French flag held high—the symbol of the French Republic that followed the crumbled monarchy. I learned about her in high school French class. I was surprised that any country's symbol of freedom would be a woman, especially a country in which women weren't granted the right to vote until after World War II. *Liberté* was a title-only promotion. La Marianne's breasts were exposed in the painting. I guess she had to earn her keep on the canvas somehow.

I looked at the picture I'd just taken of Salomé and had the same feeling as when I'd taken her picture on the trail, as if I'd somehow tainted the memory rather than preserved it. I zoomed in on her face. We'd gotten some sun. The triangle of freckles on her nose was darker, her cheekbones smartly red.

She laughed. "What are you doing?"

I held up the phone so she could glance at the picture. "You're so pretty," I said.

"Let me see again," she said, her eyes flicking to it for a second longer. "Send it to me."

"I need to get your phone number," I said as we turned onto Rue de la Poterie. I wanted her to have the picture, but part of me balked at the thought that she might use it on a dating app or send it to a guy she was talking to. This was how I saw her, how she was with me. But that was ridiculous.

Salomé rolled up her window as we pulled into the driveway, and I did the same. Nathalie watched us from the kitchen window. Her thin face was fraught, the skin seeming to hang off her hollowed cheeks.

"What's wrong with your mom?" I asked.

"What you mean?"

"I just saw her in the window . . ."

"Oh, *putain* . . ."

Nathalie rushed out the front door in her robe and slippers, an arm crossed over her midsection and a cigarette in the other hand. Her hair and clothes were disheveled, like she'd just awoken from a deep sleep. Her mouth was downturned so severely it would've been comical if I hadn't been afraid. She looked at me through the rear windshield with such fury the image of Medusa came to mind, her dark eyes frantic, the lines between her eyebrows cut deep.

Salomé got out of the car to intercept her, which made me believe this behavior was familiar. I cracked my door open and heard a low, heated exchange. Nathalie pointed in my direction with her cigarette, letting the robe slip down to expose the bony top of her rib cage above her breast.

This couldn't be about me. I hadn't done anything, had I? I hadn't even been at the house all day. It was too hot in the car, so I slipped out and collected the two coffee cups and our beach towels from the floorboard. When I looked up, Nathalie had retreated into the house.

Salomé stood still, facing away from me, her sunburned shoulders tense. When she turned to approach me, she looked like she was about to cry. "Court-en-ey, I am so sorry. She is upset, something 'as disappeared."

"What disappeared?"

"It was a ring of my papa's. It is very important to her and . . ."

Somehow, I knew what she was going to say.

". . . and I know you didn't steal it . . ."

"No, no, no."

"But she says she saw you on the cameras."

My knees almost buckled.

"I had another bad dream last night. I sleepwalked into the living room, and if I took something, I didn't mean to! I will give it back," I said, not meaning to imply that I had taken anything. "You said it yourself—everyone has crazy dreams in this house."

Salomé looked conflicted, which I understood, but I burned with the need for her to believe me. I'd go dump my backpack on the floor and go through every item until I found the ring or could prove it wasn't there.

I dashed into the house and through the kitchen to our shared bedroom. But I didn't need to dump out my bag. Nathalie had already done that.

My belongings were strewn about, including my dirty clothes. My notebook lay open on the bed. One of the cups slipped from my fingers. I barely heard the sad tinkle of ceramic breaking through the intensity of my heartbeat.

I was saying "What the fuck?" over and over as I scrambled to gather my clothes and money. "Salomé, I swear to God, I've never even been in her room, I didn't . . ." I paused, barely able to breathe.

She had to believe me. But the crease between her eyebrows was hard to decipher. She knelt beside me, and I thought she would place a gentle hand onto my shoulder, but instead she reached for a piece of the broken cup.

The front door slammed. We heard gravel crunching as Nathalie reversed the car from the driveway and peeled off down the street.

"Salomé, please. I don't want your father's jewelry. I don't even wear jewelry!" I held up my ten bare fingers as if this were proof of my innocence.

She sat back on her ankles, holding the shattered ceramic with a similar reverence as she had the bird. It must've been a precious cup, maybe her father's favorite. Of course I would come into this house and break something beloved. Without responding to my plea, she left the room. I focused on a small feather clinging to the blanket on the bed, watching it shiver at the touch of my breath. I'm not sure how long she left me sitting there, but when she returned she had a small broom and dustpan, which she left on the floor next to the smaller ceramic pieces.

She sat on the floor, folding her knees up to her chin. "This is my fault."

"How is this your fault?"

"It was maybe not such a good idea to bring you."

"I didn't steal, I . . ."

"Not you. Maman. I was being selfish because I didn't want to be here alone with her. She is sometimes *instable. Paranoïaque.*" The look on her face was utter exhaustion. "It has been a long time, but she does this before, when we were little . . . maybe every year one time. But I thought she was better now. She takes medicine."

I couldn't think of anything to say.

"When I was young, my father would tell Élise and me to leave the house and come back in a few hours, and she would forget it all, like it was a dream."

"Did she?"

"Always."

"So we should leave? Should we get a hotel?"

She kept her eyes trained on the pieces of ceramic on the floor. "I think it's best if you go to Paris now to be with your friend. I am so sorry, Cour-ten-ey."

It took a moment for her words to sink in. My first instinct was to assume we'd stay together. But I didn't know this woman or her family. I was a stranger here. Salomé still looked like she was trying not to cry. She was probably embarrassed, though she didn't need to be.

I reached for her hand. "It's okay, it's not your fault."

"It is a little funny because it was Marco I didn't want you meeting, and now look, you won't meet him anyway."

"Will you be okay here with him? You could come with me to Paris."

She squeezed my hand. "It is very sweet that you are worried about me now. I will be okay. It is my family's house, not his."

I gathered the rest of my things in silence. Salomé looked up the train timetables on her phone. "There is a direct to Angers in one hour, and you can get the TGV from there."

"What do we do until then?"

"Prendre un verre?"

I definitely wanted a drink. I was packed, but not ready. I hoisted my backpack onto my sunburned shoulders and followed Salomé out of the house. I spelled *serrer*, tapping my fingers against my thighs. But my mind kept zipping back to Nathalie's deranged expression in the driveway, the helpless sensation of waking up in their living room. Had I stolen something? I tried to breathe deliberately and evenly. The film of sweat covering my skin grew clammy. Please don't have a panic attack here.

We said nothing as we walked to the same wine bar from two nights before. The tables didn't have umbrellas, but the outdoor seating was nestled between two buildings, which provided enough shade. Sweat already soaked through my shirt under my backpack.

Salomé sighed heavily before leaning her elbows on the table. She looked exhausted. "I was thinking to go to America for a while, I would forget all of this, it would not be waiting for me, but being 'ere, I just feel it more than ever."

"I swear to God, I didn't steal anything. Or if I did, I was sleepwalking. I swear," I said, my voice verging on panic.

A look of compassion crossed her face. "Oh, Cour-ten-ey. I know."

I got myself under control just in time for the server to approach, but still, I could barely acknowledge her outside of a meek "*Bonjour*."

Salomé ordered us two Aperol spritzes. Her eyes followed the server until she'd disappeared into the restaurant.

"What is going on?" I asked. "Like, I'm having these horrible sleep paralysis dreams, I'm sleepwalking . . . then all this with your mom?"

"I agree. There is such bad energy at the house. It was never like this before, not even when she was sick."

Sick. I could practically hear Thierry using the word *malade* to describe the situation to his daughters.

Salomé said, "I think the problem is Marco. I think he is abusing her. And Maman, like I was saying to you earlier, she is not so easy to control. You can see how he does it. The cameras. I feel like either he makes her so skinny or she is not eating so she can have something to control. She would not tell me."

I wasn't sure how that would cause me to have terrible dreams unless I was sensitive to the bad energy in the house. I guessed that could be a possibility, but it seemed unlikely. Marco had mentioned that ViPi offered some sort of course in caloric restriction, which might be connected to Nathalie's thinness. I thought about telling Salomé that I'd watched those videos, but I didn't want to come across as untrustworthy to her, like I was trying to uncover something without her permission.

The server returned with our drinks. My hand was still shaking from the Nathalie situation as I brought the paper straw to my lips.

Salomé set her glass down. "I will tell you about what happened, but I don't want you to write about it."

"That's okay," I said. "I promise. I've only had one publication that wasn't about Raleigh anyway."

She held my gaze, looking skeptical. I couldn't imagine why she thought any of this might appeal to a broad American audience.

"You don't have to tell me if you don't want to," I said.

"I will tell you. But I don't know where to start."

"So your dad's book? He studied aging, and immortality—but not literal immortality, right? Was that just a buzzword for the title?"

She looked down at her hands, which were clasped together on the table. She shook her head gently and looked back up at me. "I will have to start at the beginning, much before my father. Do you know of Alexis Carrel?"

"I don't think so . . ."

"It is a scientist who kept the 'eart of a chicken alive for a very long time in his laboratory . . ."

"I think I read about him in a book about Henrietta Lacks. It was the immortal chicken heart, right? But it didn't end up being immortal at all?"

"Yes, so he was a very important scientist for France, and for the world. He won the Nobel Prize for some discoveries in surgery. My grandfather Émile would travel to Paris to work in Carrel's laboratory, when Carrel worked in France. But Carrel spent a lot of time in North America because he was an outcast in France. Most scientists wouldn't work with him because he believed he saw a . . . *une guérison par la foi*? What is this?"

"Umm, like a faith healing maybe? Just tell me in French. But slowly."

She nodded. "My father was only four when Carrel died. He said he always knew he wanted to be a scientist of some kind, like his own father. When Papa went to university, he studied genetics. And he wanted to expand upon certain elements of Carrel's research, but he wanted to add a metaphysical element."

"Metaphysical," or *métaphysique*, was one of those words that I thought I understood but couldn't clearly define. "What does that mean?"

"Science has discovered many reasons why our bodies age and die. It is not one thing, but rather several converging factors. So, my father's hypothesis was that the cure for death was not going to be a medicine or genetic mutation, but beliefs and practices that could change our biology. Then he wanted to prove that the added metaphysical elements actually did change the cellular makeup of a body. It was mostly telomeres that he was looking at . . . Do you know what that is?"

"I do, actually," I said.

"The problem with his research is that by nature, the subjects had to be human. You cannot ask a lab rat to meditate or change its beliefs around linear time. So, he worked with human volunteers, such as his own father, who lived to be one hundred and seven years old. My grandfather died four years ago, just after Papa. There were only four people in the study. Papa, his father, and two of my father's friends, who are twins."

They must've been the twins in the Polaroids.

"And now Marco has used my father's research to make his own business, because if you take his vitamins, you will live forever." She rolled her eyes and leaned forward to take a sip from the wilting paper straw.

She continued, "So, in 2001, when I was twelve, there was this scandal that resulted in my father being fired from his tenured professor status at the university where he worked in Paris. That's when we moved to Châteaubriant. And he had his first bout of cancer, which was the reason my parents gave Élise and me for why we were moving. He needed less stress in his life."

It would be almost impossible to fire a tenured professor in France, I'd think. "What was the scandal?"

"There was a huge article about him in *Le Figaro* called 'The New Carrel.' Papa had been inspired by Carrel's immortality research, yes, but Carrel was a eugenicist. It is so complicated because Carrel's research saved lives and even today serves as the foundation of some surgical practices. Yet, like many European men before World War II, he was obsessed with the idea of racial purity and 'survival of the fittest.'"

"Doesn't that seem at odds with itself?" I said in English. "Survival of the fittest and saving lives through medicine?"

"Well, Carrel just wanted to save the white people," she said. "And not all white people, but elite people from certain bloodlines. I am sure not Jewish people. He was working with this American you probably know."

I almost missed the name of his research partner because she pronounced "Charles Lindbergh" as "Sharrl Leen-berrh."

"The pilot?"

"Yes, they did many experiments together. They thought they could achieve immortality. There's a whole book about their partnership that I tried to read but I couldn't because it was full of animal experiments."

"Wow, I had no idea," I said. "I don't know anything about Lindbergh outside of being a pilot and the whole baby kidnapping thing."

"Yes, he was an engineer who built much of Carrel's laboratory equipment, and he was also a eugenicist. It was a very popular idea in Europe leading up to the Holocaust, as you can probably imagine. But anyway, after 'The New Carrel' was published, there were many other articles about Papa. Someone accused Papa of being a eugenicist because all of the people in his experiment were white. But that happened because he took a very small sample of four volunteers, and at the time, Papa thought they needed to be genetically related. Papa wrote an op-ed admitting that the study was flawed and that he should have diversified his volunteer pool when he started the experiment twenty-five years earlier, but he hadn't had the foresight. And an experiment with four people is hardly an experiment. It was supposed to offer basic insight into his idea upon which other scientists could later conduct larger experiments. He took full responsibility for the bad decision and advised younger scientists to not make the same mistake. But the tabloids started using some quotes out of context, leaving out the parts where he admitted to his mistake and asserted that scientists must be open to criticism, and studies need to be scrutinized from every angle."

"That's terrible," I said. Of course I wanted to believe her at face value, but a bit of me wondered if I was getting the whole story here. She was certainly not an unbiased source.

She blew a puff of air through her lips. "That is not the worst part," she said in English, but continued in French: "The worst part is that there were other people who wanted to celebrate him and thought he was going to purify the French population. These people almost made him into a saint for their cause. There was a media explosion about him after that. The far right defending him, the left maligning him. It seemed like every journalist in the country had an opinion on him. He hated it. He never wanted to be in the spotlight like that."

"That's really sad," I said. "And yet another reason why I'm disillusioned by journalism. I understand why you keep telling me not to write about it."

"Yes. I was so mad at the journalists, but Papa would say, 'They are just doing their job.' I still don't know how he could be so understanding. All Papa wanted was for everyone to have access to healthy aging and to enjoy their old age. And these assholes ruined the last few years of his life."

"The people who supported him have to be pretty fringe, right?"

"Oh, it is a minority, but more than you want to think it is. I'm telling you, you think we are so progressive because of our health care system, but there are the same types of people in France as those who fly the Confederate flag in North Carolina. Maybe not so much in the cities, but other places, yes. They sit in their homes watching the news that is telling them how dangerous the world is, how their jobs are in jeopardy because of immigrants, how white people are going to be the minority. And they're so afraid, even though their lives are so safe. They're the type of people that you want supporting you if you plan to become a dictator. Because of this, many people hated my family. And I understand. I would not want to be associated with that. But it was not true."

"That really sucks."

"I blame Marco," she said.

"For what? 'The New Carrel'?"

She nodded. "I know he planted the article."

"Why would Nathalie be with him if he ruined your father's career?"

Salomé's eyebrows raised. "*Le syndrome de la grenouille cuite*, I think. Do you have this in English?"

"The frog in boiling water? Yeah."

In French she said, "But at the time, none of us suspected that Marco was behind the article. He acted as incensed as we were. There's still no evidence that he did it, except that in creating a controversy, he easily identified a target market for ViPi. But I didn't put this together for many years, and when I did, I demanded that Maman leave him. But she didn't, and I still can't understand why."

"Is this why you don't have any friends in Châteaubriant?"

"Well, mostly they moved away. I still have a few friends in Paris, but I don't know. We are not very close. And I have trouble trusting new French people I meet. Because I don't know what they already know about me, and if they are eager to be my friend, it might be for the wrong reason. And then if they know nothing about me, they will soon enough." She sighed. She was done talking about it.

I was honored she'd shared that with me. I wanted to deserve her trust.

"Come to Paris with me," I said.

"I think I need to stay and make sure Maman is okay. But if you are still in Paris in maybe two or three days, I will come."

"I'm sorry it's hard to be with your family. I understand."

Her eyes softened. "I knew you would understand."

I pressed the center button of my phone. It was time to go. We left cash on the table tucked under an empty glass.

As we walked toward the station in silence, I tried to busy myself with thinking about the logistics of travel. What if there wasn't room on the TGV tonight from Angers? I'd need a hotel, too.

"Oh, look, she's there." Salomé pointed across the street.

My first thought was Nathalie, which gripped me with fear. But she was pointing to a big black dog sitting outside of a Carrefour grocery store, watching us, her long, freckled tongue hanging out as she panted.

"Loute," I said.

Salomé crossed the street. "Do you have water?"

There was a dented plastic bottle that I'd carried from the plane near the top of my backpack. She poured the water into her palm and the dog lapped it up. Loute slid down onto the sidewalk, turning her spotted belly up, which Salomé scratched.

"*Quelle* good girl." She smiled sadly up at me, but I didn't feel much like smiling, even at her cute franglais. This shouldn't be goodbye, but in all likelihood, it would be.

At the tiny train station Salomé sat me down on a bench next to a kiosk. We were the only people here. Even the *accueil* window wasn't staffed. She typed into the kiosk, something I'd done as a student before everyone started using apps.

I leafed through my wallet and limply held up my debit card.

"No, Maman is paying for this," she said, pulling a card from her pocket.

"Did she tell you she'd pay for it?"

"No, but if she is going to accuse of stealing, I am feeling like really taking from her."

"If this comes up you have to take the fall."

"What are you saying?" Her face, lit by the kiosk's dull glow, was suddenly so beautiful I couldn't look at her.

"Sorry. I mean, don't let her think I asked you to buy this."

"Don't worry. I will not throw you under a bus." She stepped over to validate the ticket at the little yellow *machine à composter*, then sat next to me on the bench. She crossed her bare legs at the knee and leaned her forehead onto my shoulder. Closeness now felt normal between us. I'd never had anything like this with a friend. I felt like I'd been missing out on something my whole life.

The arch of her foot was crusted in sand.

"Was the beach today?" I asked.

"It feels like two lifetimes ago," she said in French, still looking down.

"I want . . . more time." It was all I had.

Her hand moved to my leg, then to my hand. She slid her fingers between mine and squeezed gently. "Me too. I will call you, I promise."

Though the air was stifling, I imagined that we were wearing coats with faux fur–lined hoods, interlacing our gloved fingers, our breath mingling in the air above.

The SNCF lady came over the intercom announcing my train's arrival. As sad as I was, I was somehow thankful for this rip-the-bandage reason to leave. It would've been too hard otherwise.

The TER train rattled into the station. We turned into each other, holding tight, burying our faces in the faux fur, buttons and zippers tapping together.

"Come with me," I said once again.

"Soon. I will see you soon."

When she pulled my face to her own, pressing her mouth to mine as easily as I'd ever been kissed, the tips of our noses were cold.

CHAPTER 9

I thought about not telling Kylie I was on my way to Paris. It was short notice, and she liked a lot of notice. I'd get a cheap hotel. But then I thought about being alone tonight with nothing to distract me from replaying my every move and every word over the past few days on a tortuous loop, so I texted her before I boarded the TGV in Angers. I offered to stay somewhere else, but she told me not to be crazy.

I hadn't gotten Salomé's phone number. How could I have overlooked that? I'd given her mine on the plane, along with my email address. She would contact me. But what if she said something I didn't want to hear? What if, in the time since I had left her, she had started to suspect me? I knew I would never intentionally steal, but I *had* woken up that night standing by the bookshelf. What if I got to Kylie's apartment and opened my bag and the ring fell out?

What if Salomé hadn't meant to kiss me? She could've tried to go in for *la bise* and I'd misinterpreted and accidentally kissed her mouth. Oh my God. She was probably walking back to her house thinking, *Putain,* Cour-ten-ey thinks I wanted to kiss her, so now I can never talk to her again.

Maybe the kiss hadn't really happened. The memory of it was like memories of dreams, tinged with an ethereal quality that gave me reason to doubt it. I could swear we were wearing coats, but that didn't make any sense. My lips still tingled slightly from the connection. I lifted my fingers to brush against them.

I wasn't into women. Most of the time I felt like I wasn't into people at all, apart from the occasional outlier. Maybe I was just an asshole who was traveling and had no plans to see it through. Either that or I was the trope of the man-hating lesbian, driven into the arms of a woman only because she despised men so fervently. I was a fucking stereotype probably getting a lot of attention on 4chan.

I thought of the two hairs on Salomé's ankle fluttering when I blew on them, which sent an almost painful current through my body. How strange that I'd felt compelled to do that; how easy it became to touch her, once I was brave enough.

I tried never to think about the first time a guy touched me. Sometimes I made it months without thinking about it. Years at times. Even though it was half my life ago, I still hadn't fully processed it.

I'd gone to a football game in high school with a group, and afterward we went to a friend's house. She had a basement and her parents more or less let us do whatever we wanted. I choked down a Bud Light in a red Solo cup—I hadn't yet developed a taste for beer, only a taste for fitting in. Then I woke on the couch to the sight of my friend's boyfriend on top of me, his face rising and falling, rising and falling, inches from mine. It took me a few seconds to realize that my pants were off.

I couldn't have pushed him off if I'd tried. I must've been roofied, though that didn't occur to me at the time. But I was much too light a sleeper to sleep through someone crawling on top of me and pulling off my pants. At the time, it felt like a choice I made to just stay still, hoping everyone else was asleep so they wouldn't accuse me of cheating with Cara's boyfriend. The only other thing I remember of that night was walking home a few hours later on the side of a county road that didn't have a sidewalk, my vision spinning. I thought I was still drunk from one beer. From a distance, I smelled a dead deer, but if I turned around, I'd have to go back to Cara's. I walked on and on, and the smell became so strong I had to pull my sweatshirt over my nose. The shirt I wore underneath smelled of his body spray. I stopped walking and threw up. I wanted to scream, but I was afraid someone would hear me and call the police. I kept walking, imagining each step spinning the whole earth behind me rather than propelling me forward. When I finally passed the bloated doe, I shielded my eyes and willed myself to keep going.

The most fucked-up part is that for years I rewrote the memory and harbored guilt for having cheated on my friend. In college I'd recounted the story in a way that gave me autonomy, like I was some sort of remorseless badass who would have sex with a friend's boyfriend while she slept yards away. I left out the blood in my underwear, the way it hurt to sink down into the warm bath I drew myself once I got home. I left out how I had to pass this guy in the hallway for another year and he would sometimes wave and sometimes ignore me. I made myself believe that I wanted him to be interested in me. I left out how I wouldn't experience my first kiss for over two years despite no longer being a virgin, and how terrified I was when that finally happened, and how I didn't actually *want* the kiss, either. I left out how whenever I saw a dead deer on the highway, I had to choke down a swell of primal anger that felt like it was going to burst out of my body.

The real memory resurfaced years later, during the #MeToo movement, which, I'm ashamed to admit, was the first time I'd truly considered that men could be held accountable for their actions. I'd been taught that love was hard and relationships were challenging, even your relationship to God, which I'd never figured out either. No one ever quantified that.

I wrote in my notebook: *How often I've mistaken fear for attraction.* The train jerked, sending the tip of my pen skittering down the side of the page.

For as much time as I spent in my own head, I had done shockingly little self-interrogation on my sexuality. Was it the Catholicism? I'd switched to the regular public school for high school, and hadn't been to mass in at least ten years. I didn't consider myself religious at all, aside from the way it influenced my early education. If it was based in Catholicism, it was too deeply ingrained for me to recognize. But I didn't feel like I was wrestling with any deep-seated homophobia as much as a general disinterest in my sexuality. I saw people all around me, some of whom were beautiful, but I rarely felt attracted to them, men or women. The main difference between the men and women I found beautiful was that I knew what to do if a man wanted me.

But sometimes a kiss is just a kiss, right? There were probably a lot of women who had kissed their friend at some point and then continued to live their lives without thinking about it ad nauseam. Nathalie's accusation, her scowling face, as untrusting as an animal in a trap. Would she be able to convince Salomé that I'd done something wrong? Or *had* I?

God, the loop was starting over.

I looked at my reflection in the window. "You really fucking suck," I said to myself. My reflection grew brighter as the train traveled through a series of dark tunnels, entering the Paris metro area. If I angled my head just right, I looked like a skull, or maybe like a Modigliani portrait, with their gray, empty eyes. "When I know your soul, I will paint your eyes," Modigliani had supposedly said.

I tried to keep my hand still enough to draw a head, a face, and empty eyes in my notebook. Rudimentary nose, off-center lips. A long, graceful neck. My attempt at Salomé via Modigliani. The wavy edges gave the portrait a creepy, haunted quality.

I remembered the weight of the succubus, how I wanted it to kiss me, the beauty I perceived in what it whispered to me. It was only a dream, so why did it feel so significant? I'd been a vivid dreamer my whole life, but I almost never had recurring dreams, especially not nightmares. That hole where its face should've been, the way it tried to rip my jaw open. I shuddered. I spelled my words but the image stayed lodged in my mind even after the train stopped at Gare Montparnasse.

I'd finally made it to Paris, where I'd meant to be all along. I navigated the levels of Gare Montparnasse on autopilot, bought a carnet of Métro tickets, and hopped onto the first train that came screeching into the station. Normally I lived for these moments that made it feel like I'd never left Paris, but none of it brought me any satisfaction tonight.

Kylie met me at the Opéra Métro stop at 21h30 as promised, wearing a pin-striped button-up sundress.

"Hey, girl, hey!" she practically shouted, throwing one arm dramatically into the air, and pulled me into a hug. My arms raised to return the embrace as if connected to puppet strings. She squealed and bounced up and down, scraping the fabric of our clothes together in a way that bunched my shirt up over my belly button.

I could not match this energy. I fought the desire to extinguish her. "It's great to see you," I said, forcing a smile as I fixed my shirt. I picked up my backpack, which I'd rested against my calf. When I looked back at Kylie, her head was tilted to the side like an inquisitive cocker spaniel.

"What's wrong?" she asked.

"Oh, it's . . ." I didn't know whether to say "nothing" or "everything." I said, "I should never have gone over there." Instantly my eyes stung. I didn't want that to be true.

Kylie gave me an exaggerated frown and touched my upper arm. "Let's go back to my place so you can set your bag down. We can talk about it."

I nodded and followed her, managing, I hoped, to somewhat mask my devastation.

We walked north for a few minutes. I don't remember what we talked about, but I laughed a few times, hoping she'd forget how upset I'd looked when I arrived. A few blocks away from her apartment, Kylie stopped at a street vendor's cart. "Are you hungry?"

"Not really," I said, though I should've been.

She ordered a Nutella crepe, which didn't end up being for eating, anyway. She instructed me to hold it up while she took several pictures, some of just my hand holding it, and others with both our hands on it. I wondered what her caption would be. "Have *une crêpe* on me, *mon amie*!" Something that made me out to be a complete foreigner here. She took one bite before handing it to me. I took one bite as well. A group pushed past us, trailing cigarette smoke in my face, which mixed in my mouth with the Nutella like a chocolate ashtray. I fought to swallow the bite. On the way to throw the crepe into a garbage can, I stepped over a pile of dog shit that had already been tracked through a few times. The walk to Kylie's apartment felt like it took hours, though it was less than fifteen minutes from the Métro stop.

Kylie's apartment in the 9th arrondissement was on the third floor of a harshly renovated building whose interior didn't at all match its romantic exterior. Even the key turning in the lock sounded too clinical to give way to a home. There is no direct translation for "home" in French.

It was the same two-bedroom apartment Kylie had lived in for years with a few different roommates. Her current roommate was Mari, who was born in Japan and grew up in New York City. Kylie had mentioned that Mari was dating someone and was rarely home these days, which I was glad to hear, although I'd liked Mari when I met her on my last trip. But the fewer people to see me in this state, the better.

Kylie kept her apartment minimalistically decorated, with only a few small paintings on the walls. She displayed her books with the pages out, spines in, so they were all monochrome. This had infuriated me the first time I'd seen it. The homiest touch was the herringbone floor—probably the only part that was original to the apartment. It looked like the floor in our old place above the *serrurerie.*

I sat on the thin futon, staring at the stubble on my knees while Kylie got us some wine in the kitchen, which was really just the space directly behind the futon. I checked my phone for what had to be the tenth time since getting off the train. She would contact me, she promised. At the same time, no news was good news. At least she wasn't calling me having sided with Nathalie, newly convinced I was a thief.

The cork popped, reverberating through the hollow of my body. The surprise hurt. I slid onto the floor next to the coffee table, resisting the urge to wad myself into a ball. There was a dust bunny stuck to one of the coffee table's legs. I liked seeing something imperfect in Kylie's world.

Kylie set my wine down on the table and stood still, waiting. Reluctantly, I raised my eyes to her face. She wasn't mad, but she wasn't happy either. She was neutral, which was scarier than I expected.

"Courtney, you have to tell me what happened. Am I just supposed to know what to do for you? I literally haven't seen you in a year, and you show up four days late looking like you've witnessed a murder. Seriously, like, I want to help you, but I obviously don't know what to do."

There were so many ways to begin the story, but nothing seemed right, and nothing quite matched up with how I was presenting myself. I wished I could huddle under a blanket.

"I got accused of stealing some jewelry," I said finally, in monotone. I stared at the dust bunny rather than Kylie.

"And you didn't?"

"No, of course not! I've never stolen anything in my life!"

"Okay, well, I didn't actually know that. So who accused you?"

"Her mother."

"Who is 'her'?"

I tried not to seem annoyed for having to explain it all. "Salomé. The girl I met on the plane." I reached out and touched the dust bunny.

"Eww," Kylie said, snatching it up between her thumb and pointer finger. She disappeared behind the couch. The trash can lid banged open, then the faucet ran as Kylie washed her hands.

Kylie returned and sat on the futon, drawing her long legs up to her chest. "That seems like a setup, right?"

The implication felt sour in my stomach. "What do you mean?"

"Okay, first of all, French people don't just invite strangers over. That's like the least French thing I've ever heard."

"That's a stereotype."

"Okay, well, I've lived here for ten years and I'm telling you that has never happened to me. I mean, outside of a hookup or something. Like, she just invites a stranger to her house and her mother accuses you of stealing? Did she think you'd give her money or something?"

I couldn't entertain that thought. I reminded myself that Kylie might have known more French people than I did, but she didn't know Salomé. "No, she wouldn't do that. I'm just in shock, I think. Things were going so well. Her mom was . . . so mad. You should've seen her face, it was awful. I feel like . . . haunted by it." I shook my hands at the wrists as if I could flick the feeling off the tips of my fingers.

Kylie's mouth contorted into a scowl. "Well, fuck her, right? Who is she, anyway? You'll never see her again."

"I want to see her again. I really like her," I said.

Kylie arched an eyebrow up high, like this was just *so* typical of me. "Courtney, you probably only like her because she's French."

It took a second for that comment to land, but before I could respond, she patted my knee and said, "C'mon, you're in Paris! Don't let some batshit old crone ruin your vacation. It's almost your birthday! We have so many paintings to look at and . . . stuff to eat . . . you know?" She got distracted by her phone. "Who is . . . ? Oh," she said, smiling. She rolled her eyes. "This *mec*." She quickly typed a response and set the phone face up on the coffee table and looked back at me. "Sorry, what did you say?"

I hadn't said anything. I was still trying to process the accusation that I only liked Salomé because she was French.

Kylie's phone buzzed on the table in front of me with a WhatsApp text from someone named Mikail. Immediately she was texting again, smirking. "Do you want to go out?"

"Tonight?" I looked at my phone. It was 10:32 but the sun still hadn't completely set.

"Well, yeah, it's not that late."

"I don't know if I feel like being around people . . ."

"Come on! It'll make you feel better. I promise. We'll go somewhere where we can sit outside."

I almost told her to just leave me, but I didn't want to wait around alone in the apartment with all these wrong-way-facing books, anxious that Mari would come home, so I nodded.

"Do you want to like, freshen up a little?" She managed to sound helpful and not mean.

I nodded again.

She led me into the bathroom, where she leaned me against the counter and patted my face with expensive-smelling cream. She gently applied mascara and a light lip gloss. After she was done, I did look better. I grabbed my things and followed her out of the apartment and down the stairs, where we got into a taxi.

She spoke French with the driver and I looked out the window as Paris—"the love of my life"—slipped by. Each little round chimney on the slatted metal rooftops represented a person who had made their life here, but I hadn't been one of them. What did everyone else know or believe about themselves that I didn't? I wondered what Kylie's salary was. A schoolteacher in the US would never be able to afford to live in the equivalent of the 9th arrondissement, even if it wasn't a fancy apartment. It didn't seem to add up here either. Maybe her parents still helped her. Or maybe she was doing really well with the influencer thing. We drove about fifteen minutes to an active area in the 3rd. Kylie asked the driver to let us out and then stood on the sidewalk, frowning at the map on her phone.

"I don't see the place," she muttered, turning to look the other way down the street.

I was utterly unhelpful. I followed her down a tight alley that opened into a stone courtyard, romantically lit with string lighting and candles on each table. There was a live band and couples dancing.

A man approached us. "*Bonsoir,*" he said, giving Kylie *la bise* on her cheeks.

"*Mikail, c'est mon amie Courtney,*" Kylie said, not even trying to soften her American accent.

"Cour-ten-ey, you come from the US too?" Mikail asked after we'd exchanged *la bise.*

I nodded.

"Welcome to Paris!" he said, and before I could tell him I had actually lived in Paris before, he turned to lead us to our table.

"Will you take our picture?" Kylie asked Mikail, once we were seated. She handed him her phone and leaned in toward me. As he clicked again and again, Kylie performed micromovements, tilting her head differently for each frame. I didn't move at all. I was there to make Kylie look prettier by comparison, her arm thinner than mine because I didn't know how to position it for pictures. I was glad to be of service.

Kylie scrolled through the pictures, deleting a few, then turned the screen toward me for my approval. I nodded without really looking. She posted it to Instagram with the caption "Friends for a decade!!"

The sparkling rosé I ordered wasn't very cold and fizzed up in my mouth, making my eyes water. What exactly had Kylie meant by "a setup"? That Salomé had purposefully put me in Nathalie's crosshairs? Or that Nathalie had made the accusation to get rid of me?

I didn't want to be in public. I drank, soothed by the weight of the glass in my hand and the familiar activity it presented, despite knowing that my emotions were in a precarious spot that alcohol might not help. Mikail and Kylie were discussing something. They looked good together, if a bit related. Like Kylie, Mikail had an olive complexion, dark brown hair, and blue eyes. He had uniform dark stubble across his strong jawline. I imagined them dressed in seersucker on the cover of a magazine for people with private jets. I turned my attention to trying to count the tiny bubbles in my wine as they rushed to the surface.

"Courtney is a writer, too," I heard Kylie say. I looked up. Mikail was leaning slightly over Kylie, now paying attention to me.

"Oh, yeah?" he said. "What do you write?"

"I'm a journalist. So mostly assigned articles, but I've been trying to get into more nuanced essays about culture recently. It's not too glamorous. What about you?"

"I'm into poetry some, and fiction. I've been writing a work of science fiction for the past three years, and I'm hoping I will be able to get it published soon." His accent was softer than Salomé's. He casually swirled the red wine in his glass.

"I've just started writing poetry too. Like literally this week." It wasn't a total lie if you counted the succubus's spiraling words in an unknown language. I thought it might also give more weight as to why I wanted to stay in a small town rather than come to Paris.

"Very cool, and why did you start writing poetry this week, 'like literally'?" Mikail asked.

A succubus whispered it to me before she broke my jaw and wiggled down my throat and maybe she's still in there, bargaining some inspiration for my autonomy? "I don't know, maybe just being in France makes the words in my mind come in verses."

Mikail clinked his glass to mine. "I believe you are a writer! So very well said. Kylie, have you read these poems yet, or are they still in secret?"

"No, Courtney only arrived a couple of hours ago . . ."

I couldn't listen to them or participate in the conversation anymore. I felt like my gravitational center had been left behind, back at Salomé's house. Somehow, I was able to visualize Nathalie's room even though I'd never been inside. But I knew where the bed was, and how her dresser was covered in stuff, and how there was a sliding door that led out into the garden but the latch was broken so she hadn't used it in years. The thick, pilled curtains were always drawn so the room was dark except for a yellow lamp at the bedside. The bed was a simple four-poster frame and the mattress was old. Nathalie slept with many blankets and dark red sheets that she never straightened, causing them to twist and tangle in a way that made me nervous. The room had a distinctly different odor than the rest of the house, but how did I know that? Had I somnambulated into her bedroom? I couldn't remember everything that happened during those two nights. I could've crept past her sleeping body, somehow able to see in the dark like a nocturnal animal, and slid her jewelry box to the edge of the dresser, cracked it open. What if the succubus was controlling my brain like a virus, making me self-destruct cell by cell? What if I was still infected?

I stood up quickly and bumped the table, sending everyone's wine splashing over the rims.

"Bathroom . . ." I said, and hurried inside the restaurant. I found the door marked "W.C." and locked it behind me.

There I was in the mirror, looking okay but very tired. I got closer and poked the skin around my eyes. My pupils seemed bigger than normal. Maybe because it was dark outside? That didn't seem right. They were bigger in a weird way. Luke's were always like that too. He said it was because of his antidepressant, but I liked that it seemed as if his eyes could swallow me. I ran my fingers through the hair on the right side of my face, where I'd dreamed it was being cut. Some of the strands did seem bluntly cut. But it was hard to say.

I could still feel the gagging sensation of the succubus burrowing down my throat. I pulled at the corners of my mouth, looking into my throat as best I could in the dim light above the mirror. It seemed red, maybe more than usual. I never looked at this part of my body. I hiked my skirt up and slid my knees onto the small countertop to get closer. My pupils were growing. She was definitely in there. I got so close my teeth bumped the fogged-up glass. I reached my fingers farther down. If I could feel the spiky scaly tail sticking up from the entrance of my stomach, I'd grab her and pull her out and stab her with a shard of this fucking mirror and make her pay for stealing that jewelry and then accusing me.

I retched, sending hot vomit all over the base of the mirror and my bare knees.

"Fuck," I said, meeting my own eyes. "Fuck fuck fuck." I scrambled off the counter, covering my mouth. I backed against the wall and braced myself. I was alone, thankfully and painfully.

Someone knocked on the door. "*Occupée!*" I called. Tears streamed down my cheeks again, maybe from the vomit stinging my throat and dripping into my sandal, mostly Nutella. I wet some paper towels and cleaned myself, the counter, and the mirror, but the glass remained streaked.

Desperate for distraction or normalcy, I looked at my phone. No notifications. With a shaking hand I opened my text thread with Luke and tried to think of something to say, anything to say, but I had nothing.

No one was there when I opened the door. I dabbed my eyes and cheeks on my shirt and went to the bar.

The braless bartender leaned over and spoke incredibly fast.

"*Trois . . . shooters?*" I hadn't said that word in a few years and now it didn't sound right.

"What you want, like vodka or whiskey or rum?"

"Seriously, anything. Thanks."

She poured three shots of clear liquor and pushed them toward me on the bar. *"Dix-huit."*

I gave her twenty-five euros and waved at her to keep the change. She made a skeptical face in response to the large tip, but she didn't know she'd be cleaning my vomit off the mirror later. Two of the shots were supposed to be for Kylie and Mikail, but instead I drank them all, one after the other, and abandoned the empty glasses before the bartender could turn around.

The string lights were fuzzy as I picked my way through the courtyard. Kylie and Mikail were intertwined at the fingers, wrists, forearms, speaking up close. I sat down a little harder than I meant to, disturbing their reverie. I finished my wine and saw another waiting for me. I grabbed the glass by the stem and sank back into my chair to watch the couples dancing.

"We're going to dance," Kylie said, already standing. She slid her phone across the table to me. "Would you mind getting a little video of us?"

"Sure," I said.

She led Mikail to the dance floor.

I hit "record" but couldn't tell if it was the iPhone camera or my own eyes that had them out of focus. At least I couldn't really think about anything else at the moment. Kylie raised her arms over her head, crossing her wrists, moving her body side to side. She wasn't a particularly talented dancer but she was so pretty that even moves like that looked good. She and Mikail made a striking couple. She'd probably marry a Frenchman and get a passport. Then she'd never have to leave.

There was another couple closer to me. A young guy who looked like he was barely out of high school, and a short brunette with bangs so long they must've impeded her vision. Her white babydoll dress was loose and shapeless, but she was obviously toned underneath. She was some sort of fitness instructor for sure, or maybe she could afford a personal trainer. There was something decidedly Not French about her. I assumed she was Spanish or maybe Portuguese. She was golden, as if she'd been on the beach all summer, and her cheekbones were highlighted. Her face was innocent; her mouth popped open in surprise when her partner spun her. She looked uninvolved, like everything around her was coming to her eyes completely uninvited and she was accepting it all in passive wonder. She wasn't fooling me. She knew how many eyes were on her, how many men wished they could have a hand on the small of her back, how they would lift her hands up in a spin to make the edge of her dress rise higher. For her, to be a spectacle was a job well done. She probably felt like she'd always look like that, like she'd always be carefree, like the same sun that caressed her today wouldn't someday give her cancer. She had no idea how quickly the earth would whip around its orbit, whittling away at her options, her ability to captivate. Her sandals clapped the stone; she peered over her partner's shoulder and caught my eye. Her face remained calm, but I quickly looked away.

I stopped recording. The waiter passed by and I managed to gesture for another glass of wine. The alcohol spread out like warm butter in my stomach and I nestled deeper into my imaginary coat, wrapping myself in the comfort of anonymity. The music ended, the dancers dispersed, and I lost sight of that poor little tan dancer. By the time the next song started, my new wine and Kylie and Mikail had arrived at the table.

"Court, you have raccoon eyes," Kylie said, leaning over with a napkin from the table. She blotted my face.

"I can do it." I took the napkin from her and wiped under my eyes without really trying.

"Do you like dancing?" Mikail asked, obviously just trying to be polite, as if he wanted to dance with me.

Before I knew it, I was speaking. "I used to love dancing when I was little. My sister and I would take turns dancing on my dad's feet. I'd hold on to the backs of his legs. I remember this one time looking over and seeing my sister's face as she watched us, and realizing she was jealous. She was jealous anytime he and I shared anything special."

"Isn't your sister like ten years younger than you?" Kylie said.

"I meant my cousin."

Kylie cringed a little. I was drunk. I sank back into my chair and spelled my word. French Courtney was no longer present.

Sometime later, I followed them out of the courtyard and pressed my forehead against the window of the cab. We stomped up the echoing stairwell of Kylie's building, my stomach ready to retch again. Kylie gave me a blanket and then took Mikail into her bedroom.

I kicked my legs free of the blanket, trying to latch my sight onto the swinging chandelier. Then the words came back, timing themselves with the chandelier's spins: *Throw a hair to the magpies, the magpies, the magpies.*

CHAPTER 10

When Élise was six and Salomé was four, the family visited Thierry's family in Châteaubriant. One night, Élise woke up in the bed she shared with Salomé. She slipped out, careful not to wake her sister, and tiptoed past her parents sleeping on the other side of the room. She had a plastic mermaid with a sparkly pink fin that she wanted to take to bed with her, but Salomé had acted possessive over it earlier, which led to a fight, so Thierry declared that no one got the mermaid. It would spend the night in the bag of toys they'd brought with them from Paris.

Élise turned the corner and saw Salomé standing there, stroking the mermaid's pink hair. Salomé looked up and, upon seeing her sister, dropped the doll.

"You are in the bed," Élise whispered. "I just saw you."

"It's a dream," Salomé said.

The sisters stared at each other. This was no normal dream, but neither knew exactly why. It felt like riding a bike, whereas other dreams felt like being on a train. They seemed to have control over themselves.

"Don't touch her!" Élise said when Salomé went to pick up the mermaid.

Salomé touched the doll with her big toe.

"*Arrête!*" Élise said, a little too loudly.

Salomé acted like she was going to step on the doll's face. Élise screamed.

In the seconds after the scream, the two girls stood silently, holding their breath, waiting for the rustle of their parents getting out of bed to scold them. But nothing happened.

Salomé and Élise looked at each other. What was this they'd discovered? Unlimited, unsupervised playtime? Élise unzipped the bag and dumped the toys onto the floor between them.

This scene I watched unfold from the upper corner of the room, from the spot where the surveillance camera was now mounted.

My phone buzzed on the coffee table, pulling me away from the scene, away from Châteaubriant. I opened my eyes to the fabric of Kylie's futon.

The text wasn't from Salomé. It was from Kylie.

> Hey, we're at a cafe a couple of blocks away if you're awake.

She dropped a pin in her location, which was something I had yet to figure out how to do.

When had they left this morning? They had to have walked right past me.

Coffee was a necessity. And being around people was too, at least to keep me from combing over every excruciating detail of my own belligerence.

I checked the side pocket of my backpack for my passport. It was there. The keys to my house were there, too. I'd apparently gotten my phone charger out last night and plugged my phone in. One small victory. Unless, of course, Kylie had done it for me. She'd figure out a way to let me know if she had.

Why was I such a fuck-up? This was a microcosm for why I hadn't enjoyed more than one flash-in-the-pan success in my life. One meaningful publication for being tethered to my laptop for over a decade. If I were truly competent, I'd have many awards, enjoy the geographical freedom that so many seemed to obtain, maybe even have a functioning relationship.

The room spun. I pressed my palms into my eyes and took a few deep breaths. I needed water and coffee. I was absolutely useless until those needs were met. I decided not to change out of last night's outfit and didn't dare to check the mirror before I left.

How's your head?" Kylie asked. Her thin face and dark hair were so different from Salomé's, it almost felt weird to look at her, like there was a glitch in her somewhere.

"I'm fine," I said. I poured some water from the carafe and squinted at her and Mikail, working to maintain a smile. They both seemed to expect me to say something vastly different. Perhaps they wanted an apology. "Where's our guy?" I asked. A server came over, and I ordered a *café allongé.* Kylie and Mikail watched me closely.

"What?"

"We expected you to be a wreck this morning."

"Yeah, I don't drink much anymore and barely ate last night, so it hit me pretty hard. I'm sorry."

"You talked in your sleep all night," Kylie said. I couldn't tell if she was more concerned or annoyed.

"That's weird. I slept okay, actually." I remembered the dream I'd had of Salomé and Élise, but it wasn't a nightmare. "I hope I didn't keep you awake."

Kylie and Mikail exchanged a glance. I guess I had? Or maybe that was a glance to say that they'd been up all night with each other, regardless of me.

"Are you hungry? Breakfast's on me. I'm sorry about last night." My stomach turned at the idea of eating, but I didn't know what else to give them.

"Um, okay. I could eat. Do you want anything?" Kylie asked Mikail.

"Me, no, I will finish this coffee and then I have to go to the office for a little while," Mikail said.

"On a Saturday?" I asked.

"Sunday," Kylie said in an almost-scolding tone as if I'd mispronounced my own name.

It was still a fair question, right? It was the weekend. But I didn't know what he did professionally. Maybe this was usual for him. He wore off-white chino pants and an expensive-looking pin-striped button-up. He looked like he might have an important job. I could've asked last night. Had I asked him anything about himself? Shown any interest in him or Kylie at all? I could ask now, but I felt like no matter what I did now, it would be wrong.

"Oh right. Sorry, travel brain," I said.

They looked at each other again, that same look. They could stop doing that whenever and it would be fine by me. Mikail pecked Kylie on the cheek and stood to leave. "I'll come back tonight, if you want." His protective tone indicated they'd already discussed this. She nodded, then looked down at the menu.

I tried to busy myself with reading the breakfast options but could barely focus. I'd broken out in a gross nervous sweat.

Kylie cut through the silence. "So, what do you want to do today?"

"Um, I guess I'd like to go to the Picasso Museum, since it was closed the last time I was here. But don't feel like you have to go around with me all day if you have other stuff to do."

She kept her eyes trained on the menu. "I blocked off the week for your visit, so."

So she was really mad. I looked at the menu again. The words began to swim in tears pooling onto my bottom eyelids. I tried not to blink so they wouldn't spill over. I steadied my breath. If I cried, Kylie would feel compelled to come to my rescue, and I didn't need to further inconvenience her.

The server approached. Kylie ordered the *formule "healthy"* (the menu's name, not Kylie's franglais), which consisted of a small length of halved baguette with jam, cut fruit, and a little glass of orange juice. I got the same. I spelled *serrer* until I got myself under control.

"So how do you know Mikail?"

"We met at a party."

"He's cute."

"Yeah, I think so."

"Are you going to like, date him do you think?"

"Probably not."

I sipped my coffee in silence. I didn't know what to do. I hadn't ever been on the bad side of a friend like this, especially not because of some lack of etiquette or social blunder.

Kylie pushed away from the table. "I'll be right back."

The extent of my rudeness was dawning on me. I'd changed plans on her, then gotten so needlessly drunk in front of Mikail. We both knew I'd change our plans again in a heartbeat if given the chance. I was using her for her futon. What an asshole.

It took me a moment to notice her sitting at the table directly behind where Kylie had been. But there she was, a familiar face without a glitch. The long blonde bangs, the nose, the mannerisms. She was lifting a fork to her mouth, dabbing her lips with the napkin, laughing. I jumped up, overturning my chair.

She and her friend at the table noticed my sudden movement. Then she was standing too, looking at me. It wasn't Salomé. It was Élise.

CHAPTER 11

Élise," I said, inching close enough to talk without being overheard.

"Non, non, non. Vous voulez quoi? Vous êtes qui?" Her eyes were untrusting, like the woman my mother approached in the grocery store. I just had to let her know who I was, that I was safe.

"I was just at your house," I started. Her eyelids narrowed further. Not the right thing to say.

"Who the fuck are you?"

"Sorry, sorry. I'm Courtney, Salomé's friend from Raleigh."

"Raleigh?" Something about her softened when she heard Salomé's name.

"North Carolina."

"I know that," she said curtly. "Salomé is here?"

"Yes, well, she is in France. We were at your mother's house . . ."

Her expression dropped.

"What? Is that bad? It ended very strangely and . . . did she tell you I stole something? I swear, I didn't." I couldn't believe these words pouring from my mouth. Shut up, shut up. I steadied myself on the nearest chair. What was this look she was giving me? Pity? Fear?

She turned to her friend, who had stood up holding both of their purses, looking ready to dash out of there, and murmured in French. Élise looked just like Salomé, the same height, build, and coloration, but her movements were harsher.

". . . Court?" Kylie called from our table. "What are you doing?"

I gestured for Kylie to hold on. To Élise, I said, "Please, I just want Salomé's number. I had to leave so fast I didn't get it."

"Courtney . . . our food is here?" Kylie approached the table. "*Bonjour*, I'm Kylie," she said to Élise and her friend.

I turned to Élise. "Are you going there? To Châteaubriant?"

Élise's hands flew to her cheeks, flustered. Then, something shifted in her face. She relaxed a little. "No. I am here for my friend's wedding that was yesterday, and I didn't tell my mother that I'm in France because I don't want to see her, and if she knew, she would be upset."

Interesting. Élise didn't want to see Nathalie. I nodded, hoping she'd elaborate.

"Look, I am here for one weekend and I wasn't planning on having to deal with my crazy family."

Was Salomé included in that choice of words? "What do you mean by 'crazy'?"

Élise sighed. She looked at Kylie. "Is she safe? Like, should I not be alone with her?"

Kylie's mouth opened and closed a couple of times before she choked out, "Sh-she's okay, she just had a weird experience I think, right, Court?"

I looked feverishly between Kylie and Élise.

"Picave."

Élise said it quietly, almost under her breath. Her friend looked shocked and glanced around the nearby tables. Élise stared me down, waiting.

"I'm sorry?"

Élise produced a pen from her purse and wrote on a napkin from the table. I thought she was giving me Salomé's number, but when she handed it to me, it just said "Les Intemporels." "Meet me here at noon. I'll only have a little while before my train back to London. Please don't be weird."

"I'll be there." I folded the napkin and put it in my purse.

"Court, let's go, now." Kylie pulled my arm toward our table. "Nice meeting you," she called over her shoulder. "Don't face them," she said in a low, serious tone, and righted the chair I had overturned, almost shoving me into it. She sat with her head in her hands. This was too messy a gesture for Kylie. After a moment she peered at me from between her fingers.

"I recognized her from the pictures on the wall," I said.

"I actually don't want to know. I'm going to go to the gym. This is stressing me the fuck out, Court. I don't know what to do." Her expression shifted to complete indifference. "So. Let's eat."

"I didn't mean to scare her . . ."

"Listen, I'm not trying to be rude or anything, but you really need to take a shower. You look like you swam here. I'd be scared if I got accosted by . . ." She failed to find the right word for what I looked like, so she picked up her knife and stabbed it into the little glass jar of jam.

I caught my reflection in the blade of my knife. Even in the rippled, warped image, I could tell she was right. My makeup was more than smeared, my eyes were watery and bloodshot, and most of my hair had escaped the kind of semi-ponytail I only used while brushing my teeth. "Sorry," I said.

"So is this girl coming for your birthday?"

"Is today the twenty-fourth?"

"Did you forget it was your birthday?"

Right. My thirty-first birthday. "I haven't really thought about it."

"Well I thought you'd probably want to go get dinner or something, unless you're going to hang out with this *French girl* instead."

The dismissive way she said "French girl" pissed me off. I fought the urge to look over her shoulder at Élise.

"Please eat your food," Kylie said. How did she know? She wasn't even looking at me.

I pulled the elastic out of my hair and ran my fingers through it. I had to pretend that things were normal now. "Oh my God, do you know what I was thinking about?"

She stopped mid-chew and her eyes went up and down my face, reading me like an airport security scanner. "What?"

"I was thinking about that time"—I put my fork down to laugh—"about that time that we were going to meet that dude at Parc Monceau . . ."

"And you peed on the street and that cop reprimanded you but I convinced him to let us go because we were just stupid Americans," she finished all in one breath. She caught the waiter's attention and mimed scribbling.

Élise and her friend walked past us. She didn't turn to catch my eye as she passed.

"Yeah . . . you saved me from going to French jail."

Kylie gave me a pained smile. I decided to stop trying. I paid for the meal in cash and we stood to leave.

Kylie was preoccupied with her phone for most of the walk back. Outside of her apartment door, she stopped and looked at me. "What on earth?"

"What?"

She turned the screen to face me. "Who is this? Why did you make this video last night?"

Oh God. I took the phone from her. There was a three-minute

video of that other girl dancing, and only about five seconds of Kylie and Mikail. "Sorry. I was really drunk."

She shook her head and pulled her keys out of her purse. "Yeah, no kidding. I had to dig through your bag for your phone charger and your toothbrush, but I'm not sure if you even used it."

When we got upstairs, she brought me a folded towel from her bedroom. "Here," she said, nodding toward the bathroom.

"Thanks."

"Well, I won't be here when you get out. Be careful, the door will lock behind you if you decide to leave. I'm going to the gym and then to Monoprix, so I'll be gone for an hour and a half or so. What time are you meeting that girl?"

"Noon."

"Yeah, well, I guess I'll catch you later today, if you still want to do something for your birthday. I had originally planned a kind of fun evening, back before things changed, so now I don't know. We could get dinner if you want. I shouldn't have let you pay for breakfast. I'm sorry." She sounded genuinely sad.

"No, I've been really weird. I should be apologizing to you."

"I hope you don't hate me for saying this, but I feel like I need to. Just, be careful, okay? This is a big city and you have to treat it like one."

"I used to live here, you know." I didn't mean for my tone to be as dry as it came across, but I was fairly sure she meant to start something with that comment.

"I'm sorry, it's just that sometimes I think you make France out to be this idyllic place with no bad guys and no crime. Paris is a huge city. Yeah, not everyone has a gun, but people still get murdered here."

I didn't have time to decide how to respond. I was already speaking. "Well, you'd never glean that sort of idea off of any of your 'come for a walk with me in Paris' videos. You make this place out like if you *don't* live here, you fucking lost at life, and if you *do* live here, it's just constant Amélie Poulain fetish porn. All you do is offer a shallow, American perspective that should embarrass you. Like what the fuck, Kylie. Not all Americans come here just to bumble around, making videos about how hard it still is to pronounce *croissant* after living here for ten fucking years. Jesus Christ, why give people more reasons to hate us?"

I thought I was going to faint. I never thought I'd say those things to her aloud, no matter how many times I'd rehearsed it in my mind.

Kylie set her jaw, her throat splotchy with redness. Her nostrils flared. She was going to yell at me. I almost covered my ears, but then one perfect tear fell down her cheek. I might've thought it was scripted, had I not just launched such a torrent of insults at her.

She inhaled and held her fingers horizontally under her nose, though it didn't appear to be running. "It's just really expensive to live here, okay?" Her voice cracked on "okay." "I'm trying to supplement my income. The videos get a lot of streams."

"Well I'm sorry if I don't make for good 'content' and I'm a shitty cameraperson."

"Yeah, you are. You filmed a complete stranger last night like a total fucking creep!" she said, her voice pitching high.

We looked at each other for a few more seconds, shocked, and then she turned and went into her room, clicking the door closed behind her.

I went to the window and opened it, taking deep breaths of the hot summer breeze. I spelled *serrer* and imagined being put into an anxiety vest like Aunt Trudy's trembling chihuahua every time it rained. Kylie's words floated around my mind: *a total fucking creep*, my idyllic view of France, how I probably only liked Salomé because she was French.

I looked over the metal roofs with their dozens of round red chimneys. A couple of little boys were playing in the tiled courtyard below, lined with blooming pink flowers in planters. I watched the tops of their heads as they ran and spun and jumped, laughing together. The word *anniversaire* echoed off the courtyard walls. If I had been in the US, I might have waved at the kids and said happy birthday, and that it was mine, too. But I couldn't risk coming off as a creep again.

Across the courtyard, a gray-haired woman stuck a round placemat out of the window and smacked it a few times, sending bread crumbs sprinkling down. I slid down to my knees and watched from between the railing's wrought iron bars as the woman retreated into the depths of her apartment.

I heard a zipper from Kylie's room, probably her gym bag.

I walked up to her door. "Kyles?" I said, though I hadn't used that nickname for her since college.

"I'm fine," she said.

"I'm sorry," I said.

She took a couple of long, audible breaths, and said, "I know."

I guess she wasn't going to apologize for calling me a "total fucking creep," then. I could tell she was waiting for me to leave the room before she opened her door, so I hurried into the bathroom.

My heart stuttered at the sight of my reflection. I looked like I'd been hiking the Appalachian Trail for at least a month without a shower, and also ten years from now. I'd never seen my skin look so . . . old.

Kylie's bathroom was not a traditional French separate *salle de bain* and *toilettes.* This was more like a hotel geared toward Americans, because the toilet, bathtub, and sink were in the same room. The dark tiled tub was as big as it could be, taking up almost half of the space in the bathroom. I sat on the floor of the tub and sprayed the handheld nozzle directly into my mouth, gulping the hot water as if it were refreshing. I had to keep climbing out of my mind as it shot back to what

I'd just said to Kylie, then last night at that bar, that poor little Portuguese yoga instructor who was basically mummified in her own beauty. How had I not realized I was filming her? *Total fucking creep.* Stop the thoughts, pull harder. But, there I was, throwing up on the mirror. Shame shivered down my body. I almost gagged. The looks I was getting last night and this morning. It was like I was playing the role of the unhinged woman in a movie. I couldn't stay here tonight. I'd get a hotel. I hadn't planned for that expense, but that's what credit cards were for, right?

I squeezed my head between my knees and let my tears mix with the shower water. This was normal; I cried on many of my birthdays.

"Time to grow up," I said to myself. I really meant it. I vowed to never throw up at a bar again. Or get too drunk again. Or crash on a futon again.

Toweling off reminded me of Salomé and her lotion. The smell didn't linger on me anymore, but I wished it did. I went into the living room and swallowed two Advils from the travel-sized bottle I'd thankfully brought with me. I didn't have the energy to do anything else at the moment, so I sat on the futon in my towel and looked at my phone. No notifications, not even from Mom. They wouldn't wake up for a few more hours in America. I opened my texts and scrolled through my thread with Luke.

Auspicious. Mostly the root.

What did that mean? I Googled "auspicious." From the French *auspice*—a divine or prophetic token. From Latin *auspicium*, from *auspex* (observer of birds), from *avis* (bird) + *specere* (to look).

To look at a bird? I squinted hard at my phone, my heartbeat rising to my throat.

Why do I make you think of auspicious?

I scanned the corners and approached the half-empty bookcase. I didn't see anything that could be a hidden camera. I dumped my bag out onto the floor, looking for something, a wiretap, anything weird. Besides how hastily my belongings were shoved into the bag, nothing was different.

My fingers trembled as I went through the motions of getting dressed. I was a mannequin as I dried my hair, avoiding my own eyes in the mirror as I put on some mascara, willing myself not to cry again and wreck it. I wanted to look good for Élise, so if she ever told Salomé about meeting me, she wouldn't describe me as crazy.

I got a text from Luke, responding to my question.

I honestly don't know, it just sprang to mind at that moment.

How you?

31 in Paris!—not too shabby ☺

I tried to take a selfie in front of the window, but I was terribly backlit. I gave up. I'd never be a selfie person.

Bon anniversaire. I looked that up :)

I'll be there in 10 hours. <3

I knew he wasn't serious, but I frowned at the phone. The thought of having him here, even as a joke, wasn't comforting. What might I end up saying to him? *Why do you still text me? Just to have something to do with your hands when you're bored? You never took me seriously. You're a thirty-three-year-old songwriter with no song placements and no publishing deal who strings women along like they're just some accessory to your future success.*

The phone screen in my hand went dark. I was scowling in the reflection. I smoothed the place between my eyebrows with my thumb.

Stop thinking about Luke. I had a sister to impress.

Les Intemporels was a seedy-looking bar in the 12th, just over a half-hour ride on the Métro line 8. The place wouldn't have seemed weird at night, but the daylight exposed the griminess of the walls, and the air was still thick with last night's spilled beers. It didn't seem like a place that would be open before evening. I passed the bar without ordering anything, holding my breath, and stepped out into the small back courtyard, which was as grimy as the interior of the place.

Élise sat at a table against the wall, wearing a short-sleeved pink sweater. There was a glass of rosé in front of her, the sight of which made my stomach lurch. She stood when she saw me, perhaps a reflex to give me *la bise*, but when I approached, she didn't even extend her hand, just sat back down after I reached the table. I took my seat across from her.

"So you know," she said, gesturing to the empty chair beside her, "my husband is here, too, inside. I'm waiting for him to return before I say anything."

"Okay."

We avoided looking at each other for a minute, her out of nervousness and me because I wanted so desperately to study her likeness to Salomé.

A tall, bearded man with ghostly blue eyes arrived at the table. "Hello," he said, extending his hand to me. "I'm Callum." Oh, that's what Salomé had been saying.

"Courtney."

"Pleasure. Could you please turn your pockets inside out?"

I almost laughed, but quickly realized he wasn't joking. "Are you serious?"

His stern face told me that he was.

"I don't have pockets," I said, fiddling with my skirt's fabric to show him.

"Phone?" he said. I got it out of my purse.

"Turn it off," he said.

I glanced at Élise as if she might come to my rescue, but her face remained neutral. She studied me while I turned the phone off and set it on the table.

"Let me see your bag," Callum said. I turned it over to him so he could look through it. All I had was my wallet, my notebook, a few Métro tickets, hand sanitizer, and lip balm.

He took another look at me, maybe trying to decide if I was wearing a wire. I saved him the trouble of asking. I held my shirt up to my bra line and turned in a circle so they could both see.

When I finished my 360, Élise looked somewhat amused, but remained silent as I sat.

"Do you want to do a cavity search or are we good?" I asked.

"I'll be honest with you, Courtney, I'm not sure what you want with my wife's family, but I suggest you tread lightly." Callum's Scottish accent wasn't overwhelming. It would've even been nice to hear had his message been different. "Normally if someone came up to us on the street asking about Élise's family, we would be on the next train back to the UK. But for whatever reason, Élise seems to think you're harmless."

"I am harmless. I'm trying to figure this out myself. I don't want anything from Élise, except maybe her sister's phone number, if that's—"

"How do you know her?" Élise asked, leaning forward in her seat.

I told them about meeting Salomé on the plane. Élise listened carefully. She hardly moved while I spoke—a tiny twitch at the corner of her mouth, a slight narrowing of her eyes—until I got to the part about Salomé inviting me to Châteaubriant. There, Élise let out a huge, angry sigh that made me stop to ask, "Should she not have done that?"

Élise rubbed her temples in a slow, circular motion. I remembered Salomé telling me that Élise didn't like her. "She is so naive, my sister."

"I swear, I'm not dangerous, I'm—"

"No, it wasn't dangerous for her. It was dangerous for you."

My mouth opened, but offered no words. Salomé would never consciously put me in danger, would she? Was Élise risking her own safety to talk to me?

"I don't know why Salomé would bring a stranger into the house. Maybe she thought that having you there would keep Maman acting on good behavior . . ."

"I did get the feeling that I was there to be a buffer between them."

"Look, honestly, I just wanted to hear how Salomé is, and how things are going at the house. It's not often I get an honest update. So I wasn't sure what I was going to tell you here. But now, I think we should tell you . . ." Elise turned to her husband. "Callum, will you tell her please?" She fixed her eyes on the table and pushed a few crumbs through a hole in the metal.

"What should I tell her?"

"I mean, I feel like she should know why it was stupid of Salomé to take her there. She needs to know what she walked into." She cupped her head in her hands, resigned to listening.

"Stupid" sounded like a strong word. And "naive," too. Neither of those sounded like Salomé. Élise was being harsh to her sister, and maybe to me, as well. I went with her willingly, didn't I? "Is it Thierry's work?" I asked.

Élise flinched. "So she told you?"

"A little—enough that I knew what I was getting into. But she made me promise not to write about it."

Élise's eyes narrowed. "Why would you *write* about it?"

"I'm a journalist." Why had I volunteered that? I had to stop talking. I was in no condition to make a solid point. Élise took a sip of wine that seemed calculated, as if she'd just made an excellent move in a game of chess. Or maybe it was just my hangover that made it seem so. I had to look away as she swallowed.

Élise set her glass down a little too hard. "Go ahead, write about these assholes, but then you may be the next one asking people to turn off their phones around you."

I took a deep breath. "I'm listening."

Callum drummed his fingertips on the edge of the table, perhaps a nervous habit, but it felt a little intimidating. "It should go without saying that this conversation will remain between us."

I nodded.

"So, after Élise's father passed away, his former assistant attempted to carry on his lab work, and . . . he hasn't done a good job of keeping the work ethical or aligned with Thierry's original concept . . . though Élise and I kind of have differing opinions about the ethics of his original work. But now it's something we don't agree with at all."

"We're talking about Marco, right?"

"Yes. After Thierry died, Marco has turned it into a . . . cult of sorts," Callum continued. "Or, well, 'secret society' may be a better term."

Panic bloomed in my stomach. Salomé had alluded to this when she described Marco's charisma, but she hadn't said these words. "What do you mean?"

Élise shook her head. "Marco didn't create the cult. He marketed to them and then moved in like a *bernard l'ermite machiavélique*."

Before I could conceptualize what she meant by "Machiavellian hermit crab," Callum said, "Look, interest in immortality is as old as the concept of death. It's biologically ingrained in humans. So when a group in a rural area claims to be 'curing death' with all this fancy science based on a famous researcher, it's bound to pick up a few followers."

"ViPi, right?" I asked.

Callum said, "ViPi is a laundering scheme, but Marco works hard to make it appear like a legitimate supplement. I mean, it might be. I haven't had it tested or anything. But the targeted marketing is pretty fucked up. It's a pretty quick pipeline from 'healthy anti-aging supplement' to 'only white people are truly French.'"

I shook my head. "Does this have to do with that scientist? Alexis Carrel?"

"Kind of," Callum said. "Marco has tapped into this group of people who still idolize Carrel and his ideas. So they link this lineage from Carrel to Leduc to ViPi and buy whatever Marco sells. And then Marco turns around and funnels their money into far-right politics. He's got a small team of lobbyists trying to affect immigration policy."

"Wow," I said. "I didn't realize there were lobbyists in France."

"Ask Salomé," Élise said, her tone bitter.

"What do you mean?"

"No, not directly," Callum said. "She was supposed to head up an international think tank. She was going to be a head philosopher or something. It killed two birds with one stone. First, she was a woman, so it didn't alienate women, and she had a direct relation to Thierry, so ViPi was instantly legitimized. And then, I guess the third was that it bought her out. She was neutralized. She wouldn't bite the hand that fed her. It fed her *well.*"

I shook my head. "She hates Marco so much. Why would she work for him?"

Élise said, "We didn't know how bad he was at the beginning. At some point, though . . . there is no excuse. Everything Marco does is calculated. Even that he offered Salomé a job and not me. At the time, it seemed like a family business. Our father was still alive. But Marco, he wants to find a crack in the foundation and make sure that crack keeps getting bigger and bigger. He made it clear that Salomé was the smart one, and I should probably look for a husband."

There was a tightening of her face and neck when she said this that let on how unhealed the wound still was. Callum took her hand and kissed the back of it.

Machiavellian hermit crab still lingered in my mind. Who were these people Marco had infiltrated and used to his advantage? "Can you tell me more about the group? The cult, or secret society? Who are they?"

Callum said, "It's been around since before World War II. There's an American group of them, too."

"What?"

"Oh yeah. This shit is generations old. A few of the American Magpies are billionaires. They send Marco a ton of money, too, which he funnels through ViPi."

I gripped the edge of the table, suddenly off-balance. "Magpies?"

Élise blew air through her lips dismissively and said, "Bah, it's some nickname for Charles Lindbergh. Because of his flight that connected the United States and France, and his whole connection to Carrel. That word I said to you earlier? *Picave*—it's their code word.

It's Latin for magpie. I could tell you didn't know what it meant, and you were confused by this fucked-up story, not a crazy from the group trying to harvest my DNA or something."

"Do they do that?"

"Wouldn't put it past them," said Callum.

Throw a hair to the magpies. Why had I been thinking that? I *had* been thinking that, right? My breathing became shallow. I felt a prickling through my fingertips. I put my hands in my lap and spelled *serrer* a few times, staring down at my fingers.

"Are you okay?" Élise asked.

"Yeah. It's just . . ." I shook my head and looked back up at her. "So there are American Magpies? Who are they?"

Élise looked to Callum.

"So, there's a lot we don't know. The only thing we know for sure is that they have a lot of money, and they've invested heavily in ViPi."

"Are the French Magpies rich, too?" I asked.

"No, it's kind of the opposite here. It's mostly working-class people," Callum said.

"ViPi customers?"

"ViPi customers certainly *fund* the Magpies. And, from what we understand, there are several tiers to ViPi. Perhaps some of the most dedicated ViPi enthusiasts may eventually find their way to the Magpies."

"What kind of tiers?"

"Are they still starving themselves?" Callum said, raising an eyebrow.

I wasn't sure if that was supposed to be an answer to my question. "Nathalie is extremely thin and Salomé was upset about it. What's that about?"

Élise clicked her tongue disapprovingly. "Some immortality shit that increased the lifespans of some flies or some little worms or something. It's terrible. Like, you live in France where the food is actually good but you don't eat it. Go live in England and I can understand why you don't eat . . ."

Callum gave her a lighthearted tap with his elbow and she smiled. Smiling, she and Salomé could be twins.

"It's supposedly based on animal studies but I'm sure it's really about control," Callum said. "It's like the next level of ViPi, if you join this longevity course. They walk you through 'safe' caloric restriction and do a bunch of bloodwork. I guess Marco makes Nathalie do it to prove that they believe in it and everything."

"What are the other levels?"

Élise put her head into her hands and sighed. "I don't want to know."

"I want to know," Callum said, and they exchanged a glance. He looked at me and said, "But we don't know. After the basic 'communities' you can join via the website, it gets much more secretive."

Nobody said anything for several seconds. I almost asked, *Does Salomé know?* but couldn't bring myself to. Instead, I said, "Do you know anything about a ring?"

Élise squinted and pursed her lips. "I don't think so."

"Nathalie accused me of stealing a ring and that's why I left."

Élise closed her eyes briefly, her shoulders dropping on an exhalation. When she looked back at me, she looked dejected, hopelessly tired. "My sister, she wants so much to be close with our mother the way she was with Papa. But it just isn't possible. She is not stable. But Salomé is always hoping that things will stay good, because when Maman is good, things are good, you know? And then she . . ." Élise turned to Callum. "What did you call it?"

"Flips out."

"When she flips out, it is bad. She mostly flipped out on me and not so much Salomé when we were younger."

"Is Salomé in danger?"

Élise frowned. "I cannot answer that. Actually, that is a big reason why I asked you to meet me. I haven't talked to Salomé in over a year. I had to stop talking to everyone in my family . . ."

"Why?"

"A lot of reasons. But mostly because Marco's people follow me," Élise said.

"That's why no one knows you're here?"

"It's a pretty big deal for Élise to come to France," Callum said. "We didn't bring our phones this time. We aren't sure how they find her, but the past two times she has come here, she's seen someone trailing her."

"So when I came up to you, you thought . . ."

"Yes, I thought you were hired by Marco to watch me."

"No, I've never met Marco. I'm sorry, that must've been scary."

"It was, but, I don't know. I could tell you were sincere," she said. "Also, you looked very hungover and that is not the type of person who Marco hires."

How did we end up at the same café this morning? Should I have been worried that they were following *me*? Once, at the Salt Lake City airport, I'd run into a Taiwanese girl I met seven years before while studying in Paris. We were both on layovers, going to and coming from completely different places. We recognized each other instantly. That seemed far less plausible than this.

Élise seemed to know what I was thinking. "Don't worry. We are not following you," she said, almost laughing. "But I do want to know, how was Salomé? Did she seem okay?"

The first thing Salomé said to me was "I am sad." I thought about it for a moment. "Well, she was sad because she and her boyfriend broke up. The main reason she seemed irritated to have to be in Châteaubriant was because of Marco. And she said she couldn't go back to

Paris. But we were having a great time together. We really hit it off. I was surprised when I had to leave."

Élise gave me a look, as if she could tell we'd kissed. Maybe that wasn't rare for Salomé and her friends. I didn't like that thought.

"Well, if you hear from her, don't tell her that we are in France. I don't want anyone to know. I just wanted to celebrate with the friends who still talk to me," Élise said. "And they know not to post pictures of the celebration until we are gone."

I nodded. "I won't."

Élise finished the last of her wine. The meeting was ending. I had more questions, but I suddenly couldn't think of anything to ask, so I said, "I kept having really weird dreams while I was there. And hearing some voices from Nathalie's room."

Élise bit her lip, and I got the impression she was going to say something truly illuminating.

Callum said, "Élise . . ." in a slightly condescending tone.

"I don't care, Callum. I'm going to tell her." She looked at me, a new intensity to her gaze. "I do not believe in coincidences since my father died. And I told Callum earlier and he says it is not rational, but I dreamed your face last night."

"When there is a literal secret society–cult thing that wants to stalk you, you can't make choices based on dreams," he said.

"I know," she said, keeping eye contact with me. We held it for a few seconds. I almost said, "You were in mine, too," but before I could, Élise tapped Callum's wrist and he let her see his watch. "Well, it's time for us to go. I'm sorry that my family was harmful to you, but you should not get involved with them. You seem like a nice person."

"Is there any way you'd give me her number?"

Élise sighed. "Honestly, I don't know her number. And we left our phones in England, so I can't look it up. I think you should forget it and stay away." We all stood up. I shook both of their hands. Élise touched Callum's arm exactly how Salomé had touched mine, and said she was going to the bathroom.

"Well, goodbye," Élise said to me, adjusting her purse strap on her shoulder.

I walked, somewhat unsteadily, through the bar and out the front door. I leaned against the exterior wall as I waited for my phone to turn back on. I was waiting for it to load my messages so I could look at the texts I'd sent both Kylie and Luke to confirm that I'd written something like "throw a hair to the magpies."

"You said you're a journalist?" Callum's voice came from directly beside me, making me jump. I didn't realize he'd come outside.

"Yes, well—I write for a newsmagazine."

He glanced back at the bar's front door to be sure Élise wasn't nearby. "There's stuff Élise doesn't even know." He handed me a slip of paper with a name and a phone number on it. "I've done my own reading, mostly from this guy. But he's gone silent for almost six months, and I can't find a trace of him. Something's wrong. So watch your back. Look this guy up. For real."

I took the paper but didn't know what to say.

"That's my phone number. Please reach out if you need anything. Or if you learn anything of interest. But I won't have my phone again until I'm back in London this evening, so don't do anything too risky over the next five-ish hours."

"Okay, thank you," I said, too stunned to fully process what he said.

He peeled away and was waiting at the door when Élise emerged from the bar. She met my eyes one last time before they walked in the opposite direction.

I didn't know what to do. Maybe I should go back in and sit for a while, jot some of this down in my notebook. Did I now know more about this than Salomé did? That seemed unlikely, though I would've preferred that to the alternative.

My phone vibrated in my hand. I knew it was her before I saw the French number scrolling across the top of the screen. My thumb hesitated before accepting the call. I wanted so badly to trust her, and to not be stupid for doing so.

"Salomé."

First, a sweet, surprised inhalation, so similar to my dream that it caused a moment's panic that the succubus could travel through phone lines. But the sound immediately ceased, and Salomé's voice said, "I'm sorry I didn't call you before now. I've been taking care of my mom. But she is back to normal now. How are you? How is Paris?"

The sound of her voice instantly soothed me.

"It's okay. Actually, I've had a really weird time in Paris." I would've called it "weird" even without the experience of running into Élise, so I felt like it was okay to say.

Silence for a moment. Then she said, "Do you want to leave?" I detected a note of hopefulness there.

"Kind of. But I don't know where I'd go. Unless you think you might come here."

Salomé paused. "I want to get out of here, but I feel so guilty."

"For bringing me?"

"Yes, that, but also you know when I bought your train ticket to Paris with my mom's card?"

"Yeah?"

"Marco thought she went to Paris without telling him because he saw the charge and he was very mad. It was all a fucking mess here yesterday."

"Jesus, I'm sorry. I can pay for the ticket . . ."

"No, it wasn't the money. He has plenty of money. But I think I did not know how much he is controlling her until now, you know?"

"I'm sorry. That's terrible."

"I want to say that I'm sorry for bringing you into this mess. But at the same time, I wish you hadn't gone to Paris. I am miserable since you left."

My heart beat a little faster. "I wish I hadn't come to Paris. I wish we'd gone somewhere else together."

"We could still do that," she said. Did she sound hopeful or was I projecting?

"Let's meet in Nantes tomorrow morning." Then, if it felt right, I could find out more about how much she knew about the Magpies. Especially the American ones.

Salomé said, "Could you come here to get me?"

I hesitated, surprised she would ask me to do that. She saw what happened with Nathalie. I didn't want to say no outright, so I said, "Why? I could get the direct TGV to Nantes from Paris and not have to change trains."

Salomé sighed. "I hate that I am now making decisions to keep Marco happy, but I think, if Marco sees me leave with you, it will be easier for her, and probably for me, too. He will see I have just brought a friend from Raleigh, and you are on vacation and leaving soon."

As opposed to what? Bringing a spy into the house? But after that conversation with Callum and Élise, that could be exactly what she meant.

"I don't know . . . I'm honestly kind of afraid after yesterday." I hoped she wouldn't be offended.

"I know it is a lot to ask." There was a heaviness to her words, a longing for something just outside of her realm of control.

Right after college, I worked as a waitress in a breakfast café. There was another server, Rachel, who lived with her boyfriend, Billy. He hung around the café too much, sitting on a barstool for hours, watching her work. Once I caught him taking a photo of our schedule in the employee closet, so our manager moved the schedule into the kitchen. Rachel always wanted to take a selfie with one of the other female servers at the beginning of each shift, which she later admitted was proof she sent to him of where she was. When he wasn't around, her phone constantly lit up with texts.

Our manager was about to hire a new male barista, and I overheard Rachel approach her while I was rolling silverware. "Please don't hire that guy. I think Billy would have a hard time."

"You need to leave him," the manager said.

"I know." As Rachel walked away, her face was shockingly stoic, the expression in her eyes both vacant and determined. The manager hired a female barista.

We all encouraged Rachel to leave him, probably too flippantly, and she would nod and tell us she would, but that he wasn't always bad. Eventually she moved out while Billy was at work. The next morning, he showed up at the café before we were open, screaming at all of us about how we'd poisoned her mind and that he was going to kill her. She ended up having to move back to her hometown. That was terrifying enough, and that guy didn't have a network of spies reporting back to him.

That look in Rachel's eyes. I'd only seen one other person with that look.

"Are you in danger?"

She hesitated before answering. "Maybe. But it's not so much me I worry about. I left before and I will leave again. But for now I just want things to look . . . natural."

It sounded like they needed me to be a scapegoat so Marco would see with his own eyes the bumbling American who had upset the balance in the house, causing Nathalie to flip. Perhaps my presence would buy them enough reprieve that Salomé could leave again.

I tried to find the words to tell her that I was too scared to go back there. I didn't want to get followed by some zealot or put myself in the crosshairs of an international secret society. But the gravity of her on the other side of the phone, the expectation in that silence, begged for something else. Once again, I found myself unable to tell her no.

CHAPTER 12

The sunrise over the farmlands between Le Mans and Angers was spectacular. Dew evaporated off the long grasses in a fine mist that gave everything an ethereal, soft focus. Each little stone house enveloped in fields looked worthy of an impressionist painting. Kilometers ticked by, dotted by cows and circular hay bales, scattered farm equipment, the occasional vineyard. All this empty space in France even though it was small.

That day in Paris had butted me up against myself in a way that chafed. I'd lost touch with French Courtney. Maybe she only came out when Salomé was around. I apologized again to Kylie for what I said, and told her I was going back to Châteaubriant because of something I'd learned from my meeting with Élise, which was somewhat true. Kylie didn't have any further questions. I sensed it was a relief for her, too, when we hugged goodbye last night. I left before she woke up this morning, my thin blanket neatly folded at the end of the futon with a little note that said "*merci*."

I unfolded the piece of paper Callum gave me. The name on it was Loïc Duchêne. I tried to look him up on my phone, but the train's Wi-Fi wasn't working. It never seemed to. I probably had to pay or something. There was barely enough service to use data, but after several minutes, the search results loaded. He kept a WordPress blog with an unattractive template that looked as if it hadn't been updated since 2007. His last post was from six months ago, in January 2018. "Sous le couvert de la science." Under the cover of science. For having such an ugly website, Loïc wrote in an elevated register similar to Thierry's book, which went somewhat over my head. It would be a dead end, though, I was sure. Websites this shitty didn't make good sources. Plus there were many more likely reasons someone might take a six-month hiatus from posting on a blog than getting abducted by a cult. I didn't want to jump to conclusions.

When Salomé asked me not to write about her family, I'd assumed it was out of protectiveness for Thierry and not wanting his name to be posthumously dragged through the mud. But what if Salomé knew about this Loïc guy? Was she trying to protect *me*? If there was anything for me to write about here, it would be those American billionaires Callum mentioned. It seemed they were going to much greater lengths than just freezing themselves when they died.

I opened my notebook and wrote: *How far have their tentacles reached out across the world, enacting policies that favor their industries, or terminating those that don't?*

If there were a way to write the story without putting myself or Salomé in danger, I would consider it—or maybe I'd *want* to consider it. But the story was too big, and I was too small, too limited, too gullible to do it justice. I could send it to other, more established journalists as a lead, tacking, "Have fun, hope you don't get murdered!" to the end of the email.

I still had half an hour on this TGV, then I'd transfer to a regional TER in Angers to Châteaubriant. It was hard to believe how little I knew only a few days ago, when Salomé and I traveled this same path to Nantes, before I'd been to her home. I thought of the framed portrait of her and Élise as children in the living room. The fetal bird, forever preserved.

I closed my eyes and thought of Salomé as a six-year-old walking next to Thierry in Paris. He wore a coal gray wool trench coat. She wore a little pink puffy jacket with faux fur around the hood. Thierry had a sack of groceries in his arms. Just before they entered their building, Salomé stopped walking, looking down in front of her rain boots.

There was a small curve of flesh on the sidewalk. She knelt by it.

"Salomé," Thierry said. *"Ne le touche pas, s'il te plaît."*

From her window, she had watched the bird parents building their nest out of anything they could find in the city: strings and sticks and cigarettes and pieces of trash. Then the eggs appeared, and just yesterday, the first hatchling.

Salomé looked up at the ledge where the nest was built. There was no disturbance she could see from this angle, no cracked egg on the sidewalk. Just the little bird, dead.

She looked up at the people who passed, unaware of or unbothered by the tiny body, and that's what made her cry. She plopped onto her bottom and looked up at Thierry, eyes spilling over, begging him to save the bird.

Thierry sat on the sidewalk next to her, setting the bag of groceries to the side. Gently he scooped the baby into his hands. He told her that wasn't possible, that what was dead could never live again. But, he said, he could help her save it in another way if she wanted.

Upstairs, Nathalie looked out the window and saw her husband and daughter sitting on the sidewalk. She came down to see what had happened. Thierry explained what they were going to do, so she took the bag of groceries upstairs and returned with a small, empty jelly jar.

Thierry and Salomé got on the Métro, the little bird in the jar. They went to the university lab where Thierry worked. He told Salomé about decomposition, how it happens with bacteria and fungi, and how that's an integral part of the way our planet works. If they buried the little bird, it would soon become earth. But we have ways to stop that when we want to or need to, he said, and poured a thick, clear liquid into the jar with the bird.

"Is it bad to preserve things?" Salomé asked. "Isn't it better to let it return to the earth?"

"The vast majority of things return to the earth, so it isn't bad to occasionally preserve something," he said. "Like this." He handed her the jar. She held it up to her eye and watched the little pink bird spin ever so gently in the liquid.

"Whenever I see this bird," he told her, "I will be reminded of what a kind and gentle daughter I have. I never want to forget that." He kissed her on the head.

It was a nice memory. Had she recounted it to me? I was able to see it in such detail. Maybe it was just my imagination, but the memory felt more grounded than that.

I flipped the page of my notebook to the terrible Modigliani portrait I'd sketched while traveling in the other direction, the shock of Nathalie's flip-out still fresh. Even though Élise and Callum had told me some seriously disturbing information, I felt better now than I did going to Paris. It wasn't my fault Nathalie flipped. I hadn't stolen anything in my sleep. In my notebook, I made a timeline of the two nightmares I'd had at Salomé's house. One on Thursday, and the other on Friday.

I wrote "nightmare" and then *cauchemar*, French for nightmare. I'd thought at first that the word was "couchemar" because *se coucher* meant to go to bed. But it's an *a*: *cauche*. I didn't know if that was a word on its own or what the root might be. I was waiting for the page to load with the etymology of *cauchemar* when the train stopped in Angers.

This was the first train of the day and there weren't many passengers. I pulled my bag from the rack and stepped out onto the platform. The *gare* was starting to come to life. Someone rolled up the metal grate in front of the Relay store, and a little queue had formed in front of the Paul boulangerie. I had forty-five minutes before my next train left, so I bought a sandwich and coffee and sat in the morning sun by a fountain outside the station. I was close enough to connect to the Wi-Fi, so I did some reading.

In my notebook I'd written a few things: *Alexis Carrel*, *ViPi*, and *La science de l'immortalité.* I decided to start from the beginning. I opened a new search tab on my phone's browser and Googled Carrel.

Alexis Carrel received the Nobel Prize in 1912 for vascular suturing techniques. As Salomé had mentioned, he'd garnered the scorn of his French colleagues over his description of a miracle healing he'd witnessed in Lourdes in 1902. After that, he couldn't get a hospital appointment in France and ended up moving to North America. Charles Lindbergh was a major player in his technological advancement by creating the perfusion pump that made organ transplants possible. Carrel spent a good portion of his life in the US.

As I read further, I got into the eugenics stuff, which was as blatant as it could be—he went so far as to praise the Nazis for their swift suppression of mentally diseased and defective individuals in his 1935 book *L'homme, cet inconnu.*

So yes, being deemed "The New Carrel" would be a bad look for a modern scientist, especially one looking to do anything with genetics. Carrel had a tangled, complicated legacy: the Nobel Prize recipient, the surgeon who pioneered organ transplants, the devout Catholic who witnessed a healing miracle, the advocate for the suppression of the proletariat, the unabashed eugenicist, and the man who thought women should be educated not for their own advancement, but for the benefit of raising smarter children. This wasn't a far cry from some of today's rhetoric swirling around not-so-niche corners of the internet, packaged as something new and edgy. It was wild that these ideas were still around. Did humans never learn? But maybe that was by design, too. Maybe *that* was my angle.

No, I didn't need an angle because I wasn't going to write about it.

I searched "Salomé Leduc ViPi." There was only one search result that seemed relevant: her name in a short press release dated 2013. She was one of five people announced to be ViPi's new *"philosophes de la politique publique."* Philosophers of public policy. Salomé was the only woman.

I looked through the other search results, none of which included Salomé's name. One was a sponsored post from ViPi's YouTube channel. I clicked on it. It was a thirty-second video that broke down some of the active ingredients in ViPi. A beautiful woman appeared as a talking head against a bright green background. She said something about having anti-aging choices all around us . . . but did they *work?* The video showed the woman walking through a French pharmacy, where she was surrounded by creams and serums and vitamins, all of which promised to make her look younger. This image morphed into the woman with her entire face bandaged. Her voice-over said there are plenty of ways to *look* younger, but you will spend thousands of euros for an aesthetic change, when the real change must happen on the cellular level. Then the woman appeared in a lab coat, the words "nicotinamide adénine dinucléotide (NAD)" above her.

She was replaced by a graphic of a cell, which zoomed in until it showed a double-helix DNA that was damaged like strands of hair in a shampoo commercial. Suddenly, the strands were repaired, and the image panned out to reveal the outline of a human body with all its major organs drawn in. The voice-over said something about memory and a green check mark appeared next to the brain. More check marks popped up next to the heart, lungs, stomach, liver, and kidneys. Then a bottle of ViPi materialized on the screen.

There was a link in the video description. I clicked it and was rerouted to the ViPi website, but I had to create a user account to sign in, which I didn't want to do.

I went back to YouTube and clicked on one more video, this time a grainy recording that looked like it was filmed on a flip phone. I was surprised to see that it had been uploaded only a few days ago, though it looked ten years old.

Marco frantically paced around an outdoor stage at some kind of little festival. The wind obscured his speech, but I could tell that his delivery was meant to get the crowd hyped up, not to convince them of his scientifically sound vitamins. I wondered if this was what Salomé was referring to when she said he ranted about aging being a disease. The people in the sparse crowd punched their fists into the air, cheering wildly. After eighteen seconds, the clip ended. Weird.

I closed my phone screen and looked up. A couple of little boys were playing in the spray from the fountain as their mothers chatted nearby.

I left my backpack by the bench and walked closer to the fountain. I tilted my face upward, letting the mist settle on my throat and chest, hoping the water wasn't teeming with bacteria. I felt the sun on my face. "There is nothing new under the sun," I said quietly. The only Bible verse that had ever meant anything to me, even before I stopped considering myself a Christian. I found comfort in believing that nothing I encountered, even in my own mind, was unique. Every problem had an ancient equivalent. There were no new stories. I remember being blown away when I learned about the patriarchal bargain, that there was a name for the thing I'd witnessed my whole life and had never tried to articulate.

Similarly, there was nothing novel about the Magpies. People had been seeking immortality since they were able to understand death.

There was a Greek myth about a man who was granted immortality by the gods, but instead of having eternal youth, he continued to age without dying until he turned into a cicada.

It seemed plausible that science was getting close to understanding how to reverse the aging process. After all, some Silicon Valley billionaires were dumping money into longevity research, according to an article I'd read in *The New Yorker.* I could only assume they'd made some progress.

What if the right supplement could press "pause" on the disease attacking my mom's brain? It looked far more legit than a laundering scheme. What if ViPi was actually effective because it had some EU-approved ingredient that we didn't have in the US? If Alexis Carrel could have horrible ideas about humanity and still figure out a way to save lives, it wasn't impossible that Marco could be an abusive partner *and* have created a product that worked. Not that I wanted to support him. But the success of ViPi was hardly based on whether or not I bought a bottle of vitamins. I was ashamed to admit to myself how much the advertisement had intrigued me—particularly the green check mark beside the brain.

Even though it was the middle of the night in the US, I texted my mom to let her know that Kylie and I were taking a day trip to Orléans.

je t'aime, xoxo.

She knew what it meant, or hopefully she would. Up until recently, she'd maintained an almost two-year-long Duolingo streak, studying French. Since the diagnosis she'd dropped off, saying it was getting frustrating. I guess Alexis Carrel would've thought it ridiculous for a postmenopausal woman to take any steps toward self-improvement, even before her diagnosis. But hearing the app's little dings of approval ringing out from her phone filled me with more pride than anything I'd ever accomplished in my life.

I should've responded with more enthusiasm to her French study. It was obviously her attempt to have more in common with me. I should've been teaching her French words this whole time.

At least Salomé knew what it was like to have a complicated relationship with your mother. Even that thought churned my stomach as I remembered I was about to see Nathalie again. No. Nothing could go wrong. I'd just go get Salomé and leave. In and out as quickly as possible. I could do what she asked of me.

Since when was I so altruistic? It only took a kiss from a French person who seemed to like me for me to shove all my apprehension aside and become the American hero.

"Shut up," I said aloud to myself. I looked around. No one had overheard. Everyone by the fountain was preoccupied with their phones or their children. My train was due to arrive in ten minutes. My last chance to bail on this. I picked up my backpack and went inside the station.

I texted Salomé that I was about to board the TER to Châteaubriant.

Do you remember how to get to the house?

I remember.

I put on a downloaded podcast and tried to keep my anxiety in check. I didn't need to worm myself into every corner of possibility. I just needed to get to the town, then to the house, and back to her.

CHAPTER 13

I knew Châteaubriant now. I created a little mantra as I walked, timing my steps with the syllables: *She asked me to.* This propelled me through *le centre-ville*, dotted with centuries-old half-timbered houses among the more common sand-colored buildings. I passed the cathedral, which was markedly less breathtaking in the daytime (and while sober), and walked toward the bridge crossing the small canal where the Chère passed through town. I paused for a moment. A few days ago this channel had a foot or so of water. Now it was barely a trickle.

The sun was already brutal on the back of my neck. According to my weather app, Châteaubriant would reach about 94 degrees today, and 101 tomorrow. Besides the largest hotel in town, almost nowhere would have air-conditioning.

Strangely, I felt far less nervous about meeting Marco than I did about seeing Nathalie again. There was a small piece of me that almost looked forward to meeting him, getting to draw my own image of someone so steeped in lore, he might as well have been Judas Iscariot. That same piece of me, some tiny live wire in an otherwise defunct piece of machinery, was what kept me introducing myself as a "journalist" instead of a "columnist"—which also felt uncomfortably aggrandizing—and had prompted me to spend the majority of the ride on the TER thinking about writing a profile about Marco, called "The *Real* New Carrel."

But as soon as the thought would enter my mind, I'd shut it down, and ask myself: Then what? Send it to my *Slate* editor, only to have him tell me to stick to the *Raleigh Scene*? This was so far out of my wheelhouse, so far out of the scope of my talents and intelligence and tolerance for danger.

What if I *do* want to write about it?

The stream below me seemed to waver under my eyes, and I wasn't sure if it was a heat-related optical illusion or a visual lapse on my part. Suddenly my body grew so hot, my stomach so precarious, that I clawed my backpack off and sat on the bridge, leaning against the wrought iron barrier. My fingers trembled as I wiped my sweaty hair away from my forehead. It's going to be okay. It's going to be okay. Just walk. There's not enough time for anything terrible to happen. They need me. I pulled myself to my feet on the railing, and hoisted my bag onto my shoulders, teetering a little. Then I walked.

Salomé's house came into view. There was a new Mercedes parked in the driveway behind the Peugeot. That had to be Marco.

I went to the front door and knocked, unsure what would greet me on the other side.

Nathalie opened the door. I fought to keep my face as pleasant as possible. Salomé was behind her, very still, maybe holding her breath like I was.

Nathalie greeted me and lightly touched my elbows, kissing the air beside my cheeks.

"Are you hungry?" she asked in French.

"No, thank you, I've already eaten," I told her in French.

She stood in front of me, formidable in a way despite her tiny frame. She looked at me with an expression I wanted to read as appreciation, but which felt more like appraisal. She still hadn't stepped back to let me enter, seconds after it would've been natural.

"*Excuse-moi, Maman.*" Salomé's voice came from behind her. She gently guided Nathalie aside and stepped out through the doorway to give me *la bise.* Her smooth cheek brushed against mine. "Welcome back," she said. "I am so glad you are here."

When she pulled away, the air around my face was cool and smelled like her lotion. The closeness made me a little lightheaded. I was sure she could tell. I followed them into the kitchen, where she turned the flame off under the rumbling percolator. "Do you want some coffee?"

"Yes, please," I said.

Nathalie leaned against the countertop, her flat palm pressing on it like an anchor, and cleared her throat. My heart rate increased. "Cour-te-ney, I hope you know that I do not think you stole Thierry's ring. The truth is, the ring was stolen or lost several years ago. I suffer from paranoia sometimes. I am sorry for what I said. You are welcome here anytime." She looked at Salomé, who gave her a single nod.

I couldn't tell whose idea it was that Nathalie should apologize, and I didn't have time to think about it for long. We heard the harsh cadence of footsteps approaching from the hallway to Nathalie's room.

"Thank you," I said to Nathalie, but she was already angling her body toward the sound.

Both of them tensed. Even their breathing seemed quieter as the footsteps clipped in our direction. I braced myself with a flat palm on the counter like Nathalie.

"*Bonjour, mes belles,*" Marco said, breezing into the kitchen. He strode in my direction, his expression pleasant and welcoming. "*Moi c'est Marco*," he said, extending a hand for me to shake.

"Courtney," I said.

"Cour-ten-ey, it is a pleasure to meet you," he said in French, now grasping my hand in both of his. "We haven't had a guest for a long time. I hope you've been comfortable here."

I nodded. "*Oui*," I said, too nervous to elaborate.

Marco released my hand. He gathered his laptop and a few file folders from the dining table, and slid these into a nice-looking charcoal-colored messenger bag, buckling the latch. He remarked to the room that it was going to be a beautiful day, and that we should enjoy it because the heat wave was coming.

His French was easy to understand, just like in the videos. He picked up an envelope from the table and slid his finger under the lip to open it. He had a nice side profile and was quite a bit more handsome in person. Maybe it was the lighting. Or maybe it was because he looked ever-so-slightly younger now. He appeared to be in his early fifties, with shoulder-length salt-and-pepper hair that hadn't thinned at all. He wore a gold wedding band, though from what I understood, he and Nathalie were not married. I felt somewhat disarmed, now having met him.

After Marco discarded the piece of mail, he came up behind Nathalie and put his arms around her waist. He rocked her from side to side and planted a kiss on her neck and another on her cheek. Was he trying to convince us all that he hadn't just thrown a fit over thinking Nathalie bought a train ticket to Paris? Nathalie smiled and leaned into him, seemingly relieved to get this version of Marco. Still, there was a stiffness to her shoulders.

"Cour-ten-ey, will you be staying with us again tonight?" he asked in French.

I jumped at the sound of my name. I told him I wasn't sure and looked to Salomé for help.

"We're going to Nantes this afternoon and might decide to get a hotel close to the beach. Cour-ten-ey wants to see the sunrise over the Atlantic," Salomé said, her voice impassive.

Nathalie seemed surprised. "Really?"

Marco dropped another kiss onto Nathalie's neck. "Okay, I'm going to work. I hope the day is as beautiful as you three. Cour-ten-ey, please don't hesitate to ask me if you need anything. It was marvelous to meet you," he said in French.

I barely had time to say, "*Merci*," before he grabbed his messenger bag and left out the front door.

Salomé handed me an espresso-sized cup of coffee. "Come with me, Cour-ten-ey," she said, and went into her bedroom.

I looked at Nathalie, trying to catch her eye for a moment of closure over our previous conversation, but she was staring out the window, watching Marco drive away.

I followed Salomé. That interaction couldn't have gone better. I must've been visibly relieved when I arrived in the bedroom, because she sat on her bed and gave me a knowing look. "Be careful, he does understand English, but he will not speak it. You are thinking he can't be that bad, right?"

"I've been picturing an absolute monster. I do feel a bit better now that I've seen him in person."

"He should have a César for it. I am telling you, he is someone very different when alone. He will make you think he is the best guy in the world. But he is on the inside . . ." She pointed to her temples while trying to think of the word.

"Scheming?"

"Yes. That." She smoothed her thumbnail.

"I believe you. I promise."

She cut me a glance from under her bangs, somewhat flirtatious, somewhat omniscient. She placed her hand on my leg. Her touch unraveled the malaise that had gripped me since the moment I left her. "Thank you for coming back. It was really good, right?"

I wasn't sure if she meant the conversation in the kitchen or a more general summary of our time together. Either way, I agreed. "Yeah. Do you feel okay about leaving?"

She leaned over and pulled her laptop onto her knees. She typed, then spun the screen around so I could see. She'd pulled up hotels for tonight in Nantes. Most of the listings for rooms with two beds were over €200 per night, but I found a site offering last-minute bookings for around €120. I hadn't budgeted to have to spend any money on lodging. Though I also hadn't spent money on what I had budgeted for, like museums and a couple of nice meals.

"Should I book it for two nights?" I asked.

"How many more nights will you be here?"

"Well, technically two, but that last one I should be in Paris to fly out the next day. My flight home is at ten-thirty. Or I could get a really early train from Nantes, but that makes me a little nervous."

"You could get the hotel for only one night and figure it out later," she said.

"Okay, that's a good idea." I'd never been much of a figure-it-out-later person when it came to being on time for an international flight, but French Courtney could roll with the unknown better than the American one. I got out my credit card and keyed in the number on the booking website. "Okay. Check-in is at three."

Salomé went to the doorway and told Nathalie, who was still in the kitchen, that we were going to spend the night in Nantes. Nathalie said that she was going to need the car for a couple of hours, but that we could have it this afternoon if we could wait. They said goodbye and I heard Nathalie leave out of the front door. Outside, the car started. Salomé turned back to me with her thumbs hooked into the front pockets of her shorts.

"Well, it's just us. I'm going to take a shower and get packed. She said we could use the car this afternoon, but if we don't want to wait, we can take the train."

"Yeah, let's take the train. We can probably drop off our luggage at the hotel." I didn't want to be in the house any longer than necessary.

She nodded, then bit the inside of her lip. She stood on one foot and used the other big toe to scoot a sock around on the floor. It looked like she was writing a word in cursive.

I sensed that she felt awkward about what it would mean to go to a hotel together, which was relieving. We were on the same page.

"Salomé . . ."

"Yes?"

"Sorry. I just . . . it's okay. Don't worry."

She gave me a little nod. "Thank you. It means a lot to me." She turned to go.

I flopped back onto the bed and closed my eyes for a few minutes. I'd woken up at 5:00 that morning to get to Gare Montparnasse from Kylie's house. I slept badly knowing my alarm was set so early, and the added apprehension of going back to Châteaubriant didn't help, nor did the still mostly unresolved confrontation with Kylie. I hadn't slept well for several nights. Maybe not since I'd been in France. If I stayed in bed, I'd fall asleep. The image of that shimmery faceless thing came to mind, and I got up. I shot the espresso like tequila and went into the kitchen to see if there was more. The percolator was empty. I debated making more, but decided just to keep moving.

I went into the living room and stopped at the bookshelf where I'd woken up from sleepwalking. The security camera's blue light glowed in my peripheral vision. I shouldn't have left the bedroom. No, it's not off-limits to look at someone's bookcase. This is normal behavior. I tilted my head to read the book spines. Maybe I'd find a clue here. *Manger moins pour vivre plus* with its terrible clip-art cover; a book of Keats poetry that might explain the English epigraph in Thierry's book; and several nonfiction books about biology and genetics. Nothing especially damning. What was I expecting to see, the French translation of *Mein Kampf*?

From the way the water splashed in the shower, it sounded like Salomé was washing her hair. I wanted to pound on the door and say, "You know they have a shower at the hotel, right? And it's probably a lot nicer than this one." Why would she take the time to wash her hair now? I glanced at my phone. It was just after 9:30. I needed to chill out. I opened the internet browser and clicked to the tab with the etymology of *cauchemar*, which finally loaded.

From Old French *cauche*, from the verb *chauchier* (to press), from Latin *calcare* (I trample, tread on), from *calx* (heel), of uncertain origin. From Frankish *marā* (evil spirit), from Proto-Indo-European *mor-* (malicious female spirit), from *mer-* (to die). A shiver passed through my arms. I set my phone on the bookshelf next to the little bird. I spelled *serrer* and shook my hands. *Cauchemar* was an accurate word.

Though closed, the bird's pale lidded eyes seemed to look at me. "Auspicious," I said to myself, and picked the jar up off the shelf. "To look at a bird." Also disturbingly literal at this moment. Had Salomé told me the story of finding the bird? Or did I make that up?

The shower water turned off. I wanted to dash back into the bedroom, to not be caught at the bookshelf again, but I made myself stay. I needed to nudge into the conversation of what Salomé knew, and this would be a natural entry point. She came out of the *salle de bain*, a thin towel wrapped around her body and another around her hair. "Oh, you are always with ze bird!"

There was a conspicuous space between the two remaining copies of *La science de l'immortalité*. I thought I felt her notice it.

"So, can I ask you something?"

"Sure," she said, shrugging.

I reached for one of the copies but only slid it out a bit. "Does this put people in danger?"

"It wasn't what he wanted . . ."

"So it does?"

"Why do you want to know?"

I let go of the book and took a step back. "I was thinking about it on the train. Wondering if you—if we're complicit in something that is worse than we know, you know?"

She translated in her head for a moment. "What I do know is that my father did all of his science on trying to help people live longer and not be in pain. And now people spend money on fake vitamins. It is not fair, but not dangerous."

"I'm sorry," I said, and I was, to an extent. I wondered how much she knew about the Magpies at all, though it did seem like more than she was letting on.

"It's okay," she said, though still a little bristled. She walked through the kitchen and turned toward the bedroom. I followed her.

She pulled a shirt over her head, her shoulder blades moving under her skin like a cat's. The towel was around her waist now, and she kept it on as she stepped into a pair of shorts. She tossed the towel onto the bedpost and sat on the bed, hugging her knees to her chest.

I sank down onto the side of the bed. "I'm sorry," I said again.

Her eyes searched my face, somewhat loving, somewhat amused. "I am sorry," she said.

"About what?"

She touched my hair above my right ear and picked up a few limp strands. Her fingers got close to the place I'd dreamed someone had cut off a chunk. "I'm glad we are leaving. Being here, it makes me . . . *irritable.* What is this?"

"Irritable. Same word."

"Sorry. I know I am not being fun."

"It's okay. When is the next train to Nantes?"

"There's a tram-train that goes every hour." She looked at her phone. "And it is in five minutes, so we will go on the next one. In one hour."

"Let's just chill until it's time to leave. Do you want to watch *Broad City?*" I had the urge to kiss her forehead. Would that be too maternal? Send the wrong message? I wasn't sure what kind of message I wanted to send.

She nodded and reached for her laptop. She clicked around for a few seconds and pulled up the show, a few episodes past where we'd left off. She wiggled down onto the bed and motioned for me to do the same.

Maybe this is what sharing an apartment in Montmartre would be like.

But as what? As lovers? As best friends? As best friends who were a little bit in love with each other and held each other back from meeting other people? What if I *was* mostly drawn to her because she was French, or she was drawn to me for being American, and there was no real foundation outside of a weird fixation on each other's culture? Suddenly my body flushed hot. I couldn't push the uncertainty aside any longer.

I hit the space bar. "When I was in Paris, I thought about you the whole time. Since the plane, I haven't stopped. It's like—"

"I think about you all the time," she said without hesitation.

Though she'd given me no reason to think she felt differently, I was nonetheless surprised to hear my sentiments echoed back. I searched her face for a hint that she wasn't sincere. After a moment, I said, "It's scary. I mean . . . I'm not sure what it means. I just wanted you to know where my head's at, and all I know is that I don't know."

She smiled. "It's the same for me. Normally, I am more friends with girls."

Thank God she would name it. Now that the words had been spoken, I asked, "Have you ever had feelings for a woman?"

"I was in love with a girl in high school. For a little while, but not really since her."

"Did you sleep with her?"

She rolled onto her back and brought her fingers to her lips, smiling slightly. "We did a lot of kissing," she said, and patted the bed. "Right here."

"You mean I'm not the only woman who's been in your bed?" I feigned mild indignation.

She laughed. "No, I'm sorry, you are not." She propped herself up on her elbow and leaned over me, her hair falling around my face. "Now you are camping in a tent of hair."

"I like the tent." My head was swirling. Her hair tickled my cheeks. There was a sharpness to her breath, not unpleasant, but something you only notice when you're very close to someone. We were very close.

She glanced quickly at the camera on the wall. The sock was still in place. She returned her attention to me and kissed me between the eyebrows, then trailed her nose down my face, and, breathing in, pressed her lips to mine. I almost didn't know how to kiss her back, so unlike our first in the train station. We were somewhat awkward, but my heart was so loud that I could barely pay attention. I didn't know where to put my hands, my tongue. Her mouth was smaller than what I was used to, her stubble-free skin was silk on my fingers. I was probably not being a good kisser.

She pulled away and I couldn't read her expression.

"I'm sorry," I said. "I don't know what I'm doing."

"Yes, you do."

It felt good to hear that, but my instinct was to reject the compliment. "I've only ever been with men because I already know how to do it."

"Yes, I know what you mean. And because it is what people expect."

"Yeah, it's the assumed societal default."

"Socie-tal deefault," she said. "I like that you are so smart."

She thought I was smart for making an observation in my native language? I wanted to tell her that she intimidated the shit out of me, that I could feel her genius buzzing inside of her like a motor.

Her fingers gently roamed my collarbone. "This is so much better on women," she said, meaning the collarbone, I assumed.

I pulled the neck hole of her shirt aside and traced my finger along hers, a delicate curve like the *Serpent d'Océan.* She was right.

She kissed me again. I felt like I was sinking down into miles and miles of pillows. She slid on top of me, cupping my face, and pressed her forehead to mine, the tips of our noses touching, linked breath. She kissed me lightly three times, then pulled away.

I took a deep breath that came in ragged. My armpits were sweaty. My teeth started chattering, but it was more adrenaline than nerves. It wasn't like the dream, but still, the image of the faceless mermaid flashed in my mind.

"I will stop." She pulled away.

I wanted her to stop and I didn't want her to stop. I swallowed hard and nodded. "It's okay, I just need a minute," I said. She moved to the side and I got out of the bed. I went to the *salle de bain,* where I stripped down and got into the bathtub. I held the shower nozzle directly on top of my head and let the cool water wash down my neck and shoulders. I set it down, covered my face with my hands, and sobbed as quietly as I could.

A man would be having sex with me right now, whether or not I wanted it, because I never would've asked him to stop. It was easier for me to let it happen than to risk the humiliation of not being listened to or fear his response. Was I even attracted to male bodies or did I simply assume they were available to me?

What terrified me now was how much work it would take to free myself of all the baggage I'd accumulated over the past ten years. I wasn't ready to deem it all a waste. I felt like I'd been running, dragging a sled full of misbeliefs and bad ideas, and Salomé had brought me to a momentary halt. For a few glorious seconds, a reprieve from the sprint—*oh, this is nice*—until the sled caught up, taking me out at the knees.

I closed the tap and toweled off but didn't have the energy to mess with any lotion or air-dry serum. I put the same clothes back on. When I returned to the bedroom, she was sitting with her knees pulled up again, her forehead against them, this beautiful thing she did. I sat next to her and hugged her.

"I'm sorry," she said.

"Don't be sorry. I'm just a little overwhelmed right now."

"Did you feel dirty?"

It took me a second to realize she was referring to the shower I'd taken. I pulled away to look at her. "Yeah. I mean, not because of you. Because I was sweaty."

"Oh, good. I thought it was because you are Catholic."

"That might have to do with why I was so sweaty."

She smiled and squeezed my hand. "It's okay," she said. "You are young. There is a lot of time, you know?" She lay back down, pulling the computer onto her belly. She hit the space bar, and the show resumed. She wasn't ignoring me. She sensed I didn't want to be observed while I was processing.

I snuggled down next to her, less self-conscious now that I'd showered, but didn't watch the show. I just cried. Memories of moments like this one that had gone so badly filed through my mind. His face above mine on the couch. My back shoved against a parked car, a hand snaking up my sweater. My own voice, panting and moaning, imitating the noises of pleasure just so he would finish faster and I could enjoy the safety I'd earned.

Salomé let me cry, occasionally stroking my hair. Sometime later, absolutely exhausted, I curled onto my side, and she curled herself around me.

CHAPTER 14

D*on't open your eyes.*

Salomé's breathing had become a tiny whistle. She was still asleep behind me.

My shirt was wet against my chest. How could she sleep in this heat? The room was too bright. I didn't remember there being a lamp in the far corner. I wanted to go turn it off. I tried to look at the lamp, but my eyes felt limp, as if they were rolling in their sockets. My whole body tingled like a limb that had fallen asleep. I tried wiggling my feet and legs, my sweaty thighs sliding against each other. I pulled and pulled toward the surface, slapped my foot down onto the tile floor, and pulled some more. Somehow I managed to lurch from the bed, leaving the hot mess of blankets behind, and made my way toward the lamp, whose obnoxious light was burning through my closed eyelids. It was amazing, moving like this, the way I could barely feel my body under me, but still make it walk. I was my own puppet. I arrived at the lamp, which was like direct sunlight on my skin.

Don't open your eyes. Oh shit.

I pressed my numb hands to my eyelids, but they did nothing to block out the light. My body buzzed, every electron in every atom that built me spinning faster and faster. My hands, where were they?

I tried to touch them together, nothing. I reached for the lamp. My finger grazed something. *Don't open your eyes*—the words warbled from somewhere. I couldn't, I wanted to. My breathing was way too loud inside my head, along with a song, something with a lone clarinet, moving solemnly around like a sine wave. I licked my lips, trying to open my mouth, but I couldn't feel that either. Then a pop, a crack. My jaw fell open, and so did my eyes.

It wasn't a lamp. It was a furnace, and it burned hotter now that I could see. Salomé stood to my left. Her eyes were solid gray empty marbles. Modigliani eyes. I tried to ask her how long the furnace had been there, but my throat was full of that same gray. She looked at me, grabbed my hand, but all I could feel was a small pulse to know we were touching. We walked out of the room, past our sleeping selves in the bed. I saw my foot twitch.

We stepped into the enormous medieval kitchen, made entirely of dark stone, and shuffled into the living room. My breathing was drowning out the clarinet. It was dark outside, but there was enough light coming from somewhere that I could see the outline of the furniture. Louis was on the couch if I looked directly at him, but if I turned my head to the side, he was gone. Salomé was gone, too.

"Hey." It was a man's voice from the hallway leading to Nathalie's room.

Luke.

"Luke?" I wanted to say. "What are you doing in France?"

He turned to walk down the hallway.

"Wait!" I wanted to say.

The hallway was glowing—another furnace perhaps. Voices, too, from that direction. Pleasant. Luke's voice, Salomé's. This was familiar. I'd frozen here before, when the mermaid told me to stop. But I was invited now. I puppeteered my limbs to shuffle toward the red glow of Nathalie's room.

I'd seen this room before. The bed with its tangles of sheets, the dresser with too many dust-covered knickknacks, the forlorn thick curtains that were always drawn, even in the daytime. But I didn't remember the furnace. It blazed orange from the corner of the room, just like the one in Salomé's. I could only see it from the corners of my vision.

In my periphery, I saw three people lounging on the bed. I couldn't focus on them. Was this what it was like to look out of a fly's eyes?

"Hey." It was Luke's voice again, coming from the bed.

Someone swept into the room. From the edges I saw it was Nathalie, carrying a tray of bowls of fruit and lit candles, which she set on the bed. Candles on the bed was a bad idea, I knew, even in this fuzzy state. Nathalie craned her neck to look at me from the sides of her gray marbled eyes, the same as everyone else's. Mine must've been empty gray marbles too. That's why I couldn't see straight ahead. I didn't like that. Nathalie sat on the edge of the bed and extended her hand to me, offering an object.

A lone raspberry sat in the center of her palm. She craned her long neck toward me, cocking her head curiously to the side to get a good look at me.

"It's okay if you want," said Salomé from the bed. "It is from 'er garden."

Salomé and the two others were kneeling, watching me. Luke and someone else. A man with stringy black facial hair and a wormy skin tone. It was Marco, I realized, but he looked terrible.

"Salomé," I wanted to say, but my throat was still full.

"It's okay, Cour-ten-ey," Salomé said.

"Cour-ten-ey, do you want?" Nathalie asked, still extending her palm. I angled my head away so I could bring her offering into focus. The raspberry was gone, replaced by a razor blade that glinted in the light of the furnace. I reached for it.

My hand came back bloody. A thin, stinging line in the center of my palm. I tried to assess it through the corners of my eyes, but I was suddenly lightheaded and fell to my knees, slumping doll-like against the side of the bed.

"Don't hurt her," said Salomé, monotone like the clarinet. She and Luke stood next to me now, facing Nathalie and Marco, who had puddled onto the bed like a Dalí clock. He must have gotten too close to the furnace and melted.

My arms hung at my sides. I felt blood dripping from my fingertips, but couldn't lift my other hand to apply pressure. I sensed the puddle-man sliding off the bed and onto the floor, where he stationed himself directly under the flow of blood. I struggled to move away, but my chest was pinned to the bed.

Nathalie watched me through those gray eyes, her face tilted eerily away, her mouth drawn tight in a smirk. She stepped toward me and reached tenderly for my hand, easing my body away from the bed. I knelt in front of her while she wrapped a white bandage around the cut. Sensations started to return to my body, tingly and unpleasant.

On the floor next to me, Puddle-Marco was gaining energy, vibrating like he was about to explode into a wave and crash against my body.

"Stop!" I wanted to say, but my limp jaw was hanging open. I tried again and again to speak.

I felt it slither out through my mouth, seeping from the depths of me. The air around its scales shimmered like heat rising from asphalt as it wound its way around Nathalie's neck. A silver boa. Nathalie's monochrome eyes could be looking anywhere, but I felt them on me.

Salomé's hand flashed in front of my face, brushing my eyes closed. "Don't open your eyes, Cour-ten-ey," she said, and dropped down and away from me, a splash on my ankles. Then Luke dropped on my right, *splash*, and then I dropped too, as if flushed down a pipe and to the sea.

CHAPTER 15

I kicked my legs out and felt grittiness. I took a few deep breaths. My throat was raw. What a terrible dream. I patted the bed next to me. Salomé wasn't there. There was a dense object behind me, and for a moment I thought it was a person, but it was my backpack. Water rustled and coolness rushed over my feet. I sat up, struggling to adjust my eyes to the darkness.

The sliver of moon provided enough light to see the water rushing away from me, rippling around something large. I tried to focus my eyes on the shape. All at once, it came together—a skull and fangs, partially submerged in the dark water. *Serpent d'Océan.*

I crouched on the sand, watching the water and snake for a long time. The tide had risen to the algae line on its metal ribs, where Salomé and I had stood not long ago. How long ago?

A dream-within-a-dream. *Mise en abyme.* My vision was the same as usual, so at least this dream wasn't as scary. But there was something too real, too tactile about it to be a dream. I decided to test it.

"I didn't mean to come here," I said aloud to the snake.

Yet here you are. Its voice came from within my mind, like the mermaid's, but it was male. *People show up, from time to time. They always claim it was an accident. But really, it takes an enormous amount of effort to get here, doesn't it?*

I liked the voice. It was comforting. "Why would they put a work of art in a place that's so hard to get to?"

Do you value convenience over significance?

I thought about it. "I mean, I'm American." I think I wanted the snake to laugh, but it didn't.

What else do you want to know?

"Are you a god?"

No, I'm a sculpture.

"Yeah, I know. I meant are you a sculpture *of* a god?"

You don't know that I represent the fall of man, original sin?

"Of course. But not every culture will have the same interpretation of snakes as Christianity."

What would you like me to represent?

"I don't know."

Well then I'm afraid I can't help you.

"So I can just pick something?"

I can't guarantee the sculptor would agree with you, but he doesn't have to.

The beach was empty. I walked toward the water and stood for a long time, as the tide rushed forward and backward between the statue and me. At some point I realized my feet were tired, so I dragged my backpack to the edge of the beach, where a stone wall separated the sand from the walking path. I leaned against the bag and watched the statue. It was suspended, like the embryonic bird.

My body felt strangely calm and alert at the same time, somewhat like the relief you feel after vomiting. I sensed the absence of fear as if that were itself a tangible entity. I had recently been afraid. But of what? If I closed my eyes, I could almost hear the remnants of someone screaming far away, from the other side of a long tunnel. I didn't know what to do, so I waited to wake up.

The sunrise came from behind me, warming the sky and inching toward the watery horizon. I wasn't sure if I'd slept or not. I lay motionless with my back against my bag. I wiggled my toes against the rocky sand and cigarette butts. Two people ran by with dogs, and even the dogs avoided looking at the human on the ground.

I sat up. The tide was inching away now. Nearby, a sea bird tried tasting a cigarette butt before dropping it and pausing to stare at me. It flew away as I brushed off the small pebbles stuck to my face.

Why was I still here? Had I actually slept on the beach?

"Hey," I said, a little surprised by the raspiness of my own voice.

The statue didn't respond. I stood up and brushed off my arms and legs. I felt hungover. My hands searched my lower back for lacerations. No, kidneys seemed intact, though they ached in a way that meant I needed to drink some water.

Better move along. Anywhere. Don't think, just go. Hoisting my bag onto my back almost toppled me over. The inside crook of my elbow stung when I moved my arm. There was a small bruise and a tiny puncture over the vein.

The only thought I had was to not think about it. I had to get to another location. I walked along the beach, trying to look inconspicuous, until I found the parking lot and the café where Salomé and I had gone a couple of days ago, or whenever that was.

I sat at a table outside. It was so early they hadn't yet put the Aperol umbrellas up. I wondered if they were open. The same young server from before peeked out of the café's doorway, then retreated back inside without coming over. I found my purse inside my backpack and pulled out a five-euro bill.

I spread my fingers wide and pressed them into the table. It was wooden, poorly stained, and bleached under the relentless sun. The pattern of the wood grain looked like flames leaping up from behind my fingers. I stared at my burning hands for a few minutes, and had the realization that I was being extremely present, how we're supposed to be all the time. But it wasn't intentional; it was because my thoughts and memories were contained behind a levee of static.

"*Bonjour.*" The server stood back from my table.

I asked him for a carafe of water and a coffee, then returned to studying my hands, palms up this time. Grime had seeped into every crevice and line. I kept my eyes away from the bruise and puncture. Not yet.

My phone. I ripped open my bag. It was there, in the front zippered pocket. Thank God. But the battery was dead.

The server came back with my water and *café allongé*, which he set down with a little clatter. I asked him what day it was. He looked suspicious but told me it was *mardi*, Tuesday. I must've appeared visibly relieved by this news, because he kept the skeptical look when he said, "*Deux euros trente.*" I gave him the five and told him to keep the change.

My vision was still a little shaky, as was my hand as I guided the coffee to my lips. After a few sips I managed to find my charger and the power converter in another pocket of my backpack. But there was nowhere to plug in my phone. I would have to go inside. I'd have a little more coffee first, get my bearings. I was going to get through this, one piece at a time.

You are in Saint-Brevin, on the western coast of France, at a café.

It is possible no one knows you're here.

You don't know how you got here.

Your plane leaves on Wednesday.

It is now Tuesday.

How much money do you have? Good question. I'd spent some money on a hotel in Nantes. Maybe I'd gotten abducted on my way there. I booked that hotel while sitting on Salomé's bed, moments before we kissed. Had that really happened? And where was Salomé?

Salomé. Oh my God. I left my bag at the table and went running down the path to the beach. I stood on top of the stone wall and called her name, but not very loudly because my throat burned like I had swallowed sandpaper. My voice disappeared into the wind. There was no sign of her. I clutched my hand over my chest and looked out at the dark blue ocean. What if the tide had carried her out there? Or what if she'd left me here? A gust of wind nearly blew me off the wall. I bent over at the waist, trying to catch my breath.

One reasonable step at a time. Call her. Which meant charging my phone.

I ran back to my table, gathered my phone, charger, and power converter, and went to the café's door, which was propped open with a cinder block. The server was behind the bar, counting bills in the register. There were a few tables inside, each with the chairs turned upside down on top. The overhead lights were off.

Were they open? "*Vous êtes ouverts?*" I asked.

"*Pas encore*," the server said without looking up at me.

God. They weren't even open.

"*Il est quelle heure?*"

"*Six heures et demie.*" Six-thirty in the morning.

"Jesus Christ, I'm so sorry, I didn't realize . . ." I said in English.

He waved at me to not worry about it, rather good-naturedly, I thought, given the circumstances.

"Excuse me, but would it be possible for you to call me a taxi to take me to the train station? My phone is dead," I said in wobbly French, referring to my phone as "*mort*"—the literal word for dead, but I didn't know if that was right for electronics.

He nodded and picked up the landline phone behind the bar. After a few seconds he spoke into the receiver, ordered the cab, and hung up. "*Quinze minutes*," he told me.

I thanked him profusely.

He nodded toward a hallway and told me the bathroom was that way. His face and voice remained so stoic, I wasn't sure what he was implying. But I thanked him and walked in that direction. The lights flickered on automatically as I stepped into the dark hallway.

The bathroom was no bigger than an airplane bathroom. Sitting on the toilet, I had to lean against the wall to avoid the sink. I tried to pee but there was barely anything to come out, and what did stung like the beginning of a UTI. I didn't feel like I'd been assaulted, so that was good. I finally worked up the courage to look at my arm. The bruised spot stung as I opened my elbow. I brought it close to my face and smoothed the skin with my thumb. A clear needle indentation. Blue-purple bruising. Black dots blotted my vision. I fought to keep my breathing steady.

If a needle goes into your arm, there are two options: something goes in, or blood comes out. A useless technical third option is that a needle goes in and comes out with no other action, no addition or subtraction. But that's unlikely, right? Why would someone go to the effort to stick you with a needle right in the crook of your elbow if they didn't mean to tamper with you? What if the needle hadn't been sterile? When was the last time I'd gotten a tetanus shot?

I stood up and held the door open with my foot, not wanting to be closed in there. Finally, I dared to look into the mirror.

"Fuck."

Mascara and dirt streaked down my face. My neck was crusted with dark sand, and my lips, I saw with a pang of shame, showed the telltale stains of too much red wine. There were several strands of dry kelp sticking out of my hair. I started there, tugging the sea plants out of the tangled mess, which covered the porcelain sink with a fine mist of dirt and sand. I threw the plants away in the tiny trash can by the toilet, and tried to clean out the sink with a few handfuls of water.

I washed my hands thoroughly before cupping some water onto my face and neck. I remembered being in a swimming pool as a kid and saving a praying mantis from drowning. I'd set it on the pool deck and watched it frantically running its arms and legs over its wings, its antennae, drying and soothing itself. I watched it from eye level, standing shoulder-deep in the water. It knows its body as well as I know mine, I'd thought, and the idea felt profound. I'd never looked at bugs the same way after that. I wanted to tell Salomé that story. I knew she'd appreciate it. Now I was the one frantically running my hands over every inch of my body, cleaning, searching for injuries. Salomé might be doing the same thing, but where?

I dried my face and neck on a paper towel, then wiped out the sink with it. I was looking a little better. At least a cab driver wouldn't refuse to let me into the car.

"*Mademoiselle?*" The server's voice carried down the hallway. I'd been getting "*madame*" more often these days.

I hurried to the front of the café. I asked him if he'd seen a woman my age, blonde? It was implied that she'd probably be in the same state as me. My voice shook. I made at least two errors in just that sentence.

A small grimace crossed his face when he told me no. I could tell he knew something had gone very wrong for me over the past few hours, but he was as involved as he was willing to get.

I thanked him again and left. The taxi waited in the parking lot. I got in and asked the driver to take me to the train station. He turned on some club music with bass so loud it rattled the car doors. I noticed, for the first time, that I had a headache. I wondered briefly if I could've just walked here, but as we climbed onto the suspension bridge spanning the Loire estuary, which looked a lot like the Golden Gate Bridge, I realized I couldn't have walked this far with a huge backpack. How did I get here?

Each time I thought of Salomé, a hot rush of dread consumed me. Had she driven us here? Had she abandoned me? I reflexively touched my phone every few minutes, forgetting it was dead. But I had to wait.

There was something relieving about not being able to access all my thoughts, being forced to take each moment as it came. Something like drunkenness but not exactly. Under different circumstances I might've enjoyed it. I watched through the window as the driver wound through the unremarkable little town. The buildings were bland and uniform, like touristy beach towns in America. Even the smooth pavement lacked character. Maybe I'd suffered a head injury and lost my Francophilia. Maybe this was what France looked like to other people.

CHAPTER 16

The first thing I did in the train station was plug in my phone. There were only a few people milling about at this hour, and all of them passed right through to wait on the outside quai for the next train to Nantes. Once that train left, I was alone except for the workers in the Relay store.

As soon as my phone gathered enough battery to turn on, I connected to the *gare*'s Wi-Fi.

A few belated "Happy Birthday" texts came in. Three appeared from Salomé, two from yesterday at 7:38 p.m.:

Did you leave?

Désolée. Pardon, pardon. I wish we could talk about this.

Then one more at 10:22 p.m.:

Did you take the car?

Why was she sorry? Where was she? Which car, the Peugeot? I couldn't drive that car if I wanted to. The thought that whatever happened to me could've been Salomé's fault or intentional on her part felt so sacrilegious I refused to let it take root in my mind. I opened Salomé's contact and forced my trembling fingers to call her. A network tone followed by a French robot with a woman's voice told me I needed to purchase minutes. But I was on the Wi-Fi? I texted her instead:

> Are you okay? Where are you? I'm in Saint-Nazaire and I don't know why.

The text indicated that it was delivered, so her iPhone was on, wherever it was. This small piece of evidence, along with her texts, helped me relax a little. She was alive, and she was worried about me.

I opened my banking app. There was still almost a thousand dollars in my checking account, but there was a fifty-six-dollar pending charge from what appeared to be a restaurant. On my credit card, the most recent charge was the hotel in Nantes. Had I even been there? Maybe the restaurant charge was from my night in Paris when I got so drunk. My head throbbed. Had I become such a bad alcoholic that I'd gone on two benders in three days? Or had someone drugged me? Maybe Marco or one of his Magpies?

I looked for familiarity. I'd been in dozens of these small-town train stations. There were only four tracks, a few kiosks, a bathroom that cost fifty cents, a Nescafé vending machine, and a Relay store. I could navigate this.

Nobody was around, so I left my belongings unattended so my phone could keep charging and went into the Relay, where I bought a big bottle of water. When I got back to my phone, I had no new texts.

I'd performed the most functional tasks. Now I had to make a decision. I looked at the SNCF timetable on my phone. There was a TGV to Paris in ninety minutes. The last-minute fare was €109. The regional train to Châteaubriant in forty minutes would cost €22 and was over two hours long. But my hotel was in Nantes, right? If I went there now, I'd only have a few hours before checkout. I looked up hospitals on Google Maps. There was one not far from the train station. I'd have to get another cab. But I wasn't ready to go sit in a waiting room for hours, saying, "*Je ne sais pas.*"

Trying to recall anything prior to the serpent made me light-headed. I leaned my head against the wall behind me as I tried to collect my thoughts, but there were none to collect. The levee stood solid as ever. In a way I was thankful for its protection, the way a body might go into shock so it doesn't die from pain.

I felt the remnants of a huge surge of adrenaline and could still hear an echo in my skull of someone screaming—an angry scream, not a fearful one. I needed to talk to Salomé before making a decision. There were trains all day. I had electricity, Wi-Fi, and water. I was safe, for now.

A flash: Salomé smiling at me from across a table. When was that? The first night at the wine bar? Maybe she and I had gone out again, gotten wasted, and somehow got separated? Roofied, even?

Her last text haunted me.

Did you take the car?

I wanted to talk to someone, but it was 2:00 a.m. in Raleigh. I could call Kylie, but then I'd have to admit that I'd gotten into trouble, which for some reason she seemed to predict. I'd rather sit here for twenty-four hours until my flight home than admit to her that she was right.

I didn't want to wonder if Salomé was to blame here or to scrutinize myself for having trusted her. I just wanted to be right about somebody. Even flirting with the idea that Salomé had caused this made me almost physically ill. I wasn't that stupid.

Then I remembered the one other phone number I had. I opened my bag and dug the slip of paper out of my purse.

It's Courtney. Things got weird. I need help.

Seconds later, my screen lit up with an incoming FaceTime call. Tears burned the backs of my eyes when Callum's face appeared.

"Where are you?" he said immediately.

"The train station in Saint-Nazaire, which is pretty close to Nantes."

"How did you get there?"

"The train station or Saint-Nazaire?"

"I guess both."

"I took a taxi to the train station. It just seemed like somewhere I would have options. But I don't know how I left Salomé's house yesterday. I think Marco must've drugged me. I don't remember anything from last night."

"Jesus Christ, are you okay?"

"I mean, I'm alive. But I don't know where Salomé is. She texted me a few hours ago, so I think she's okay, but I don't know for sure. She hasn't responded to me this morning. Should I go to the police? The hospital?"

"Hold on, Courtney," he said, and his screen went fuzzy while he looked at a different app. "Did you say Saint-Nazaire?"

"Yes."

"Okay, yeah, I have a guy out there, I think. In the network."

"What network?"

Callum's face came back into view. "They call it 'La Résistance.' He didn't even try to pronounce it with a French accent. "Do you want me to call someone to come get you?"

Yes. That was my first instinct. I desperately wanted to be with someone. But I wasn't even sure I should trust Callum. The only person I wanted to see or talk to was Salomé.

"Courtney?"

"Yeah, sorry. I'm just shaken up. Who is this guy?"

"His name's Tim Diop. I met him here in London, actually, but he lives out there during the summers, from what I understand. He's safe, and he speaks fluent English and French. He'll know about the local police and whether or not you should go to them. I mean, if I were a secret society, the first people I'd try to recruit would be the local police, but he'll have a better understanding of that. He's connected to that journalist I told you about, ex-boyfriend or former boyfriend. But it's up to you. You could also just get on the next train to Paris," he said. "You have a friend there, right?"

If I got on the train, I might not have cell service or working Wi-Fi in case Salomé tried to get in touch with me. I wouldn't know whether or not she was okay for the entire two-and-a-half-hour trip, and then, if she wasn't okay, I'd be too far away to help.

"I want to speak to Salomé before I go anywhere else. And I think I'd like to have that guy's contact information at the very least. I want to have someone to call."

"Let me give him a call, and then I'll get right back with you. And if you haven't heard from Salomé in fifteen minutes or so, I can have Élise come up with a reason to call Nathalie and find out if she's there. We'll get this sorted."

"Okay, thank you."

"I want to tell you not to worry, but well . . . yeah." He hung up.

I felt a little better knowing I might not be alone for the next several hours. I looked around the train station. It was still quite empty, though a few more people had trickled in, all staring at their phones while they waited for the next train.

What happened to us? Was the sun beating down on her, lost

somewhere, separated from her phone and wallet? What if she *was* on the beach this morning, just a bit farther down, and I hadn't seen her? Her phone could've been on the floorboard of some stranger's car, dinging with my texts while she regained consciousness on the beach. Or whatever they put into my arm, they could've given her too much . . .

I remembered Salomé calling me just after my meeting with Élise and Callum. The comfort I found in her voice all but erased Callum's warning. She asked me to come back to Châteaubriant, ostensibly because it would be safer for everyone if Marco saw her leave with me. If I was being honest with myself, she probably could've asked me to come back because Nathalie had just made a batch of cookies, and my stupid, lovestruck ass would've gone.

What if she still worked for Marco? Had she lured me right back into his trap? I had to close my eyes to stop the little pattern on the linoleum floor from swirling.

My phone vibrated. She was FaceTiming me. I answered immediately.

Her face was framed by white pillows. Thank God she was okay.

"Salomé," I said, nearly breathless.

"Hi," she said. Her tone was somewhat distant, her eyes puffy.

"Where are you?"

"At my house. Where are you?"

I wished she'd show a flicker of emotion so I'd know if she'd worried about me the way I'd worried about her. "I'm at the train station in Saint-Nazaire. I woke up on the beach. I'm so confused . . ."

"Did you take the car?"

"No, of course not."

She sighed. "This is what I tell them."

"Wait, so Marco and Nathalie think I took her car?" What the fuck?

"Yes, this is what she said last night. After you left she flipped out again. She has never flipped two times before. I know she is not thinking right, but it is . . . what's the word . . . suspicious? I mean, the car really is gone, and so are you."

I was scrambling to organize the information, but it still hurt that she suspected me, even a little. Though I'd just had similar thoughts about her. I remembered what Kylie said: *It sounds like a setup, right?*

"I can't even drive a stick shift. What happened last night?"

She recounted us waking up from our nap and deciding we were hungry. Nathalie still wasn't back with the car, so we went to get some food in Châteaubriant—none of which I remembered.

"You surprised me, you smoked two cigarettes . . ."

My hand flew to my throat, which was still scratchy. "I've never smoked a cigarette in my life."

"I mean, I watched you do it. I found it weird. It didn't seem like you."

Had my throat not felt the way it did, I wouldn't have believed her. But there was an undeniable plausibility to her words. I really had no justification to question her story.

"What happened next?"

"You don't remember anything?"

"I swear to God."

"We shared a bottle of wine, but we weren't like, shit-faced, you know?"

I glanced at the puncture in my elbow, still unable to give it a close look. I'd never heard of intravenous roofies, but it must've been something like that. "What happened after dinner?"

"We came back here to get our bags. Marco was here, and he started screaming at us, kind of like Maman when she flips except he was just being himself . . ."

I felt the echoing remnants of the timbre of his voice and flinched.

"I kind of remember that, I think. Why was he screaming? What did we do wrong?"

"He was saying things about how we think we are so clever, but he knows everything that's going on. I think he was taking cocaine. I've seen him scream before but not like this. I did not believe he was doing this in front of you. So I was screaming back at him, and then you were gone. And I think maybe you went to get your stuff from the room, but you were gone when I tried to look for you. I was so embarrassed, I was crying. I understand Marco is not your problem and you are a very new friend, so why should you stay while a madman is screaming at you? But still, I felt abandoned that you went to the hotel without me. We had a good dinner. At the same time I am thinking, Oh sheet, she decided not to spend the night with me because I kissed her. I looked for you everywhere, I even walked down to the *gare*. I went to the cathedral, then back to the restaurant, and to the wine bar. I walked around until the sun set. The whole time I am calling you until my phone died. Then I went home."

"Hold on a second." I opened my call log. Forty-three missed calls from Salomé. As unsettling as it was to see forty-three calls I didn't answer, it was relieving to see her story add up.

I went back to the FaceTime screen. "It's like you're telling me a story I'm not a part of. I would never leave without at least saying goodbye to you, no matter what Marco did. When did your mom say I stole the car?"

"When I got back from looking for you, Marco and my mom were flipping out, screaming at each other. Maman was accusing you of stealing the car, but it really was gone. I went into my room and was hiding all night. I was so embarrassed for what you saw, and I just wish you took me with you. I was very sad."

"I think Marco must've drugged me while we were napping, because that's the last thing I remember. And then I woke up on the beach." I closed my eyes and tried to keep from crying, but my next few words still came out strained. "I'm freaking out. I don't know what to do or where to go. My bag is with me, so it seems like I was trying to go to the hotel I booked in Nantes."

"On the *bitch*?"

"Yeah, by that skeleton statue." I'd said this already but she obviously hadn't caught it before.

Something new crossed her face, like she may have put something together that she didn't want to tell me. "How did he give you drugs?"

"When I woke up, I found this," I said, flipping the camera to show the inside of my elbow.

"What?" Her eyebrows knitted together.

I flipped back to the front camera, now a little more aware of how terrible I looked. The puncture was almost all of the concrete evidence I had, but I suddenly felt ashamed by it. Except for the sand still clinging to various parts of my body, I looked like one of those girls stumbling home from a club in Berlin while everyone else was on their way to work. I wondered if her suspicion had now turned to me, thinking that I was some loose-cannon fuckup who got blackout drunk and ran away from a party to go do heroin. But a part of me almost wanted that to be the case so I could do anything to fix it rather than sit with so many unknowns.

"Do you feel okay? Like physically?"

"Now that I've had some coffee and water, I just feel a little hungover, besides the fact that my memory is almost blank except for a couple of flashes. I think I should go to the hospital," I said.

She bit her bottom lip and looked away from the camera, trying to maintain her composure. She looked back at me and said, "I can't believe this. Is anything missing?"

I was sure she meant my cash or passport, but I said, "I have all my organs, if that's what you mean."

Her face softened, a small sound in her throat to acknowledge my joke. I liked that my humor landed with her, even under these circumstances. Her presence on the other end of the phone was a balm to my chafed nerves. I was able to take a deep breath and tell myself everything would be okay. I felt the phantom remnants of her touch—a cool emptiness in my palms where her hand should have been. I knew it made empirical sense to suspect her more, but I only had the instinct to be close to her. The idea that she could be behind this mess just felt wrong. I said, "I don't want to go to the hospital alone. Will you come with me? I really don't want to try to explain in French what happened."

She nodded, thank God. Her screen paused as she searched on her phone. "Of course I will. Nantes would be better, I think. We can meet at the *gare* and go to the hospital. And then you will have many direct trains to Paris for later."

"Yes, let's meet in Nantes," I said, glancing up at the timetable. "There's a train every half hour from here."

"Okay, will be like eleven-thirty before I will be there. The tram-train is not running today. I will get a TER, since I can't ask to borrow my mother's car. It is not here."

She paused for a moment, then said, "How did you get to the *gare*?"

"A taxi. I swear, nothing like this has ever happened to me before. I'm usually very organized." I didn't know what else to say.

"I know," she said. "I believe you. It will be okay, Cour-ten-ey."

"Okay. I will meet you at the train station in Nantes."

She ended the call.

I looked around. There were a few more people now. A man in his late forties with very short hair and glasses walked by so closely he almost brushed my knee with his messenger bag. He looked out of the window at the quai and made an odd noise deep in his throat. Then he sat in a seat directly opposite me, and placed his bag at his feet.

There was a flourish of crinkling as he pulled a pastry from inside the bag, eating it directly from the small paper sack.

He looked at me. I dropped my gaze to my sand-crusted feet. I realized I'd been staring at him with a look of absolute terror. I needed to chill out, which would be hard to do for obvious reasons. The phone in my hand vibrated and I almost leapt from my seat.

From Callum:

> Tim is coming to meet you right now. I told him you were at the train station. He said 2 minutes.

I pressed the soles of my feet into the floor to ground myself, spelling *serrer*, but my legs still trembled. I wanted to wrap my arms around myself, curl into a little ball, and just cry, but I didn't want to draw any attention. Why did this guy have to sit across from me? Was he watching me? Following me?

With a shaking hand, I uncapped my water bottle and tried to guide it to my lips, but I spilled it down the front of my shirt. The man saw me and averted his eyes. He had to be a Magpie. He might've been following me all the way from the beach. There was no way he'd gotten close enough to drop a tracking device in my bag while I wasn't looking, right? I had left it unattended for a minute while I bought the water. But he hadn't been nearby yet, right? These people were probably so sophisticated with their tracking methods, I'd never realize if they were actually after me. Why had I been so stupid as to leave my bag unattended?

I heard the urgent squeal of a rubber-soled shoe on linoleum behind me. I looked over my shoulder and saw a young Black man walking quickly, scanning the station. His eyes locked on me, and he came straight for me. Please let this be Tim.

"Courtney?" he said with a British accent, rounding the corner of the row of seats.

"Tim?"

He sat next to me and extended a hand. Mine probably felt clammy, so I pulled it away quickly. "Sorry." Before he could say anything I leaned in and said, "I need to get out of here, and I need to get rid of all my stuff, I think it's bugged, I think this guy is following me!"

Tim glanced across the aisle at the man, who had since finished his pastry and was still looking at us. Tim put his warm hand on my shoulder. "Let's go outside, yeah?" He stood and picked up my backpack. I unplugged my phone and followed him through the station's automatic doors.

The second Tim stopped on the sidewalk, I ripped open my backpack's zipper. He let it slide off his shoulders. Digging through my clothes, I said, "That guy back there, he was staring at me, and I think he might've put something in my bag . . ."

Tim dropped to his knees and helped me pull my clothes out of the bag. Just the small suggestion that he might believe what I told him almost made me cry. I covered my face with my hands and tried to breathe, but my shoulders started shaking. No, keep it together. Don't draw any more attention.

I looked up and met Tim's eyes over my gutted backpack. He was young, maybe only twenty or so. The look he gave me was rooted in understanding, not skepticism.

"Hey, let me tell you something that might make you feel better," he said.

"What?"

He gently reached to the side of my head and pulled a large strand of kelp out from the back of my hair. I had no idea how I'd missed it in the café mirror and FaceTime.

"Maybe that's why that guy was staring at me," I said.

"I reckon that's why," Tim said. "You definitely look like you've just had the roughest night of your life."

"You're right, that actually does make me feel better." I looked down at my stuff on the dirty sidewalk, too humbled to be embarrassed.

"I got this." Tim repacked my bag while I tried to calm my breathing. "Are you alright? I mean, physically. Are you injured at all?"

"The only thing that seems to be wrong is this," I said, extending my elbow so he could see the mark. "Should I go to the police?"

His face dropped when he saw it, but he didn't seem entirely surprised. "Yeah, I don't like that." He zipped my bag up and we both stood. "I won't tell you what to do. I'll just give you the information I know. I dealt with the police a lot after my friend disappeared, and they couldn't have been more unhelpful."

"What if the needle wasn't clean?"

"I totally get why you'd worry about that. But also, these are pretty sophisticated scientists, assuming it was the higher-tier Magpies we're dealing with, which I do. They'd use a sterile needle. They just would."

I could feel my bottom lip shaking but I couldn't stop it. I reached out and grabbed his hand, unsure how he'd react. He clasped my hand in both of his, warm and dry and grounding.

He leaned closer, making sure to meet my eyes. "If you want to go to the hospital, I will take you on my scooter, but I can't go in with you. I'm sorry. I need to be careful of how much attention I draw to La Résistance, at least for the time being."

I nodded, letting go of his hands. "No, Salomé is going to take me to the hospital in Nantes."

"Salomé is coming? Salomé Leduc?"

"I'm meeting her in Nantes in a little while. Do you know her?"

"I don't." There was a hint of trepidation in his voice. After a pause, he said, "Well, I know it's been a harrowing morning for you, so it's totally understandable if you don't feel up to going to a stranger's house while you wait. But I thought I'd offer to take you to my father's apartment so you could get more cleaned up. If you aren't comfortable with that, we can go to a café around here. Either way, I'd like to make a record of whatever you can tell me about what happened to you."

"Where is the apartment?"

"It's just round the corner, two streets over. No pressure."

He clasped his hands in front and waited for me to think it over. Not that my brain was functioning. I knew it was stupid to willingly go into a stranger's apartment after what I'd just been through. Tim seemed trustworthy, but what did I know? Though Callum appeared to be on the right side of this mess, and he vouched for Tim, which was a big vote of confidence. My other option was to go back into the train station.

"I'd like to get cleaned up," I said. I couldn't handle fearing every person who showed up in my line of sight until I got back to Salomé.

We walked away from the train station. "Is anyone following us?" I asked.

"Stop looking around," Tim said. "People are going to look at you for acting weird."

I tried to scan more casually. "I'm probably just paranoid."

"With good reason," Tim said. "They do follow people."

"Why?"

"Intimidation, information. I don't think it's ever happened to me. But Callum and Élise always get trailed, he's told me." We stopped at an intersection. Tim pressed the button to allow us to cross.

Across the street, servers were setting up terrasse umbrellas at a café. The morning traffic had just picked up. The flow of cars came to a stop in front of us, and the light changed for us to cross.

"Are you afraid they'll follow you?" I asked once we were on the other side.

Tim reached into his pocket and withdrew a set of keys. "Yeah, sometimes. But if they are, I don't want them to know that I know." He approached a nondescript door between a pharmacy and a lawyer's office.

"We're already here?"

"This is it," he said.

I followed Tim up a narrow, winding staircase, my eyes perfectly level with his butt. His father's apartment was on the fourth floor. Climbing past the second floor, the air got hotter.

"It's going to be unbearable up here this week," Tim said. "The fans do nothing. I'm starting to wonder why I don't live in London during the summer and here the rest of the year." He unlocked the door and held it open for me.

Their apartment was small and sparsely decorated. Thin red curtains were pulled across the windows to block out the sun, which gave the whole room a rusty tint. There were a few framed pictures on the tables on either side of the black leather couch, but the walls were bare. A massive bookcase took up an entire wall on one side of the room, every shelf stuffed with books and papers. A tall fan near the one open window blew warm air around. It smelled like they'd eaten fish last night, the air still thick with an oily tinge.

Tim set my bag on the floor and rolled his shoulders a few times. He went into the bathroom and returned with a folded towel. "Take your time. We'll talk once you've cleaned up," he said, handing it to me.

The towel was so warm it felt like it had come out of the dryer. I thought of Luke and of who I was just weeks prior, snuggled in the warmth of his laundry, only disturbed by my own mind.

I took my backpack into the bathroom and shut the door. I was glad to shower but not thrilled to be alone. There was nothing odd about the bathroom, no objects that could double as a camera. I undressed and checked out what I could see in the small mirror. No additional scrapes or bruises, though my shoulders and neck were bright red from sunburn.

I grabbed the shower attachment and sat on the floor of the tub, too tired to stand. I squirted some apple-scented Le Petit Marseillais body wash into my hands and lathered it through my hair. The puncture on my arm stung as suds ran over it. Someone had been close enough to my body to insert a needle into my arm without my knowledge. I knew I was probably washing evidence down the drain, but it wasn't the first time.

A moment from last night hit me in a flash. I'd been in a car. Wipers scraping across a dry windshield, a mistaken flick of the lever. Moths splattering across the glass. There were no other cars on the road. A raspberry. I couldn't look directly at it, only sideways.

A car was the only means of transportation that made sense. A train would've taken hours. Châteaubriant was far too small to hail a passing taxi. There wasn't an Uber receipt in my inbox or a charge on my card. The only thing that made sense was that I'd been in a car and that, if I'd had a plan to return the way I came, it didn't work out. According to Salomé, both Nathalie and Marco had been at the house last night. So either I'd magically learned to drive a stick shift and stole the car, or there was someone else involved that neither of us remembered.

I quickly turned the water off and got out of the tub. I wrapped myself in the towel and stared into my open bag. The skirt I'd had on for several days was covered in sand. I dusted it off over the trash can but still made a bit of a mess on the bathroom floor. My legs were past spiky, but I didn't care. At my current point on Maslow's Hierarchy of Needs, "shave to be publicly presentable" was not a priority. That was kind of nice, but I wished I hadn't had to be abducted to get there.

I chose a sleeveless top that wasn't too dirty. I dressed quickly and went back into the living room. Tim sat at a barstool at the kitchen counter holding a half-eaten apple between his thumb and third finger. With his other hand, he scrolled his phone.

"Better?" he said, looking up.

"Much, thanks." I reluctantly glanced at the puncture. It was bruising slightly. I had to brace my hand against the wall to steady myself. Maybe whoever drugged me was also the driver of the car.

"Do you think something went in, or blood came out?" Tim asked, watching me.

"Something went in. A drug. My memories of last night are almost nonexistent." I shivered with disgust.

"Take some deep breaths."

I struggled to control my breathing. "I'm just . . . I'm lucky to be alive right now."

Tim nodded, his eyes sympathetic. "Yeah, mate. You don't even know the half of it. Can I get you anything? Something to eat?"

I sat on the couch. "No, I think I'm too panicked to eat anything."

"Makes sense. Coffee?"

My fingers were shaking, but I accepted. Tim threw the apple core away and crossed the kitchen, where he popped a Nespresso pod into a little machine, which rumbled against the countertop at the volume of an airplane engine. Tim steadied it with his hand to mute it slightly. When it finished, he brought me the tiny steaming cup. "Okay. Are you ready to talk?"

"I guess so."

"Basically, you have two options. You can tell me what happened and I can make sure you safely get on a train to wherever you're going, or you can learn more. But that would mean joining La Résistance."

"I don't even live here," I said.

"I know. You don't have to."

I thought about it for a minute. My vision was still shaky, maybe more from a lack of sleep than anything. I didn't feel like I'd be able to retain any real information given to me.

"Have you ever picked anyone else up? Like me?"

"No," Tim said. "But my dad has."

"Who was that?"

Tim smiled. "So are you joining?"

I exhaled deeply. "You won't tell me anything unless I 'join'? Do I have to sign anything or something?"

Tim laughed. "No. It's not a highly organized vigilante group or anything. It's more a group of people deemed as 'safe' by this guy Bernard. I'll tell you about him later if you join. There are probably twenty of us or so in northwestern France, and a few more around the rest of the country, and then Callum up in London."

It seemed borderline offensive to use the name "La Résistance" for something so informal. Though the informality was what made me feel at all comfortable. Tim wasn't asking for my signature in blood or for any type of collateral. "I feel like I'm supposed to ask if there's a catch?"

"Yeah, the catch is that you have to realize how fucking dangerous all of this is, and you have to grapple with that. But obviously you haven't avoided danger by not knowing."

I just looked at him.

"And, of course, you can't reveal our identities in any compromising ways . . . but that should go without saying. And it may not apply to you, not living here and all, but if another member calls you like Callum called me this morning, you do everything you can to make yourself available to help."

"Okay," I said. "Tell me what you know."

"Welcome to the Resistance." He opened his arms to form a wingspan and looked from side to side, smiling.

"Is this the headquarters or something?"

He laughed again. "No, sorry. I'm just joking."

"I'm not in the headspace to pick up on humor."

"Okay, well here's how I got to know about it all. Last summer when I was here I met someone on a dating app. He lived in Nantes. He was a reporter for a regional publication for the Pays de la Loire, but he wanted to cover more serious stuff."

"I can relate," I said.

"I really liked him, but there was a bit of an age gap, and I don't live here year-round, so we decided to keep it casual until I graduated from uni. We texted a bit, FaceTimed once or twice after I went back to London. And he told me he was working on this huge story about a secret society that originated in the 1930s, but the paper wouldn't touch it, so he'd started reporting about it on a personal blog."

"This is Loïc, right?" I forgot his last name. "Callum told me to check out his blog. I looked it up on the train back from Paris. And . . . holy shit, Loïc disappeared, didn't he?"

Tim nodded. "He stopped returning my texts, so I figured he'd met someone else and felt weird that we were still talking. But I'd check his blog, not just because I wanted to keep up with him, but because I'd put it together that the group he was reporting on was this group my dad had warned me about when I was a kid. They're called the Magpies."

"Really? You knew about them before?"

"Yeah, their rhetoric is super racist and xenophobic, so the immigrant communities are aware of them in general. My dad's Senegalese. He's a French citizen now but still, the Magpies are anti-immigrant, particularly for those who aren't white. When I was a kid, my dad was just like, 'If you ever hear people talking about magpies or immortality, get the fuck out.' Except he didn't say 'fuck,' 'cause I was like, eight or something. And he never really said much else about it. It felt more like superstition than truth to me back then. It wasn't until Loïc started writing about it that I pieced together that this was the group Papa had warned me about."

"So Salomé's sister told me that 'magpie' is a reference to Charles Lindbergh."

"Clever, isn't it," Tim said flatly. "Yeah, it's definitely tied to America. They get a ton of funding from these Silicon Valley billionaires who are trying to live forever."

"Callum mentioned that. But I don't really understand how a billionaire's personal quest for longevity or immortality or whatever could affect French politics."

"It's definitely a long game they're playing. They send money wherever they can promote white nationalism. This is like, you know, funding news channels, paying pundits to say certain things, funding lobbyists to keep business regulations as minimal as possible, et cetera. They stoke fear within working-class people through social media bots and skewed news stories, trying to get them to vote a certain way. Then they bribe the local politicians they help to get elected, which translates to a national level, and then an international level, and before you know it, the entire world is set up for them to be royalty, right? They can exploit whomever to mine their electric car batteries and underpay the workers in their warehouses and fire everyone the second they start to unionize, but it won't matter, because they own the news stations and the local governments, right? There's nobody to stop them."

"I mean I get that part, but I still don't understand the immortality piece of it."

"I said it was a *long game*. Like *forever* long. They're trying to get their guys in office and keep them in office for as long as humanly possible—or like, as long as *inhumanly* possible—to keep this little club of the world's richest people as rich as possible, literally forever.

Like imagine that the current US president could live for another five hundred years and just keep on stuffing his friends' pockets while they also got to live forever?"

I reflexively made a scoffing sound, though I didn't mean to be dismissive. Tim looked at me and said, "I'm serious. I know it sounds absurd, but you have to believe that these people would say yes to this arrangement, no matter the cost—and I don't just mean money. And Marco Angevine supposedly holds the key to immortality that all these guys want. Which he hopes to package and sell for a sticker price of a billion euros."

"What's the key? Surely not ViPi?"

"This is what Loïc wanted to figure out. But they're super secretive, as you can imagine. They're not easy to infiltrate. So, a few weeks after Loïc stopped returning my texts, I noticed that he had stopped updating his blog, and then it disappeared. I tried calling and found out his phone had been disconnected. I got kind of suspicious so I told my dad. He's a professor at the University of Nantes. He's pretty well connected. He looked into it and found that Loïc's mother had filed a missing persons report. My dad got in contact with her and she told him the police got into Loïc's computer and determined that he had up and moved to Peru to live with this woman he'd been messaging with for months. And of course his mother knew that wouldn't happen. I guess whatever Magpie was attempting to catfish him didn't do enough due diligence to find out that he is gay, but Loïc was obviously just playing along."

"Wow," I said.

"Oh, the story's not over. So Loïc's mom gave my dad the name of a man who had reached out to her about Loïc, and this guy, Bernard, was how my dad ultimately joined La Résistance. But here's the crazy part. My dad spoke with Bernard for the first time one afternoon, and literally two days later, he gets woken up in the middle of the night by

Bernard calling. There was a girl who was found disoriented, walking across that huge suspension bridge between Saint-Nazaire and the beach at Saint-Brevin. She was taken to the hospital."

"Did she have . . . ?" I gestured to the inside of my elbow.

"Yeah," Tim said. "I'm gathering that it's a thing they do. But I'm not sure what the purpose is just yet."

"What happened to the girl?"

"She was a student at the University of Nantes and a reporter for the school paper. Somehow she was looking into the Magpies for an article. She didn't take any of my dad's classes, but she knew who he was. He went to sit with her in the hospital, where he recorded her testimony, as Bernard asked him to. She was so desperate to leave that she asked Dad to drive her to the airport the next day, and she went back home to Switzerland. She withdrew from all of her classes and they haven't heard from her since."

"Who is this Bernard guy?"

"He told my dad he was Thierry Leduc's colleague. I think this '*résistance*' thing is half personal vendetta for his friend, and half out of an ethical concern."

We both fell silent for a moment. I didn't know what to think.

"Loïc's blog? It's still up," I said.

"Yeah, that's me. I assume some Magpie was assigned the task of scrubbing the internet of Loïc's name. I made a free WordPress account and put it back up at a cybercafe. Well, just that one blog, though. It's the only one I had, because I'd copy/pasted it once and emailed it to my dad. There are also some weird videos of Marco that make him look much less polished than he prefers, and I reupload those whenever they get pulled."

"I definitely thought that Loïc's website looked pretty shitty," I said. "No offense."

"It looked better when he kept it," Tim said. "Finished?" He nodded toward my empty espresso cup. I handed it to him. He walked over to the sink and rinsed it. He stood with his back to me for several seconds after he turned off the faucet.

"I'm really sorry about Loïc," I said. "He sounds like a great guy."

Without facing me, Tim said, "He is."

"Do you think you'll be able to find him?"

Tim turned, his expression more vulnerable than I'd expected. "I have to try."

"I'm sorry," I said again. I wished there was something more specific to say.

Tim cleared his throat. "So I'm unclear as to how you got involved with all of this in the first place."

I told him how I met Salomé on the plane. He would probably think I was insane for traveling with a stranger, or for going back to Châteaubriant when she asked. But as I spoke, his face didn't betray any judgment. "Élise told me that Salomé worked for ViPi years ago. I looked it up but barely found anything. She's not involved anymore," I said. Then I quickly added, "She hates the whole thing."

Tim considered this information. "It makes sense that he'd try to recruit her, with her lineage to Thierry and everything. That's his claim to legitimacy. So, wait. Have you met Marco Angevine?"

"Yes, only briefly."

"What was he like?"

"He was welcoming. Charming, even. Salomé said he should have a César for it. She told me that the day before, he'd freaked out at her mother for buying a train ticket that was actually for me, and that last night he'd screamed at her and accused me of stealing their car, which I don't even know how to drive."

Tim pursed his lips together and nodded slowly. "Is he crazy or on drugs or just playing out of the abuser's playbook?"

"I've wondered the same thing. Salomé mentioned that she thought he might do a lot of cocaine. But something else weird is that Salomé asked me not to write about her family. She told me it was because reporters had a feast over her dad's career downfall in the early 2000s, but it makes me wonder if she knows about Loïc."

"Write about it? What do you do?"

"I'm a journalist."

Tim's eyes widened. "Jesus Christ, when were you going to say that?"

"I'm not an investigative reporter. I just write for a local newsmagazine. I shouldn't even call myself that. It's a reflex or something."

He was quiet for a few seconds. "Well, if you don't write about it, you probably won't end up like Loïc. But that makes me think that she knows about him."

I turned these thoughts over for a few seconds without coming up with anything to say.

Tim said, "Do you want to write about it?"

"Fuck no. I mean, I'd love to see it get exposed, but I'm not the right person to do that."

Tim propped his chin on his steepled fingers, elbows resting on the kitchen counter. I'd read somewhere that body language experts claimed people only did that when they felt superior to someone else, but it didn't seem that way with Tim. "Loïc was at a little regional publication, and he took this on."

"If you're looking for the next Loïc to carry this torch, I'm only going to disappoint you."

"No, I don't need to find someone to do it. *I'm* going to do it. Not just for Loïc, but for everybody who stands to be harmed by this group."

"Are you a journalist?"

Tim smiled. "I'm going into my final year of an audio journalism degree. I'm developing a deep-dive narrative-style podcast like *Serial* as my final project. To be honest I've been thinking about it for a while, and even talked to Loïc about it. He had been on board to help write it." He became more animated when he said, "This whole thing sprang out of the alliance between Lindbergh and Carrel. You're the American piece here. And I can be the French piece, *and* the British piece, 'cause Lord knows they're probably implicated too. And we can trace the roots of this back to our countries' gross imperialist pasts . . ."

I closed my eyes, resting my head on the couch. Colors danced across the backs of my eyelids. I felt that I could fall asleep at any moment.

"Okay, then what? We'll just disappear too?" I said, my eyes still closed.

"There's always a certain amount of danger that comes with the job, wouldn't you say?"

I looked at him. "I think it might shock you to learn what absolute insipid fluff I'm paid to write."

"See? Don't you want to change that?"

"I've been telling myself that as long as I'm being paid to write, I'm winning. You know, while that work is still available."

"Look, I've thought a lot about it. And while laying low might seem like the safer choice, I also think it's reasonable to assume that they already have a target on my dad's back, especially after that university reporter incident. I don't want to just sit around and wait for them to go after him. I want to do something substantial enough to actually call attention to them."

"I don't know. This sounds like way too big a risk for a school project."

Tim came and sat next to me on the couch, leaning toward me. "No, no, let me be clear about this. It would *satisfy the requirements* for my capstone project. But my advisor has deep ties to the BBC, and many alumni from this program have gone on to get their shows aired. It's not just for a grade. This is probably the best shot at breaking the story that I'll have for years, unless I get a great job right out of school. But the project has to be good enough to really turn his head, you know? And this is."

I didn't know what to say. It did sound like a great project. It also sounded exhausting and dangerous. Suddenly the fact that he'd done so much to help me this morning felt cheapened. "So you're doing this resistance stuff for your career? Not to . . ." I stopped myself before I said, "help people," but the implication was strong enough.

"It's not an either/or. So Loïc turned me on to this American journalist, Ronan Farrow?"

"Yeah, the Harvey Weinstein exposé guy?"

"I have mad respect for him. He's become a bit of an idol for me."

"Yeah, I agree. But his parents are movie stars. He has a certain level of protection . . . probably physical and financial, that affords him the ability to take that kind of risk. I don't really have that. Do you?"

Tim shook his head. "But that's the best thing about him. He could've grown up to be such an entitled nepotism guy who like, founded a tequila company or something, and had nothing else to show for himself. But he fucking blew this case out of the water, taking down one of the most powerful people in Hollywood, and on top of that, he's an out gay man. I feel like he's cleared the path for a new level of integrity in journalism, don't you?"

Tim was right. I read Farrow's piece in *The New Yorker* last fall. But I'd spent the following months, during which the men we used to admire toppled like dominos, paying much more attention to the hordes of average women with stories like mine, not focusing so much on the journalism aspect of the #MeToo movement. That was probably more evidence to the fact that I wasn't cut out to be a real journalist.

"Aren't you a little interested in it? This could be a career-making story for you," he said.

I was so tired. "I thought it was your project?"

"We're encouraged to collaborate, because that's what happens in the real world. I'd produce and host. You'd write. I'm a good storyteller but not the best writer."

I didn't want to tell him what I was thinking: There was no way I'd risk my safety for someone else's senior thesis project. But wasn't he risking his safety for me? I said something equally true. "I know this is going to sound pathetic, but it's more important for me to not betray Salomé than it is for me to have a career-defining story. Is that insane?"

Tim sighed. "It's not insane. But I think that if she saw an exposé of the Magpies as a betrayal, then she isn't the type of person you should be loyal to."

I shook my head slowly. "It's more than that. Her mother is in danger. I think Salomé would love to see the Magpies fall and ViPi shutter. And she probably has all the information needed to do that—or at least, access to the information. But she's treading very carefully so her mother doesn't have to bear the consequences."

He looked at me for a long moment. "Of all the—let's call them 'characters'—in this story, she's the one I know the least about. Did anything weird happen with her? Do you have any reason to suspect that she brought you into this intentionally?"

"I don't think so." I put my head back and closed my eyes again for a few more seconds of almost-rest.

Tim said, "Do you think she *wants* you to write about it? Be the person to pull the trigger, so to speak?"

I cracked my eyes open and stared at the ceiling. I was getting tired of this journalism-saves-the-day conversation. "No. I don't even remember when she found out I was a journalist. She may have already invited me before I told her." Why was it so hard for people to believe that we just liked each other right away?

"Have you looked through your phone for clues from last night? Any recent searches in Maps? Social posts? Sent emails or numbers you dialed?"

I'd almost forgotten that deciding whether or not to expose the Magpies wasn't our most pressing matter. "A little. Salomé called me forty-three times last night after we got separated." I lifted my eyes to make sure he was listening. "So that part of her story checks out. I didn't pay for a taxi and it doesn't seem like I've spent any cash. But let me see if there's anything else." I looked through the apps he suggested. My last internet searches were the etymology of *cauchemar*, Alexis Carrel's Wikipedia page, Salomé's ViPi job, and those clips of Marco. Besides that, there were no clues.

I found Loïc's WordPress blog and copied a paragraph into Google Translate.

Under the Guise of Science
By Loïc Duchêne
7 January 2018

Thierry Leduc was a polarizing figure in life, and more so after his death. His scientific advances were inherited by his wife, herself a scientist, whose reputation is much more polarizing than that of her late husband. Nathalie Leduc is a physics prodigy born in Paris. During her stay at the higher superior school in Paris, she received several awards in many disciplines, including physics, computation, and biology. His thesis, which won him the Panofsky Prize for physics, is undeniably a masterpiece, although it has drawn criticism for being unethical. Now, separated from education and most of society, Leduc's genius is hijacked, used to inspire well-meaning and uneducated citizens to trust and invest in the sect of the Magpie.

"Huh," I said.

"What?"

"I'm just reading Loïc's article 'Sous le couvert de la science.' I put it into Google Translate. I'm too tired to try to read it in French. At first I thought it was talking about Thierry's thesis and awards, but now I'm realizing that the translation should've said '*her* thesis, which won *her* the Panofsky Prize.'"

French possessive pronouns changed for the gender of the noun, not the gender of the subject. I hadn't realized Nathalie was a scientist, but it made sense. Salomé had mentioned she was from "a family of scientists" and that Nathalie was an abstract thinker.

Leduc's genius is hijacked.

"Yeah, she's a physicist. Or was a physicist. That is well documented," Tim said. "So you spent time with Nathalie too, right?"

"Yeah, and it was . . . weird. Nathalie was starving herself. And I was having these horrible nightmares, and woke up sleepwalking once, and then Nathalie accused me of stealing something of Thierry's." Just as I said this, my screen lit up with an incoming FaceTime call.

"It's Callum," I said to Tim, and accepted the call.

"Are you with Tim?" Callum asked.

"Yes, I'm at his apartment."

"Good. Hey, mate," he called to Tim.

"Hiya," Tim said back.

"I've called in sick to work today," Callum said. "And I dunno. I just got a spark of inspiration and called one of the IT guys at the office and paid him to hack into Loïc's Google Drive."

"He was able to get in?" Tim asked. "I tried a few times but wasn't able to."

"It was harder than most, he said. There were a few extra layers of protection on it, but he's a pro."

"The police didn't go through his Google Drive?" I asked.

"I don't think so," Tim said. "They said he bought a plane ticket to Peru and checked into his flight, so that's all the evidence they needed to prove that it wasn't foul play." Tim rolled his eyes. He leaned into the camera's frame. "What do you see?"

"He hasn't checked his email in months. The inbox is full. Also, he had all of the Peruvian woman's emails sorted into a folder called 'Mariana'—in quotes, because obviously he knew she was fake. I haven't seen anything else of interest, but I'm just now getting into his unpublished blog drafts. I'm using Google Translate, which is better than it was a few years ago, but it's still kind of confusing."

"Actually I was just doing the same," I said.

Callum clicked around on a computer. "So Loïc has twelve unpublished blog drafts. And one is very concerning."

"Why?" I asked.

"There's going to be a summit. An immortality training. In Châteaubriant in August. Loïc had even pieced together an incomplete guest list, or at least what it was before January."

"Who's on it?" Tim asked.

"It's five guys. The three Americans I've never heard of. They're venture capitalists and tech guys, apparently."

He listed three of the blandest-yet-douchiest names imaginable. I'd never heard of any of them. I shook my head and looked at Tim, who did the same.

Callum continued, "There's a Brit who calls himself the BioBard, whom I've looked up and found to be just a banker's son, but he's started up a whole social media movement around longevity, where he's doing all these fringe treatments and publicly logging his bio-data and has millions of followers. I couldn't imagine being remotely interested in the resting heart rate of a twenty-nine-year-old keto-carnivore who sleeps in a hyperbaric chamber, but evidently a lot of people are.

Anyway, I wasn't surprised to see that tech mogul, Sinclair, who's trying to fuck everything up for the whole planet."

"He's the only one I've heard of," I said. Sinclair was the cherry on top of the Silicon Valley tech bros—the one who was closest to launching a space tourism company. Of course he wanted immortality; he was planning to colonize Mars and would certainly want to be the King Martian for much longer than the twenty years or so left in his normal human lifespan. I knew that much about him, but realized I strangely didn't know if Sinclair was his first name or his last. I'd never cared.

"So basically, whatever Marco has to offer these guys is so cutting-edge and valuable that they're all coming to meet him in Châteaubriant in less than two months?" I said.

"Appears so," said Callum.

"Can you send me the Google Drive contents?" Tim asked.

"As long as you know that everything you do on Google is highly traceable. I keep getting so engrossed in this and then remembering that I'm walking right into the crosshairs of something I don't understand. I haven't even told Élise about all this Loïc stuff," Callum said. "She is going to be livid. I've promised more than once to stay out of it."

Tim's jaw muscles pulsed. "I want to see it," he said. "I don't fucking care about these assholes. What if he left some clues? What if we can find him?"

"Okay, I think you should," Callum said. "I'll send you the login information." The screen went blurry for a few seconds, and Tim's phone buzzed with an incoming text. "So, Courtney, what's your next move?"

"I'm going to meet Salomé in Nantes in about an hour."

"Really?" Callum said, an edge to his tone.

"She was going to take me to the hospital to get my arm checked out. I mean . . . should I not?"

"Sorry, I don't mean to tell you what to do . . ."

Tim said to Callum, "Do you know something about her that we don't?"

"I wouldn't say that. Actually, I don't know her much at all. The only time I've ever been in the same room as her was at our wedding. She and Élise had a bit of a falling-out a few years ago and haven't been close since."

"I don't think that means she's dangerous," I said, looking from Callum's face on the screen to Tim.

"But didn't she work for the company? And her mother still does? I think she's got some pretty sketchy ties to these people, and from what I can tell, she might be trying to protect them," Tim said.

Callum said, "I don't think she's outright dangerous, but you should operate under the assumption that she's being followed. I'll assume you've never been trailed before. It's terrifying. Sometimes I think that's the main reason Élise married me, to make a more permanent liaison with the UK." He laughed, but it seemed like he really thought that could be the case. "Just watch your back. If I were you, I'd be on a train to CDG, where I'd probably sit with my back against the wall until my flight."

I knew he was right. But I also knew I wasn't going to do that. I was in too deep. And it wasn't only because of Salomé. I couldn't pinpoint the exact moment in the past twenty minutes when I'd started wanting to work on the project with Tim. It felt as if my brain had decided without me. What if we could create something that exonerated Thierry's name while implicating Marco and stopping the summit, and also draw international attention to the Magpies? Being a part of something like this could change my career, but it wouldn't necessarily mean I had to become a politics writer or investigative journalist. Maybe it would just help editors consider saying yes more often when I pitched those "nuanced essays" I longed to write. Like Tim said, this wasn't an either/or situation. If I presented it honestly to her, I had the sense that Salomé would grant me permission. Not only permission, but she would make it possible.

To Callum, I said, "You're right, you *don't* know her. I just . . . what if she could be the biggest source of information? She might be able to grant us access to stuff we'd never know about otherwise." I didn't have it in me to imagine what would happen if I was wrong.

Callum said, "Well, you know where to find me. Keep me posted, will you?"

"Of course, mate. Thanks. Cheers." Tim ended the FaceTime and smiled at me.

"So I take it you're on board?"

"If I can get her permission. Then yes. I'm in."

Tim and I looked at each other. A hot breeze fluttered through the curtains, rustling the stacks of papers on his dad's bookshelf. There wasn't anything to say. Only the shared knowledge that we had agreed to at least walk up to the precipice together. Beyond that was for our future selves to decide.

CHAPTER 17

Salomé's train was due in ten minutes after an hour of being stalled out on the tracks. It was now half past noon, and already so hot that the workers were striking. Several other trains had been canceled. The heat would break later, so the trains would be running again by nightfall. At least that's what I told myself so I could postpone worrying about getting to Paris. There would be plenty of options. I'd make it happen.

Tim had ridden the train with me to Nantes. He went to the university to talk to his father. He told me he'd ask to borrow his dad's car for the day so we wouldn't be dependent on the trains. He left before we knew that Salomé's train was delayed, which meant I was alone with my thoughts for almost an hour. I busied myself by finding a place to plug in my phone. I sat, as Callum suggested, with my back against the wall.

At first I looked at Instagram as a means of distraction. I saw that Luke had gone to a waterfall with two women who didn't mind being photographed from behind in bathing suits. Good for them. And that's why you don't look at Instagram to try to feel better.

I got out my notebook and flipped through the pages, hoping I'd stumble upon a clue of sorts. That's what would happen in a movie. But I found nothing new or unexpected. I wrote some sentences:

I had the unmistakable feeling of being in a coat before Salomé and I parted, when we kissed for the first time. But that couldn't be true. This is how memories tarnish and warp over time. In five years, maybe I'll tell the story and say it must've been Salomé's birthday because I remember that big coat with faux fur lining on the hood, the tip of her nose being cold on my cheek. Then Salomé will say, "Are you crazy? You don't remember the heat wave? It was so hot that people died in their houses and the trains were stopping on their tracks as the workers went on strike. It was summer. It was your birthday, not mine."

This could be an interesting way to open the story. And if I was writing and Tim was producing, I wouldn't get the copy returned to me with a big red slash through the last three paragraphs.

I drew a slanted line across the paper, demonstrating the Aristotelian rising action. This might be interesting, getting to outline a story with a narrative arc, based on listener experience, rather than by laying out facts from the most important to the least. I marked a few dots along the line. *Episode One: Meeting Salomé. Episode Two: The Succubus. Episode Three: Thierry Leduc. Episode Four: Marco Angevine. Episode Five: Carrel and Lindbergh. Episode Six: The Magpies. Episode Seven: La Résistance. Episode Eight:*

My pen hovered. It already felt exploitative. I couldn't put her name in episode one like that. I couldn't put her name in the project at all. What was I thinking? Narratively it made sense to tell it from my point of view, but did I want that? I shouldn't even think about this until I'd gotten Salomé's permission. Assuming she would give it. And if not?

I didn't want to be the type of woman who turned away a career-making opportunity over a potential crush. But I also didn't want to be the type of person who abused a friend's trust. Maybe I could fictionalize it and use avatar characters? No, that would defeat the entire purpose of the story. And had I forgotten how dangerous this could be?

I was thinking about dumping my notebook in the trash when the SNCF voice came over the intercom announcing the arrival of a TER from the direction of Angers at track four.

I gathered my belongings and headed toward track four. The ground trembled, accompanied by a squeal from around the bend. The train hobbled its way into the station, packed with miserable-looking passengers.

The doors opened. A string of people passed me, and then there she was with her arms outstretched, her hair messy and stuck to her neck, dark circles under her eyes. But I found her more beautiful than I remembered. Not "effortless." Tangible, complicated.

"*Bonjour*," she said, and kissed beside my cheeks, wafts of herbal lotion and sweat.

God, it felt good to see her. I pulled her into a hug. I couldn't help but smile, just having her with me again. When we pulled away, she smiled too, exposing the little overlap of her front teeth. Then she looked from side to side, scanning the train station. My hands slid from her upper arms, where I'd been awkwardly touching since we stopped hugging.

I became aware of all the people around me for the first time since the Saint-Nazaire train station. I looked behind her, searching the crowd for anyone who looked suspicious. "Did anyone follow you?"

Without turning around, she said, "I don't think so." She touched my arm, and I flipped it over so she could see the puncture in my elbow. She gently smoothed it with her thumb. It stung a little under her touch, and I flinched. She got her phone out of her pocket. "I will get a car to take us to the hospital."

"Wait," I said. She looked up from her phone. "This is going to sound crazy, but I don't think I want to go to the hospital."

"Why not?"

"I just don't think I'm going to get the answers I need there."

I couldn't tell if she was surprised or not. I was somewhat surprised myself.

"That depends on what you want to know." She looked at me deeply, her chin tilted up slightly due to our small height difference. That same expression from the car, defiant, but inviting. For the first time, I felt like her equal, not a bumbling American. I knew too much to be taken lightly, and she knew that. But at the same time, I wanted to make sure she understood that I wasn't some unscrupulous journalist who would recklessly exploit her family. I would be the real deal, but only with her permission. But I couldn't say all of that here.

"Salomé," I said. Just that, hoping it would convey everything.

She held my gaze, her eyes very still. "I think you are right. About the hospital. And . . ." She touched her sternum, her finger idly drawing a tiny circle. "Let's go find somewhere to talk."

To talk. There were too many things. My mind felt like a traffic jam, and then there was the heat, wiping away any shred of energy I could muster. I nodded.

I'd never been to Nantes, but I didn't even perceive it. I followed her along the sidewalk with my backpack bearing down on me, sweat dripping down my arms, staring at the ground so I wouldn't trip. The pavement was uneven, and on the other side of the road, a construction crew was jackhammering, kicking up a cloud of gravel dust that coated the inside of my mouth.

We turned off the main road and walked down a narrow street lined with shops, some of which were closed due to the heat wave.

"I need to stop soon," I said. "I just can't carry this anymore."

"Let's go 'ere." She pointed to a small, dimly lit corner bar with red shutters on a tiny stone side street. If not for the A-frame chalk sign advertising their showing of a particular sports game, I wouldn't have realized it was open to the public.

Inside the bar was like a cave. It was crowded, probably because word had gotten out that it was cool inside. Most of the patrons were men huddled around the bar watching soccer on the one TV. We'd barely been inside for ten seconds before they erupted into screams, clapping each other on the back. Salomé grabbed my forearm. We scanned the crowd, but none of the men around the bar gave us a passing glance. I followed her to an empty table tucked in the back corner.

I searched for something truthful to say that didn't sound too dramatic or accusatory. "It's hard to tell if I'm dreaming."

"If you're dreaming then so am I."

There was a little LED candle on the table. I flipped it over and found the switch to make it flicker, then set it on the table between us.

"*Trop romantique*," I said.

That was a stupid thing to say. She looked away, and so did I, trying to think of how to recover.

She spoke first. "I thought you would never speak to me again."

"Why would I do that?"

"Because I scared you when I kissed you."

"That was the least scary thing that's happened to me over the past couple of days," I said.

"I hate this. I'm sorry, it was stupid of me to bring you 'ere . . . All morning, I think of nothing except you waking up alone, outside, and with . . ." She tapped the inside of her elbow.

I wanted to address the kiss before the moment was superseded by everything else. "I don't know how to say this, but I'm aware of the stereotype of the lascivious French woman, and I don't want you to think I'm just trying to experiment with you because of that."

She looked down at the table.

"'Lascivious' is like . . ."

"I know what it means," she said, meeting my eyes. She looked like she might cry. "I am not sure how I feel. I worry that you would think I was just wanting to hook up with someone because of breaking up with Justin. Which is maybe true, a little, so I am sorry for that."

Had I ever considered that I could be a rebound? Somehow that realization was both painful and relieving. All I could manage was, "Yeah." I squinted at one of the TVs behind the bar.

A server came by. Salomé asked for sparkling water. I asked for *la même chose*—the only thing I seemed to order on this trip. She also ordered a vegetarian pizza, which was a great idea. I was sure I needed food, though it was hard to be hungry in the heat.

When the server moved away, we sat in silence, avoiding each other's eyes. Salomé picked up the LED candle and spun it gently by the fake wick. That familiar grace in her movements, the coolness. I didn't know what to say. After several seconds of silence, I said, "There's something about you that makes me feel like lying to you would be a mortal sin. But I know people don't feel the same way about me."

She stopped twirling the candle. "I know you are not lying about the car."

"How?"

She smiled somewhat coyly, as if she'd wanted me to ask. "I don't know how to tell you . . ."

"Say it in French."

"No, I don't know how to tell you because it sounds crazy."

The men around the bar screamed again, and one shattered his pint glass against the wall, making us both clutch our hands over our hearts.

"I don't know why people do these things," she said. We laughed as the panic subsided, as if we didn't have a very real reason to be on edge.

The moment was slipping away. Suddenly I reached across the table and took her hand. "I'm pretty far past thinking things are too crazy to believe. I promise to believe you."

She sat perfectly still except for her hand that was in mine. There, she lightly squeezed. She looked me in the eyes. "Do you ever feel me? Inside your mind?"

The space between us was thick like water. All of a sudden, there was a word, an acknowledgment, of this unnamed sensation. I felt like we could meet in the middle like a couple of synchronized swimmers. I didn't know how to respond. I took a shallow breath. "I think so," I said. "When did this start?"

"I'm not sure. I want to think it has been like this the whole time. Maybe since the Fête, or maybe since the plane?"

I couldn't pinpoint the moment either. It wasn't terribly obvious. It was just easy to be with her in a way I wasn't accustomed to. Things I didn't know if she'd told me or I'd imagined. I had the naive thought that maybe this was simply what it was like to be with a woman, but that idea quickly dissipated into feeling exposed. There were too many things in my head that could scare her.

"What all have you seen?" I asked.

"Enough to know that you are not lying to me. It's more that I just know who you are."

I nodded and looked down at my lap. I couldn't explain it, but I felt the same way.

"Enough to know that inside of you is beautiful," she said.

"Dude, I can't have this conversation here." I dropped her hand and scooted my chair back, putting my forehead on the edge of the table. I didn't realize I was crying, but the fabric of my skirt was dotted with tears. I inhaled, making a terribly snotty sound. I was disgusting. It took me a minute to gain my composure and look at her.

"It's okay, he has put the pizza there, *dude*," she said, her head gesturing to the empty table next to us. The server had left our pizza and Perriers there.

I laughed and dried my eyes on the bottom of my shirt.

She got up and brought the food and drinks to our table.

"Have you ever felt like this with someone before?" I asked when she sat down.

She pulled a slice of the pizza onto her plate. "Élise." She used her fork to lift a thin ribbon of fresh basil off the pizza and twirled it in a drop of grease. Her nostrils flared slightly as she breathed. She then shook her head lightly as if dismissing her own thoughts.

"What?" I asked.

She seemed to consider what to say for a few seconds, but then her eyes flicked to mine. "Cour-ten-ey, I have to get Maman out of here, and I don't know how."

"Like out of Châteaubriant or out of France?"

She shook her head slowly. "I don't know. Both. Neither. I don't know. But she is going to die here." As if her statement reminded her of the pizza on her plate, she finally took a bite.

"Do you think Marco is physically violent to her?"

"It depends on what you mean by 'violent.' I don't think he hits her. But I think he is making her starve by putting her as the leader of the calorie restriction ViPi group. And psychologically, I'm sure."

"Do you think she knows she's being abused? Sometimes it takes people years."

"The last time I saw her, before I went to the US, she would not admit that anything was wrong. She came to visit me in Paris. She was excited about the things she and Marco were working on together. And she had a lot of money. Much more than she used to. She gave me two thousand euros to pay my roommates to keep my room empty for me. She was happy for me to travel and see the world. But there was something she was hiding. It was like, every time she looked at me, there was so much . . . *désespoir* . . . what is this?"

"Like . . . desperation?"

"Yes. There was desperation behind her eyes."

"I've sensed that too. Her eyes kind of look . . ." I stopped myself, searching for a nicer word than "lifeless."

"Sans vie."

"So that's new?"

"Oh, yes."

"I guess I just realized she used to be a scientist," I said.

"Did I tell you?"

"I wish that's how I knew." I opened my phone's internet browser to Loïc's blog and slid it across the table to her.

She read a little, then scrolled to the bottom of the page, skimming the text. "At least he knows she is the smart one." She looked up. "I'm not surprised this exists. How did you find it?"

"Callum showed it to me."

"Callum, my *beau-frère*?"

"I have so much to tell you."

Salomé sat very still while I recounted seeing Élise at the café in Paris. I kept waiting for her to question my story, but when I finished, she said, "Did she seem okay?"

"Élise was afraid of me at first, but . . . I don't know how to describe it. She recognized me. And she said she didn't believe in coincidences. Callum wanted to warn me about the Magpies, and probably to make sure I wasn't one of them, but I got the sense that Élise met with me because she wanted to hear about you."

"I miss her," she sighed. I realized I didn't know what had really happened there, but that could wait.

"Evidently this journalist has disappeared," I said.

"*Putain* . . ." she said under her breath. "This is why I tell you not to write about it."

"I thought you just didn't want any more attention brought to it."

"If it would clear my father's name, I would welcome it," she said in French. "As long as I was sure that Maman would be safe, too. I don't know what it will look like when this whole thing topples to the ground. Who will be caught in it."

"I understand. I promise I will tread carefully. But there's something I assume you don't know. This morning, Callum hacked into this journalist's Google Drive and found his unpublished drafts, and we just found out that Marco is evidently hosting an immortality summit in Châteaubriant in August, and it seems way more serious than just ViPi stuff." I paused, letting her process.

Salomé shook her head. "I wonder what he has figured out." She turned away from me and squinted at one of the TV screens behind the bar, where soccer players darted around the field like bugs under an overturned rock. The men screamed again. Salomé flinched, but kept her eyes on the screen. I could see her mind turning.

"I need to know what you know. You obviously know about the Magpies, right? You used to work for ViPi . . . What was your job when you worked for him?"

She told me that Marco had hired her when she'd finished her graduate program in 2012. For two years, her job was to help her father write another book. He was sick, so the work was slow. When they finished it, Marco took the manuscript. Things were different then with Marco. He was Thierry's former assistant, not Nathalie's lover. ViPi was just a startup. And Salomé really thought that Marco loved her dad. So when he approached her to come on board to build a philosophical think tank adjacent to ViPi, she was excited. She'd studied philosophy, and it's hard to get a job that utilizes that subject without becoming a professor.

At first it was just Salomé and three men basically thinking about different policies through a lens of benefiting public health and longevity. Salomé had very much liked the job at that point. Slowly, though, they started discussing more tangentially related ideas. What if a certain public policy went away in favor of a private one? What if we were, in fact, living in a simulation? Would that mean that the point of "life" was to win?

What if the government *paid* women to raise their kids at home? quickly turned into: How many generations would it take to establish women not going to school as a norm? Sometimes Salomé would pump the brakes and tell them these thought experiments sounded insidious.

Her coworkers would condescend: "We're just thinking hypothetically, Salomé." But it wasn't hypothetical. They generated reports that were shared widely, and often by groups that Salomé didn't want to be affiliated with. She started to feel like she was contributing to something that could go very wrong. But she was making a good salary and was able to afford a nice one-bedroom apartment in Paris. Whenever she thought about quitting, she'd realize she wouldn't be able to afford such a place on a professor's salary.

A few months after Thierry died, Salomé emailed his editor about the manuscript. He told her he had never received it. She then called Marco, who claimed another publisher was working on it. Nathalie found the file on Marco's computer and sent it to Salomé. It was hardly recognizable. It diverged significantly from the version she and Thierry had written, which focused on the advancements in understanding of cellular immortality since his first book, as well as some philosophical musings on the subject. From his deathbed, Thierry had written that he believed the quest for actual immortality would rob people of their lives more than staring death right in the eye.

But Marco had skewed several things, which fit with the "New

Carrel" identity Thierry had been trying to escape for the past thirteen years. Thierry had written a chapter that outlined various studies that, like his own, had failed to use a diverse test group, which resulted in biased outcomes for decades, particularly in medicine and technology. But of course that chapter was gone. In reading the manipulated draft, Salomé learned that Marco believed we live in a simulation—that it wasn't simply a thought experiment for him. He didn't think anything was real or that all people experienced consciousness. The mission of his life was to win the game, and he had put these words onto Thierry's pages.

"Literally win it?"

"Yes, literally. He thinks he is playing something, and he has to break all the rules to win. I honestly think it's a new mental illness that we will see more and more in the near future."

Salomé traveled from Paris to confront Marco about the manuscript. He said he wasn't planning on getting it published, but rather distributing it internally within ViPi.

"I've never seen Maman so mad," she said. "She filled up the sink and threw his computer into the water. She told Marco, 'If that manuscript ever resurfaces under my husband's name, I will kill you, and you know that I can.'"

"Whoa."

"Yeah. It was intense. That's when I quit working for him and went to work at the café. But ever since then, Maman has been like a puppet. I don't know what happened to her. It is so sad."

Just a few nights ago when we'd drunkenly walked past the cathedral, I had so naively said I wanted to be her.

"I'm sorry," I said.

"For what?"

"For assuming that your breakup was the worst thing going on in your life."

She hadn't gone with Justin because she was deeply in love with him. She had hoped he could be her Callum, someone who could offer her a chance at a different reality.

What came out of my mouth surprised me. "I want you to come back to Raleigh with me. I want to get you out of here. I'll pay for it. I'll put it on my credit card." This would far exceed my budget of approximately one hundred dollars a day, but I didn't care.

Her face didn't change. She reached for her water and took a long sip, during which I was suspended, thoughtless, as I waited for her response. When the bottom of the glass clinked down to the table, she said, "Okay."

"Really?" My smile was bigger than I wanted it to be.

"Really."

"I'm leaving tomorrow. Well, I mean, I'd actually like to go back to Paris tonight, if possible. And we can still help your mom, but I think we can do it from afar."

"I will have to go home to get my stuff."

"You can use my stuff. And we can get you some new clothes in Raleigh."

"I don't have my passport."

Damn. There was no way around that one.

I got a text from Tim:

ça va?

Jesus, I hadn't told her about Tim yet. Part of me wanted to forget it all and just go to Paris.

"Do you know about La Résistance?" I asked.

"You mean the twins?"

"The twins?"

"The colleagues of my father. I know they have opposed Marco for a long time. They tried to get me to join their group but I went to America instead."

I remembered the pictures of the twins from Thierry's book, photographed on the same day every year. "Is Bernard one of the twins?"

"Oui, Bernard et Gérard."

I turned over my thoughts. I needed to do this right. I couldn't risk Salomé feeling like I'd tried to deceive her. "I've been talking to this guy, Tim, who is part of the resistance. It sounds like a lot of the money from ViPi comes from American funds. Tim is thinking about producing some sort of podcast about this whole situation, and it sounds like he has a legit connection to the BBC. I just wanted you to know. It could actually be pretty big. Maybe it could even exonerate your father's name."

Her face remained neutral. "And you are going to help him?"

"I need more than your permission. I need your help."

She looked down and smoothed her thumbnail, then locked eyes with me, a new intensity to her expression—calculating, cunning. I got the sense that she was many moves ahead of me, but that we were on the same team. "Are you sure? It could be dangerous."

"I think so."

"I know where Bernard lives. It is just outside Châteaubriant. He tries to get me to talk to him since Papa died, and I cannot make myself do it. I know he will say things I don't want to know. But he will have all the answers."

"Do you want to go there?"

"Yes. And I want to meet Tim. Are you sure we can trust him?"

"As far as I can tell. Callum put us in contact. He came to meet me at the train station immediately."

"Does Élise know him?"

"I'm not sure."

She nodded slowly. "Okay. Call him."

When Tim answered, I said, "I told her everything. She's going to help us."

He exhaled into the receiver, out of relief or trepidation, I couldn't tell. "How?"

"We're going to talk to Bernard. Do you want to go?"

My phone buzzed with incoming texts. I glanced at the screen. They were from Aunt Trudy.

> Courtney when are you coming back?? I took Els to hospital . . . she is okay but she caught her stove on fire and burned her hand. The stove and the ventilation hood are ruined. The fire trucks came and everything. Could have been a disaster. . . . .

The next text was a picture of the burned stove. The vent hood was charred black. I stared at the photo, unable to fully process what I was seeing.

Another picture came in from Trudy of a package sitting on my mom's welcome mat.

> This came

I zoomed in. It was from France. The return address label was from ViPi.

"What?" I said aloud.

"Cour-ten-ey? Is everything okay?" Salomé said.

"Courtney?" said Tim's distant voice.

I snapped the phone back to my ear. "Sorry," I said. "What did you say?"

"I said I'll come pick you up in my dad's car. Share your location."

We hung up. I tried to figure out how to send him our location, but my fingers were shaking.

Salomé gently took the phone from my hands. "Share the location?" She tapped around on the screen and then returned it to me.

"My mom . . ." No matter how little I divulged about her burning her hand, the story had to end with me expressing how selfish I was for being here. But I couldn't do the shame spiral now. It didn't seem right to expect Salomé to comfort me through it.

". . . got this package delivered this morning." I opened the photo from Trudy and turned the screen to her. "It's from ViPi."

Salomé's eyes narrowed.

"How did Marco get my mom's address?"

"I'm sure he has a lot more than your address." Salomé touched the place between her eyebrows and winced as if she suddenly had a headache. "Cour-ten-ey, I hate to say it, but I do not think just going back to Raleigh will keep us safe from him. That's his message here. I had just started to think that we could escape together, and then, from Raleigh . . ." She mimed detonating a bomb with her thumb.

"Do you think Bernard could help us?"

Salomé shook her head slowly. "I don't know. But if anyone can, it's him." She motioned for the server to bring us our check. We'd barely eaten any of the pizza.

I watched her open her purse and pull out some cash. She gently smoothed the bills before placing them in the tray. It felt good to imagine someone there with me when I'd have to handle Mom's appointments and inevitable decline. I liked the idea of coming home from Mom's house or nursing home and Salomé being there, maybe pouring me a glass of wine and getting me to watch a show I'd never watch alone. But wouldn't that be a boring life for her? And what if I was living with my mom? Would Salomé want to come with me then? What a terribly unsexy life for such a vibrant, brilliant young person.

But the banality of life seemed to be what she was seeking, a respite from what she'd come to expect here. Perhaps she'd sink into blissful anonymity in Raleigh.

But then there was my mind. Once the novelty of our uncanny connection wore off, she would notice how I twitched and jumped in my sleep, even with no succubus involved. How, at any given moment, I could instantly be hundreds of miles away from the present, away from her. She'd soon notice that I wasn't with her the way she deserved, as everyone who got close to me eventually noticed.

"I need to call my mom later. Don't let me forget."

She nodded. "I will remind you."

I knew she would. Maybe it would be different this time. Maybe my mind wouldn't scare her off. Maybe it would be better with her around.

CHAPTER 18

There were very few other cars on the road between Nantes and Châteaubriant. The pavement undulated with heat. Salomé sat up front, next to Tim, and I stared out the back window, watching the fields and small plots of farmland pass by. The fields went on and on, occasionally accompanied by a quaint farmhouse or rows of grapevines.

I'd first seen this region when I studied in Aix-en-Provence as a high school junior. The program took us on a weekend-long bus excursion to several Loire Valley châteaux, Chenonceau and Blois and Chambord, which were a little southeast of where I was now. I remember thinking it was one of the most beautiful places I'd ever seen. I'd loved France for a long time, and, I realized with a tinge of sadness, maybe I didn't know it as well as I thought. Maybe I was being punished for a lifetime of glorifying this place and who I was when I was here.

The GPS prompted Tim to exit to another highway, which sent us winding through a tiny village. Its gray stone buildings were so close to the road it seemed like I could reach through the window and touch them. Their black roofs were streaked with age, the doors and windows all charmingly askew. I hated how frivolous I felt for loving France.

Salome turned around in the front seat to look at me. I had the instinct to smile, to let her know I was okay back here, but I couldn't bring myself to. The texts from Aunt Trudy sat like a brick in my stomach.

Tim stopped the car to let a mother duck and several ducklings cross. Salomé worried aloud about their little feet on the hot pavement. They waddled down to a small algae-covered pond and slid in.

Salomé and Tim spoke in French. After discussing how Tim had met Callum, she asked about Tim's dual citizenship.

It was interesting to watch Salomé interacting with a French peer. Her tonality was flatter. She spoke faster and used a bit more slang than she did with me. I hadn't realized to what extent she had gone out of her way so I could understand her. I caught most of what they said, but I stayed quiet.

Tim told her how his parents met while his dad was at the Sorbonne and his mom was on a weekend trip to Paris during her last year of college. Several weeks later, back at school in London, his mother found out that she was pregnant. Tim said he had always known his parents to be good friends and had never thought to wish they were a couple until someone suggested it to him around the age of twelve. Even then, he realized that adding romance into their family unit would jeopardize it. He had attended a *lycée français* to ensure he kept up with his French fluency, and his father had taught him enough Wolof to speak with his Senegalese grandparents. I liked the idea of an intentional multicultural and multilingual family like that. Tim's life sounded curated, whereas mine was cliché: married middle-class heterosexual couple has baby, man cheats, divorce ensues. But of course, I was only hearing the abridged version of Tim's story.

A few narrow country roads later, we stopped in front of a stone farmhouse, its blue shutters closed against the sunlight.

At the sound of our car doors closing, a dog started yapping inside the house. We walked the stone path to the front door. Before we could knock, the knob turned. The person behind it had to yank twice to free the door from its swollen frame. He was a slender man with brown hair that was graying at the temples—the young-looking twin from the photos in Thierry's book.

"*Bonjour.* Bernard Menoret," he said, revealing a missing incisor. A wire-haired dog strained against his arms, flicking its tongue toward Bernard's mouth when he spoke.

Tim and I introduced ourselves. Salomé stepped forward and exchanged *la bise* with Bernard, giggling when the dog intercepted and licked her cheek. Bernard held the door open for us to enter.

Several oscillating fans blew at full speed, but the inside of the house wasn't much cooler than outside. Bernard let the dog down and it raced ahead of us, claws scratching on the tile, then beelined back and jumped up Salomé's leg, yipping and whimpering. Most of the French dogs I'd ever encountered acted mature off-leash, like that dog Loute, but this little thing broke the mold.

"*Ça suffit!*" Bernard said, pointing a finger in the dog's face. It backed off.

We followed Bernard through the house, which was cramped with antiques and smelled faintly of rotting vegetation. The kitchen countertops were covered with loose eggs and onions with dirty roots, the green parts lying wilted over the side.

Bernard led us through the open back doors and into the yard, which was basically a tiny farm on a plot no bigger than two acres. Chickens huddled under the shade of a freestanding stone chimney from a house that must've been on this spot long before the current one, which appeared to be at least two hundred years old itself. The little dog zoomed between two crudely plowed rows of vegetables. The scene was delightfully haphazard; tomato plants peeking over sprawling squash vines, and lean-to trellises teeming with cucumbers. A short chicken wire fence bulged around the bottom of the garden, struggling to contain the growing plants like an overstuffed pillow.

Bernard instructed us to gather around the table (which was really a giant wooden spool turned on its side) under the shade of an enormous tree. Then he went back inside and clattered around in the kitchen.

Salomé hadn't spoken since she first greeted Bernard. Her eyes were fixed on a rooster strutting alongside a hen, forcing her out of the chimney's shade. Salomé's cheeks were flushed with heat, but the rest of her face was pale. She was smoothing her thumbnail again, perhaps her version of spelling.

Bernard returned with a selection of drinks on a tray: coffee, a carafe of water, and small glasses of pastis. He sat and wiped his beaded brow on a handkerchief from his front shirt pocket. He didn't ask us to prove we weren't wiretapped, just held his hands palms-up and said, *"Bienvenue à la résistance,"* to Salomé. He had been waiting a long time for her to show up.

Salomé looked on edge. She responded rather flatly that she hadn't been in the country. Bernard said he understood and that he was glad to see her. He then exchanged a few pleasantries with Tim, and asked about his father.

"He asked me to find out if you've had any contact with the University of Nantes student journalist," Tim said in French.

Bernard said he hadn't been able to contact her since her return to Switzerland.

Tim pulled up the invitation to the summit on his phone and

showed it to Bernard. "We just got access to Loïc's Google Drive today and found this. Do you know anything about it?"

Bernard paused and patted his front shirt pocket, pulling out his glasses case, and put on a pair of readers. He took the phone from Tim. "*Roh, là là là là.*" He must've read the text three or four times. Finally he looked up at us from over his glasses. "No, this can't happen. We have to stop this." His tone was serious.

We stayed silent for a moment, processing.

"What is going on?" Tim asked. "Loïc never would've just left the country like that, especially not when he was this close to exposing the Magpies. Did they threaten him into leaving? Extort him? Or is there some sort of mind control? Hypnotism?"

"You're on the right track." Bernard dabbed his forehead with a handkerchief. He shifted uncomfortably before looking directly at Tim. "I want to be honest with you . . ." His voice caught in his throat. "I regret to tell you this, but I think there is almost no chance of Loïc being alive." He paused, seeming to debate whether or not to place his hand on Tim's shoulder. "I'm sorry. I had a lot of hope for Loïc, but he got too close."

Tim stared at the ground, jaw set.

"I'm so sorry, Tim," I said.

"Just give me a minute." Tim got up and wandered across the yard to the overflowing garden. He knelt down, hooked his fingers into the chicken wire, and let out a few loud sobs. Bernard pushed away from the spool table and walked into the house.

Salomé and I looked at each other. I was surprised that Tim was so unprepared for the possibility of Loïc's death. "Do you think I should . . . ?" I said, meaning should I try to comfort him.

She shook her head gently. She was right; he needed space. She touched her sternum with two fingers in that reverent way and squeezed her eyes closed.

A hen flapped onto the table, startling me. Salomé opened her eyes, her face softening when she saw the hen, who stuck her beak into Salomé's water glass. Salomé tipped the glass to help her, and the hen filled her beak and tilted her head back, letting the water run down her throat. Something about this made me want to cry. Salomé gently ushered the hen into her lap, where she stroked her like a cat. The bird closed her eyes and made little clucks of pleasure.

Bernard returned to his seat with a nondescript black binder. He glanced across the yard, where Tim was still crouched by the garden, and suggested we give him a few minutes.

"Would it bother you if I took some notes?" I asked.

Bernard's light blue eyes came to rest on mine. I didn't know what he knew about me, if anything. Salomé had called him briefly to ask if we could come over, and she had addressed me as an American friend. Nothing more.

"Of course not," he said.

"I'm a journalist . . ." I hoped I could convey the rest of my thought without having to say it: *and I just learned that the two other journalists who were involved in this story are either dead or have gone into hiding.*

Bernard nodded. "As long as you are with Salomé, I think you will be relatively safe."

"Why do you think that? I was abducted last night." I wasn't sure how to say "abducted" in French, so I said *kidnappée.* I extended my elbow so he could see.

Bernard put on his glasses again and leaned over to examine the puncture mark. "Like Florence, the student," he said.

"What kind of drug was it?"

"I'm not entirely sure, but I have theories," Bernard said. He looked at Tim again, who had made no progress toward returning to the table. Even from across the yard, I could see the sweat shining on Tim's arms in the full sun.

Bernard seemed to have a lot of information. I wondered why he wasn't in danger like Loïc, or if perhaps he was. I asked him.

"I am partially responsible for the science their whole enterprise is based on. And me being alive and appearing young is an important piece of their sales pitch. The experiment continues," he said, and gestured up and down his body. From what I knew, he was the same age as Thierry, which meant he would be close to eighty at this point. He looked thirty years younger.

"But, the real thing that protects me is Nathalie. I'm like family," Bernard said. "Thierry's best friend from childhood. I loved Thierry as much as my twin brother. Nathalie would never let anyone come after me, not as long as she can help it. Emotions aside, I've always thought that Nathalie would keep me around as a final exit strategy, so if she ever needed to escape, she had someone to facilitate it. I think that moment will come any day now."

"But if Nathalie's keeping you safe, who's keeping Nathalie safe?" I asked.

"That's a very important part of all of this. The truth is, Nathalie is the true holder of the technology I assume he plans to sell or teach at this summit. If Marco controls her, he controls the technology. She could devalue what he has if she were to start to share it on her own, or deny him access."

Dévaluer. It was the same word in English and French. So it all came down to money. Marco would completely devalue Nathalie's life before he would consider losing money.

Bernard nodded toward Tim, who was coming toward us, wiping his eyes on the backs of his wrists. He sat beside Bernard at the table, his face hardened. Bernard placed his hand on the back of Tim's shoulders and patted him a few times. It was always interesting to see men console one another.

Bernard flipped open the binder. In the left pocket was Thierry's book, *La science de l'immortalité.* The rest of the binder appeared to be crammed with newspaper and magazine clippings and the yellow pages of several legal pads covered with slanted handwriting.

"*Alors,*" said Bernard. He squinted at the top page and scooted the binder closer and farther from his face. "*Alors.*"

There was a grainy black-and-white picture embedded in the article. I leaned in. A young, serious-looking Thierry stood between Bernard and his identical twin, all wearing lab coats. Thierry looked so much like his daughters. He had a more masculine version of their nose, their same cheekbones, their eyes.

"*C'est Gérard,*" he said, pointing to his twin in the picture. Bernard had apparently been missing the tooth this whole time.

"This picture was taken in 1985, on our forty-fifth birthday," he said. "Look." He flipped to a tab at the back of the binder that held a sleeve of the original Polaroids from Thierry's book. They had continued to take the pictures after the book's publication. I looked at the 2017 photo. Gérard looked like an old man.

"How did you decide who was the control?" I asked in English.

Bernard mimed flipping a coin. "Let's start at the beginning," he said in French, leaning forward with his forearms on the table.

I flipped to a new page of my notebook and held my pen poised.

"Could I make an audio recording?" Tim's voice was still deflated, but he pulled his phone out of his pocket, ready to work.

"Of course," Bernard said. "Everything I am about to tell you is indisputable fact and part of public record."

Bernard did his best to speak clearly for me as he went on, "My twin brother, Gérard, and I met Thierry at elementary school. We were friends through high school, which is where we became interested in science. It was Thierry's idea to all apply to ESPCI University. That's where Émile, Thierry's father, had worked in Alexis Carrel's Parisian laboratory. Émile very seldom saw Carrel, as Carrel did most of his work in North America, but he had a team working in Paris as well. Thierry was only four years old or so when Carrel passed away. Somehow in all the lore created by the Magpies, they made Thierry out to be Carrel's assistant or student, but the truth is, they were separated by more than a generation. However, the scientific lineage was there."

Bernard explained how Thierry followed in his father's footsteps, studying genetics. "Thierry and my brother and I were particularly interested in the burgeoning field of gerontology, basically answering the question of why we age, and how we can slow down that process. We were working to perfect a technique of removing cells from a host and using a combination of low temperatures and a concentration of certain compounds to slow the cells' rate of aging. Then we would inject the solution back into the host to see if the DNA in the altered cells could affect the DNA in new cells. Fruit flies and mice, mostly. The results were mixed.

"Then we graduated and went our separate ways. Thierry finished his doctorate in genetics and was offered a position at the university. I went to teach in Nantes, and Gérard went to Lyon. We lived our lives. Gérard married and had two sons. I never married, and we all thought Thierry wouldn't either.

"By the early seventies, transcendental meditation was popular, and Thierry spent a summer in Nepal. He had long hair—*un hippie.*" Bernard laughed under his breath, perhaps for Salomé's benefit. He looked at my notebook page, which I had covered in a mixture of shorthand notes in French and English. He waited for my pen to stop scratching.

He continued, "The monks Thierry encountered in Nepal were known to live well into their late nineties and beyond thanks to meditation, which lowered stress, and in turn created physical benefits that Thierry planned to isolate in the lab. It wasn't new information that lower stress had beneficial effects on physical health, but no one had yet been able to pinpoint the actual cell-level physiology at play, even though Lindbergh had tried with hypothermic chambers. Thierry hypothesized that these benefits could be artificially simulated in the lab, multiplied thousands of times over, and then injected back into the cell donor. Could a body be convinced it had spent years in calm meditation and reap the cellular benefits even if the life it lived had been incredibly stressful, like that of a head of state?

"After that, Thierry returned to his job at ESPCI, teaching genetics, and chipping away at his research in his spare time. Around this time, he secured some funding and brought Gérard and me to Paris to work with him. We were back to testing on fruit flies and mice, but this study needed human subjects. We tossed a coin to see who would serve as the control, me or Gérard. Gérard won. Well, no. I won. Gérard had to meditate for two hours a day with Thierry. Thierry's father—the other volunteer for the experiment—and I received the multiplied stem cell infusions from them on a monthly basis to see if we would benefit from their meditation. Thierry's father ended up outliving Thierry, which was anecdotal but very interesting. And you saw the picture of my brother. At my last visit to the doctor, I was told I had the heart of a forty-six-year-old. By my own calculation, I only age two hundred and forty days out of the year."

Bernard paused to take a sip of pastis. Tim picked up his glass of water and held it to his forehead, though it didn't look very cold.

Bernard went on, "In 1986, Thierry met a brilliant physics student by the name of Nathalie Boucher. Her thesis project collided with his theories about the link between longevity and mental control in ways he'd never considered."

Bernard licked his finger and flipped through the tabs until he got to a thick section of yellowing paper that had been typed on a typewriter. He turned the binder to face us.

PROJECTION ASTRALE COMME REMÈDE CONTRE LA MORT

"Astral projection?" I said in English. I'd heard of it before in a couple of movies. "Is that like lucid dreaming?"

In French, Bernard said, "Lucid dreaming can be a toehold into astral projection, like meditation, but the goals are very different. Meditation is the first step, having any control over your own mind. This can lend itself to lucid dreaming, which can then lend itself to the control needed for astral projection. But it isn't a simple process, and these things can all be mutually exclusive as well."

Salomé leaned forward and pulled the binder closer, scanning the top page and then another.

"Does this make sense to you?" I asked.

She got to a page with a diagram of a human body surrounded by insane-looking math equations. "Maman called it *la marche nocturne*..."

"Like . . . nightwalking?" I watched her eyes move across the papers, waiting for her to blow a puff of air and dismiss it as Nathalie's instability. But she nodded.

Tim asked if Bernard believed Nathalie's thesis.

"Well," Bernard said. "Yes and no. Yes, because Nathalie had somehow been able to calculate the physics of consciousness—something so solid it held up to the scrutiny of some of the brightest minds in physics. It proves something we all know innately: When we die, consciousness exits the body. It's after that moment that is up for debate, as far as religions and philosophies go." His next sentence in French was completely lost on me.

"I'm sorry, I didn't get that," I said, turning to Tim.

Tim translated in his mind before answering me. "I think how I'd put it is . . . Nathalie proved that it is possible to stay with that consciousness long enough to retain agency."

"Retain agency? What does that mean?"

"You find a new body," Bernard said in a slightly apologetic tone, as if to make up for the fact that we wouldn't be able to believe him.

Salomé crossed her arms over her chest, her mouth turned in a slight frown.

Bernard explained that Nathalie's thesis opened a whole new dimension of longevity for Thierry. Before, the longevity he'd been philosophizing over only encompassed some generations of fruit flies and mice who lived 50 percent longer than their parents, and two willing human volunteers who risked no adverse effects. He had never had to consider the ethics of his research, as he considered it natural for man to want to live a long, healthy life, and it was his duty to help them do it.

Nathalie, though, represented something totally different. She theorized that someone could live forever—evidence, at least on paper, that consciousness could be truly immortal. But now it involved someone else. The next body. This raised so many questions of ethics for Thierry, not to mention the legality surrounding it.

"Thierry wouldn't even share what he was working on with us," Bernard said. "He kept it a secret because he knew there was no way we would entertain the idea." There was an edge to Bernard's voice, if only slight, that revealed some lasting anger.

Salomé's nostrils were flared, but besides that, her face remained stoic, arms still crossed.

"Oh my God," I said in English. I looked at Bernard. "Wait . . . is Marco is going to pitch immortality through astral projection at the summit? Astral projection is the 'technology'?"

Bernard breathed in like he was about to launch into a long sentence, but he muttered, "*Euhhhh . . . voilà.*" From what he could tell, *someone* would be teaching the participants about this, whether it was Marco or Nathalie, he explained in French.

Tim scoffed. "Carrel wanted to offer immortality to elite white people, and—surprise—that's still what's happening today, though it's in a different package."

No one said anything for a moment. I slid the paper with Nathalie's thesis closer to me and examined the diagram.

"Wait, is Thierry still around, then? Did he not really die?" Tim asked.

"If my father were still alive I would know it," Salomé said, bristling.

"Thierry is not alive," Bernard said quickly. "But Marco had pitched the idea to Thierry and Nathalie that when Thierry died, he could astrally project into Marco's body and go on with his research."

Salomé gasped, but she didn't look surprised. She looked angry.

Bernard said that Nathalie had been desperate for Thierry to project into Marco's body, and that for a little while, Thierry had even considered it. However, at the end of Thierry's life, he told her he was ready to die, and that man shouldn't try to live forever. Nathalie begged him to reconsider, but he maintained that it was unethical and very unlikely to actually work. Bernard and Gérard remained close friends with Thierry until the end, and he expressed this dilemma over the phone only two weeks before he died. Until then, Thierry had been secretive about what he and Nathalie had been working on. At the time, Bernard thought that Thierry's mind might've been slipping, and didn't believe him until recently, when he'd accessed Nathalie's thesis from the university archives.

Bernard paused. I thought about the clip I'd watched of Marco professing his love for being alive. Would he willingly give up his life for Thierry? Or would he remain alive, in some shared consciousness?

"What would happen to Marco if Thierry had projected into him? Would he die?" I asked.

"I don't know. I don't know if anyone knows, until we find a person who has served as a vessel for an astral projector. If we could talk to Loïc, maybe we could know."

Tim pressed his hand to his forehead. "My God." He looked across the yard.

"It's just a theory," Bernard said. "But Loïc's mother hired a private investigator who was able to get airport security footage from Lima, and Loïc was on tape, scanning his passport and walking out of the airport, where he got in a cab. He didn't have a suitcase. The driver dropped him at a hotel, where he never checked in. There is footage of him walking away from the hotel, and that's all we know. This is why I don't want you to get your hopes up."

"You think they made him kill himself?" Tim's voice strained to remain calm.

"Maybe," Bernard said with a small wince. "I can't rule it out until Loïc is found alive."

"How long could a projection last? I mean, if the projector wasn't dead. They'd have to be unconscious in some other way, right?" I asked Bernard. Even if someone managed to buy a last-minute direct flight from Paris to Peru, I imagined it would take at least fourteen hours to get there, and that was only the flight.

"I believe the projector is asleep, or in a lowered state of consciousness. I think they would have to use medical intervention in a case like Loïc's."

Medical intervention. The term made me queasy. "You mean like, needles?" My whole body felt clammy.

Before Bernard could answer, Salomé said, "Marco goes on these 'business trips' for days at a time. Do you think he's unconscious somewhere, terrorizing people from the inside?"

"We still don't know if he has the ability. But maybe."

"So we're saying that someone—Marco or whoever else—drove

Loïc's body like a car all the way to Peru and what, made him walk straight into the ocean?" Tim's eyes darted between the three of us.

Like a car. I'd been skeptical, even looking at Nathalie's thesis, covered in mathematical calculations I'd never begin to understand. I would believe that someone had implanted a mind-control device into my body while I slept before I believed that I'd been a vessel for an astral projector.

Bernard held up his hands, asking us to slow our questions. "You know I don't have a definitive answer. But I do think it's a possibility."

"Do they just practice on random people?" Tim asked. "How would that work?"

"Thierry told me that he learned using magpies," Bernard said.

"Like, birds or cult members?" Tim asked.

The dreadful feeling spread over my body, my pulse rising in my ears. I gripped the edge of the table to steady myself. It was true. Every cell in my body knew it was true. The conversation went on, but I struggled to listen.

"Birds. They are good vessels. They can fly, they're inconspicuous, and there are a lot of them."

"Did it hurt the bird?" Salomé asked, putting both hands back on the hen still perched on her lap. Of course she would worry about that.

"I don't believe so," said Bernard, sounding very far away from me. "But of course we can't ask the bird to describe what it was like to be inhabited."

My head was swimming with the absurdity of this story, this group, the idea of astral projecting at all. Then there was the fact that Bernard was not a professional investigator, but a bored retiree on some sort of reputation-clearing vendetta for his friend. It didn't make empirical sense. But far more terrifying was how I knew I could spend the rest of my life doing the mental gymnastics required to convince myself that this hadn't happened. Even considering that exhausted me further. I closed my eyes. Out of the haze of thoughts came a memory, as visually clear as watching a film, but just as removed, as if it weren't originating from my own mind. The interior of the Peugeot, the scraping windshield wipers, the orange streetlights illuminating the bridge over the Loire. I was in the driver's seat. I was the only body in the car, but I wasn't alone.

The succubus I'd dreamed had burrowed down my throat, scales and all, had taken control of my body as if it were simply a shell. A *Machiavellian hermit crab.*

"It's . . . psychedelic, really," I said quietly.

The three of them looked at me.

After a few seconds, Salomé spoke. "The car." Thank God she didn't make me say it.

"Marco?" Tim asked.

I looked to Bernard, expecting him to remind us not to jump to conclusions. But he studied me, nodding. "What do you remember?"

"Not much," I said in English. "Just . . . driving." I closed my eyes again. "I was having nightmares . . . like a succubus sitting on my chest. And in some of them, I was in Nathalie's room, but everything was wild, like a bad LSD trip or something." I looked at Bernard again, desperate for him to contradict me. "Maybe I'm wrong. Maybe I was just having bad dreams?"

"No, Courtney," he said in French. "What you're describing is very similar to what Florence, the student reporter, told us."

Tim's attention snapped back to Bernard. "Does my dad know about this?"

I barely heard Bernard's response: No, Bernard wasn't confident enough in the theory to spread it widely. I couldn't stay still any longer. I had to move. "Can I just—" I stood up and walked toward the garden, the periphery streaking green as my eyes filled with tears. I heard Salomé following me, and once we were far enough away to not be overheard, I turned to her.

"Tell me you didn't know." I tried to whisper, but I had little control over my voice. "Please tell me you didn't know. Please." I didn't know if I meant about the Magpies or the astral projection or all of it.

"Cour-ten-ey," she said softly. "I want to tell you something. Come sit with me." She led me toward the little stream at the back of the property, where we sat in the hot grass, the sun merciless on the backs of our necks.

On a stone in the middle of the stream, a large turtle sunned with a smaller turtle perched on its back. Lucky cold-bloods, they probably liked this heat. We watched the turtles for a few moments, collecting ourselves.

With her gaze still on the turtles, Salomé spoke. "When I was little, Maman used to tell us a story about how she could walk around town in the body of a cat. She would tell us these stories like . . . what is it called, *des contes de fées*?"

"Fairy tales?"

"Yeah. Like what she sees through the eyes of a cat. We loved them."

"But you thought they were just stories?"

"No," she said softly. "We believed them." She shook her head. "Remember how I told you that Élise and I could play in our dreams when we were little?"

Had she told me about the mermaid toy? Or did I dream it? "I saw that, I think. You and Élise and a mermaid."

"You were in a pool, and there was *une mante religieuse*." She held her hand up to eye level, indicating where the praying mantis had been in my line of sight.

"I . . . I wanted to tell you about that. And the bird?"

"I wanted to tell you about that, too," she said.

"What is it?" I asked.

"I don't know. It seems like something that happens when someone . . ."

I suddenly realized what she was about to say. "You can do it too, can't you? Nightwalking?" I could stick with the euphemism if it made it easier for her.

Salomé pulled a blade of grass out of the ground and smoothed it with her thumb. "At first it was just playing in our sleep. But later, as I got better at it . . . I learned that I could nightwalk *as* Élise while she was sleeping."

"How old were you?"

"I started it when we moved to Châteaubriant. I was twelve. I only did it for a short time. I stopped when I was thirteen and she was fifteen. I didn't realize how fucked up it was. I just wanted to hang out with her friends and would sometimes do it before a party or something. But then Élise was going to a doctor to be put on medication for having such terrible dreams, and I knew it was because of me. Whenever I nightwalked as Élise, she had nightmares and would be upset for days. So I stopped, but she took the medication for years. It had such bad side effects. She was falling asleep at her desk at school. Her grades weren't good. We were concerned about her passing the *bac.* I realized this could mess up her entire future, so I told her what I'd done. That there wasn't anything wrong with her. She didn't need the medication. I thought she would be happy to know, but she was so angry with me. We barely talked for two years, and even after that, we are not the same."

What was she telling me? That *she* had projected into me?

Salomé said, "It was so long ago, I had stopped believing it was real. I convinced myself that it was just my imagination. But then, the other night, when I 'eard you have the bad dream . . . it was easy to tell myself that it was jet lag, being in a new place."

"What are you saying?"

Her eyes grew wide. "It wasn't me," she said. "I will never do something like that again. I am feeling profoundly stupid. And I think . . ." She held the back of her hand to her lips. "I think a lot of the choices I made in the past year have been so I can avoid it. Like, I knew Marco did business with bad people. But I didn't know how bad the situation really was. I'm pretty sure he is making her starve herself for some stupid experiment, he put all the cameras so she doesn't know when he is watching her . . . he put the tracking thing on the car . . ."

"A tracking device?"

"Yeah, that's how he found the car this morning," she said.

"But if he projected into me and made me drive the car, wouldn't he already know where he left it?"

She paused, carefully considering what to say. "Cour-ten-ey, I'm sorry. But I don't think it was Marco."

Before the words fully sunk in, I knew she was right. I closed my eyes to brace against another wave of dizziness. The memories of the lost night played on the backs of my eyelids. But they weren't mine. They were Nathalie's.

CHAPTER 19

It was all there: My reflection in the bathroom mirror, my arm lifting itself, snipping, the chunk of brown hair falling into the sink, which I wiped away. Holding the end of a pantyhose tourniquet between my teeth as I shot a syringe of clear liquid into my vein. Then the images got less distinct: Salomé across the dinner table, a raspberry on a tarte, eating more and more because I wouldn't have to report these calories, feeling like I was getting to see a version of my daughter that she reserved for anyone other than me. Realizing, with a fair amount of surprise, that she seemed more interested in this American girl than I'd initially thought. It was true that I'd thought about dying and living in this body, getting to move continents and stay friends with Salomé. At first, I'd even thought: Salomé brought me a way out. But my only decent escape plan was ruined in a single look from my daughter, the flame of a tea candle reflected in her eyes. Then the car, the windshield wipers, the statue rising from the lapping water. Thierry's voice. What did he say?

I shook my head, my eyes still closed. "I remember it now, I think," I said to Salomé.

"What do you remember?" Salomé asked.

Thierry's voice washed into my mind as gentle as the water rushing over the base of the *Serpent d'Océan*: *You will have to kill him.*

Nathalie cried out of my mouth, a cry of desperation. *I can't.*

I forced my eyes open. "She's going to kill Marco."

Salomé's eyes were wide, but before she could respond, I said, "She thought you brought me to the house so she could inhabit me and kill her own body to escape Marco." My voice got louder, though I tried to keep it under control. "And I just need to hear you say that you didn't do that. Just tell me you didn't do that."

Her eyebrows rose in a silent plea. "No," she said, almost a whisper.

The ground beneath me swayed. I collapsed onto my side in the fetal position, where I watched a bee wiggling inside an orange flower just in front of me, coating its fuzzy legs in chunks of pollen. I closed my eyes, halfway wondering if I was suffering a heatstroke. When I was in high school, a football player had died of heatstroke on the field during practice. What if I died here? Who would take care of my mom? Would they pay to ship my body back to the US, or bury me in France like Jim Morrison? That would be one way to set up permanent residency.

I laughed under my breath. It was either that or hyperventilate.

Salomé echoed back a tiny laugh. I propped myself up on my elbow to look at her. Even this much movement made me dizzy.

"Why are you laughing?" she asked.

"I just thought that maybe if I died of heatstroke they wouldn't ship my body back to the States and then I could be a French resident, finally. Why are *you* laughing?"

"It is not a good reason to laugh, but I was thinking 'ow you were a stranger last week and now you know more about my family than I do. And you just wanted to go on vacation. Oh, my God," she said, laughing harder. "This is so fucked up."

Bernard's voice cut across the garden. "*Hé!*"

We looked up to see Tim slumping off his chair.

Salomé jumped to her feet and pulled me up. We ran across the yard. Bernard was fanning Tim's face with the binder. By the time we got there, Tim's eyes were rolling open again.

"He's too hot," Bernard said.

"*Ça va, ça va,*" Tim said.

Bernard jogged inside and returned with a cold bottle of white wine, which he pressed to Tim's cheek. Tim's breathing steadied.

"Drink some water, Tim," I said, handing him his glass.

He assured us that he was okay a few more times, but he was clearly unsettled. We needed to go somewhere cooler as quickly as possible, but there was nowhere to go.

Bernard continued to fan Tim with the binder, but he looked at me, seeming to wonder what Salomé and I had discussed across the yard. I looked at her, and she gave me a barely perceptible nod to go ahead.

"We think we figured it out," I said in English. "It was Nathalie projecting into me. Not Marco."

Bernard didn't seem entirely surprised by this revelation. "Are you sure?"

"I can remember what Nathalie was thinking at times."

Tim gestured for Bernard to stop fanning him. "*Merci, merci,*" he said.

The page of notes in front of me was unintelligible. This wasn't a story yet—at least not one we could tell to anyone who wasn't at this table. There were too many loose ends. Tim looked beyond exhausted. I'd need to take the lead on this if we were going to walk away with enough material.

Once Bernard was back in his seat, I said, "I have some more questions, if you don't mind."

He nodded.

"So, this plan for Thierry to project into Marco. Was Marco serious about it? Was he planning to essentially give up his life, or do you think he was planning to sabotage it, and he would just masquerade as Thierry?"

Bernard said, "I've thought about that, and I think they're both plausible. Especially before Thierry's death, Marco was desperate for recognition and would take it in any package, even if that meant essentially being a martyr for the cause. Or he could announce to all the Magpies that he was Thierry, therefore assuming all of Thierry's recognition in the scientific community."

Bernard reached across the table to tap Nathalie's thesis. "But this became Marco's link between Thierry's research and the Magpies. Marco's idea was to find a group of young people who would voluntarily function as vessels for geniuses, artists, and, most importantly, politicians who were nearing the end of their body's lifespan. So a person's ability to expand and finish work could span multiple lifetimes."

We all looked at Salomé as if she would offer an explanation for everything. She was sitting very still. "This idea of immortality for geniuses . . . he introduced this to the philosophers when I worked for him," she said. "We were discussing the hypothetical ethics of it. This was around the time I quit. But it makes me wonder if the other people I worked with ever figured out that this wasn't hypothetical."

"So, do we know who all has the ability to astrally project?" I asked. Salomé held my gaze, giving me a pointed look. I would follow her lead on that.

"I don't know," Bernard said. "Not many people have enough control of their astral bodies to pull something like this off. The only people I am sure have projected are Nathalie and Thierry. I pray that Marco hasn't developed the skill himself. But this summit is worrisome, as is the information that Marco is often gone for days at a time.

It seems likely that Marco has the ability. If he doesn't, perhaps he is going to force Nathalie to teach it at the summit."

"Or they're trying to sell something else entirely," I said.

Bernard raised an eyebrow. "We can't rule out that possibility, though I don't know what it would be."

We were silent for a few seconds. Salomé's face was pale. Tim slowly fanned himself with the copy of *La science de l'immortalité* from the binder. I didn't know what to ask next. Then I remembered the text from Aunt Trudy. I got out my phone and opened the photo of the ViPi package.

"Bernard, what do you think of this? It arrived yesterday evening at my mom's house." I showed him the picture.

He zoomed in on the address label. Then, giving me a serious look over his glasses, he said, "This is a threat."

"It's more than that. It's weird because I was looking into ViPi, and I'm embarrassed to admit this, but I thought for a moment that maybe it could be beneficial for my mom. She has Alzheimer's. Like maybe there was an ingredient they can use here that we don't have in the US. It's like he could read my mind. I think that's what the threat is—that he knows what I was hoping for."

Bernard nodded. *"Exactement."*

"It could also be website traffic analytics. I'm sure he uses that information to his advantage, not just for targeted marketing but for occasional intimidation," Tim said.

I didn't like either thought, though Tim's was a lot easier to comprehend. In English, I said, "I just looked it up for the first time yesterday. That's too fast for international shipping, right? He must've sent this before I even met him. Like the day I got to Châteaubriant."

"He wants you to know that you're devastatingly predictable," Salomé said in French. "I'm sure he saw you on the security cameras and found out who you were, ran a background check on you, found out about your mother, and in anticipation of all the shit he knew I'd say about him, he sent it."

"Really?"

She shrugged, a little too casually for the situation. "He's like that," she said. But she couldn't know for sure why Marco sent the package. She was probably trying to keep me from worrying that the special little psychic connection we shared might leave us vulnerable to others—though it seemed like it might. What if "nightwalking" pierced some sort of veil, or somehow uploaded my thoughts and memories into a shared drive that anyone else who had nightwalked had access to?

I didn't have the mental energy to consider this. It was hard to focus on the greater problem when we were literally fainting from the heat. It was almost 5 p.m. I hoped that meant we'd made it through the hottest part of the day.

I watched Salomé turn over her thoughts. This time tomorrow, we'd be on a plane back to Raleigh, if everything went as planned. But if something went wrong, I wouldn't be able to wait for her. And if she decided not to come with me for whatever reason, I'd have to leave alone.

As much as I didn't want to consider that option, I knew that when the time came, my legs would carry me to the train station. I might be exhausted, sweaty, crumbling under the weight of my backpack and the unbelievable mess of the week. I might be crying, not wanting to let go of her hand, or I might be walking alone. But no matter what I was leaving behind, I would get home to my mother.

CHAPTER 20

Salomé called Nathalie several times on the short drive to the Leduc house, but she didn't answer. We were going to grab Salomé's passport and suitcase. Salomé wanted to see Nathalie before she left, to at least say goodbye, and encourage her to let Bernard help. I understood why she wanted to do that, but my plan was to sit in the car. I didn't want to see Nathalie ever again.

Bernard followed in his own car. If we found Nathalie, he would confront her about the summit and offer to help her dismantle it, if she was willing.

"And what if she isn't willing?" Tim had asked before we left Bernard's house.

Bernard didn't have an answer. "I want to give her the option first."

Tim, Salomé, and I didn't speak much on the way to Nathalie's house. We pulled onto Rue de la Poterie. The Peugeot was in the driveway, but the Mercedes was not. Salomé hoped aloud that this meant Nathalie was home alone.

Tim parked on the street in front of the house. Salomé gave me a long glance before she got out of the car and went inside.

Bernard parked behind us, then came and sat beside me in the back seat while we waited.

Tim was reading Loïc's blogs on his phone.

"So how much of this did Loïc know?" I asked.

Tim told us that Loïc had figured out just about everything. He had traced the history of the Magpies back to the early 1930s. He'd identified the main donors from the US. He puffed air into one cheek when he said, "But the one thing he's wrong about is trying to legally attack ViPi for being a laundering scheme."

"Why's that?"

"He seemed to think it was the weakest link and was planning to get ViPi embroiled in legal bullshit with the government, but it seems to me that Marco would've made sure all of that was watertight. And maybe going about it from that direction drew too much attention to him," Tim said.

Bernard shook his head in pity. "If Marco can astrally project, then none of this matters. It doesn't matter where we are on the planet. He can find us, and he won't be recognizable to us. It doesn't even matter if he goes to jail."

I'd been thinking about this since we'd left Bernard's house, except I hadn't been worried about Marco as much as I had Nathalie. These "rules" of projection would apply to her too, right? If Salomé lived with me, would I basically be a portal for Nathalie to visit her daughter whenever she wanted? Or perhaps she would go through with her plan to live as me?

Tim turned in his seat to look at me. "Do you think Salomé brought you here for that purpose? To deliver a new shell for Nathalie to live in?"

Bernard stiffened.

"No," I said immediately. "No, I don't. I asked her."

Tim's small laugh had a sardonic edge to it. "Like she'd tell you."

I fixed my eyes on the front door, holding my breath. Tim was right, as much as I didn't want it to be true. I had been prioritizing my desires more than my safety, and I seemed to be confused about both of those things—just the same high school girl who wanted her assailant to smile at her in the hallway.

Just then, Salomé reappeared out the front door, pulling her suitcase behind her. As soon as I saw her, the worries dissipated.

Tim popped the trunk for her suitcase. She slammed the trunk closed, then got into the front seat and placed a charcoal-colored messenger bag on her knees. I recognized it from the morning I met Marco, the same bag he'd taken with him when he left for work.

"She wasn't there, but her phone was. She must've walked somewhere and didn't want him to track her," she told us in French. "Her room was locked."

"You're sure she wasn't in her room?" I asked.

"She locks it when she leaves the house," Salomé said.

"Do you have any idea where she could've gone?" Bernard asked.

"I have two guesses." She looked at me in the back seat. "Courten-ey, will you come with me?"

"Where?"

In French, Salomé said, "Right around the corner. I think my mom might be there. I want to check, anyway." To Tim, she said, "This is Marco's," and handed him the messenger bag.

Tim unzipped it and looked inside. He pulled out a bunch of samples of vitamins in plastic sachets that said "ViPi" in the Papyrus font. They looked cheap.

"Just to come out in piss, you know. What else is there?" Salomé said.

There were two issues of *Le Figaro* newspaper, folded so neatly they appeared unread. He checked out the other pockets but found nothing of importance.

"You can just wait for us," Salomé said to Tim and Bernard. "We won't be long."

Tim nodded and went back to reading Loïc's blogs. I felt bad making them wait, but at the same time, being inside an air-conditioned car was far more comfortable than being anywhere else. Tim seemed okay now, but he clearly hadn't felt well since he fainted. I was going to do everything I could to be on a train to Paris later so he wouldn't have to drive me.

There was no part of me that wanted to go look for Nathalie. I didn't want to see Nathalie at all. But I was too tired to protest, so I got out of the car.

Salomé and I walked on the shoulder of Rue de la Poterie. Before, when we'd walked to town, we'd turned left, but this time, she took a right and walked toward an old redbrick church with a small graveyard across the street.

I'd never felt heat like this, endlessly compounded without the reprieve of air-conditioning. And I'd grown up in the American South, where a summer rain would turn pavement into a sauna and you could get a sunburn through your car window. The sweat left cumulative layers of hardened salt on my skin, pulling at the corners of my eyes, constricting around my neck when I turned my head. I felt like a human stalagmite.

Salomé came to a halt at the cemetery gates. "*Oh putain, non!*" she muttered. Down a few aisles of raised graves—I wasn't sure if the correct word was *mausolée* or *sépulcre*—a fairly new one was dotted with fluttering black feathers. She marched across the fine gravel and didn't stop until she'd climbed right onto the concrete slab of the grave. I jumped a little at the brazenness. She picked the feathers away one by one.

"Sometimes they do this," was the only explanation she gave. She handed me a bouquet of about twenty of them and tossed the rest onto the ground. They were real, so inky black they shimmered tints of blue as I turned one between my fingers.

The inscription on the structure read:

LEDUC

THIERRY ÉTIENNE

NÉ LE 14 JANVIER 1940 À CHÂTEAUBRIANT

DÉCÉDÉ LE 5 MAI 2014 À CHÂTEAUBRIANT

Repose en paix notre cher papa

Salomé sat cross-legged on the slab of stone, propping her head in her hands, elbows on her knees, watching me twirl the feather. "The Magpies, they make him their . . . saint or something."

In French, she said, "These people don't know my father at all. It's strange. I don't know how to describe it." She paused. "I miss him."

I made a small move toward her and she patted the stone, inviting me to sit. I'd never climbed onto a grave, at least not knowingly. I put my hand on her back and she did the same for me, the closest thing to an embrace we could bear in the heat. I couldn't recall ever knowing anyone I could touch so casually.

"You thought Nathalie might be here?" I asked.

"Sometimes she comes to remove the feathers. But it's so hot, it makes sense she isn't here." She swung her legs a couple of times as if we were sitting on a dock, our toes dipped in the water. "But I also needed a minute away from the men. Just to stop investigating my family for 'alf a second."

"Yeah. Thank you. I know this is terrible and hard."

She looked from the epitaph to the little pile of feathers on the ground. I wondered if bringing me to sit on her father's grave was supposed to be proof to me that he had actually died. I felt a surge of pity for her, no matter what her level of involvement had been. She never wanted it to come to this.

She extended her legs in front of her, then brought her knees to her chest, wrapping her arms around her shins. "A few days before he died, Papa asked me if I would live my life over again, exactly as it had been, if I had the chance. I told him yes, and that made him happy, because that meant he had given me the best life possible. But now, I don't think I would, because that would mean I'd have to lose him twice," she said in French. She leaned her cheek against her knees and closed her eyes. "I asked him the same question. Would you do it all again? And with no explanation, and no hesitation, he said, 'No.'"

My mother's death loomed on the horizon like a distant milepost I couldn't look directly at, though I knew someday I'd have to. I'd almost started anticipating the relief as much as the pain. The pain of losing her exacerbated by the pain of never being close in the first place, time fleeting by, robbing me of the chance to get my shit together and try harder.

Sweat streaked down our faces, cutting through gravel dust, and dripped off our chins. We could no longer fight the heat or even mention it.

In only a few hours, we'd be at the air-conditioned airport, where we'd find a corner for the night. Salomé could rest her head in my lap to sleep. Maybe we could wipe ourselves down with cool water in the airport bathroom. Stranger things had been done in airports, I was sure.

I said, "So where is the other place Nathalie might be?"

Salomé looked at me. "That old school. Marco uses it as his 'office.'"

Perhaps that was the real reason she had taken me there that day. Not to learn about Guy Môquet, but to see if anything was amiss. But I was too exhausted to ask.

"What are you going to say to your mom? Are you going to confront her about . . . using me?" I wasn't sure what vocabulary to use for astral projection.

"I'm going to tell her that I know. And that if she does this summit, I will not be in her life anymore." She paused, letting her legs drop down again. "Cour-ten-ey, I know you want to go now, and I understand. But I worry that if I don't see my mother before I leave, I might never see her again."

I had nothing to say. She was right. I had to give her this chance.

"Look," she said, turning her phone screen toward me with the SNCF timetable pulled up. "The last train to Paris is at *vingt-deux heures trente.* We have four hours."

Four hours. She said that like it was a good thing.

"Dude," I said.

"Yeah, 'dude'?" I had to stop calling her that.

"We haven't looked into the visa requirements for you to reenter the US. You were just there for ninety days, right? I think you have to be gone for longer before you come back in."

She exhaled. "Sheet, I did not think of that."

"I hate all this bullshit. Why can't people just be where they want to be?"

She pressed off the mausoleum to stand up, then helped me stand. I put my hands on her shoulders to steady myself. My vision trembled. Her skin beneath the freckles was red from sun. I almost said, "I love you," but I stopped myself, though it would've been true, to the extent of my knowledge. I pulled her to me and pressed my lips against her forehead, rough with salt. I breathed in the scent of her scalp, which smelled like rainwater. It wasn't a kiss, just an instinct to be close to her, while I still could.

I wished there was a way to describe how deeply I felt her presence. All the words were negative: "possessed," "inhabited," "obsessed." Those weren't right. I felt like a little cottage that she had made into her home, tending to the rooms and garden with care.

"We will figure it out," she said when I pulled away.

"I'll stay with you until the last minute," I said. "Whenever that is."

She took one last look at her father's grave. In French, she said, "Goodbye, Papa. Please protect us. We might need you."

CHAPTER 21

Tim drove us past the château and the scummy green pond that had seemed so romantic on that first night. We pulled onto the school's driveway and plunged into an eerie twilit darkness under the dense canopy of trees. I felt eyes on me from the thicket. My first thought was they were judging me, condemning me. Or maybe they were protecting us. Loïc, watching us continue his work. Thierry, if he was truly as opposed to this group—cult, or whatever it was—as Salomé made it seem.

We broke into the clearing, where the daylight smoldered on. The top of the old school was lit by a bright stripe of yellow sunlight, reflected sharply off the third-story windows.

At 6:45 p.m. the sun had barely begun its descent and would take at least four hours to set. By the time it was low on the horizon, I would be on the way to Paris. God, please let that be the case.

We got out of the car. Salomé tucked her sweaty bangs behind her ear, trembling out of fear or heat exhaustion or both. I reached for her hand and caught it between mine, squeezing lightly to steady her.

She sighed and said, "Wait here. I'll go first." She pulled away and walked around the back of the building, where she disappeared from sight.

I crumpled to the ground in the shade of a giant tree. Burning jabs coursed through the back of my thigh. I jerked to the side to see if I'd sat on an anthill, but it was just a stinging nettle plant that had gone through my skirt. I didn't even get up. I was too tired to be bothered to move for an inconvenience as small as pain. It almost felt good, this discomfort, unrelated to real danger or the heat.

Ten years ago I'd gone to a Saturday market in Paris and overheard a woman buying a bunch of *ortie* for tea. The farmer who sold the nettles reached for them with her bare hands, and the customer reacted with surprise. "Don't they sting you?"

The farmer's dark hair was streaked with gray. She smiled and said, "Yes, they sting me," with no further explanation. I wondered where she was now, if she'd staved off arthritis because she let herself be stung, how pronounced that gray streak had become. I stood and examined the red welts forming along the backs of my thighs. "I sat in nettles," I said to Tim, who was leaning against his car. His gaze was fixed on the side of the building where Salomé had disappeared.

He nodded and sat on the gravel, checking first for nettles. He rested his back against the car. Poor Tim.

Bernard had parked beside Tim but hadn't gotten out yet.

I turned back toward the building, choked by vines, roof more moss than shingle. On the lower left window were two little smudges left by our foreheads.

A black-and-white bird flew from behind the building and into the trees, where it perched on a branch, screeching. Another followed.

Tim gazed up where the magpies settled and said, "*Putain . . .*"

"Cour-ten-ey, come help!" Salomé's voice echoed against the trees.

She didn't sound scared or threatened, but the word "help" sent me running toward her, stomping through the high grass, around the side of the building, and down a staircase that descended to a basement door propped open by a brick. The sounds of agitated birds poured through as I jerked it open. A flurry of black collided with my face—hard, smooth beak and wisp of feathers—before it flew up and away.

Salomé stood in the doorway wearing thick leather falconry gloves. She looked almost surprised to see me. "Sorry," she said, then beckoned for me to follow her into the dark basement. I covered my ears to brace against the cacophony of screaming birds.

It smelled like a zoo, rank and earthy. My eyes adjusted to the dim greenish light from the line of bulbs along the ceiling. Along the back wall were the kinds of things I expected to see in a laboratory: shelves of beakers, tubes, all pretty cheap-looking, perhaps leftover storage from the school's chemistry classes. They were covered in several years' worth of dust. Against the far wall were birdcages, about a dozen in all. Some were empty. The rest made such a calamitous noise that along with the odor was almost a sensory overload.

Tim opened the door behind me and immediately covered his nose with his shirt. He moved the brick to prop the door open wider, casting a stripe of daylight across the room.

Someone was seated at a long stainless-steel table in the middle of the room that looked like it belonged in a morgue, not a two-hundred-year-old abandoned schoolhouse. It took me a few seconds to realize it was Nathalie, head in her hands, her bony chest leaning against the table's edge. Her body language read like someone suffering from a migraine. With all these screeching birds, she may not have known I came in.

"There are more gloves there," Salomé said, tilting her head toward the end of the table. She unlatched a cage and reached in, murmuring to the frightened bird. She clasped the bird between her gloved hands, pinning its wings safely to its sides. Its feet pedaled the air as she walked it across the room. I stepped in alongside her.

She let go of the bird at the open door. "Help me."

I didn't particularly want to handle the birds, but I pulled on the gloves. Nathalie sat still, eyes closed against the endless noise. Surely the birds hadn't been this loud for long before Salomé showed up. No one would be able to work in here, if not for the noise then for the smell.

I crossed the room and looked into one of the cages. A magpie battered itself against the cage door, flashing its pointy black tongue out with each cry. I wasn't confident I would be able to pick it up. I'd never held a bird before, or even been very close to one. The magpie's eyes were solid black beads, but there was sentience there. The bird knew we were freeing the others and was anxious to go. I wondered if he had access to the memory pool like we did. What if this bird could remember me walking down that road in the middle of the night and passing the dead deer? Maybe it saw me saving the praying mantis and wondered why I didn't just eat it.

Salomé already had her next bird in hand and was crossing the floor. "Hurry," she said.

I opened the cage and grabbed the bird, but I only got one wing down. I worried I was squeezing too hard. It writhed against my hands as I ran to the door. I pitched it into the air and it took a few flaps of its wings to right itself, but made it into a tree.

Salomé looked annoyed with me. "You have to be more careful."

"Sorry," I said. I opened the next cage for her to reach into, which was a much better system.

Tim walked slowly next to the shelves of beakers and lab equipment, surveying the collection. He picked up a glass bottle and gently dusted it off on the bottom of his shirt before placing it back on the shelf.

"Cour-ten-ey!" Salomé said. She was crossing to the final bird's cage. I hurried over and opened it for her.

Once she let it go, a balmy silence fell over the room, except for the unnerving buzzing of the overhead light bulbs. Nathalie was no longer at the table.

"Where did she go?" I asked, looking around.

"She is there." Salomé nodded to where Nathalie's feet were sticking out from under the table like the Wicked Witch of the East. There were bird droppings and straw all over the floor. I couldn't believe she was down there. She was probably dizzy from the heat and malnourishment.

Nathalie looked from me to Salomé to Tim. Her eyes were glossy as usual. Maybe she was always drunk, though that would be a lot of calories to report. She had one hand on her belly, the other on her heart. She appeared to be doing a breathing exercise. Her face was expressionless, maybe dissociated. Whatever the case, she didn't seem upset that we were here. Maybe she was slamming her hand down on the self-destruct button because it was her only way out.

After a few seconds, Nathalie's voice cut through the room in French. "I am so tired."

Salomé stepped forward and dropped to her knees at Nathalie's side.

Nathalie flopped her arm over her eyes. She heaved a shaking sigh and said, "I am done. I am sorry," in English. With her eyes still covered, she said, "Who's that?" in an equally weary tone.

"Tim," Salomé said.

Tim said in French, "I found Courtney after you abandoned her at the beach this morning."

Tim used *tu*, which signified a level of friendliness that didn't seem appropriate between him and Nathalie.

Salomé hesitated, then said in French, "We know about the nightwalking."

Nathalie didn't seem surprised. "Who told you?"

"Bernard Menoret."

Nathalie almost laughed under her breath. "Bernard. He has been chasing me for years."

"He's outside," Salomé said.

"Bernard is here?" There was hopefulness in her voice. She slowly sat up, with Salomé's help, and climbed to her feet.

Bernard must've been listening at the door, because he pushed it open at the mention of his name. Bernard and Nathalie were cordial given the circumstances, greeting each other with "*Bonsoir.*"

Nathalie's hands trembled as they fluttered to her face. Despite her tiny size, she gave off the energy of a balloon that was full to the point of popping, a visible, almost tangible freneticism that was magnified by the incessant buzzing of the light bulbs. She looked at Salomé and said in French, "I'm in trouble, my darling. I don't expect you to understand."

The only other time I'd seen a person look so fragile was my mother when I found her on the floor beside her bed the day my father left. What was this pity I felt for her? I should be screaming, pounding my fists against her bony shoulders.

Bernard said, "Nathalie. We're listening."

Nathalie said, in English, obviously for my benefit, "This isn't what I wanted. This isn't what Thierry wanted. What Thierry and I conceived was an idea of volunteers. People who wanted to fuse with someone brilliant or famous, who had so much left to offer the world through their science or their art, but needed another lifetime to accomplish it. Marco was supposed to find people willing to be hosts. But Marco found a group of people who wanted immortality for themselves. The Magpies existed long before us and had been seeking immortality in a variety of ways, but their resources were limited, as was their science. Marco brought it all together. And they have paid us a lot of money . . . how could I say no . . . ?" Nathalie cupped her hand over her mouth. "This is my fault. I taught him."

"Why did you teach him?" Salomé asked, sounding more curious than accusatory.

"I don't know. I thought I had to," Nathalie said, almost in a whisper. She looked directly at me and said, "But you know what it feels like now, don't you?"

"What?"

"This transcendent connection. I thought I would never feel it with anyone other than Thierry. And then, as Marco learned to share the astral space, we got closer and closer, and he saw me in ways I had never felt before."

"Couldn't you see that he was bad, then?" I asked.

She dropped her gaze to the dirty cement floor. "He wasn't always like that. He changed. And by the time I saw who he truly was, it was too late."

My brain struggled to make room for this information. There were so many things I wanted to ask her, but all I could think of was, "Did you make me cut my hair?"

"You remember?" Nathalie said.

"I was half awake. It was terrifying."

Nathalie looked genuinely surprised. "I think it is different for everyone. But yes, I always cut a little 'air before I take someone anywhere. They will only do it if they think they are dreaming. It does not hurt anyone."

"And what about this?" I pointed to my inner elbow.

"Just something to make it easier on everyone."

"What was it?"

"*Kétamine.* It is very safe. But it helps the vessel not push me out."

I pulled out one of the stools and sat. Ketamine was a hallucinogen, right? No wonder it felt like a bad acid trip. "Tell me you used a sterile needle, Nathalie."

She managed to look offended. "Of course."

I hadn't felt angry before, but now it felt like a swarm of bees was pummeling the inside of my chest. "Fuck you," I said, this time letting myself speak so loudly a spray of spit flew from my mouth. I didn't look at Salomé or anyone else. I wanted to see Nathalie squirm under my gaze.

Nathalie sighed. "I didn't mean to leave you there. I brought your bag so you wouldn't be without your things in case we were separated."

Was I supposed to thank her for that? "I can't drive a stick shift! What if you'd been woken up while I was driving?"

Salomé gasped. "I woke you up," she said to Nathalie. "I woke you up while you were nightwalking and . . ."

Nathalie nodded. "If my body is woken up while I am projecting, I spend the next several hours in a terrifying state of delusion and confusion. It has always been like that. I've used pills and other medication to keep my body asleep, but lately they have stopped working."

Salomé said, "So each time you flipped out, since I was a child, it was because of this?"

"*Oui*," Nathalie said on an inhalation. "We tried to keep it away from you, but it takes so much practice to project, even into a bird. And I was training your father. We had to do it every few days to maintain our level of skill. Most of the time it went well."

"I know you considered projecting into me and then killing your body," I said.

Nathalie looked at me, unblinking. "I thought about it."

"And what would happen to me? Would I live in a fucking nightmare for the rest of my life?" My voice verged on a shout, loud enough that a few of the glass beakers on the shelves rattled.

Nathalie's reply was quiet. "I don't know."

"Nathalie, you have other options," Bernard said from across the room.

Nathalie twisted her frail body in his direction, as if suddenly recalling his presence. "You don't know the terror I live in. I cannot do anything on my phone that Marco doesn't trace," Nathalie said in French, her eyes wild. "Even calling my own daughters can become a debate. He knows I could render the most lucrative part of his business obsolete if I decided to share the knowledge for free. He knows I'm the only person who could . . ."

We all waited in silence while Nathalie caught her breath, steadying herself on the table.

She turned to Salomé, her face softening. "I was going to bring you, too, to the statue last night, so we could speak with Thierry together. *Serpent d'Océan*'s location is at a particularly thin part of the veil. I've recently discovered that I can access Thierry's consciousness when I'm near it. I was going to tell you it was me. But when we got home from dinner, Marco was there, and he knew I was projecting without his permission. I'm sorry I left you with him. I was running out of time."

Salomé looked as if she'd been slapped across the face. It almost sounded like Nathalie was implying that Thierry condoned her actions. "What does Papa say about all of this?"

Tim cleared his throat. He said, in French, "If I may, as a more impartial person here, I think we should look at the facts. There is no crime. Even if you called the police and told them that someone astrally projected into Courtney, what it will look like to them is that she stole a car. Marco could file a police report about it in ten minutes' time. So, instead of wallowing in this revelation, it'd be best to discuss our next move. How might this all work to your benefit?"

I wasn't sure I'd understood him correctly. What was he saying?

Tim continued, "And Nathalie is right. She is in danger, and the more you all pretend like she won't be in more danger if she tried to leave, or tried to tamper with Marco's empire, the more delusional you sound. Marco is a powerful person who occupies himself with other very powerful people. You saw what happened to Loïc." He then looked at me. "Courtney, I'd take whatever benefits he might offer you. My sense is that he could get you a French visa in one phone call. And Salomé," he said, turning to her, "you're in an amazing position to get whatever you've always wanted, too. If you want funding for your animal rescue center, Marco could get that for you. You're basically royalty to his community."

Salomé and I both stared at him, trying to make sense of what he was saying.

When was the last time I'd heard Tim speak English? There was new calculating shrewdness in his eyes. Why hadn't I noticed it before?

Tim scoffed. "As if I wouldn't know where you'd gone, Nathalie. You take me for a fool."

Nathalie said, "*Oh, putain.*"

Salomé took a step backward to create a tiny bit more distance between her and Tim.

Tim clapped his hands together once, looking delighted with his big reveal. "I'm glad to know what you've been planning, Nathalie."

Nathalie screamed a horrible, reverberating shriek. She picked up a stool and lifted it over her head, the tendons in her thin arms stretching taut. Before she could throw it or charge at him, Tim's body swayed violently, his joints crumpling like a dropped silk scarf. Bernard lunged toward Tim, catching him as he fell, and guided him to the floor. Tim's eyes rolled back until we saw only the whites.

I tried to rush to Tim's side, but my knees buckled as soon as my feet touched the floor. I slumped forward and fell to all fours on the grimy cement. "I almost fainted," I tried to say to Salomé, but my voice echoed from far away.

I felt tugged downward by a gravity deep inside my body. The edges of my vision blurred, and suddenly Nathalie's hands were on the sides of my face. Just before I lost consciousness, she said, "You must fight back."

CHAPTER 22

I tried to breathe through it. The energy pushed its way from the depths of my body, rushing out like a current. It didn't hurt. All I felt was release.

Then I was cool. There was a pillow under my cheek. I opened my eyes. I was curled on my side in a small, yet comfortable, bed. It was familiar. I sat up.

The room was dark due to the closed shutter. I got out of bed and crossed to the window. I pulled the rope on the side to roll up the *volet.* Bright sunlight sliced across the room, growing wider with each tug of the rope.

The floorboards were smooth under my bare feet. I opened the windows and looked out at the cobblestone street below. The locksmith was putting his key into the shop door, just arriving to work. Paris. My apartment.

I went out into the living room. It was how Kylie and I had left it, but slightly nicer. Instead of the folding table we'd gotten for fifteen euros from Leboncoin, there was a solid wood table covered with a spread of cheeses and fruit. I went over and picked up a fuzzy little apricot, bringing it to my lips, breathing in its sweet-and-tart smell.

The produce store right around the corner on Square Carpeaux had the best apricots.

"Oh good, you're up." Salomé's voice came from behind me.

She was barefoot, wearing a simple white linen dress. She approached me, gliding over the floor. When I thought she would stop, she took a step closer. She maintained eye contact as she lowered her head and took a bite out of the apricot in my hand. She pulled away, leaving a drop of juice on her lower lip.

I leaned forward and kissed her, tasting the sweet drop. There was nothing awkward about it. We did this all the time. She hooked her fingers into mine and led me gently back to my bedroom. She sat me on the edge of the bed and straddled me, pulling the dress off from over her head. The apricot fell to the floor with a little thud.

I closed my eyes and saw bursts of colors behind my eyelids as she kissed me, shimmery blue on our inhales and soft rose on our exhales, which tickled across my cheek. The dewy words of the poem spiraled through my mind, not only words or sounds, but somehow both, neither. She sat up and grasped the bottom of my shirt, pulling it up. I lifted myself onto my elbows to help her. She maintained intense eye contact, and before she brought the shirt over my head, she said, "I want you so bad, baby."

I shifted slightly, stiffening my arms so she couldn't lift my shirt any higher.

"What?"

"You 'eard me. I want you so bad, I want you to fuck me, baby."

No. This wasn't right. I had to get away from this. "I need to go to the bathroom," I said, and wiggled out from beneath her.

"Don't leave me 'ere, Cour-ten-ey." She flipped onto her back and crammed her fingers between her legs, moaning as she arched her back against the bed.

I couldn't look at her. I went into the main room and to the little green basket of apricots. I picked one up and examined it. Not a single blemish. I turned to look at the apartment. I didn't live here anymore. Slowly, the realization came that none of this was real. I struggled to remember the last thing I'd seen before I opened my eyes here.

"Is some-zing wrong, Cour-ten-ey?" Salomé's voice came from the bedroom in an almost cartoonish French accent.

The school basement. The birds. Nathalie's warning: *You must fight back.*

Salomé appeared in the bedroom door, completely naked. She walked slowly toward me, placing one little dovelike foot in front of the other, hips swinging from side to side. This Salomé's breasts were larger and rounder. She had no pubic hair. I didn't know how the real Salomé preferred to groom her pubic hair, but this cheap facsimile infuriated me.

"What are you?" I said. As soon as the words left my mouth the air around me became thick with electricity, as if I could dig my fingers into it and claw through. I tried paddling my hands against nothing. The buzzing sensation grew brighter, louder. Salomé got close to me and kissed me again, fiercely this time, biting my lip so hard I tasted blood.

Don't open your eyes.

No no no no. I knew what I would see when I was free of her embrace. The sunken spot. I felt the void of it under my lips. I pulled my head away, pushed her hard with both of my hands. I covered my eyes and rushed into the kitchen.

"Cour-ten-ey, don't leave me," she called. "I have some-zing for you. A beautiful poem, to start your career as a real writer, to inspire you every day for as long as you live."

I turned on the electric stove eye. When it glowed orange, I slapped my hand on it. Pain seared through my arm. I screamed and fell backward, clutching my hand to my chest. It didn't work. I'd have to find another way through.

I tried to inspect the damage, even though I knew it wasn't really my hand. I uncurled my fingers. My palm was shiny and red. And I had too many fingers. I wiggled them each, one by one. There were seven. *S-E-R-R-U-R-E*, I spelled. The noun for "lock," a word I'd always wanted to spell, but it didn't fit across five fingers in a satisfying way.

S-E-R-R-U-R-E. S-E-R-R-U-R-E. S-E-R-R-U-R-E. I held my hand directly in front of my face, blocking out the kitchen and any memories that could come with it. This place was meant to be a distraction. The seven fingers twitched one by one. My periphery was buzzing, but I kept my eyes focused on my fingers. *S-E-R-R-U-R-E.* I felt Marco's gravity on the other side of the buzzing. I needed to be closer to him, I knew instinctively. I tried to get myself into his orbit.

My eyes closed. When they opened, I was in the middle of a giant hall with a rounded ceiling and walls lined with shelves of thousands of books. There were leather couches and plush velvet reading chairs, luxurious rugs, the warm glow of lamps, and potted plants in every nook.

Marco sat on a crimson-colored velvet chair, tucked between a bird of paradise plant and a bookcase. He didn't look like the real Marco. This was the pallid and wormy version, more like a bad Madame Tussauds wax figure than a person. Still, there was a smug expression on his face, a slight curl of his lip under his stringy mustache. Maybe this was just how my consciousness perceived him so I'd be less threatened.

Fuck this guy. We were both in my body, were we not? I had to have the upper hand here. I strode toward him. He held up a hand as if to stop me, but I kept going. "Get out!" I screamed. The sound waves from my voice ricocheted back and hit me in the face, stinging like hundreds of needles. I stopped, covering my face.

"I gave you everything you wanted. Your old apartment where you can live with Salomé and fuck her whenever you want. It wasn't to your liking?" Was he speaking French or English? His mouth wasn't moving. It was just something I could hear.

I was afraid to speak aloud again. I tried responding without speaking. "That's not what I want," I thought. "I want you to leave. You aren't welcome here."

"I'm not some sort of ghost you can exorcize by saying I'm not welcome. That's not how this works."

"This isn't real!"

"Normally I don't tell people this so early into our relationship, but I suppose you should know. It's not real out there either. It's all made up. Everything. The systems. The order. The money. The laws. It's all fake. Some of us sink, and some of us swim. And some of us build boats and go into uncharted territory. It's always been this way. And I think of this as not the final frontier, but one of the least explored, yet most accessible. So yes, it is all made up. But if you walk to the window and look out, you'll see Paris, just as you remember it. And the more receptive you are, the more control you have over your experience. Nathalie's ridiculous idea of using ketamine to subdue her recipient doesn't illustrate what can be in it for them. You can design everything. You could have everything you want."

"What, I'm supposed to *stay* here? While you drive my body around like a car? What the fuck?"

There was a strange sound, a rapid series of taps. I looked at Marco's hands, which were folded over a book on his lap. *Tap-tap-tap-tap. Tap-tap-tap-tap.* His fingers were shiny, metallic. They were knives. Was this my imagination, or was it his?

"Wait, are we going to fight?" I said aloud, accidentally, and felt the air sucked out of my lungs like a vacuum. I grabbed my throat and coughed.

"I certainly don't want to." *Tap-tap-tap-tap.*

I wanted to scream, to hurl myself at him, wrap my hands around his throat and squeeze as hard as I could, but my body wouldn't do anything. This probably wasn't even Marco's consciousness I was talking to. It was probably some avatar he was using to distract me while he used my body to convince Salomé to act in his best interest. She would know it wasn't me, right? Or maybe he was holding me hostage as leverage against her.

The air around me warbled, thick and viscous. The buzzing started again, though distant.

"Can't you just accept a gift?" Marco said. "You ungrateful American." *Tap-tap-tap-tap.* The tapping frightened me. The air thinned a bit; the buzzing subsided. No, that's not what I needed. It seemed the thickness was what I could move through, as though the less I invested in perceiving this space as real, the more I could manipulate it.

I looked up at the domed glass ceiling. The sky was cloudy and gray. I kept my eyes trained on the sky. I had to anchor myself into the real world. What was there? My mom. The dings from her phone as she did Duolingo. The set of cloth napkins in her kitchen that still smelled like Gran over ten years after she died.

The air buzzed and warped. This was what I wanted.

Tap-tap-tap-tap.

"Don't you see what I'm trying to build here? And yet here comes the American hero. You, just like your ancestors, must think you are entitled to everyone else's successes, everyone else's empires. You know it is in your blood to not let people have what they've worked for. But here is your chance to leave it alone, and look what I can give you in return."

No. Pull harder. The spiderweb by Mom's front door, where I saw her initials spun in silk: *EW*, Elspeth Woods, and I said, "Mom, look." Before she knew what I was talking about, she swiped at the web with a broom and I watched the dark round spider retreat into the safety of the porch's rafters.

The air was so thick, it was becoming hard to breathe. It shimmered in front of my face. I reached out my hand and found the space in front of me solid enough to press against.

Tap-tap-tap-tap. Marco stood from his chair.

I thought of Salomé's lips pressed against mine, the tent of hair, the way her fingers slid across my collarbone. The honey-sick feeling in my stomach when we were close.

"Cour-ten-ey?" I heard her voice all around me, warped, as if it were traveling through water. "Cour-ten-ey?"

I paddled the air, thinking maybe I could swim in it, and my hand hit something hard like metal. It was invisible except for the wavy undulations. I felt for it and realized it had distinct rungs. A ladder. I hoisted myself onto it and scrambled for the ceiling.

The ladder shook beneath me. The sound of metal on metal. I didn't have to look down to know he was climbing after me. I hurried up and up toward the domed window.

"Cour-ten-ey!" It was Salomé's voice, very far away.

"I'm coming," I thought. I got to the top and pressed against the windowpanes. I pushed as hard as I could, but there was no way I could move the glass. Marco's metal fingers scraped the rungs below me. I had only a few seconds to break through.

I couldn't help but scream as I pushed with everything I had. Instead of sound, the skeleton of a snake exploded out of my mouth like a cannon, shattering through the window before coiling back into my throat. I shoved upward, upward, and felt hands on my arms as I slapped my way onto the roof.

"Cour-ten-ey, are you there?"

I opened my eyes.

"Cour-ten-ey." I reached for her and she wrapped her arms around me. I was on the bird shit–covered basement floor.

"What's happening?" I gasped, gripping the back of her shirt.

Salomé's face was streaked with grime and sweat. I looked wildly from side to side, scanning the room for the others. I didn't see them.

"Help me. Marco . . ." I struggled to catch my breath.

"I'm with you," she said.

Then everything went dark. I was falling backward.

I opened my eyes to see the library walls melting down my periphery in slow motion, like a watercolor painting in the rain. Cold raindrops pelted my face as I fell.

I had no awareness of where the floor was or when I would hit it. My feet were above my head. I was falling headfirst, watching the strap of my sandal flapping, when suddenly I had the instinct to take a huge inhale, just before I plunged into water.

It was warm and dark. I flailed, pumping a stream of bubbles out of my mouth. I saw which way the bubbles traveled and followed them, cracking the surface just as a huge clap of thunder ripped through the sky.

The ocean swelled beneath me, at first bringing me closer to the beach, but then dragging me back out with the tide. My mouth and nose filled with briny water. I coughed. It wasn't real. I had to be able to control this. Another swell of the tide pushed me almost all the way to the shore. My arm bumped something cold and hollow. My eyes weren't adjusted to the darkness enough to see it, but I knew what it was. I clung to the serpent's aluminum rib as the water rushed back out.

I went around the side of the statue and climbed into its mouth, finding shelter from the pelting rain. I gripped one of the fangs as another wave crashed over the top of the skull.

I didn't want to fight Marco. I didn't trust myself to be strong enough or smart enough. I didn't even feel him anymore. He must've been at the surface, interacting with Salomé.

"Marco! Where are you?"

He won't come unless he feels you gaining power over him. Right now he has you exactly where he wants you.

How did I know that? The words had come from within me, just as they had when I'd stood alone in front of the statue a few nights ago.

"Thierry?" I said aloud.

I'm here.

His paternal presence softened my fear. Maybe he could just tell me where the exit was and all of this could be over. "Please, what do I do? I don't know what to do."

Reject him. He will try to overpower you. Don't let him.

Reject him? What did that mean? Maybe I'd have to act as my own immune system, identifying and attacking the intruder, except it would have to be mental. I could show him that even though I didn't have a flourishing meditation practice, I was still the master of my own mind. Why couldn't my spelling count as meditation?

I spelled *S-T-O-P-S-T-O-R-M* across my fingers, which were now five again. I timed the spelling with my breaths. But nothing happened. I was distracted.

You have to find him before you can push him out.

"Marco!" I shouted into the wind. I didn't know how this would work. Would I suddenly join him in whatever universe he was creating, or pull him into mine? I screamed his name over and over, hoping that whatever he was doing, whatever level of lucidity he was experiencing looking out of my eyes, he was distracted.

I could feel his gravity now. A streak of lightning lit the sky, and I saw him standing on the beach. I tried to call out to him, but like in the library, my voice came flying back like shards of glass. I stopped. I was afraid he'd leave, just having muted me, so I scrambled out of the statue and waded through the shallow water toward him.

He stood on the beach with his arms crossed like an unimpressed babysitter. "Shut up," he thought.

I hadn't thought past this moment yet. I tried to think of a response that would keep him from flitting back to the surface, even for a minute longer. But suddenly, my body seized in a flash of heat, and Thierry's voice said: *Move.*

I lunged forward. Just behind me, a boulder crashed into the sand, leaving a crater several inches deep. The sand I stood on started to crumble into the hole. I scooted back onto firmer ground. This wasn't real, right? It couldn't actually hurt me. But the boulder looked solid enough.

The sound of rushing air and rock slapping against wet sand surrounded me. Boulders plunked down all around me in a small circle, and then more on top, and then more. I cowered and covered my head, but nothing touched me. It was happening so fast I barely had time to register that he was building a trap. By the time I looked up, the wall encircling me was twice as tall as my body. More and more rocks zipped into place, until the tower was so tall, the opening was a pinhole.

I was at the bottom of a well. The walls wept a shiny liquid. The earthy, coppery scent of blood. He was trying to deter me from climbing out.

I imagined a rope ladder unfurling down the side, but nothing happened. I imagined the well filling up with water so I could float on the surface, but that didn't happen either. I smelled smoke from a campfire. How could anything be on fire in this storm?

I felt Marco leave, blinking off like a light bulb. He wasn't out there anymore. Shit.

"Thierry?" I tried to say aloud, but the moment I opened my

mouth, it felt stuffed with cactus spines. I almost cried out at the pain in my cheeks but managed to stay quiet. I sat on the sand and started pulling them out, my mouth filling with blood.

Stop. Just get him back.

I wished Thierry could be of more help. This was all his problem, wasn't it? I spat blood and spines onto the ground and nodded. This was a distraction. Even though it felt real, it wasn't. I had to get back to Marco.

I curled onto my side and held my hand in front of my face. The smoke was thicker now. Was he trying to suffocate me? It was too dark to see it, but I spelled *serrure* again and again until the air thickened and the extra fingers were back. This was the key. *S-E-R-R-U-R-E. S-E-R-R-U-R-E.*

The buzzing got so loud, so hot in my ears, but I kept going. I didn't want a ladder this time. I was going to pop through to wherever he was and surprise him. The pressure grew. It was terrible, like diving down to the deep end of the pool, the pressure in my ears like a screwdriver pressing down, and then—

The basement floor again. I sat up.

Salomé was on her knees on the floor beside me. Tears dripped off her chin. "You win," she said in French. "Marco, you win. Use my body, but let Cour-ten-ey go, please, please let her go. I surrender."

I tried to reach for her hand but I couldn't move. I still didn't have control over myself.

"Leave Cour-ten-ey alone for the rest of her life," she cried out. "I surrender, I surrender."

I felt him leave me. The lightness returned to my limbs. I slid my hand over to hers. The second we touched, her eyes locked into mine, and everything in my periphery froze in place. The space between our eyes became a tunnel. I walked into it, my footsteps echoing off the walls. I moved forward in the darkness, closer and closer to Salomé.

Then my toes were at the edge of a steep drop-off. There was a strong wind blowing upward. I wasn't afraid. I knew I needed to go down to the source of the wind, so I closed my eyes and let myself fall.

My feet hit the ground in motion. It was night. I was outside, running through the woods, my arms stretched out in front of me. My foot caught a root and I pitched forward onto the ground. There was a woman screaming. Salomé. I called her name. I held still, straining to hear over my breathing. The screams came from all around.

I climbed to my feet and turned in a circle. Where was she? A freezing wind cut through the trees, and my body shivered violently. I gripped my jaw to keep my teeth from chattering. I couldn't pinpoint the source of the screaming. I called her name, but the wind snatched my voice, sucking it far away.

My eyes were adjusting to the darkness. I was surrounded by trees. A pale light gently tinted the sky straight ahead of me. The sunrise. I walked in that direction until I came into a clearing. There, outlined by the pastel colors of the rising sun, was the school.

I was wearing the same skirt and Chacos I'd been wearing the day before, but it was cold out now. I looked at my hands. Five fingers. I wasn't sure if this was real. Maybe I'd somehow left the basement.

The woman screamed.

"Salomé?" I called into the trees. "Tim?"

I smelled smoke again. I walked across the pebbled driveway and around the back of the school. Maybe the screams were coming from the basement? By the time I got behind the building, the screaming had stopped. The embers from a small fire glowed near the edge of the woods. I approached cautiously and knelt by the fire, warming my palms. Its gentle crackle soothed me.

Something on the other side of the fire caught my eye. Something pale and fleshy. The realization hit me with a jolt: toes splayed limply out to the side, connected to a foot that did not seem to have life in it. I stood.

She was on her back.

"Salomé?" My voice was weak.

She didn't move. I approached slowly. At first I saw only her eyes, fixed on the sky. Then, as my eyes adjusted, I saw the redness around her pale throat.

I touched her hand, gently at first. I said her name again. I grabbed her shoulders, shaking her, crying out. I pinched her nose with my fingers and breathed into her mouth like I'd seen in the movies, but I didn't know what I was doing. I did this until it was obvious it wasn't working.

How long did I kneel there, holding her in my arms, rocking her back and forth, sobbing into her hair? It felt like hours. I remember screaming Tim's name, screaming for help in French and in English. By the time I gave up, the sun had risen. I lay on my side next to her, unable to have a single thought until a few ants crawled across her arm and broke me from my suspended consciousness. I had cried so much that the skin beneath my eyes was chapped. My throat was raw. I breathed raggedly through my mouth.

I wondered if I was actually dead. Maybe when the plane hit that patch of turbulence, it crashed into the North Atlantic. Maybe this whole weeklong fantasy was that burst of DMT as my brain died. Somehow that seemed more realistic than everything else I thought had happened.

And then she moved. A twitch of her hand, then her forearm.

"Salomé?" I sat up. I reached out to touch her, but found her body cold and stiff.

It was the ants. Thousands upon thousands of ants were underneath her, lifting her up, trying to carry her away like a magic carpet.

"No!" I screamed, grabbing her by the arm and pulling her to me. I wrapped myself around the back of her, curled her into a little spoon. The ants tickled. I felt them going through the neck hole of my tank top. I buried my face into the back of Salomé's neck. Magpies screeched from the trees. The air was so thick with smoke, it was hard to breathe. I looked over my shoulder and saw the school building on fire.

There was something about the smell of the smoke that made me remember what Marco said in the library—nothing is real. But did that matter? I could spend the rest of my conscious existence in this world or dimension. Marco was showing me what my life would be like if I kept opposing him. One disorienting hellscape experience after another. The words "white hot rage" came to mind, and maybe that's what it was that crept in next. Something vaguely recognizable as anger, but more absolute, more sinister.

I remembered Nathalie saying I'd have to fight back. But I didn't feel Marco anywhere. This space, wherever I was, did not seem like it was under my control. Then I remembered the tunnel I'd walked through, the look Salomé gave me the moment she invited Marco in.

Holy shit, I realized. I was in Salomé's body. Did I have any control here? I spelled *serrure* several times. Nothing. What did it mean that Salomé was dead in her own body?

I would've thought there were no more tears left in me, but I wept. I've never experienced such deep, desolate sorrow. I wanted my mom. I know I cried out for her, and each time I inhaled to call out again, my mouth and throat filled with ants. I tried to spit them out and swallowed a bunch. Finally I lay still so the ants could eat me.

I thought of my mom right now, probably sitting on the couch with one of Gran's crocheted blankets over her legs because the AC would be blasting throughout the house. Maybe she was watching the Game Show Network, her favorite as of late. She'd recently taken to the habit of fingering the beads around her rosary even while doing other tasks. She didn't realize she was doing it. She'd just pick it up and go bead-by-bead, which had disturbed me when I first noticed. It felt like a countdown of sorts, sand through the hourglass. Now that I thought maybe I'd never see it again, I wished I'd had more compassion. I wished I'd turned off the TV and asked if she wanted me to pray with her.

There were so many things I wished I'd done differently. I spelled her name. *E-L-S-P-E-T-H. E-L-S-P-E-T-H. E-L-S-P-E-T-H.* She'd never felt like an Elspeth, she'd told me many times, and had wanted to give me the gift of normalcy with "Courtney." I always thought I would've made a good Elspeth. I spelled her name until the image of her sitting on the couch with her rosary merged into another vision, one of her and Trudy about eight years ago, waving to me from in front of the airport's automatic doors. I dropped them off before their "big trip"—a cruise to Cozumel. They smiled and waved, wearing matching floppy-brimmed hats and white capris. I remember thinking it was silly to take a cruise rather than a true adventure, and didn't hide my opinion from them. Now I just hoped it was fun. They deserved to have fun. Then I saw her before that, in her early fifties, shortly after the divorce, lying on Gran's couch with an ice pack on her forehead, her eyes swollen and red. Gran brought her a glass of iced tea and set it on a coaster.

"Mom," my mother said, and Gran placed her hand on her head. She stroked for a few seconds before walking away.

I saw Mom holding me as a baby in the middle of the night, sitting in the nursing chair as the mobile spun gently over the crib. She was exhausted but she'd wanted this so badly. I saw her at forty-one, holding up the pregnancy test, her hand over her mouth, trying to stifle the smile. She'd seen two lines before and it had never resulted in a baby she could rock in her arms. But she felt it in her heart that this time it would.

I hoped she got what she wanted. But she probably hadn't. I was not a good daughter. If it's possible for a child to always have one foot out the door, that was me. Trying to go abroad, trying to find ways to leave. Trying to break the mold by not having my own family. I'd spent most of my adult life trying to find a way out, and now I would give anything to spend one more day in that old house, going through the boxes of antiques and heirlooms that made me feel so trapped.

E-L-S-P-E-T-H. There was a finger for each letter now. The air thickened. I didn't want to pass from one imaginary realm to the next, constantly hoping the next one would be real. This had to be the way out.

I felt Marco in this space with me. But I didn't have the energy to open my eyes, let alone sit up and confront him. Leaves shuffled under his feet. The air between us hummed, heavy and potent. My fingers moved, all seven of them, and I spelled my mother's name.

"Court." My mother's voice, not far away. Marco was just trying to torment me. But a soft hand moved across my face, wiping away the ants. "Open your eyes." I did. It was her. I knew it was just a hologram, but I sat up and fell into her embrace.

"I'm sorry," I sobbed into her chest.

"Sorry for what?"

"I hope you got what you wanted," I said. The ants crawled from me to her, connecting us like a map of waterways that existed long before people drew arbitrary borders. I watched them file across the thin skin on my mother's forearm, two by two. The more I watched, the more I was aware of their deliberate movement. They took hairpin turns at precisely the same spots, traveling the same pathways as the ants directly before them.

A thick wind howled around us. I felt Marco in the trees. I didn't know if I was supposed to kill him, or banish him from Salomé's body, or push him so far down that he could never resurface. I didn't want to do any of it. I just wanted to ignore Marco, and maybe I could think of something later after I'd rested.

The ants left a trail of gold dust behind them on our skin. My mother's body and mine were now connected by a series of coiling lines, like what I'd seen in diagrams of electron orbits. The ants walked faster. I sensed I was being given a tool, but I had no idea what it was or how to use it. I touched Salomé's hand, and the ants from my hand walked to her, trailing gold dust onto her.

"You could've had your choice of realities." Marco's voice came from all around. "But I can't trust you to take what you've been given and mind your own business. You've left me no choice but to get rid of you both."

"You're literally using her body right now as some sort of fucked-up playground," I thought. "I don't follow your logic." I immediately wished I'd said nothing. Each time I engaged with him, my energy was further drained. Maybe if I ignored him, he'd burn up in his own fury. I decided to stop giving him the satisfaction of an exchange.

"Oh, but your logic falls short, mademoiselle. There is no scientific basis for the ownership of a body. The soul's implantation is random. Scientifically speaking, it is possible that with the twitch of an atom in another galaxy, your consciousness could be expelled from your body, and you'd have no say in the matter."

My mother looked at Salomé, now crisscrossed with golden lines. She pulled Salomé into a sitting position between us. I leaned forward, wrapping my arms around both of them. Mom and I rested our foreheads together. As the ants marched on, the golden pathways seemed to become binding, securing the three of us into one. It felt nice. I wondered if this was what it felt like to be a baby marsupial, outside your mother, but tethered safely.

"It is far more natural for us to have the choice of bodies than it is to leave it all to chance," Marco droned on. "We have the opportunity to allow great people to be even greater. What if Stephen Hawking had not succumbed to his disease? What if Einstein had lived past the expiration date of his body?"

What if... what if... I slipped further away from being able to care what Marco was saying. It was almost like falling asleep, this warm and inviting place. I felt the ants' pathways lifting off of us, encircling us. My eyes were closed but the vision appeared inside my mind—the golden rings swirling and rotating around us like a force field, the way the skin between our foreheads had fused, our hands and arms shrinking in toward our hearts, fetuses growing in reverse. We were becoming each other's source of everything, shrinking and expanding at the same time.

"You can't ignore me forever, Courtney. Your body will dehydrate and rot right there on the basement floor—"

As soon as he said that, I felt a new density inside myself—my body. I could access my body. I sensed Tim leaning over me, holding my hand. The rings around my mother, Salomé, and me spun faster and faster, so fast they blurred into a solid golden orb.

Marco kept talking but his words became muffled. I could feel the hard cement under my back. The heat wave. I tried to move. I spelled my mother's name though I no longer had fingers. But my real fingers were responding, grit and roughness beneath them.

Tim's voice joined in the muffled chorus of Marco's. I pulled toward Tim's voice.

He was calling my name. His British accent. I pulled and pulled, nearing the surface. The pressure grew heavier. The walls of gold around me were solid now, the light bulb was buzzing above my head, Tim was squeezing my hand, my mother's body was my body was Salomé's body, the air around me was thick and red and wet, there was a pressure in my ears so intense I almost screamed, but my mouth was no longer a mouth, or perhaps it wasn't yet a mouth. I needed to inhale to relieve the pressure. The golden orb around us had reached such a density that it was going to either implode or explode.

"Courtney!"

I took one last pull toward the sound, one final aim, and then the sphere exploded and I hurtled up, back through the tunnel, into the light.

The eerie bulbs hummed directly above me. Somebody was screaming. It was me. I sat up. My voice echoed off the back wall of the stone basement.

Arms around me. Tim. My heart pounded against his chest. I breathed in the soapy, salty smell of his shoulder along with the revolting odor of the basement. I expected to feel other hands on me, cool and comforting, with the scent of herbal lotion, but when I looked around the room, Tim and I were alone.

CHAPTER 23

Tim and I emerged from the basement and saw a black mass of smoke curling up into the sky, the last remnants of the sunset glowing behind it. We both knew it was Nathalie's house.

We hurried to his car and crossed the town in minutes, neither of us speaking, just keeping our eyes fixed on the dark, churning horizon. It was almost 11 p.m. One hour until tomorrow, when I needed to be in Paris, and I didn't know where Salomé was.

Rue de la Poterie was blocked by fire trucks. There was a news van and a reporter speaking into a microphone, jets of water arching upward and onto the smoldering house behind her.

"Did Salomé come here?" I scanned the faces of a small group of onlookers through the passenger seat window.

"I don't know," Tim said. "When Marco projected into her, she just took off."

I'd smelled smoke in there. Did that mean that Salomé was in the house? My hand gripped the door handle, opening it before the car had stopped.

Tim hit the brakes. "I don't want to be seen here. If there are any Magpies around, or any watching on the news, you know?"

"No, of course, just let me out," I said, already halfway out of the car. "I'll meet you over by the cemetery around the corner." I hurried toward an ambulance where I saw Nathalie and Bernard sitting in the back with oxygen masks over their noses. There was a pet carrier between them.

"Where is she?" I yelled to them as I neared.

Nathalie's eyebrows rose and pinched together over the top of the plastic breathing apparatus.

"Where is she?" I said again, my voice pitching higher.

Nathalie's mouth moved under the oxygen mask, her shoulders raised and lowered. I knew what she said: *Je ne sais pas.* I tried to read Nathalie's expression. She wasn't panicking—or at least, she wasn't ripping the mask off and trying to run back into the building to look for her daughter. But she appeared disassociated, blank. I guess most people would be while they watched their home burn to the ground.

"Has she been here or not?"

Nathalie shook her head.

I ran to the side of the house with the wisteria vine and tried to go behind it, but a firefighter reprimanded me. The heat was unbelievable. I wouldn't have been able to get around the side of the house anyway.

Neighbors from the houses on each side were evacuated into the street, carrying their laptops and photo albums. The glass on every window on the side of the house left standing shattered in tandem. The crowd gasped.

An old woman holding a birdcage covered with a sheet approached me. "Was there anyone inside?" she asked in French.

"*Je ne sais pas,*" I told her.

If I could just calm my mind, maybe I could look inside and find her. I tried to breathe. I tried to spell. I closed my eyes and waited to feel her. She wasn't dead. I would know.

My phone buzzed in my back pocket. I grabbed it.

It was from Luke.

Bonjourrrrr :D you back? I'm on my way to Raleigh.

I slid the phone back into my pocket.

The crowd cheered, drawing my attention back to the house. The firefighters had succeeded in quelling the flames. Now the remnants of the house smoldered in thick gray smoke.

The woman next to me said, "Oh, thank God, thank God," in French. She lifted the cage to face-height and peeked under the sheet. "We're going to be okay, *ma belle.* We can go home."

I was watching her speak to the bird when I felt someone behind me. I turned.

She was dirty. There were scratches along her bare shins and her hair was drenched with sweat. The ambulance's flashing lights lit her in blue. Everything around me, the fire trucks, the spraying water, the cries of the firefighters, blurred to nothing. She grabbed me and pulled me close.

"Cour-ten-ey," she said into my neck.

I pulled away and we held each other's faces, smiling and breathing hard through tears.

"It's you," I said.

"C'est moi."

We both looked at Nathalie, who watched us from the back of the ambulance. Salomé ran over and hugged her. She then bent down to look into the animal carrier at Nathalie's feet, sticking her fingers through the grate.

"Where is Marco?" I asked when she returned to me.

She touched my arm. "Let's go somewhere to talk."

We walked away from the flashing lights and sounds of rumbling motors, down Rue de la Poterie and around the corner. When we were far enough away from anyone to risk being overheard, she said, "Maman did what she had to do. She fixed everything."

"What do you mean?"

"Marco, he fell asleep on the bed with a cigarette. Which, I don't know if you know, Marco smoked like, *all the time* at home, but never in public because he was trying to look so healthy, you know?" she said.

It sounded like she was telling me that Nathalie had started the fire while Marco's body was inside, but I didn't say it aloud, just in case.

We approached the edge of the graveyard. I looked toward the mausoleums through the wrought iron fence. "Your dad was in there," I said, hoping she would know what I meant without further explanation.

"Did he help you?"

"I think so." It would be hard to describe. I could remember it all, but words didn't seem adequate.

"He helped me," she said.

"You saw him?"

"I could hear him."

"Me too." I thought about Thierry telling Nathalie when she was in my body at the *Serpent d'Océan* that she'd have to kill Marco. "I think he was helping us keep Marco distracted so he wouldn't know what Nathalie was doing."

She considered this, and a little smile appeared on her lips. She shook her head. "Marco messed with the wrong people."

"What happened to you? Where did you come from just now?"

"I was by the river," she said. "I think Marco was trying to get back to the house. And as soon as I woke up, I saw the smoke, and I knew."

After a few seconds I said, "Did Marco interact with you? Like, in my body?"

"Yes, he did. But he did not pretend to be you like he did with Tim. He just threatened to never let you go if I didn't give in to him. He was telling me all the things I could have if I stopped resisting. He was like, 'You can have so much sex with your girlfriend all the time' or something like that."

I almost laughed. "He showed me this weird porno version of you."

She scoffed. "I hope he is really gone. But I'm not sure how we will know for sure."

Tim sat in his car between the church and the cemetery, talking on the phone with the window rolled down. He waved when he saw us coming, as if we would somehow miss him. He mouthed, "Papa," to us, pointing to the phone. We nodded.

"We're going to talk for a minute," I said.

Tim asked his dad to hold on for a second. "We're all who we think we are, right?" he said to us in English, just to be clear.

"It seems that way," I said.

Salomé stepped forward and took Tim's free hand in both of hers. "Thank you." They exchanged a few quiet words before she released his hand. The trunk opened and Salomé got her suitcase from it. "Let's go in here," she said to me, nodding toward the church.

My legs felt unsteady as I climbed the stone steps to the red wooden door. I thought we might sit on the steps, but to my surprise, Salomé pushed the door open.

Salomé flipped the light switch by the door, which lit a series of oddly modern sconces underneath the stained-glass windows. Saint-Jean de Béré was not an ornate church by French standards. White stucco walls with some kind of gaudy fresco-looking statues mounted near the windows. It was much colder inside. I remembered what Nathalie said about how these buildings were constructed at certain angles to stay cool. That conversation felt like years ago.

Salomé sat on a pew near the door. I settled down beside her.

There was a little smudge of ash on her cheek and dried bird shit on her shins. Mine, too.

"My father came to church here when he was a kid," she said, looking around at the stained-glass windows. One window depicted a young woman in a silver robe that barely clung to her shoulders. She knelt at the feet of her mother and the king, holding the platter with John the Baptist's head.

"This is where you get your name," I said.

She looked at the window of Salome and sighed. I thought she might say something about having seen this imagery when she was young. "You know I can't come," she said, turning to look at me. "I can't leave Maman alone with this mess."

I did know, for so many reasons. I pressed my feet into the smooth stone floor, trying to get my legs to stop shaking. "Did you ever intend to come?"

She sniffled, and a tear slid down her cheek. "I did."

"Maybe, in a couple of months, if you still want to, you can."

"Yeah, I want to," she said, wiping her cheek with the back of her hand. She looked at the windows again. "Maman did what she had to do."

"I know." I found the energy to move, and pulled her hand to my lips. I kissed the backs of her fingers. The salt from her tears on my tongue may have been the most intimate thing I'd ever experienced.

"I'm so sorry, Cour-ten-ey. I'm worried that I ruined your life, and you just wanted a vacation."

"My life is not ruined. And it wasn't really a vacation."

She crinkled her nose, skewing the triangle of freckles I'd first noticed on the plane.

"Did any of that really happen?" I asked.

"For me, the thing I can't believe is that you stayed with me. There were so many times where it would be easy for you to say, 'Fuck this,

I am going.' But every time, there you were again." She laughed. "Do not say it's because you are American. I know not all Americans are like that."

"How'd you know that's what I was about to say?" I smiled.

"You are always saying this!"

It felt wrong to laugh, so I looked at my filthy hands, which were still trembling. I needed to go. Still looking down, I said, "Almost as soon as I met you, I knew it wouldn't be easy to say goodbye."

"Then we will not say goodbye. We will say *au revoir*."

"*Au revoir* is going to hurt, too." I couldn't look at her. If I did, I'd cry.

She pulled me into her arms.

Once we let go, I forced myself to stand. My footsteps echoed through the church as I walked alone to the front door. I didn't look back until I was outside, where I turned to watch the big red door slowly close behind me. Tim was waiting in the car, still talking on his phone. He told his dad he'd call him when he was on his way home and hung up.

As we drove away, I watched the church door, waiting for it to fling open, for Salomé to run through, calling for me to wait for her. But of course it never did.

Charles de Gaulle Airport was shockingly bright. I squinted and followed the signs to security, tailing the lines of people I could only assume hadn't just navigated multiple astral planes.

Once I got to my terminal, I used my last two-euro piece to buy a single shot from a Nespresso vending machine. My hand shook so hard I spilled coffee down my chin. I found a seat and opened my notebook, but saw the words "Magpie, secret society, American billionaires, obsessed w/immortality at any cost" and snapped it closed.

My phone buzzed in my hand. A text from Salomé. Adrenaline charged through my fingertips—could she be here? But the text she sent was better than that.

appelle ta maman ♡

She remembered. It was 3 a.m. in Raleigh, but Salomé was right. I shouldn't wait. I called my mom. I didn't know if she'd even answer. Maybe she had her phone on do not disturb while she was sleeping. But after five rings, she answered, "Hello?"—whereas in the past, if I'd called her at 3 a.m. while traveling, she would've said, "Courtney, are you okay?" upon answering.

No. I wasn't okay. I started crying, telling her how sorry I was that I hadn't been there for her. I apologized for being such a selfish adult child. Then I held my breath. Would this be the moment she wouldn't know who I was? But when she spoke, she said, "Are you done being so hard on yourself?"

"You're okay? You're not upset with me?"

"I wanted you to go!"

"Mom, I'm going to move in with you now, okay? Please don't fight me on this. I want to spend this time with you while we still have it. Okay?"

"I want to spend time with you, too." I could hear her smiling.

"Maybe when I get back in a few hours, we could order a pizza and binge a new show?"

"I can't wait, Court." There was a little lift to her voice I hadn't heard in a long time.

CHAPTER 24

Wednesday, July 25, 2018

My old bedroom in Gran's house is familiar in a nice way. This is where I lived for a few years after the divorce, until Mom bought us a little house in the suburbs. The teddy bear whose head I cut open looking for a camera sits in a rickety antique high chair in the corner. I've asked him for forgiveness more than once. The maple tree that didn't clear the first story when I was in middle school now engulfs the whole second-story window, shrouding my bedroom in shadows for most of the day. There is a nest of blue robin eggs on a branch near the window.

I take a picture of the eggs and text it to Salomé.

Not yet.

I ended the lease on my attic apartment and have been moving my things slowly. I have until the end of the month, technically. I've reconciled the pain of letting go of my own place with the opportunity to rise to the occasion for my mother. There will be other apartments to contain the future mundane moments of my life. Maybe in Montmartre.

Mom has been doing well. She has a hard time remembering who Salomé is when I bring her up, and tends to tell me the same story over and over, but for the most part, she seems like herself. It's strange to know that despite my finally being willing to get to know my mother as a person, she may no longer have the ability to draw a comprehensive picture of me. I'm committed to giving her the opportunity, though, and equally committed to believing that if she had the choice, she would choose to know me. Even when we've clashed a bit, mostly over the unusual proximity, we've managed to stay positive. "Count our blessings," Mom says.

Not long ago I would've tried to reframe that in a less religious way, but now I just let her have her blessings. Somehow it feels nicer to think of someone—not necessarily God, but maybe a guide or an ancestor, or Thierry himself—leading me to Élise and Callum, rather than forcing myself to accept that it was all random. It's what I want to believe, anyway. What would be the point of dismissing the magic in a truly sensational story?

Mom and I have spent most of our long summer evenings on her screened-in back porch, drinking iced tea and talking. I'm making audio recordings of her stories, though I don't know what I'll use them for. Maybe a collection of essays, or maybe just to hear her voice when she's gone.

Mom's hair, which she always kept short, has now reached her shoulders. She always said a woman over thirty shouldn't have long hair, but it seems she's forgotten her old rule. I love her looking so wise—like an Elspeth. I always favored my dad more, with our gray eyes and dark, heavy eyebrows, but I see myself in my mother's mannerisms. Whenever she's thinking through what she wants to say, she touches her bottom lip with two fingers and taps lightly. I never realized I did that too.

A couple of nights ago, on the porch, I asked my mom if she'd live her life over again from start to finish, just the way it happened, if given the chance.

She smiled and swirled the ice cubes around at the bottom of her glass with the hand that had sustained the burn. The new skin that had grown under the bandage now appeared both delicate and angry. She thought about it for a long time. Then she said, "No, I don't think I would. Because as strange as it may sound, the past few weeks have been some of the happiest of my life, and I don't know if it would be worth it to do it all again just to get right back here."

"Really? You aren't scared?"

"I am scared," she said. "But I'm more afraid of what you'll have to do to take care of me than I am of dying."

My eyes wanted to dart to my phone, which was recording our conversation, or to the pulsing of fireflies in the azaleas behind her. I wanted to flinch, deflect, tell her not to worry about it. But I made myself hold her gaze.

"Do you still believe in Heaven?"

"You know, a few years ago, I thought that whenever I caught a whiff of my mortality, I'd double back down with the whole religion thing. But now that I'm at that point, I can't seem to bother. It's mostly because everything I do now feels like its own form of praying, but not necessarily to God. Is that terrible?"

"No, Mom. That's not terrible. I know what you mean."

"It's strange, though. I never felt this way before."

"Do you finally feel like an Elspeth?"

"I suppose I do," she said. "When I was little, I was Elsie. Elsie and Trudy. I went to Elspeth when I was about twenty, but Trudy never made the change to Gertrude . . ."

I had at least three recordings of the same story. It sounded like what Salomé recalled Thierry saying in his final days. I felt a pang of longing, not unlike looking across the rooftops of Paris. Could Mom and I have had this all along? It was easy to blame my mother for not opening up to me, but I hadn't been open, either.

I opened my notebook and wrote: *But there is no way around, no way out. Only in, deeper, and more, and more.*

Salomé and I have communicated almost daily since I returned from France. We haven't really broached the subject of what is next. Things are still in disarray for her. Half of her family home burned down, the fire taking many of her father's belongings and writings with it. The little bird on the bookcase is gone.

There has been no sign of Marco. Nathalie doesn't know what would happen if his consciousness was able to just wander, like a ghost, without finding another body to inhabit. But she senses that he is gone. We all do.

Only two families stepped up to help Salomé and Nathalie, opening their homes for a few days after the fire. But for the most part, the residents of Châteaubriant seemed to silently rejoice in the Leducs' misfortune. Or not-so-silently, as with the insurance claims adjuster who said the French equivalent of "you reap what you sow" to Nathalie while standing on a piece of charred rubble. Even the active members of the resistance were reluctant to embrace Nathalie, as Bernard could never tell them what she did to stop Marco. Salomé doesn't blame people for not rushing to their aid. She says she is more relieved to know how tarnished Marco's reputation had become than she is disheartened by the lack of community.

None of the Magpies tried to come to their rescue because the day after the fire, Nathalie had filed the paperwork to dissolve ViPi. Both ViPi and the Magpies are now getting unwanted national attention through write-ups in *Le Monde* and a few other reputable publications, many of which cite Loïc's research. Both Tim and his father were interviewed for the *Le Monde* piece but opted to remain anonymous. Bernard's picture was front and center with the article, which also included quotes from his twin brother. None of the billionaires were mentioned—a quick Google search showed that Sinclair owned the parent company of many of these publications.

Tim and I have completed our episode outline, which uses Loïc's story as the main narration mechanism, following Loïc in a close third person, showing him learning more, infiltrating deeper, and communicating with the Peruvian woman he knew to be Marco. Then, when Loïc disappears, Tim himself becomes the new first-person narrator, trying to unearth what happened to Loïc and continue his work. I've been deep in research mode, reading everything I can on Alexis Carrel and Charles Lindbergh, a part of me concerned I'm walking across a minefield. But at the same time, I'm compelled to see it through. It feels good to be working on something of substance.

A couple of days after the fire, Salomé and Nathalie relocated to the small town of Cazères, near Toulouse, where Nathalie's estranged parents retired. But Salomé doesn't plan to stay there long-term. She might come to Raleigh in a couple of months, once she is able to fly into the US again. For now, we are both spending our time trying to understand our mothers better.

I go downstairs and drink a cup of coffee on the back porch with Mom. The day isn't hot yet, but it will be. A couple of deer coming from the direction of the park pick their way through the backyard clover, stopping to look at us, their large ears trained in our direction. I breathe in the North Carolina air, pine needles and humidity. No boulangerie within walking distance, but that's okay for now.

Later, I return to my room and crawl into bed, pulling my laptop onto my bent knees. I delete the junk from my inbox. I have a new assignment, another listicle: "The Ten Best Food Trucks in Raleigh." At least the research will be fun. I don't mind writing these to pay the bills while I'm working on something big.

An email alert pops into my inbox from Kylie's YouTube channel. She's just uploaded a new video. I click the link. The video is titled "Making Sense of the French Visa Process." In the video, she breaks down exactly which visa she has and how long it permits her to work in France. Then she lists several other visas and their basic requirements. I watch the entire eighteen-minute video without cringing, except for when I remember what I said to her in Paris. I click the thumbs-up button. Several people have already left comments telling her they love her new content. Some ask if they can hire her as a move-to-Paris consultant. Her response to all of these comments is: "Bien sûr! :) :) :)" I scroll through and like all of her responses.

I close my laptop. It's almost 9:00, which is 3:00 p.m. in France. Our meeting time. I walk over to the window to check the nest. The three blue eggs lie serenely next to each other. A few of the parents' stray downy feathers flutter in the breeze.

My phone buzzes on the nightstand.

I relax on the bed, rest my head on the pillow, and close my eyes. I spell *serrure*, spending a whole breath on each letter. The backs of my eyelids become a tunnel, which I've become accustomed to navigating in the dark. There's a little fall that tickles my stomach, but then I feel solid again.

I'm standing on herringbone floorboards, looking out of open windows as a teenager bikes past, a young woman standing on the foot pegs behind him, her arms draped languidly around his neck. The sun is setting behind the metal roof of the building across from me. The sounds of people cooking and laughing mingle from the open windows of the apartments across the street. Pigeons peck around the cobblestones below, cooing softly.

"Cour-ten-ey?"

She's behind me, setting a bottle of rosé onto the round dining table.

I cross over to her and kiss the air beside her cheeks, which smells like Salomé.

"It's always Paris at sunset," she says.

"Sorry, I don't think I can help it."

"No, it's okay." She looks around at the thick beams crossing the ceiling and the defunct fireplace stacked with books. "*Pas mal.*"

We sit at the table. Salomé uncorks the wine and pours two glasses. We clink them together. She tucks a strand of hair behind her ear and it falls right back out across her cheek. Gazing out of the window, she crosses her legs at the knees, leans back into her chair, and sighs. Outside, night is falling. One by one, the warm lights of Paris flicker on, each little apartment glowing bright from within.

ACKNOWLEDGMENTS

Salomé took a long time to write, and therefore I have to thank a lot of people. And because this is my first time writing an acknowledgments page, I can't simply list the names. This project is not mine alone.

Mackenzie Williams, how did I get so lucky as to have you as an agent? *Salomé* is a product of your support, creative input, and incredible professionalism. The words "my agent" still feel so special to say, especially knowing it's you I'm referring to. You have altered the course of my life.

Tarini Sipahimalani, from the moment we first spoke on June 24, 2024—Saint John the Baptist Day, aka Courtney's birthday—I knew we were a match. I was trembling before our meeting, but you instantly put me at ease. Ever since then, you have guided me with the same steadfast grace.

To the rest of the Putnam team, I cannot thank you enough for the way you've made my dream a reality. Thank you for your professionalism and patience with a nervous debut author. I am lucky to be in your hands.

In December 2017, I emailed my then-coworker (now friend) Stephen Turner with a very early, incomplete draft of chapters one and two. He told me he liked it, so I kept writing. Thank you, Stephen.

I brought one chapter a month to share with the Paper State Writing Club in Nashville. They would eventually read many, *many* drafts. After sharing the first few chapters, Jessica Pearson said, "I want more from these two!" so I kept writing. To the Paper State: Jessica Bates, Jordan Taylor Sloan, Dawson Wells, Amy Head, Isi Stone, Kate Bradley, Adam Nicholson, Stephen Simmons, Carly Myracle, Lane Scott Jones, Sarah McCarthy, Chelsea Hall—I could not have done it without you. The "Salomé" cake made it more real than the Publishers Weekly announcement.

Thank you to my draft one beta readers in 2020: Jessica Bates, Priya Handa, Jeph Porter, and Kyle Nachtigal, who all gave me invaluable early feedback.

I sent the next drafts to my Sewanee School of Letters classmates Mina Manchester, Lisa Williams, Lisa Shanahan, Katie Todd, and John Haman. I have to give credit where credit is due: the "key" idea from the final act (that's all I'll say here to avoid spoilers) came from John Haman during a two-hour phone call in which he brainstormed with me when I was on the verge of throwing the manuscript in the garbage.

Speaking of my Sewanee family—this book would not have been published without Ryan Chapman. Ryan, thank you for your patience, your editorial genius, your belief in this manuscript, and for the doors you opened for me. I quite literally owe this publication to you.

Jamie Quatro generously stayed on a Zoom call with me far past its scheduled ending, combing through the manuscript to offer edits and suggestions. I keep her advice on a constant loop in my mind as I revise.

To Justin Taylor, Chris Bachelder, Sidik Fofana, and all the other people I met at Sewanee: Thank you for creating a learning environment as special as the School of Letters. In a world where writers—especially those in MFA programs—can be disastrously competitive,

I am lucky to have found such a supportive community at the School of Letters. To my SoL cohort: I hope you all see the publication of this book as *your* success. I know it won't be long before we're celebrating your words in print.

Christy Lynch was a key player in the production of this novel. First, she encouraged me to apply to Sewanee. I was in Christy's car when I got the email from my future agent saying she'd like to represent me. I was so surprised I ripped off my glasses and threw them onto the floorboard, and Christy later bought me a glass of champagne. Thank you, Christy, for being not only a great friend, but a trusted advisor on everything writing and publishing.

To my early editors, Jennifer Chesak and Karen E. Bender—thank you for your advice and your support. You were right about so much!

To my "French realness" readers: Victorine Lamothe and Hollis Hampton-Jones, *merci.*

To Victorine, who went from an Instagram acquaintance to offering to let me catsit for her in Paris multiple times (in the very neighborhood where Courtney lived as a student, no less!), you have a true gift with your editorial eye. I await your debut with anticipation. All my love to Édith and Odile.

Madison Fitzpatrick, thank you for reading and taking two hours to discuss the novel with me, though we'd never met in person. (We will!)

To Shannon Lee Miller, my instant bestie, someone I met and thirty seconds later knew I would die for: Your enthusiasm in your beta read and in your professional advice has gotten me through some tough moments. I love you so much.

To my parents who encouraged me to write long before I figured out how to earn money doing so, as well as Whitney Washington and Georgia Reagan, who were there from the beginning. To my best friends, Dr. Mitra Adhami Waite and Dr. Erika Porter (I couldn't help but add your credentials because I'll never stop being proud of your accomplishments)—thank you for your undying support and for cheering me on through my MFA, which may have been less grueling than a PhD, but you never made me feel like it was less important. To my professors at the University of Montevallo: Dr. David Callaghan, for challenging me to match creativity with knowledge, Dr. Stacey Ayotte, for convincing me to major in French, and Dr. Clark Hultquist, for keeping up with me over the years, continuing to encourage me, and even meeting up with me in Paris.

To Marie Pope, my best friend in every lifetime, for convincing me that I could *be* an artist rather than be destined to support one. Please consider this my matching tattoo, about fifteen years late. "You must *not* shrink." Growing alongside you, loving you, and being loved by you is the greatest gift.

Thank you to my therapist Morgan Guthrie, who on more than one occasion has said, "You have a *very* active imagination," and encouraged me to use it for good.

To the other artists who have engaged with the story of Salome over the centuries: Oscar Wilde, Aubrey Beardsley, Richard Strauss, Al Pacino, Jessica Chastain, to name only a few. I know there will be more to come.

To the authors and creators of the materials I used as research and inspiration:

Huang Yong Ping, the sculptor of *Serpent d'Océan*, who passed away the day after I completed my first draft of *Salomé* in 2019.

Borrowed Time by Sue Armstrong.

The Immortalists by David M. Friedman, who also wrote *Wilde in America*. (See, I'm not the first person to find interest in Oscar

Wilde *and* the Carrel/Lindbergh partnership. There truly is nothing new under the sun.)

Immortality, Inc. by Chip Walter.

Gene Hart and the Astral Doorway Podcast.

Elif Batuman's *New Yorker* profile "Céline Sciamma's Quest for a New, Feminist Grammar of Cinema."

The Immortal Life of Henrietta Lacks by Rebecca Skloot, which introduced me to Alexis Carrel back in 2017 just as I started writing the first pages that would become this book.

Deanna Sorenson's song "Conjure Folk" for the image of initials in a spiderweb.

My cat, Diana, was consistently in the room while I wrote this book—often between my laptop and me (at times making it difficult to write), sometimes curled under my bent knees, sometimes on my lap, sometimes at my feet. Bringing me gifts of puff ball toys to make sure I had enough to eat and reminding me to drink the water in my glass before she stuck her paw into it. Much of this novel was written and revised between the hours of 5 and 7 a.m., and Diana made sure I got up.

Kyle, thank you for knowing what it takes to be a working artist. Thank you for making my meals while I worked full time and went to grad school and wrote a novel. For all the needs you anticipated, for all the pep talks, and for the times you simply understood. You have truly embodied the word "partner." Thank you for being willing to travel to the edge of a continent to crawl into an aluminum snake's mouth during an epic heat wave with a girl you barely knew.

And finally, to the woman who switched places with me on a flight from Newark to London in 2017: We didn't talk at all, but still, you got me thinking.

Photograph of the author © Melissa Madison Fuller 2025

Leslie Baird is an author and ghostwriter. She holds an MFA in fiction from Sewanee, the University of the South, and lives in Europe. *Salomé* is her debut novel.

VISIT LESLIE BAIRD ONLINE

LeslieBairdAuthor